C000003506

The Doll
That Cried

by
Anne E. Randell

**Grosvenor House
Publishing Limited**

This book is published by
Grosvenor House Publishing Ltd
Link House
140 The Broadway, Tolworth, Surrey, KT6 7HT.
www.grosvenorhousepublishing.co.uk

This book is a work of fiction. Any resemblance to
people or events, past or present, is purely coincidental.

A CIP record for this book
is available from the British Library

ISBN 978-1-83975-753-2

To my family for their wonderful support

Books by the same author:

Next Time It Will Be Perfect

Look Right, Look Left, Look Dead

Down, Out and Dead

The Push

The doll was beautiful and must have cost a small fortune. Her pale pink dress, with its smocked top and flowing skirt, looked freshly ironed. A white jacket and socks piped with lace completed the outfit. Blond curls framed a face so flawless that no human could ever replicate it. She sat mesmerised, deep blue eyes staring at the body lying on the floor.

Chapter 1

As soon as I opened the dining room door on Monday morning, I rang 999. I felt strangely calm, though I'd never had cause to dial that number before. Normally I go straight to panic mode when anything untoward happens, but this left me feeling composed. Having given the necessary information (name, address, and the fact there was someone asleep on my front room carpet, someone I couldn't rouse) I was told an ambulance was on its way. I was going to make a cup of tea, but they arrived before I had time to pop on the kettle.

Unfortunately, I fear that my best room will be besmirched forever, but I must say the paramedics were excellent: softly spoken and most reassuring. However, for some reason they sent for the police. I didn't like them as much but at least they covered their shoes before entering and donned the funny over suits you see on TV dramas. I was glad there was no danger of unsolicited dirt entering the house. They had arrived surprisingly swiftly and were here for ages, then said I must accompany them to the station to answer some questions. I couldn't think what they wanted to ask me, as I told them I had no idea how a man came to be comatose in my front room, the one used only rarely. My children had to go to my parents' house. I didn't want Harriet to go, she's an excellent nanny, brilliant with Adam, but Mum doesn't like anyone else to be involved and the police said Harriet could leave and they'd speak to her later.

A rather officious looking officer told me that it was a body in my house: a body as in dead. In my dining room. That had nothing to do with me. Nothing. Or I don't think so.

'Sorry to disturb you on your day off, sir, but uniform informed us that they'd discovered an unusual death. I would have overseen the initial investigation myself, but it's a strange situation. The owner of the house, Mrs Susan Winters, reported it two hours ago. However, the pathologist has just told me that death occurred at least thirty-six hours ago and maybe longer. There are other things as well, sir, but you really need to see for yourself. Looks like murder, but it's the weirdest crime scene I've ever attended.'

DCI Harvey Tarquin had been enjoying his favourite activity: walking, a trip to the Lake District chosen, the early spring sunshine unseasonably warm, but the request from his DI that he return as soon as possible couldn't be ignored.

It took less time than expected for Harvey to return to Fordway, the small market town where he'd been a Detective Chief Inspector for four years. He had chosen to work and live in the town for its proximity to The Lake District, and the coast, with both Blackpool and Morecambe less than an hour away. Manchester was even closer, for the rare occasions when he needed the dubious delights of a large city. For once, the traffic was light, too early in the day for visitors to want to leave the glories of the Lake District. No hold ups on the motorway and the roads in town clear. Serena was waiting for him, the front garden of the detached property swathed in daffodils, their golden colour belying the very idea of death.

'Good morning, again, sir. So sorry to call you back, but you really need to see this. The SOCO team has just left so you can view the room minus extra bodies.'

'Yes, I rather think one will suffice.'

Smiling at her boss's levity, a most unusual phenomenon, she continued. 'Alfie Morrison is still here, somewhere in the back garden. He thought you'd want to speak to him, get the pathologist's take on the situation.'

Intrigued, Harvey followed Serena into the house. The long entrance hall was pristine, the small table and wooden cupboard gleaming. A light beige rug looked as though it had been cleaned recently and seemed to have been positioned with the aid of a set square. The overall appearance was one the DCI failed to achieve after hours of cleaning.

'This way, sir, the body is in the dining room. It's the husband: Gerald Winters.'

As they approached the room they were joined by the pathologist. 'Heard you arrive a few minutes ago. I was enjoying the sunshine but would recognise the sound of your elderly Honda anywhere.' Shaking hands with the man who had become his friend, Alfie Morrison added, 'Talk about a show home, the whole place is more germ free than my dissecting room. Might as well perform the PM on the kitchen table! Shame to spoil your day off, believe you were wandering around Windermere as lonely as a cloud, and yes, I know it's the wrong lake. However, however, however - I feel the repetition is necessary - you do need to see the crime scene.'

Allowing Harvey to enter the dining room ahead of them, the others stopped in the doorway, awaiting his reaction.

Despite the brightness of the day the room was in darkness, thick velvet curtains drawn across the bay window. Switching on the main light Harvey stood surveying the surreal scene. A body was lying full length on the carpet, arms by his side, palms up, like someone engaged in the relaxation at the end of a yoga session. Harvey had tried yoga one Wednesday evening in the local Parish Hall and had been too embarrassed to return, having been told his snores once prostrate had reduced the rest of the group to helpless giggles.

The DCI stood stock still. The central light illuminated the scene which looked like the set of a Victorian melodrama. A doll was positioned to the right of the deceased's head and appeared to be staring at him. To his left a tray, covered in a lace mat, held a meal.

'Words have vamoosed, or any that would make sense. What is going on?'

Alfie spoke for him. 'The position of the body indicates that it was sited; moved into place post-mortem. Someone took great care to lay him out, to make him look respected, even cared for. No one, and I do mean no one, dies looking that controlled, or indeed comfortable. He was made to look ordered; the best word I can think of.'

'Can you give an indication of the cause of death?' Harvey knew the pathologist wasn't one to guess.

'Sorry, you'll have to wait for the PM. You're welcome to the show, I know how you love a good cutting and sawing.'

'It's the doll that gets me,' Serena had moved into the room to stand by the toy. 'She's the most amazing doll

4

I've ever seen, such a wonderful outfit and just look at her face: perfection. I bet if I moved her, she'd cry. I had a much less impressive doll when I was little and any time it moved water ran down its cheeks. As a youngster I was really chuffed by that and used to keep moving Cindy who cried every time she changed position. I pretended to be her mum, drying her tears.'

Receiving a look that told her she was off on one of her many tangents, Serena reverted to professional mode. 'The strange thing is that she seems to be keeping watch, like a dog does when its master dies. Is that why she's placed so close to the head?'

'Why place it at all?' Harvey had discovered some words. 'So many whys here. Why the laying out of the corpse? Why the doll? And why the meal? Why is that on the floor and not on the dining room table?'

Serena stared at the tableau. 'Maybe he was expected to wake up and eat it. I glanced under the cover earlier and it's quite a feast: melon and Parma ham, a full roast main course of beef and Yorkshire pudding with all the trimmings, and what looks like a crumble of some sort with a jug of custard beside it. I love cooking, but my efforts seldom, well if I'm truthful never, look that good.'

'Unfortunately, like the body, it's been there for too long, so I won't be enjoying it whilst I do the PM. And before you ask, I will do that as soon as humanely feasible.' Alfie knew the DCI would be asking for the results post-haste.

Noises of children playing could be heard from upstairs, accompanied by a baby's distressed yell.

'Why in the name of all that's holy, is anyone still in the house?'

'Susan Winters, the woman who reported the body, is waiting for her parents to collect the children. Apparently, they live quite close, but were in Manchester this morning shopping and didn't have their mobiles switched on until recently. We've told her that she will then need to accompany us to the station to help with our enquiries.' Pausing, Serena continued, 'She seemed surprised by that and asked why it was necessary. When you meet her, sir, you'll think that she's at least as strange as the weird spectacle in this room.'

'I don't suppose there's any CCTV in the area.'

'No, the nearest is in town, so won't be any help' It wasn't the reply, the DCI had wanted.

I'm in prison! Have you ever been incarcerated? Have you slumped to the bare floor as the cell door clangs shut; the key turned with a finality that renders one breathless? Have you suffered a panic attack and battered on the each of the four walls, thinking one of them might give way and provide an escape route? I know the exact dimensions of my new space: six strides by four. A bed and toilet the only furnishings. What one might call minimal.

I have spent hours in this cell in the bowels of our local police station, but already it feels like a lifetime; one for which I have not been prepared. I was bundled from the back of the police car, taken to a small room, though palatial compared to my present surroundings, and spoken to, first by the duty solicitor and then by two officers. Nothing made any sense. How long will I be here? How will the children cope without me?

She, the solicitor asked to represent me, (call me Jessica, though I preferred Miss Lawson, far more professional) explained the next step, the reason I'm here, what the procedure will be, how long I can expect to be held, but I failed to understand. Words tumbled from her mouth, the bright pink lipstick at odds with the situation, but I didn't hear them. All I could think was how very young she looked, hardly old enough to be classified as an adult, let alone be part of the judicial system. She's an attractive girl, but surely an adult, a lady, a female of mature years should be dealing with me. The one in front of me looked as though she was part of a come-to-work-with-dad-day. I was then questioned by a very ordinary-looking policeman: middle height, middle aged, middle everything, and his extremely attractive sidekick: blond hair fashionably styled, make-up perfect and a suit that must have cost a month's wages. My no comment interview wasn't well received (scowls from him; a subdued sigh from her). He, full of his own importance, then informed me that I would be held overnight, pending further investigation. I must have slept; neither the rock-hard bed nor the harsh blanket preventing a few hours of blissful unknowing.

Sleep, the uninterrupted kind, is a luxury not experienced for seven and a half years. I could tell you exactly how long it is since I was allowed more than a couple of hours without someone demanding my attention. Since the birth of Hannah, who will be eight in early July, I have never gone to bed and known that I would be allowed to remain horizontal. This morning a loud knock on the door and a breakfast tray delivered by an officer awoke me.

'Can you tell me why I'm still here?' I asked.

'Sorry, love. Someone will be with you soon.'

Chapter 2

Nine Years Ago

There are days, indeed moments, that change the course of one's life: for better or worse. The trouble is that they aren't sign-posted, no warnings of what lies ahead or whether turning right is the correct direction. Sat Nav unavailable.

It was Gerald Winter's first experience of acting as best man, his cousin asking him so near the date that he wondered if the preferred choice had given backward. He was used to talking to people, his job in a bank meant he dealt with the public every day. This felt different. He knew he was expected to be both erudite and funny. That was the purpose of the best man's speech: to make people laugh, deliver humorous anecdotes about the groom (as cringeworthy as possible) and entertain the assembled guests.

'Try to embarrass him. That always goes down well,' had been his brother's advice. 'That incident at his eighteenth party when he got roaring drunk is a start.'

'I could advise them about the new Fixed Rate Bonds arriving soon or our advantageous mortgage deals, but I've never been able to tell jokes. Either I forget the punch line or tell them so badly no one is amused.' From the look on Eric's face, he knew his brother agreed.

His duties in church passed without incident. He kept the groom calm - not an easy task, the bride almost twenty minutes late - and the ring was passed without clanging to the stone floor. The reception was in a local hotel, two hundred guests in attendance. As he stood to speak, Gerald realised that the paper in his hand was waving like a wind-blown flag, the words moving in and out of focus might as well have been in a new language. He felt like a war time code breaker, and the situation felt at least as serious.

'That was a great speech.' The young woman standing in front of him sounded serious. 'I loved the bit about Harry falling into the swimming pool and being rescued by a dog.'

Gerald was smitten. Love at first words, his in absentia.

'Are you OK?' As there was no reply, she continued the conversation that was becoming ever more one-sided. 'I'm Sue, the bride's second cousin by marriage, or something like that. I believe you're her new husband's cousin, so we must now be related!' If only they had said goodbye; lovely to meet you. Neither could envisage what unhappiness the following decade would bring.

This morning, a new lawyer. Thank goodness. The schoolgirl no longer in attendance. It was then that I realised the situation had the potential to become serious. Mr Harding told me he'd been appointed by my father. I knew the name as Dad is a magistrate and has often joked that should we require the services of a solicitor Oliver Harding is the man one wants. 'He'd have got Jack the Ripper off, had that case come to court.' Doesn't feel funny now.

Mr Harding looked the part: tall and dignified, his dark hair streaked with grey...attractive on a man. Wearing a three-piece suit that didn't come from a local retailer, he oozed confidence, though none rubbed off on me. Shaking like someone suffering from drug withdrawal, I stumbled onto the chair he held out.

A man who spends his life employing only the most appropriate words, he introduced himself in seconds, small talk redundant. Then it was down to business. Almost certainly, he was trying to help, to give me advice, but each sentence felt like the next instruction in a game called *Your Future*. I found it almost impossible to concentrate and heard myself muttering words even I found incomprehensible.

'I suggest that you say as little as possible. No comment is, once again, perfectly acceptable. At this juncture we don't know what evidence the police have. Having spoken to the man in charge, DCI Tarquin, I don't think they have much, and I have to say I'm surprised that you were brought here, and indeed held overnight. Today's interview is scheduled for 10 a.m. I doubt they'll ask for a plea but if they do I suggest you say not guilty.'

Pausing to see if I was taking in anything he was saying (I wasn't) he continued, telling me that the police could hold me for 24 hours before they had to charge me, and that period would expire at lunch time. 'They can apply to the magistrates (surely not Dad) to hold you for up to 36 or even 96 hours. After that they must either charge you or, more realistically, release you.' It was only later, much later, that his words came back in all their dreadfulness.

Thirty minutes later I was led into a bleak room, totally devoid of character. Magnolia paint had obviously once, in a former incarnation, been applied liberally, but the walls were long overdue a fresh coat. A large table stood in the centre, a recorder at one end. Four utilitarian chairs sat in pairs opposite each other, the two police officers already in situ occupying two of them. The high window at one end was covered in mesh, though how anyone could contemplate it as an escape route was beyond me. A ladder and double-jointed agility basic requirements.

'Interview commencing ten o'clock, March 19th DCI Tarquin, DI Peil, Mrs Susan Winters and Mr Harding present.'

'No comment.' Two words that felt as though they were deciding my future. The male officer, whom I now knew to be a Detective Chief Inspector, the exalted position making me think once again that my situation might be serious, was clearly even more irritated than yesterday with my succinct responses.

'I must advise you, that should this case come to court, a no comment interview does not impress either the jury or the judge. The words will be used as part of your evidence and they have the propensity to indicate guilt.'

The female sitting beside him had obviously been cast as the good cop and smiled encouragingly at me.

Strangely, I cannot recall any of the questions except the oft repeated, 'Mrs Winters, why did it take you so long to dial 999, to ask for an ambulance or the police?' After what felt like hours I was returned to my cell, the threat of a further meeting making it feel even more claustrophobic.

I hadn't expected visitors. I'm sure it's unusual. Perhaps the idea was that they could persuade me to be more forthcoming. Dad was there with a change of clothes. I could hear my mother's voice telling him what to bring. I'm sure Gerald followed him into the room, standing at the back, incommunicado. Dad was obviously upset and talked more about Mum and how Adam had kept her awake most of the night. I felt like saying welcome to my world, but he looked so distraught that I managed to restrain myself. Perhaps I should have insisted that the nanny accompany the children. At least the girls appear to have slept well.

I thanked him for arranging my legal assistance. 'I'm sure I'll be home soon. Oliver Harding doesn't seem to think the police have much that might incriminate me. It will be good to get back to the children.'

Dad gave me a look that shouted louder than words: he knew how hard I found my life, always at the behest of my family. Five children under the age of eight being somewhat of a challenge. I had told him often enough that I had no freedom, no time to be myself. I had become a mother and a wife. Without doubt in that order. 'Give my love to Mum and say how much I appreciate what she's doing.'

Chapter 3

A whirlwind romance, others warning me that three months was too soon to know enough about Gerald to embark on a life together. I was eighteen and so knew it all. Meeting at a wedding reception seemed so apposite. Serendipity in full working order. Unfortunately, I looked no further than a day straight out of a fairy tale: walking down the aisle in a beautiful dress, enjoying a romantic honeymoon in the Maldives, then nurtured for the rest of my life. I longed to be called a wife, sadly it was my ultimate ambition. I had never excelled at school, leaving as soon as possible to work in a local shoe shop. I told anyone who'd listen that one day I would walk out in the highest pair of heels I could find: my feeble attempt at a joke. My dilemma was that I either needed a husband to provide for me or find a better job. So, husband it was.

Gerald is twelve years my senior and was already gaining promotion by the time of our somewhat starry-eyed first meeting. A deputy bank manager sounded so grown up...and prosperous. I was wooed. Flowers by the bucketful, outings to the kind of restaurants I'd never visited, trips to the opera (outside my comfort zone) and an unforgettable weekend in the Lake District. He proposed beside Coniston and I was the archetypal Mills and Boon heroine. He told me he loved me, adored me, that I was the woman who made him whole. I believed him.

I used to be so confident, knew what I wanted from life. Well, a husband was always on the wish-list, but I should have been more patient, not fallen for the first one who seemed to fit the bill: handsome, prosperous, attentive, and available. From July to October that year he was everything. My new, gloriously unforeseen, world. I had never expected to feel such joy; the gods were not just smiling on me but beaming down. Gerald had planned and booked the honeymoon, my task to pack walking shoes and layered clothing.

Glorious weather, pretty bridesmaids, my parents dressed to the nines and Gerald, my oh so handsome groom, made the wedding day perfect. According to Dad, my dress of ivory satin and guipure lace cost more than some third-world countries' annual budgets. What an unforgettable occasion, caught on thousands of photos.

My experience of holidaying abroad had been weeks in Majorca, Ibiza and Portugal, my parents happy to spend hours lazing beside a variety of imaginatively designed pools, buffet meals suiting Mum's erratic digestive system. Switzerland was certainly different! A top hotel in Zermatt with a view of the Matterhorn that had my new husband (oh, how I loved that word) drooling.

'It's one of the most famous peaks in the world and changes its appearance every time you look at it. Wait until you see it at sunset, it's mind-blowing.' The world-famous mountain and the rest of the scenery quickly became boring, one mountain looking very like the next, though even I had to admit that the Matterhorn was rather impressive. Gerald knew all the names and heights of every peak we saw and was surprised and probably disappointed by my lack of enthusiasm. Walks were interminable and to be told that we'd only done ten miles made me want to weep. My blisters developed blisters and my socks were regularly covered in blood. Saturated might be a more accurate description.

'I told you to bring comfortable walking shoes, you should have realised we'd be hiking. You work in a shoe shop for God's sake so surely you could have organised your footwear. Even you know that boots need to be broken in.'

Looking back at those comments, made in the cold voice I was to know so well, the one employed whenever I failed to respond appropriately or made a mistake, should have alerted me, the warning words being *told, should* and *even you*. Three days into the marriage and reality surfaced, a deep-sea diver suffering from the bends. Unfortunately, it seemed rather early to opt out. Had I done so I would have been spared so much heartache, though I wouldn't have had the children, all of whom I adore.

Seven days into the honeymoon Gerald suggested that we start a family. 'No point waiting. We've both said we want children and I earn enough for both of us. Us, and a son.'

'People will be counting the months on their fingers if I get pregnant this week.'

'Let them. He will be one hundred per cent legitimate!'

'Anyway, how do you know it will be a boy? Might be the other kind. Fifty-fifty chance.'

His reply should have got the alarm bells not ringing but clanging. The ones that foretell of catastrophe. The ones that should have made me run, flee, get as far away as possible.

'If the first one's a girl, we'll try again. And again. And again.'

Oliver Harding wanted to see me. Another interview (I knew they weren't cosy chats) loomed. 'The DCI hasn't disclosed all the evidence against you. I'm hoping it will become clearer this time. If there is enough evidence against you; if you enter a plea; if the police take it to the CPS, sorry Crown Prosecution Service, the ones who then decide whether it's in the public interest to instigate a trial; if...' I had stopped listening. Too many "ifs". Each escalating in seriousness. I was once told that doctors are encouraged to give their patients the worst-case scenario: a touch of indigestion possibly heralding a quadruple heart bypass. Obviously, lawyers do the same.

'Will I go home to my family after the interview? My children need me.'

'I'm afraid I can't say. It depends on what happens in the next hour.' My lawyer was hedging his bets, as he must have done so many times before.

Preparing for the interview, Harvey Tarquin experienced the excitement that was present at the start of any investigation. This should be an easy case to solve. Should being the most hopeful, but not necessarily the most accurate word available. So often cases that looked straightforward turned out to be anything but, and others were solved with far less effort than at first seemed possible. Turning to Serena Peil, the Detective Inspector he knew well and whom he regarded as one of the most professional members of his team, he updated her on the forensic team's findings.

'Obviously, Mrs Winter's DNA is all over the place. It is her home, so that's no help. Her husband's DNA is, naturally, also present. Her parents came to collect the children so theirs will have to be eliminated. There's also the nanny's, Harriet Devizes, who has apparently scarpered, back to her home somewhere in Cumbria.'

Once the forensic bods finished, both officers had revisited the house and inspected every room. 'I can't get over how unusual it felt, a family home with a difference. There was something odd. Something I can't put my finger on. So many toys, all neatly stacked. Such an abundance of clothes, all hanging in the wardrobes. However, there was an absence of photos and most rooms looked strangely minimalist. No pictures on the walls, no extra cushions or throws.'

Serena smiled. 'Well, sir, as far as the minimalist look goes, my sister, the one who lives in Preston, is obsessed with keeping her house tidy. Every night when my nephew and niece have gone to bed, she restores order to the chaos they created and makes the place look immaculate. Used to drive my brother-in-law mad, maybe one of the reasons he left. Mrs Winters is perhaps the same, can't stand anything out of place. I bet it would be an incredibly different scene at times. Four little girls and a baby must make Armageddon look peaceful.'

'I bow to your superior knowledge. However, I grew up with two younger brothers and our house was never, and I do mean never, orderly. I still say there was something not quite right inside 14 Wordsworth Avenue. We've got permission to keep her for another

24 hours, but we don't want another no comment interview. When I saw her lawyer a few minutes ago, to suggest that Mrs Winters becomes more cooperative, he gave one of those looks that said he knew we didn't have much evidence against her and that he would continue to advise her to be non-committal. Damned annoying.'

A second Bed and Breakfast. Last night wasn't as peaceful as the first with a new neighbour yelling and cursing. When the officer delivered my food, he said she was suffering withdrawal symptoms and was well-known to them. 'She's an alcoholic and drug user, a regular, always causes a disturbance. This time she's in real trouble. Assaulted a man in a pub, then the officer who was trying to arrest her. Must be due a spell at Her Majesty's Pleasure.' Did he think the same about me?

Sleep eluded me, and I almost joined in with her incessant shrieking. Oliver, my new best friend, repeated that they will have to release me at some point. Or, he added, charge me. Despite my lack of rest, I understood him only too well. 'You must prepare yourself for lengthy meetings today.' Meeting was his word, the one that turned out to be totally inappropriate as I suffered a two-hour grilling which left me feeling like a sheet pushed through a mangle, the old-fashioned variety of laundering endured by former generations.

I'm pretty sure Gerald popped in again. I say popped as he was only allowed a few minutes. He said everything is OK and I'm not to worry about the children. It was kind of him to come and I felt slightly more positive after seeing him. I know the girls will be all right without me, but I wonder how Mum is coping with

Adam. He's the most demanding baby, far harder than any of his sisters, though at the time each of them felt like fighting a never-ending war, no days of R and R. Dad admitted she was up with him several times the first night and I doubt if last night was any different. He never sleeps more than a couple of hours. The doctor says he should be sleeping through by now. But what does he know? I've tried everything and Adam still demands my company at least three times every night.

'What a monumental waste of time. We got nowhere.'

Feeling as frustrated as her boss, Serena suggested a break, coffee and cake essential, followed by a series of visits. 'We need background information: her GP, parents, the nanny and any friends in the area. Someone should be able to enlighten us.'

'Susan Winters is definitely a one-off. I can't recall such a bizarre session. I'll admit I was floundering. There are only so many ways one can ask the same question. What happened in her house last weekend didn't seem to cover it. She was strong enough to maintain her uncooperative stance for a two-hour interrogation. That takes some doing. If she was involved, you'd think she'd have her story ready by now. And if she wasn't, even more reason to have her version of events on display, if only to get us off her back.'

'Her story that she didn't go in the front room for almost two days sounded implausible, though my parents always kept the dining room for special occasions, mostly Christmas and birthdays. The rest of the time the door was kept closed, the only exception being when the room received its weekly clean, something I never thought it needed.' Serena knew her boss hated it when she made personal comments and she suffered a stern look.

'Apart from the irritating no comment answers, that was about all she did say. If, and I've a feeling it's a very big if, she was telling the truth, that would explain the delay in phoning for assistance.'

'Sir, when you said the word body, she looked surprised. Then, when you asked whether, or not she realised that death had occurred in her dining room she murmured something about being busy with the children. We need to visit Susan Winter's parents. They should be able to tell us more about their daughter.'

Chapter 4

Walking into the incident room, Harvey and Serena were met by a uniformed officer saying he would like someone senior to accompany him to 120 Rose Avenue. Familiar with the new estate where the roads had been beautified with flower names, ones that had caused weeks of letters in the local paper, people joking that at least the council had stopped short of naming any Chrysanthemum Close or Delphinium Drive, he asked what had happened.

Edward Stones was nervous, making him falter. 'Well, sir, well…we had a call an hour ago, maybe less than that. A woman's body has been found in the kitchen at that address and…'

'O.K. Constable Stones, that's enough information for now.' Failing to thank the young officer, Harvey informed Serena that they were going straight back out. 'You might as well come as well young man. I imagine it will be a new experience.'

Crowds had gathered outside the house which was cordoned off with the police tape familiar from the television. The PC on duty took their names, and once they had donned suits and boots, they entered the property. The small house felt cold and empty.

So jittery, he sounded like an actor who was having trouble remembering his lines, PC Stones muttered, 'Her son found her and phoned 999 and the call was put through to us. He was terribly upset and said he couldn't stay. He needed to go home and phone his dad and his brother who both live abroad. Apparently, his parents divorced, and his father now lives in Spain with a new partner. I've got the son's address and said someone would be round to see him later.'

This time remembering to smile at the young officer, Harvey asked him to follow him into the kitchen. Seeing his reaction to the body slumped on the floor he asked him if he wanted to leave. 'I think this is early days for you.'

'My first one, sir, but I'd rather stay and get used to it.'

'In my experience that never happens and indeed shouldn't. What we have here was a woman who until recently was very much alive. We know she was a mother, and probably a daughter, sister or friend. Her life has been cut short. That is invariably one of life's tragedies.'

Apart from the deceased the kitchen looked pristine. Modern units suggested it had been recently updated and gleaming white tiles lined the walls. Money had been spent on the American-sized fridge, gas cooker and the kind of microwave that did everything, though singing and dancing might be beyond it. The small pine table was set; cutlery for one was accompanied by a stainless-steel salt and pepper set large enough to contain a year's supply.

Nora Ederson had been an attractive woman, but death was doing her no favours. A large pool of congealed blood surrounded her head and had seeped into her hair.

'Looks as though she slipped and fell whilst cooking. These tiles can be lethal if they get wet.' Realising his faux pas, he grimaced and apologised. 'Sorry, sir, not the best words to use.'

'I agree. However, never ever assume anything. We need the doctor to come, and even more helpful the pathologist. I don't suppose you've attended a PM.' From the look of terror on the young man's face he knew the answer. Sometime soon he would have the pleasure of his first post-mortem.

A few minutes later, Harvey was pleased to see the doctor arrive. Natasha Cardiff was well known to him and he was always impressed by her business-like attitude. Immaculately dressed, she looked as if she was going out for lunch at a posh restaurant, not dealing with police matters and a cadaver. Tall and slim, with long curly brown hair, no one would guess the things she witnessed. Not one to waste words on trivialities she knelt by the body. 'Time of death is going to be hard to estimate before the pathologist does his bit. All I can say, with absolute certainty, is that this poor woman has been dead for some time. Maybe even a week, or longer. I'll pronounce the time of death as 2 p.m. today, but you'll know more after the PM.'

Pausing, she looked at the officers and asked if they were treating her death as an accident or something more sinister. 'She obviously suffered a blow to the back of her head, with the usual volume of blood any head wound creates, but the thing is, and I know this isn't my job, I couldn't help noticing that she has a large bruise on her cheek which, in my opinion, is not consistent with the fall that killed her. She might have had more than one dizzy spell, stumbled, and hit her cheek earlier, then blacked out later and fallen against a cupboard.

However, to me it looks suspicious, but I'll let the expert tell us more.'

Harvey was annoyed that he hadn't noticed the mark on the woman's face. The case had suddenly become far more interesting. Time to leave the room to the Scene of Crime Officers and go and talk to the son.

Chapter 5

Nigel Ederson was strangely calm, as though the events of the day had not yet fashioned their gruesome impact. That would come later. Harvey had seen every reaction to the death of a loved one and knew not to read anything into the son's demeanour.

'I thought Mum was on holiday. She was supposed to go away for a week. She loves Malta, goes every year, guaranteed sunshine. Since she and Dad got divorced - he walked out a month after paying for the new kitchen that he wanted more than she did - she goes on her own, says she is surrounded by people at work and it's good to have some time to herself. When I didn't hear from her, I wasn't bothered. She often fails to text or email when she's away. Likes to tell me all about it when she gets home. She was due back yesterday, so I thought I'd surprise her and call this morning. When did she get back? Do you know how long she's been lying there?'

There was no easy way to say it, Nigel would find out soon enough, so Harvey told him that in-all-likelihood his Mum hadn't been away, the doctor saying she'd probably been dead for over a week. 'We found her suitcase upstairs half packed, the outward-bound label in place on the handle.'

'God. No. That's horrible. Awful.' A long pause ensued Harvey afraid the news had been too much. 'I thought at least she'd had a great final week. She's been through a lot recently: the divorce and then the issues to do with her work. Poor Mum. Not fair. All last week I kept imagining her in the hotel she booked on the front in Mellieha, enjoying the food and sitting in the sun. I can't believe she didn't go. If I'd gone round earlier, could I have done something?'

'Probably not. The way she hit her head death would have been quick. I doubt if there was anything anyone could have done, even the professionals.' Leaving a gap, hoping some time would encourage the young man to talk, Harvey spoke softly. 'If you're up to it, can you tell us about your mother?' Harvey had noted the divorce and the mention of *issues* and could ask about both later. For now, it was enough to get the young man talking.

'She was a wonderful mother, always there for me and Ralph. She supported us in everything we did. When Ralph opted out of university after two years, saying the course wasn't for him, she helped him to start an online business. She wasn't that computer literate herself, but he came back to live at home, and she financed him for eighteen months until it took off. Dad wasn't pleased, said he should have stuck it out, finished his degree, and then pursued his idea on the internet. I don't think Dad wanted him living at home again and it was one of the many things my parents argued about. I can't say that was the main reason for their divorce, but it didn't help. When it happened, the divorce was acrimonious with bad feelings on both sides.'

'Was your mother financially secure following the split?' Harvey knew that money was often the cause of arguments, and indeed violence.

'Mum worked all her life, apart from time at home when Ralph and I were tiny. We're only nine months apart so she always joked that she was only allowed to enjoy one maternity leave. To be honest, she loved her job so much that I bet she missed it when she was at home with us.'

'What did your Mum do?'

'She was a senior midwife at Parkside Nursing Home. Mum was good at her job. That's really an understatement. She won the Midwife of the Year award twice and I've heard people say she virtually runs the place.' Nigel wasn't aware of his use of the present tense. 'Last year a group of new mums wrote to the paper, saying how amazing she was.' Breaking down Nigel said he needed to speak to his dad again. 'They weren't on good terms, but he sounded upset when I phoned him earlier. I promised to Skype once it had all sunk in.' Harvey thought that wouldn't happen any time soon, but knew the young man needed time on his own.

Nigel's final remark was unexpected: 'Can we talk later, there are some things I need to tell you.'

Wanting to know the cause of death before any further discussion, the PM results vital, Harvey said he would contact the young man to arrange a time to talk.

The following day the lowering skies made the morgue, housed in a hospital annex, hidden from public view, look bleaker than normal. Alfie Morrison was prepared: the tools of his trade laid out ready for the onslaught.

The pathologist had made the rest of the day free to conduct the two post-mortems, two bodies found twenty-four hours apart and both looking suspicious and in need of his attention. His technician had brought Nora Ederson first. The body, awaiting its final onslaught, was lying unceremoniously on the steel table, bright lights illuminating the scene that was about to make a Hammer Horror seem innocuous.

'Good day, my dear friend.' Harvey wasn't sure if Alfie Morrison was speaking to him or the corpse. 'What a sad state-of-affairs. You look far too young to be on my table. Rest assured I will do my best to find out what happened to you.'

Turning to look at the policeman, he beamed. 'And a very good morning to you, Harvey. And who is this young man, looking so unbelievably happy to be here?'

Introducing Edward Stones, Harvey explained that he was new to the force. 'It's his first PM.'

'First time will be hard, but you'll soon get used to it.' Winking at Harvey, he added, 'Well, most people do! Now do we know anything about the lady in front of me?'

Although they had been friends for years, the DCI still found Alfie's enthusiasm for his job out of keeping with the man who he knew suffered bouts of depression. When his wife had walked out (no explanation forthcoming) the previous year, Harvey had been so worried about him that he had insisted he go for help. Pills and counselling seemed to have improved the situation.

Bending over the table he laughed, a sound that seemed alien in the austere surroundings. 'I don't think my usual football chants are appropriate for you, my dear, I can't imagine you effing and blinding on the Kop. Perhaps silence is the more respectful option today, though I will have to give a running commentary on everything I do: I need to record my findings.' Turning to PC Stones, he added, 'I'll let you into a secret, the dour policeman will not be watching, but he will have to listen. I'll keep it simple and hope it's not too disconcerting.'

Turning to gaze at the table holding the body, he removed the sheet. 'Now. I can't name you after one of my heroes. The next man receiving my attention is going to be James Milner. He's such a versatile player. Great on the wing, in midfield and full-back…different terminology for defence, not that Liverpool had much of one at the weekend. Three goals against us in the space of fifteen minutes. Oh, one interesting fact: Milner came on a free from Manchester City. The bargain of the century.'

Smiling, Harvey said, 'Define interesting.'

'I am sorry to be interacting with those less cognisant with the finer aspects of the Beautiful Game. Seeing Edward Stones baffled look, the DCI explained that the pathologist was a football fanatic and invariably named the cadavers after his heroes. 'He'll start singing in a minute, but I warn you it's not a pleasant sound. Even worse than the drilling and sawing!'

'Tell me, young whipper-snapper. Which team do you support?'

'None. I've never got into organised sport and can't stand the money involved.'

'Well, blow me down. You look too normal to be a Man United fan, but I can see you on the terraces of some club, screaming and yelling. Though maybe not, you'd probably be one of the polite ones encouraging the lads to do better. So, no sports at all?'

'Chess is my game. I represented my school and university and was on the county short list. My dad taught me when I was very young, and I've always loved the game.'

'Chess? That takes brains, so not for me. You'll be telling me next that you like tiddlywinks!'

Blushing, Edward said he'd been his primary school champion every year.

'I wouldn't admit that at the station if I were you. Now to business.'

Knowing the routine, photographs of Nora Ederson clothed, then naked; cutting, sawing, and weighing about to begin, Harvey did what he had trained his mind to do and removed himself, at least mentally, to a more pleasant environment. Much to his amazement, once the process was under way, PC Stones stepped forward and watched the performance: the word Harvey used for Alfie's post-mortems.

'Harvey, DCI Tarquin, I'm talking to you. I know this is the last place on God's earth you want to be at this moment, but I think you might just want to know what killed the lady on the table.'

Apologising, Harvey muttered that he did indeed want to know the cause of death.

Smiling, Alfie said he'd send the reports through, 'By close of play! I'll start on Mr Winters after lunch, so you'll receive them in an amazingly short period of time.'

He knew Harvey thought that one post-mortem was more than enough, and that DI Peil had been asked to attend the second.

Driving back to the station Harvey realised that spring had vamoosed, with the speed of one of the latest Ferrari's which had been reported to accelerate from zero to 62 mph in 2.4 seconds. Winter showers, the seasons in reverse, had been forecast by a new weatherman who thought it was amusing to announce the forecast in raincoat and sou'wester. He had delivered the grim news far too cheerfully, serious reporting a thing of the past. When his final comment had been that global warming wasn't winning the day, Harvey had been tempted to throw something at the television, especially as the item preceding the weather had been about the glaciers disappearing in the Alps. The Lower Grindelwald Glacier, the *Unterer Grindelwaldgletscher*, at the edge of the stunning town in the Bernese Oberland had shrunk so dramatically that the lower part was no longer in existence. He remembered as a child walking up to it when it was at the edge of the village and being awestruck by its grandeur.

Patience was not one of Harvey's traits and he paced his office, unable to concentrate. It was late afternoon when Serena and Edward returned to the police station and informed him that Alfie had promised to forward the reports A.S.A.P. Finally, after what felt like days, the waiting interminable the reports arrived, Alfie Morrison being his usual efficient self, had written them up and forwarded them with a speed that Harvey found impressive. The pathologist's comment about two for the price of one made Harvey smile and he decided to start with the one he had missed.

Dr. Alfred Morrison. BSc; BM; MRCPath

Post-mortem: Mr Gerald Winters

Persons present:
DI Peil
PC Stones

On March 18th at approximately midday my presence was requested at 14 Wordsworth Avenue. A man's body had been reported lying on the dining room floor. On examining the deceased, I estimated that life had been extinct for over 48 hours. No reason was forthcoming for the delay in reporting the death.

It appeared to me that the body had been moved, post-mortem. The deceased was lying full length on the carpet, in an unnatural position following a sudden death. A doll and a tray of food had been placed beside the body.

He was a man of 39 years, approximately 1.8 metres in height and with a weight of 76 kg. Dark brown hair with some signs of grey developing. No scars, tattoos, or any other distinguishing features. His right elbow had recently been broken and was in the process of healing.

The deceased was dressed in a white vest, black Y fronts, a three-piece grey suit, white shirt, dark blue tie, black socks, and black outdoor shoes.

To begin the PM, photographs were taken of the man, clothed then unclothed. The body appeared to be well nourished. The only operation scar was to the right elbow. The break must have been severe to require surgical intervention.

The liver showed signs of alcohol abuse; the lungs looked to be those of a non-smoker.

Stomach content showed he had consumed a meal several hours before: fish, chips and peas, plus coffee. Whisky had been consumed a short while before death occurred. Large quantities of Oxycontin Oral used as an opioid to control pain and Temazepam were also present.

Harvey read the report several times.

Arriving at the conclusion, he gasped. It wasn't what he'd been expecting.

Conclusion

The deceased had been dead for approximately 48 hours by the time I arrived at the scene, some rigor mortis - which lasts approximately 72 hours - still evident.

The man had suffered a catastrophic reaction to the ingestion of excessively large quantities of Temazepam and the opioid Oxycontin Oral. The NHS has issued a black box warning concerning the effect of combining such drugs: "Taken together there is a very real danger of severe drowsiness, slowed breathing, coma and death."

Gerald Winters died from a quite staggeringly excessive overdose of drugs he must have been told must not be taken together.

Alfred Graham Morrison

Allowing himself a few minutes to consider the findings, he turned to the second report. Although he knew what to expect, it still made uncomfortable reading.

Dr. Alfred Morrison. BSc; BM; MRCPath

Post-mortem report: Mrs Nora Ederson.

Persons present:
DCI Tarquin
PC Stones

On March 19th at approximately 11:35 my presence was requested at 120 Rose Avenue. A woman's body had been discovered on the floor in the kitchen. On examining the deceased, I estimated that life had been extinct for between 7 to 10 days. She had suffered life-threatening blood loss. The blood, both behind her head and on the kitchen cupboard to her rear had congealed. There was a deep laceration to the back of her head and bruising to her left cheek.

She was a woman of 54 years and approximately 1.7 metres in height and 63 kg in weight. Medium length blond hair, pierced ears with small pearl studs in situ, an historic 2 cm length scar to the left of her mouth. No tattoos, or other distinguishing features.

The deceased was wearing indoor clothing: white underclothes, a blue blouse, dark blue trousers, and a grey cardigan. She had suede slippers on her feet.

Photographs were taken of the woman, clothed then unclothed. The body appeared to be well nourished. There were no operation scars, but the female had given birth. The cause of death was the deep laceration to the back of her skull which caused a fatal intracranial haematoma. Death would have been instantaneous. No bones were broken as-a-result of her fall, but there was a small abrasion inside her mouth, consistent with contact with her teeth. Bruising was evident on her back and on her right leg, most likely due to falling.

On examination, her internal organs were in good condition for a woman of her age. The liver showed no sign of alcohol abuse, though there was a slight lightening in keeping with blood loss. Her heart was in excellent condition as were the lungs.

Stomach content showed she had recently consumed a small meal: cheese sandwich, yogurt, and tea. Paracetamol was also present.

Not wanting to add to the queasiness that was developing, Harvey skipped over the weights of the various organs, the essentials that had once made her a living, breathing person. He knew the end of the report was what he wanted to read.

Conclusion

The deceased died sometime between March 9th and March 12th. She displayed no signs of natural disease.

The cause of death was the traumatic injury to the back of her head. That is consistent with her head coming-into-contact with the kitchen cupboard covered in her blood.

There was nothing to indicate that she was in danger of falling: no early signs of visual impairment, neuropathy, cardiovascular disease, Dementia or Parkinson's.

The bruise on her left cheek could not have been caused by the fatal fall but may have been the result of a previous, less serious stumble. However, it must be viewed as strange that such a healthy woman had two falls in a short space of time.

No defence wounds were present.

Alfred Graham Morrison

Having wanted to be alone to peruse the findings, he now demanded the company of his DI. Moaning like a child who'd not got the birthday present he'd asked for he muttered, 'No bloody use. Absolutely no use at all. We already knew ninety-nine per cent of Mrs Ederson's P.M. and could have written it ourselves, and the remaining one per cent tells us nothing. Even a ten-year old could have told us she died when her hard head hit an even harder surface. What we still don't know is whether she fell or was pushed. Smoke and mirrors; mirrors and smoke, that's all we've got.

'Gerald Winters' P.M. is slightly more interesting, a lethal dose of drugs in his system.' Pausing, he glared at Serena. 'So, what have we got? A woman who might or might not have been assaulted and a man who might or might not have deliberately taken his own life. Both could be murders. One might be, but not the other.'

'Do you think the two are linked, sir?'

'Let me put it like this: I've a strong feeling if we solve one then we solve both. And I'm more and more certain the proverbial foul play is involved. Far too much of a coincidence to discover two stiffs in our small town, neither with a valid explanation. I apologise, not the best word: two bodies far more appropriate.' Sighing, Harvey continued, thinking aloud. 'A push that led to an unfortunate out-come? Pills taken in error?'

Serena stared into space. 'Do we think either of those scenarios is correct? A deliberate assault and a poisoning are far more likely. So, as we've suspected, we have two murders to investigate.'

Chapter 6

Sunshine and a deep blue sky belied the event the two officers were investigating. Leaving the market town behind, each minute appeared to add to the cost of the dwellings. Mr and Mrs Page lived in a large, detached house situated at the end of a tree-lined road that led onto the fells. The views were spectacular. As they were shown into the front room a Rachmaninov piano concerto was playing softly in the background, one of the less well-known ones, not the one made famous by *Brief Encounter*. The room itself was beautifully furnished, the three-piece suite covered in a rich burgundy brocade which was replicated in the floor length curtains hanging at the large picture windows at opposite ends of the room. The thick carpet felt soft enough to sleep on. Lamps of varying sizes added to the comfortable scene. In a far corner a few toys stood to attention, like soldiers on parade waiting to be inspected. A dummy lay in the middle of the glass-topped table, a tray beside it already in position with a dainty milk jug and matching cups and saucers. It was not the usual type of home the police were accustomed to visit.

Once the introductions were over Mr and Mrs Page sat like animals stunned before slaughter. Sylvia Page looked exhausted and kept fidgeting with the fringe on her chair. 'This is beyond belief, we never thought we'd be involved in such a situation.'

If Harvey was surprised by her choice of words, he didn't show it. Richard Page stood nervously and left the room. After an interminable wait he returned carrying a second tray with a pot of coffee and home-made cake. As he dispensed the refreshments, he murmured, 'A terrible turn or events.'

Once again, the words sounded inappropriate.

Having suggested that Sylvia Page might be encouraged to talk if she was asked about the children, Serena opened the conversation by saying that Mrs Page must be finding it hard looking after five youngsters. 'My mum finds two grandchildren exhausting, especially when they stay overnight.'

After what felt like minutes rather than seconds, Sylvia spoke. 'I do feel a little on the tired side this morning. Adam is a gorgeous little thing, nine months next week, just starting to pull himself up. He's been crawling for weeks, very advanced. The trouble is he doesn't know day from night, and I was up with him four times. At my age I need my sleep. Not the beauty kind, that went long ago, but the pensioners' variety: as often and for as long as possible.'

Serena nodded in sympathy. 'And you had the four girls. Did you have to get them ready for school and nursery?'

Sylvia Page gave her husband a quick glance, then said that he had been a great help and that they were much easier than Adam. 'However, I hope that normal service will be resumed very soon. I presume that Susan is in the clear, that you won't be questioning her again. Children need their mother, especially babies.' Moving her head up and down in agreement, Serena was starting to feel like one of the annoying nodding dogs some misguided people thought looked cute in their car's rear window. 'It's really too early to tell. We might need to question her further.' She had never believed in lying to relatives.

Thinking the meeting was moving more slowly than the traffic in rush hour (what a misnomer that was) Harvey addressed the woman sitting so near the edge of her seat that he expected her to leap up and run away. 'Mrs Page, can you tell us about your daughter. Anything that might be helpful.'

'Why are you asking about Susan? You'll let her go. Surely, there's nothing I might say that can help you. Why do you need to know about her?' Harvey knew the mother was being defensive. Mothers were notorious for protecting their offspring: lying for them and providing false alibis, thinking they were protecting them. Harvey was used to those scenarios. Why then, did this feel different? Why was everything about this case starting to make him feel slightly nauseous, his body's way of reacting to a bizarre situation. Afterwards, he was to say to Serena that he felt out of his depth, a non-swimmer in need of a lifebelt.

'Mrs Page, Susan will probably be released, pending further investigation. However, she remains a person of interest (a dreadful cliché, but a more appropriate phrase eluded him) and it would be most helpful if you could give us some background: what she was like as a child; how she is now.' He refrained from saying how obdurate she had been during her interviews or how he was convinced there was something not quite right.

After a lengthy pause she began, speaking so quietly both officers found it difficult to hear and Serena asked her to speak up.

'Susan was a very lively child. She wasn't academic, in fact we got her extra help, especially when exams were due. The Lawrence Road Tutoring Centre helped her, especially a lovely tutor called Penny Morris...we still exchange Christmas cards.' Looking around, she was obviously thinking how to continue. 'Susan was more into sport. She played netball at county level for the under sixteens, and she was an amazing gymnast, entered competitions and has so many cups and certificates that they fill a shelf and an entire wall in her old room. Susan had a great social life, always lots of friends. Not finding schoolwork easy, she had no interest in going into the Sixth Form and left school at sixteen.' Pausing to look at Serena, she asked if any of that was what they wanted to hear.

'Anything you can tell us might assist us, so please carry on.'

'Bubbly, that was the word I'd use to describe my daughter back then. Wonderful at telling jokes, she could remember punch lines and would have us in fits. Several nights a week, and every weekend, she'd be out with friends. She liked a drink but knew when she'd had enough, not like some of the young people you see in town. Easy company, that was her. We're her parents but she never gave us any trouble. She was happy to stay living at home, even when some of her friends moved out to rented flats. Richard used to joke that she was too comfortable, that the service at home was too good: meals put down, washing done and a taxi service ever ready - like the batteries!'

Sylvia Page stopped. An uncomfortable silence filling the room. 'Oh dear, sorry, not the time for humour. Things changed and not for the better when she met

Gerald. He's a pleasant enough bloke and a good provider...he recently got a huge promotion at his bank. It came with a large pay rise. Susan said he was now a trouble-shooter, called to other branches to solve problems. The downside is that he's away a lot working throughout the Northwest. Sometimes he's away for weeks at a time and Susan finds it hard to cope. The nanny is good with the baby, but there are the older children who need a lot of attention. We help as much as we can.' Harvey waited for the but, eager to hear what would follow.

'Yes, well mannered, hard-working and very fond of our Susan. He was her first serious boyfriend. At eighteen no one knows what they want, or what's good for them, and she was bamboozled by him. No one had paid her that much attention before and she was flattered. When she told us they were engaged, we begged her to wait, to at the very least have a long engagement. She'd only known him a few months, not long enough to be confident he was the one. However, despite our best efforts they married. Susan was still eighteen and Gerald was just thirty-one. Too much of a difference for our liking. Far too much.'

'Mrs Page, we can see you're upset. Shall we take a break?' More drinks were suggested and accepted.

Harvey followed Richard Page into the kitchen. 'We are so sorry to upset your wife, but it's in the strictest confidence and is giving us some background.'

'Sorry? Strictest confidence? My wife has suffered enough and doesn't need some plods getting her to relive it all. You have no idea what the years have been like since she married that control freak. The situation has almost killed our daughter. Susan's a physical and emotional wreck and so is Sylvia. We put on a brave face when we see our daughter, and she knows we are always there for her. No doubt after a break my poor wife will tell you the rest.' The final words were delivered with such venom that Harvey heard himself deliver a further apology.

More drinks consumed (Harvey wondered how often he had sat drinking tea or coffee he didn't want) the only sound was the ticking of the Louis Quinze clock sitting on the ledge above the fireplace. Sylvia was ready to continue.

'A honeymoon baby is seldom a good idea. A couple need time to adjust to living together. We were shocked when Susan told us she was pregnant. Morning sickness lasted the entire nine months, accompanied by swollen ankles and terrible backache. All unusual in one so young. Following Hannah's birth, she'll be eight in the summer, Susan suffered a severe bout of the baby blues: post-natal depression. She's now endured five pregnancies: Hannah, Abigail who's six, Lara aged four and a half, Esther just over three and Adam. All because Gerald wanted a son. Don't get me wrong, we adore Adam, he's a real cutie, but Susan struggles constantly with motherhood. She does her best, but we get the feeling that nothing is too good for Gerald's heir. That's what he called him the day he was born. That birth was a physical torment, so much harder than the others and she was ill for weeks, well months. She's never fully recovered. When I think how she used to be it breaks my heart.'

Putting an arm round his weeping wife, Richard snapped at the officers.

'That's enough. I must insist that you leave. I do hope it has been the kind of background you want.

Please don't call again. I'm sure you can show yourselves out.' Richard Page looked as angry as he sounded.

As he reached the door, the DCI turned back, like a television cop wanting his moment when the vital question breaks the case and asked where the children went to school. 'I imagine the youngest ones will still be at nursery, so those details would also be useful.'

'Susan home-schools them all. She didn't like the local schools and thinks she can do a better job.' Richard Page sounded belligerent and repeated that they could leave.

Smiling at the angry man, Serena attempted to defuse the bad feelings. 'It's very quiet for a house with five children.' As if on cue, a wail emanated from a nearby room.

'Oh, that's Adam.' Sylvia Page almost ran into the hallway. 'I need to see to him. The girls are all upstairs. They are good at amusing themselves.'

'Goodbye inspectors.' Richard Page had followed them and shut the door firmly.

Once they were back on the main road, Harvey groaned. 'That's got to be one of the strangest ninety minutes I've ever experienced. We were not, and I mean not, being told the whole story. I'm not sure what they were hiding, but I'd bet my pension we weren't told many truths.'

'Did you notice that Sylvia Page looked at her husband both before and after everything she said. It was almost as though she was checking that what she was saying was acceptable. I agree that it's what wasn't said that's probably more interesting, but I wonder if he's a control freak like the son-in-law. And there wasn't much love lost with him. She was obviously sorry her precious daughter married Gerald Winters.'

'What did you make of her body language, Serena? You're the expert on that.'

'Interesting. If we'd been interviewing her as a suspect, I'd have had my suspicions and thought she might be feeling guilty. I'm sure she was prevaricating. Arms crossed, little eye contact, except with her husband, drink spilt and extremely fidgety. They could all be signs of fabrication. Or, of course, it's simply that she's upset that her daughter might be in trouble. That's got to be distressing. No one likes being questioned by the police, makes even the totally innocent nervous, so her attitude might simply be down to that.'

Harvey exploded, so loudly Serena jumped. 'It's just struck me. We should have followed it up. Susan is home-schooling the children, yet Mrs Page had already told us that her daughter wasn't academic, that all her talents lay in physical activities: netball, gymnastics and socialising! What in the world is she doing trying to educate her offspring at home?'

'That's a good point. The oldest daughter, Hannah, is almost eight, so should be in Year 3. I remember seeing the homework my niece had when she was in that year group. The numeracy made my brain cells work overtime and as for the spellings they're supposed to learn, they'd have been beyond me at that age.'

'Your question about the older children made Mrs Page jump. She told us they were extremely well-behaved and quote, "so much easier than Adam". I would love to know what the look her husband gave her at that moment meant. I think we will be talking to the Pages again.'

'Sir, I think our next interview should be with the nanny. See what she has to say about working for Susan Winters. I'll ask her to come to the station in the morning. Clare Jennings can observe.'

'Yes, and in the meantime, we'll let Susan Winters return to her brood.'

Chapter 7

The Winters' nanny, Harriet Devizes, had been asked to attend the station for a chat, although she was sure that was a misnomer. On receiving the phone call, she panicked.

'They just want to talk to you, nothing to worry about,' had been her mother's initial comment. 'They are obviously treating Mr Winter's death as suspicious and will want as much background information on the family as possible. Just answer their questions and you'll be fine.'

'What if I say something wrong? I was told to keep a lot of things to myself.'

'If it helps the police, you must forget what he said. From everything you've told me he was a bully, but he can't stop you now.'

'It's Susan I'm worried about so I can't tell them everything. It wouldn't be fair to her.'

11 a.m., the time etched on Harriet's brain. The DI had suggested it to allow time for Harriet to travel from Cumbria, not always the easiest journey. Arriving at the austere police station three quarters of an hour early she walked around the block a few times. There was a café opposite, but she was too nervous to go for a coffee.

The building looked even more menacing inside and she wondered if her legs would carry her to the front desk. Giving the duty sergeant her name, she looked like a candidate who realised she hadn't revised for an important exam.

DI Peil came down to meet her and took her to the interview room, the one that was the least oppressive. 'I love your layered look, very smart.' Serena was glad her boss couldn't hear her. She was impressed by the effort the young woman had made with her appearance: hair newly washed, the dark brown bob suiting her oval face. Dark trousers were topped by a pale blue blouse and multi-coloured waistcoat.

The nanny looked younger than her twenty-one years and appeared to be petrified.

'You don't need to be nervous we just want some background on life with the Winters. As you must be aware, we are treating Gerald Winters' death as unexplained (Harriet thought that sounded less serious than her mother's word "suspicious") and anything you tell us will be treated as confidential.'

The mood in the room changed as DCI Tarquin entered.

'Miss Devizes, you are not, at the present time, being charged with anything and are here voluntarily to aid our enquiry into the death of Gerald Winters. However, should you wish to have the assistance of a solicitor, one can be provided.'

Good cop: bad cop. It hadn't been discussed beforehand, but that appeared to be the way the boss wanted to play it.

'This is an informal interview (where had chat gone?) but so that we can remember everything I am now going to switch on the recorder.'

Interview with Harriet Devizes

Present: Harriet Devizes, DCI Tarquin, DI Peil

DCI: Thank you for returning to Fordway, Miss Devizes. You have been offered and declined the opportunity to have a solicitor present. Please will you confirm that for the audio tape.

H.D.: Yes, that's correct. I really don't think I need one.

DCI: We believe you have been working as a nanny for Mr and Mrs Winters. Could you tell us when you were appointed and started looking after the children?

H.D.: I qualified as a nanny last summer and saw the advertisement the Winters placed on an online site called *NannyforYou*. I'd trained in London but was keen to move back north as my family live in Cumbria, in Kendal, and I wanted to be closer to them. I had an interview in late July and started straight away.

DCI: Could you tell us what the job entails.

H.D.: I look after Adam. He's almost nine months now and a real little sweetie, crawling and pulling himself up on the furniture. He almost took his first step last week. Normally I do days, 8 a.m. to 6 in the evening, though when Susan, that's Mrs Winters, is having one of her off times, I stay in the spare room and have Adam with me overnight. He could be described as nocturnal and is awake and wanting to play several times each night. I don't think he's ever slept through and Susan gets stressed when she loses too much sleep.

DCI: Miss Devizes, you said you don't normally stay overnight at the Winters' house.

H.D.: No, I rent a small flat in town, on West Road. It's not brilliant but it's all I can afford. I'd have been happy to live in, but Mr Winters didn't want that.

DCI: You've said you look after Adam, the youngest of the children. Do your duties also include caring for the girls?

H.D.: No. No, I don't have anything to do with them. When I was appointed, it was made very clear that it was the baby I was to care for. It had been a difficult birth, and then with him not sleeping Susan was exhausted and needed help.

DCI: But she's not too tired to see to the girls.

H.D.: They are...really easy...no trouble...so Susan doesn't need my help with them. When they do get too much, her husband takes time off work and sees to them. Oh, that won't happen now.

DCI: A few minutes ago, you spoke of Mrs Winters, and said, "Susan gets stressed." Can you tell us what you meant by those words?'

H.D.: Well...she has sort of meltdowns and days when she can't even get out of bed. I hear her weeping and on one occasion she was ripping up some clothes. I know she's admitted that she has periods of depression and suffers from almost constant anxiety. Mr Winters was very impatient and told her to be grateful for everything he'd given her. Oh dear, I shouldn't have said that, but I couldn't help overhearing his tirades. Oops, not the best word but he really lost it at times.

DCI: I can assure you that anything you say will be treated as confidential and may well aid our enquiries.

H.D.: Thank you. I just feel so sorry for her. Things have never been right in that house. My mum keeps telling me to leave, but that would be deserting Susan and I do love Adam.

DCI: "Things aren't right in that house". Can you tell us what you mean by that?

H.D.: It's just a most unusual set up. Susan isn't well and Gerald was, I'm sorry to say this, a bully. He made no allowance, none whatsoever, for her fragility. I'm sure she doesn't want to keep producing babies and all the pregnancies have affected her both physically and mentally. Sorry, I'm not a doctor, it's just how it seems.

DCI: Miss Devizes, you are no doubt aware that a serious incident occurred at 14 Wordsworth Avenue sometime over the weekend. Gerald Winters' body was found in the dining room early on Monday morning and his death is being viewed as suspicious.

Did you go into the front room at any point before Mrs Winters phoned 999?

H.D.: No, I was looking after Adam and Susan told me not to go into the front room, not that I ever do. In fact, the only time I've ever been into that room was at Christmas. We all had dinner in there on Christmas Eve, then I left to go home to spend a few days with my parents. I can't believe what's happened. I just can't. He wasn't a nice man, but he didn't deserve that.

DCI: Would you like a break, Miss Devizes, or a drink?

H.D.: No thank you, it's just not something you think will happen to someone you know.

DCI: When you're ready, can you tell us in as much detail as possible, your timetable over the past four days.

H.D.: Last Friday, seems ages ago now, was a normal day. I arrived just before eight and gave Adam his breakfast, then changed him and as it was a pleasant morning, I walked around Elizabeth Park with him. He loves the ducks and we sat and talked to them for ages...he makes funny noises when he sees them. We stopped at the shops on the way home, the Spar on the parade near the park as Susan had asked me to get a few things. Adam was tired when we got home, had some lunch then slept for ages - he'd had one of his nights. I did some housework for Susan, not part of my duties, but she gets overwhelmed as

51

Mr Winters expects it to be just so. I played with Adam later in the afternoon, then gave him his tea, bathed him and put him to bed.

DCI: And what about the weekend?

H.D.: Unless Susan is unwell, I have the weekends off. I met some friends in Manchester and we went to a club in the evening, then I stayed at Paula's, she's a friend, a girl I went to school with. Home mid-afternoon Sunday and catch up on shopping and cleaning. Monday morning, I went to work as normal... normal until Susan told me she was ringing 999. Considering what she'd just found, she was surprisingly calm, and I heard her speak quietly on the phone.

DCI: It seems unusual that you left Mrs Winters at such a time and so quickly. Would it not have been better to stay and help with the children?

H.D.: Susan told me to go, she said her parents would look after them. I've never taken to Mrs Page, her mother, and I know she doesn't like me around when she comes to see Susan. I've never been to the Pages' house. I was somewhat shaken so decided to go home, back to my mum and dad's.

DCI: Thank you, Miss Devizes, you've been most helpful. I'll get this typed up and ask you to sign it.

Harriet Alison Devizes

Walking out of the interview room, Serena grimaced. 'Is no one, and I mean absolutely no one telling us the whole truth? More prevarications, maybe not lying, but not divulging anything they don't feel comfortable saying. You could call it lying by omission.'

'Any thoughts DS Jennings? You were observing, something I find hard in the middle of an interview.'

Clare Jennings was one of his best officers, and he was keen for her to be involved.

'Well, sir, Harriet was extremely nervous beforehand. That might be because she's never had dealings with us. She told you she'd never been inside a police station, or she might have been afraid of what we'd ask. She was extremely fidgety and didn't like some of the questions. The transcript doesn't highlight how long she waited before answering, or just how uncomfortable some of the questions made her. She was fine talking about Adam, and to a lesser extent Susan, but the rest troubled her. It was as though she had to plan what to say.'

'What we didn't pursue was why her parents wanted her to leave the job. A nanny looking after one small baby doesn't exactly sound onerous. And she had evenings and weekends off.'

'I thought it was interesting when she said she helped Mrs Winters with the housework. Maybe that was when the home schooling was taking place, though she claimed it was to keep Gerald Winters happy.' Clare hoped her comments had been helpful.

'DS Jennings give her a quick ring and ask about her parents' misgivings. Make sure you record her answer.'

Chapter 8

Needing to clear his head, Harvey had gone for a walk. The day wasn't very spring-like, but the many daffodils and tulips were showing off, like actors hoping for Oscars, each one trying to outdo the next. Elizabeth Park was almost empty, most people at work, just the usual array of dogs plus owners, enjoying their time outdoors.

'Good morning, not the best of weather, but just look at those flowers. Nature in all its glory.' The voice came from an elderly man who was obviously keen for a chat, his Labrador straining at the lead to be let off.

'O.K. Bernard, you can run wild in a minute, I'm having my relaxation first.'

Twenty minutes later, Harvey had no idea what the conversation had been about. He was almost certain the pensioner had done most of the talking, hardly surprising as all he could think about was a nanny who was as much of a conundrum as her employer.

'Lovely to talk to you, enjoy the rest of your day.' The DCI thought that was most unlikely.

Returning to the station, he was greeted by Clare Jennings.

'I phoned Miss Devizes and asked about her parents' concerns. I said it was just something we wanted to follow up. Well...as soon as I finished speaking, she burst into tears and said she didn't want to talk about it, that she'd volunteered more than enough information

- her exact words - earlier. I then pulled the *this is a murder investigation, and we could re-interview you under caution* line. There was a prolonged pause at her end, so long I thought she'd put down the phone.

'She then started to make up some convoluted story about her mum being a worrier and forever concerned about her. Apparently, and it's all on the tape, her parents can't forget when she had a minor breakdown during her final year at school and they don't want her "overdoing" things.

'To be honest, sir, I think she made it all up. During the silence, she'd had time to create a believable scenario, one I didn't believe. I think it was another load of cock and bull, a phrase my grandma loves. We'll soon have enough to start a farmyard!'

'Thank you for trying DS Jennings. It may come to an interview under caution, with a solicitor present.'

'Sounds like another no comment one!'

Bradford Street surgery was situated in a pleasant area on the edge of town. A Victorian building that had once housed a rich factory owner and his family, and no doubt many servants, had been rejuvenated to serve those for whom the NHS was deemed inappropriate. Four floors of well-equipped rooms were now used by privately funded doctors and practice nurses. There were several treatment rooms, the aim being to encourage people to attend instead of filling A and E with minor injuries. Other rooms were labelled Counselling, for those needing a different kind of help.

A rather brusque receptionist informed Harvey that Doctor Lennon was just finishing with the last patient of the morning.

'I get ten minutes, if I'm lucky,' Serena said after the pair had sat in reception for almost half an hour. 'Must be something serious, so the fact we've got to wait doesn't really matter. My aunt was once in for well over an hour, I know because I went with her. She was told…'

'DCI Tarquin, the doctor will see you now. Top floor, last door on the right.'

Rarely needing to see a doctor (he knew how fortunate he was) Harvey found walking into the room strangely disquieting. Doctor Lennon was on the wrong side of middle age, grey hair and a lined face made retirement look imminent. Introductions completed, Harvey asked about Susan Winters.

'Mrs Winters has been my patient since she was born and over that time, I have had cause to see her on many occasions. However, she remains my patient and as such I must abide by the doctor/patient code of confidentiality. I therefore fear that I can be of little assistance.'

Determined to remain calm, not the feeling he was experiencing, Harvey explained that they were dealing with a rather serious incident and anything the doctor could tell them about Susan Winters would be treated as confidential. 'Obviously, should it become pertinent to our enquiries it might be necessary for you to divulge further details' Harvey knew he was sounding pompous.

Following a long pause, the doctor stood and paced the room. Sitting down again, he stared at Harvey. 'This is extremely difficult for me, but what I'm about to say may help…both you and Mrs Winters. I have overseen each of Susan's pregnancies. They have not been easy for her, not easy at all, and she finds being a mother somewhat problematic. The new baby, Adam, is brought to see me on a regular basis, often with a slight snuffle or the kind of rash babies are inclined to develop.'

After pausing, obviously deciding how much more he could say, he continued. 'Susan is a young woman who has suffered, but more than that I don't want to, indeed can't, say. I would just ask you to treat her gently. There are times when she is near to not coping. Not coping at all.'

'Thank you, Doctor Lennon, that is helpful. Just one more question: can you tell me where Mrs Winters had the children?'

'As far as I recall, but I don't tend to get involved with the actual births, she had the first two at Parkside Nursing Home. In this area there are three choices: the maternity unit at Preston General, at home aided by a midwife, or Parkside Nursing Home, a rather expensive establishment between Fordway and Blackburn. Only the wealthy have the advantage of being able to give birth there. It has an excellent reputation, though of course nowhere is perfect. I always got the impression that the Winters were quite well off and an upmarket facility suited them. When Gerald Winters needed a small operation on his arm, he came to us. I remember him saying it wasn't that he didn't trust the NHS, but if he paid the op could be done straightaway. We are licensed to undertake minor surgeries.

After stopping for a moment, he continued. 'The other children were home births with a private midwife engaged.' Pausing again, he appeared to be thinking how much more to say. 'However, and this may sound like a criticism, he baulked at paying any extra for his wife's mental problems, giving the time-honoured phrase that she "needed to pull herself together and get on with it." I always found him rather impatient and lacking in empathy and over the years I think he has added to his wife's anxiety. 'We offered some counselling sessions for Susan which he refused. It seemed to me that he was the one who made all the decisions and I'm not sure if he ever gave her the option to attend for appointments here. I don't mean to speak ill of the dead, but that was my impression of him.

'That really *is* all I can say. She's a pleasant young woman and wants to do her best, indeed is desperate so to do. I'm extremely sorry to hear the police are involved and that there is a problem. I assume you're in the same boat, not able to disclose too much.'

Thanking the doctor for his time, the officers walked out. 'He described it as a problem Yes, a body on her dining room floor might just qualify as that.' Serena sounded disappointed. It felt as though they had learnt nothing.

Harvey turned to face her. 'You know I said that the parents were keeping something back, well I think the doctor was trying to tell us something whilst maintaining his precious doctor/patient confidentiality. He said something. I'm just not sure what.'

'Sir, the thing I can't get out of my mind is that the doctor said that Mrs Winters gave birth at Parkside and we know that Nora Ederson was a midwife there...and I don't believe in coincidences!'

The Pages sat over lunch which neither of them wanted. Sylvia was lost in her own thoughts then said, 'Richard, you know we've never had dealings with the police before today. They were here for almost two hours and their visit has left me drained, both physically and mentally. I wonder who else they are talking to and how much they will discover. We've learnt to cover up so much, and I now wonder if we've done the right thing. All I know is that a mother will do anything for her child. Anything.'

'Stop worrying, Sylvia. He's out of our lives and that's all that matters.'

I've been released. My house is a crime scene, so I'm not allowed to go home yet. The DI said she was sorry not to be able to give me an idea of when we can return. Mum and Dad are being kind, almost overwhelmingly so: looking after Adam, making sure the girls are comfy and plying me with meals that I don't really want. It's not the same as being in my own house, but better than the police cell. I've always known they didn't approve of Gerald, and he comes to see me when they are in another part of the house.

I'm not sure it's him, and we don't speak. How I long to get back to normal.

Chapter 9

Driving to work, Harvey found it hard to concentrate, almost failing to stop when green turned to amber. Two murders reported in so short a period of time was a first. One a well-respected midwife, dead for a week, the other, a body that had lain unreported on a dining room floor for up to two days.

Walking into the large central office he was pleased to see that two boards had been set up, the two victims displayed prominently. He knew the importance of seeing them as real people who had been alive, years ahead of them, their lives cut short. The rest of the team were already working, and the DCI felt like a child arriving at school after the register had been called: the rest of the class busy learning that week's spellings.

Not one to waste words on apologies, he launched in. 'D.I. Peil, I'd like you to visit Parkside Nursing Home.' It wasn't politically correct, but he knew he'd be uncomfortable in such a female environment. 'You can speak to Nora Ederson's boss and hopefully some of the nurses who knew her. I'll go back to talk to her son. His final remark left me intrigued. He indicated there was something we needed to know.'

Arriving at the nursing home, Serena thought she'd seen less well-appointed hotels. The reception area was plush, with deep carpets and a range of tasteful watercolours on every wall. The young receptionist looked like one of the beauty consultants in Boots, her make-up and hair immaculate. Her name label said she was called Olivia.

As soon as Serena began to explain the reason for her visit, Olivia burst into tears.

'Sorry, but we're all in a state of shock. Nora was the best, the very best midwife, and such a lovely person. She always stopped to have a chat and ask after my family. She was so lovely when Mum was ill. Do you know what happened? How did she die? I just can't believe she won't be here anymore.'

Muttering condolences, Serena asked to speak to the matron. She'd looked at the nursing home's website and seen the old-fashioned title was still used.

Ten minutes later, she was sitting in Petra Moreton's office. The space was large and well-furnished with an oak desk and the kind of upright chair designed to aid a bad back: ergonomic and rather expensive. Four wingback chairs surrounded a low coffee table and a long settee sat in front of French windows which overlooked a garden that obviously benefitted from the attention of at least one gardener. The fabric that covered the settee and chairs matched the pale lemon self-patterned fabric of the floor length curtains framing the view. Several paintings adorned the walls. Serena thought her boss would be struck by them: all similar in style to the Impressionists in his office.

Mrs Moreton stood to welcome the officer and suggested they sit by the glass-topped coffee table. Wearing scrubs, she looked like a more junior member of the nursing team. Seeing Serena looking at her dark blue short-sleeved shirt and trousers, she said, 'I like to do the job I was trained for and the one I still love.

Paperwork can wait. The mums and babies are why we're here.'

'Thank you for your time, Mrs Moreton. I realise how busy you are, but you will have heard about one of your senior midwives, Nora Ederson, and…'

Obviously upset, her voice wobbling, the matron interrupted. 'I can't believe it. None of us can. Not Nora.' Fighting a losing battle with the tears that had been threatening to fall since Serena entered the room, she spoke, so softly that Serena had to lean forward to hear her.

'Nora Ederson was probably the best midwife with whom I've ever had the pleasure of working. She was utterly professional, on many occasions staying well after her shift should have ended to see a delivery through. She was awarded the Midwife of the Year accolade several times and both staff and mums adored her. They say everyone is replaceable, but in Nora's case that will be hard.'

'How long had Mrs Ederson worked here?'

'She was here long before I was appointed. I'd say getting on for at least three decades. I've been at Parkside for twelve years and she was very well established by the time I started. I took over from Miss Simpson. I do know that Nora started here as a junior midwife and gained her promotion very quickly. You might want to talk to Imelda Simpson, I think they kept in touch. When she retired, she moved up to the Lakes, but Nora spoke about meeting up with her at weekends.'

'Mrs Moreton, the police are investigating the circumstances surrounding Mrs Ederson's death. Is there anything else that you could tell me that might aid our inquiry?'

A prolonged silence made the hairs on the back of Serena's neck twitch. There was something.

'I don't know what to say, how to put it, but Nora wasn't herself recently. She was quiet and withdrawn, totally unlike her usual outgoing bubbly style. She wasn't due any holiday leave but came to me one Friday after her shift and asked how soon she could book a couple of weeks off. It was most unlike her; she was normally punctilious about sticking to her schedule. She looked upset, but either wouldn't or couldn't tell me what was wrong. Fortunately, I was able to give her some leave a week later. She was grateful and said she'd book herself a last-minute holiday, that she needed to get away. Once again, she didn't elaborate. I wish I'd pressed her more.'

Allowing the matron to compose herself, the tears now flowing freely, Serena said that people often found it hard to speak about personal problems.

'Can I ask how she died? All we've been told is that one of her sons found her in her kitchen. Such a terrible shock for him.'

'It's very early days and I'm afraid I can't say much, but thank you for your time, and if you think of anything else that might be helpful, please ring this number.' Serena was certain there was more.

A journey that should have taken Serena half an hour took almost double: an accident had brought the town to a standstill. Harvey was waiting, impatience personified.

'You took your time.'

'Sorry, sir, two lorries involved, each thinking they were so important that they had the right to be first under the low bridge on Forrest Road.'

Ignoring her excuse, Harvey launched in. 'There's more to our midwife than we first thought. Her son was extremely forthcoming.'

'Well, sir, according to the matron at Parkside, Nora Ederson was the twenty-first century's Florence Nightingale, though there are…' the DI was interrupted, the end of her sentence left hanging as her boss said they should speak privately.

Once in his office, the door slammed behind them, Harvey began. 'Yesterday we were told that Nora was a model of propriety, an outstanding practitioner, a superb professional (Serena knew from long experience that her boss became garrulous when he thought a case was developing) loved and adored by everyone. From what I've gleaned today, that was not, and I do mean not, the whole story.'

Pacing the room, another trait of which the DCI was unaware, he began, talking as though he was addressing a party-political conference. Serena knew better than to do anything other than sit still and listen.

'I've just spoken to Nigel Ederson on the phone. He told me that over the years his mother had received several, a word he reiterated more than once, pieces of hate mail. When the first one arrived (many years ago) his mother ignored it, saying that new mums were extremely emotional, that giving birth was a traumatic experience. When I asked what it said, Nigel couldn't recall the exact wording but was almost certain it included the words "incompetent" and "negligent".'

Despite knowing her boss expected her to remain silent, Serena asked, 'Did she keep the letter?'

'No, and I was just coming to that. Nora didn't follow her son's advice and destroyed it. Apparently, she had a fair idea who that one was from and said she was sorry for the woman whose early labour made the baby unviable: too underdeveloped to survive. As there were no more letters Nigel assumed it was a one-off from a distraught woman. That was until they started to arrive on a regular basis. When I say regular, I mean every twelve to eighteen months.'

'Did his mother have any idea who sent the subsequent ones? Can they have been from the same person?'

'Nigel says he asked his mother about them, but she refused to tell him anything. He's not sure whether, or not, she knew who had sent them. All she would ever say was that women got extremely upset when anything went wrong and looked for someone to blame. He remembered her saying, "My job is the best in the world when things go right, and a new mum has a healthy baby in her arms. However, it's the worst, the agonisingly worst, when a baby doesn't make it or is born with something wrong."'

Looking at Serena he asked if the matron had given any indication that all was not well.

'No sir, or not in so many words, but I had a feeling that she wasn't telling me everything. She did say that Nora had been quiet and withdrawn during the last few weeks and that it was most unusual for her to ask for extra leave.'

'Did she mention anything regarding a complaint the nursing home received about eighteen months ago? Another gem her son shared.'

'No, sir. I gave her my card and asked her to contact me if she wanted to add anything.'

'I somehow think there's a lot the matron might want to add. Maybe want is the wrong word, needs a much more appropriate one. We will invite her to come into the station. Make it formal.'

Chapter 10

Even the innocent experience a feeling of guilt, wondering what they've done, when invited to attend an interview at a police station.

Petra Moreton arrived early. Obvious care had been taken over her appearance. The nurse's scrubs had been replaced by a black suit, the darkness relieved by a red blouse and matching accessories. Looking extremely nervous she sat down in the interview room. No cosy chat envisaged.

Marching in, like a major about to review his troops, Harvey announced that DCI Tarquin and DI Peil were present to interview Mrs Moreton in connection with the death of Nora Ederson. Sounding as angry as he felt, Harvey began the interview.

'Mrs Moreton you have been asked to attend today to give us more information about Mrs Nora Ederson.' A short pause was added, the matron looking even more discombobulated. 'I don't like it when one of my officers is not told the full story. It wastes everyone's time.' Giving the matron time to absorb his words, he continued. 'DI Peil was told by you that your employee was an outstanding midwife with many years of service at your nursing home. Unfortunately, very unfortunately, we now know that was not the full story.'

Looking as uncomfortable as a vegetarian faced with a sirloin steak, Petra asked what the inspector meant.

'Oh, come now, Mrs Moreton. You can't have forgotten the accusations levelled at Nora Ederson less than two years ago. They never made the press, but I have learnt that the internal investigation lasted weeks and that Mrs Ederson was suspended for six of them.'

'And fully exonerated. When I told DI Peil that Nora was an exemplary midwife, I meant it. The accusations were malicious and without substance. The poor woman went through hell whilst everything was investigated.'

'Despite that, we need to know what the accusations were.'

After a prolonged silence Petra Moreton began to speak. 'As a midwife one sees everything: the joys and the tragedies. The latter bring a range of accusations, each one followed up and if necessary, acted upon. Changes made where deemed necessary. The one relating to Nora was from a woman who had experienced a prolonged and difficult labour. The main accusation against Nora was that she left the woman with a young, inexperienced nurse. The baby's heartbeat was growing weak, and the nurse didn't call for a doctor in time and the baby didn't make it. Dead by the time the doctor was able to deliver the little girl with forceps. It had been far too late for a C section. Nora had assumed that the nurse would know to ask for help if it was needed. Indeed, she had expressly told her to do so. That was a strong part of her defence, plus the fact she was in another suite delivering twins, one of whom was breech. She didn't know anything until it was too late.

'The unfortunate mother was so damaged that future childbirth is highly unlikely and although she had been warned that any labour would be difficult – she has a very small pelvis and had been advised to have a Caesarean section which she had refused point blank, having been adamant that wanted to go ahead with a vaginal delivery.'

'Once the Home's authorities had concluded their investigation, I assume the mother was told their findings.'

'Yes. She was invited to a meeting and took the report as well as could be expected. She was still grieving the loss of her baby. Returning home to an empty nursery must be agony and there were a lot of tears. We've not heard any more about it. Nora was shaken. Badly shaken. It took time to recover, but the staff were unfailingly supportive.'

'We'd like the mother's name, and of course the father's as well.'

'Mr and Mrs Henderson. At the time they lived near Elizabeth Park, but I heard they moved down to Dorset to be nearer family.'

Harvey knew that didn't rule them out. Vengeance wasn't interested in a few hundred miles. 'If you have their forwarding address that would be helpful.'

'Can I ask. Are you treating Nora's death as suspicious?'

'There are aspects that we need to clarify. Just one last thing, Mrs Moreton. Were there any other accusations levelled at Mrs Ederson? Did she mention any she'd received at home? Ones that didn't become official?'

A shake of the head was followed by a quiet, 'No. None that I'm aware of and I think she would have told me.'

Or maybe not. What other secrets had the midwife been keeping?

Thanking the matron for attending Harvey marched back to the incident room. 'Time is finite, and we seem to be wasting most of it. Progress nil. We're like a team that can't score, no shots even on target. Surely tomorrow will bring something.'

Chapter 11

Tomorrow brought rain that battered the windows, one of which was leaking, a small puddle forming on the well-worn floor. The wind was growing to the predicted gale force and the team came in dripping, even the short dash across the car park soaking them, umbrellas useless.

'I don't know about anyone else, but I had the heating on full last night and took a hottie to bed.' Serena's superfluous comments received a stony look.

Harvey hated small talk and thought the adjective described it perfectly. Getting straight to the day's agenda he asked for everyone's attention. 'Edward Stones has now been assigned officially to our investigation. The powers that be, in their infinite and no doubt divine wisdom, want us to deal with both local murders.' Groans were followed by various expletives. 'Yes, not ideal, but like the Light Brigade ours not to reason why. Fortunately, I believe that the young PC will prove to be an asset. He impressed me yesterday, and I asked for him to be transferred. The lad is inexperienced, but he is keen to learn and most enthusiastic. I'm sure you all remember how that felt! Many moons ago for some of you.'

Allowing for the smiles and brief laughter that followed his last comment, he continued. 'He's a degree entrant to the force (groans) so will in any case be fast-tracked, so we'd better make the most of him whilst he's with us.'

Looking at Serena he said, 'DI Peil, I'd like you to act as his mentor. Let him shadow everything you do. You're the one who knows about body language in interviews so make sure you pass your knowledge and insights on to him.'

Turning to look at Clare Jennings, he said, 'DS Jennings we've been told that the girls in the Winters' family are all home-schooled. I know it's legal, but somewhat on the strange side if what Susan's parents say is true, that their daughter isn't academic. Certainly not the Brain of Britain. I want to know the ins and outs of home-schooling: how one goes about getting permission; what the follow up checks are and who undertakes them; and what curriculum the children should be following. In state schools there's the National Curriculum but does that apply at home? I'd like to know if the children are required to take any tests.'

Clare stood, her modus operandi when speaking in a meeting. 'Sir, D.I. Peil asked me to follow up a lead from your interview with the Parkside Home's matron. I was staying late so I tracked down the new address and phone number for Mr and Mrs Henderson in Weymouth, the ones who made the complaint against Nora Ederson. To cut the story short, it was Mrs Henderson's mother who answered the phone. She's house-sitting as her daughter and son-in-law have been visiting friends in Chicago for the last ten days. They were therefore out of the country when Mrs Ederson was killed.'

'So not the kind of suspects it's worth pursuing! Unless anyone fancies a trip to America.'

'Three funnies in one morning. He must have tried some of the Class A drugs the squad sequestered at the weekend.' The comment went unacknowledged.

PC Stones walked into the room, his suit freshly pressed, and his shoes and shirt so bright he seemed to counteract the rain still hammering on the windows. His six-foot two frame was topped by black hair combed into submission the curls barely noticeable. 'Good morning, sir. I've been told to report to you.'

After introducing him and remembering to welcome him to the team, Harvey told him he was working with Serena. 'Listen, watch and learn and you won't go far wrong.'

Folders were distributed with lists of people who needed to be interviewed. 'To start with we are concentrating on the body at 14 Wordsworth Avenue. That is the home of Mrs Susan Winters. By the end of the day, I want written reports with every bit of information you have gleaned about the Winters: from neighbours, friends, relatives, other mums and Tiddles the neighbourhood moggy. What was the state of their marriage recently? How much did they socialise? What do work colleagues know? How does Susan Winters spend her days? Do the children play out? Do either the parents or the children have many friends and if so, do they go to the house? And most importantly did anyone see anything late last week or at the weekend?

'I came in early and had a fascinating, and rather illuminating, conversation with Eric Winters, the deceased's brother. When he was told about his brother, he came straight to Fordway. Apparently, he's lived in France for several years. We'll collate all our findings later. We need to know everything there is to know about Susan and Gerald Winters. There's something "off" about that family and if we find out what it is, we may be nearer to solving the man's demise.'

Gazing around, Harvey reiterated his last point. 'Someone must have seen, heard or been aware of something at the house. I want to know what. Time of death is estimated some time on the Friday evening or possibly very early Saturday morning, but the body wasn't reported until the following Monday morning. Find out the who, why, where and when. Anything, some minute detail might be vital, so please, please make sure you record everything.'

Unable to keep still, an increasingly common occurrence, Harvey was prowling around his room, stopping at regular intervals to view his array of Monet's and Van Gogh's. He personified the phrase, "I don't know what to do with myself." More than anything he wanted to discuss the meeting he'd undertaken with Eric Winters. Sitting down he looked at the transcript he'd made. He didn't need it as he recalled the meeting verbatim.

'Gerald and I were twins. He was born five minutes before me so always claimed to be older and without doubt my superior. We were identical: in looks if not temperament and interests. At home we had separate bedrooms, just as well or World War Three would have broken out. When we went on holiday, we had to share a room. They might as well have had an invisible Berlin Wall down the middle: his side was immaculate, clothes hung up, dirty linen in a bag ready to go home, and all his books, comics and games set out at right angles on the table or tucked away in a cupboard. My side looked as though the war had begun. I've never been tidy, drives my partner nuts.

'Gerald was the academic one at school: maths, further maths and science all grade A at A level. I was more into the arts and loved to draw, sketch and paint. No wonder he became a bank manager and I make my living selling my paintings to the tourists in the Dordogne. I'm no Renoir or Cezanne, but I sell enough to make a reasonable amount of money. Jonathan, my long-time partner, and soon to be husband, is a photographer and he's good! Prizes won and work exhibited in London, Paris and New York.

'Despite our different personalities, as children Gerald and I got on surprisingly well and stayed in close contact once we were adults. That is, until he got married. It was a fairy-tale day: cloudless blue sky, expensive outfits (Susan looked beautiful and smiled for England), lovely old church in Willesden, as you know just outside Fordway, overlooking the fells, great buffet at The Elms. As I said, Susan looked the part, but I was concerned about the age difference. She was only eighteen, over a decade younger than my brother and obviously far less familiar with the world.

'I acted as best man, neither of them bothered that Jonty was there. When it was my cousin's do (ironically where Gerald and Susan met) someone told me that he hadn't even contemplated asking me to do the honours as he didn't like the fact that I'm gay. However, I digress.

'So, nuptials successfully completed, off they went on honeymoon and that was the last time I saw them. For the first couple of years Jonty and I were living down on the south coast and we suggested, on a regular basis, that they came down to visit. There was always some excuse: pregnancy (by the time they returned from holiday Susan was already expecting Hannah), one of the children was ill or there was a crisis at work. Our suggestions that we venture north were met with similar responses.

'When we moved to France (the Dordogne is perfect for our work as artists) the only contact with my brother was the occasional email and Christmas and birthday cards. Theirs always included photos of the children, a good-looking quintet, and thanks for the presents we continued to send. Strange to think I've got four nieces and now a nephew I've never met.'

'So, am I correct that you've never been to their house?'

'Unfortunately, that's the case.'

'It's not that I don't believe you, but would you mind providing your fingerprints? Really to eliminate you.'

'That makes it sound serious. Are you thinking my brother didn't die from natural causes?'

'At the moment we're keeping an open mind.' When had he started to speak in clichés? 'You've said you had very little contact with Gerald, but can you tell me when you last spoke to him?'

Eric took time to reply. 'Probably last Christmas, or it might have been on our birthday: February 21st. It's strange; I have made a great deal of effort to try to speak to him recently. Did I have a premonition that it might be the last time, or did I just want to share my exciting news, though I doubt he'd have come to my wedding? However, I never got through, it always went to the answer phone and he never called back. Jonty and I are adopting a baby, well he's a toddler, ten months old, called Pierre, a real little cutie. I wanted to tell Gerald that he was going to be an uncle. Since our parents died, within six months of each other, Dad to cancer and Mum a heart attack, we should have grown closer. Too late now. Far too late.'

No two families were the same and most hid their idiosyncrasies from public scrutiny. Despite this Harvey felt uncomfortable. No explanation had been forthcoming about the sudden cessation of contact between the siblings, who according to Eric had once been close. He had used the words confused, disappointed and unfathomable and had added that Jonathan (Jonty) had wanted them to come over unannounced and visit the family.

'To most people that would sound sensible. However, I was convinced that there was a reason Gerald had cut contact and it would have felt like an intrusion, an act of aggression, and we know where they lead, to turn up uninvited. At the back of my mind, I was convinced that he would, one day, ask to see us.

'Susan was not to blame, of that, I'm sure. From the get-go she was under Gerald's control. That was one way the age difference manifested itself. I remember one night, a few weeks before the wedding, the four of us were out for a meal (Jonty had an appointment in Manchester and we then spent the weekend in Fordway) and Gerald told Susan exactly what she was going to eat. When she whispered that she didn't like steak cooked rare, he said it was the only way to eat it and she had better get used to it. The poor girl almost balked, but she finished every-last morsel. Afterwards I told my brother that he needed to ease up, that for a relationship to work it had to be a partnership of equals, each allowed to enjoy their differences. A chilling look was his response. Maybe I should have spoken to Susan, but the opportunity never arose, Gerald an ever-watchful guard dog.'

Harvey reran the conversation in his head. Why had Gerald broken all contact with his twin brother? If, what Eric had said was true, they had been close, right up to the day of the wedding. Harvey had been disappointed to hear that both their parents were deceased, unfortunate as they might have been able to add to the story. And there was a story. Of that he was certain.

Chapter 12

First to give Harvey an update was Clare Jennings. Despite her recent engagement, her fiancée Rick a teacher at the local secondary school, and regular talk of weddings, venues, dresses, and bridesmaids, (Harvey switched off when she was talking to Serena) she continued to be one of Harvey's most reliable officers, sometimes seeing things others missed, and he valued her judgement.

Over the past eighteen months she had changed from an unfashionable girl whose outfits consisted of dark trousers and plain tops to an escapee from the catwalk. 'I don't spend any more, just take ages shopping,' was a comment he had overheard. Today's outfit was a long-sleeved maroon dress that swung out from the waist. Ankle boots in almost the same colour completed the look.

'Good afternoon, sir. I investigated home schooling. I looked it up online and went to the local Education Office. The info online said, and I quote: "It's not the responsibility of the state to educate a child." That came as a surprise. "The state must provide adequate establishments which must be available for every child. However, no parent is obliged to make use of such facilities." I assume they meant schools! "It is a parent's right to educate a child at home if they think they can do a better job."

'Now here's the thing I found fascinating, and if I'm honest, disturbing. When I went to the Education Office, I spoke to Mrs Tomkins. She's the one who's in overall charge of home-schooling. She told me that anyone can home-school their child, without giving a reason and that - wait for it - there is no legal duty for the local authority to monitor the provision the child or children are receiving. It seems that home visits are rare, or only carried out in extreme circumstances. That seems to be when social services are involved or there's been a bereavement in the family. Help is available from the local authority but there is no legal requirement to follow the National Curriculum. If, and she said it was extremely unusual, there is cause for concern, that the child is not being taught adequately, the authority can ask for a School Attendance Order, stating that the child needs to attend a school.'

Pausing for breath, Clare looked at her boss with a wry smile. 'Now the most interesting thing of all. There is no record of the Winters' house having been visited. But when I asked if that was unusual, Mrs Tomkins said it wasn't.'

Walking in, Serena looked like a toddler who had been given too many toys and didn't know which to play with first.

'Sir, I've put the information I gleaned from the neighbours on your desk. Interesting reading, the Winters certainly didn't do much socialising and even after several years no one seems to have known much about them. I'll leave you to read the transcripts.'

After a short pause she continued, 'Also Susan's doctor phoned a few minutes ago. He was obviously unsure what to say, muttering about professional confidentiality again, but apparently, he thinks it might help us to know that he did refer Susan for counselling last year. Her parents had rung him, in obvious distress, and said they would be more than happy to pay for treatment if he could suggest someone good. The woman she went to see might be willing to talk to us. I don't mind going on my own to see her.'

Nodding, Harvey said he was only too happy to let her go alone especially as there was only room for one police officer at a time to lie on the couch. 'Don't let her psychoanalyse you. You might not like what she says!'

Walking into his office, Harvey was aware how dull the day continued to be. It didn't help that his window let in very little light. He hoped it wasn't a warning and that the case would remain in the shadows. Picking up the first statement, he was pleased to see Serena had got a signature at the end.

Mrs Tara Summers

We've lived here for five years, moving in after Susan and Gerald. Our houses aren't exactly side-by-side, there are small plots of land either side of the Winters'. No idea why they haven't been built on. I digress. In all that time I've hardly exchanged a dozen words with her, though he can be slightly more friendly, at least passes the time of day. We exchange Christmas cards, but they've never been to the Boxing Day party we always host. Every year Jim sends an invitation, but we've never had a response.

I know they've got several children, but when I suggested they might like to come round to play (one time I had the paddling pool out, a glorious summer's day and Sam and Isaac were having great fun) she said that the girls preferred their own company. She must home-school them as they don't go to Otterton Road Primary where all the local kids go. It's a shame as it's a really good school, always gets Outstanding from Ofsted.

You never see them playing out, but we hear them in the back garden. They sound as if they're having fun, though with the usual squabbles. My two are friends one moment, enemies the next! Gerald once told me they always prefer (his word) to stay inside. That's strange in such young children. I think Susan's scared of letting them go too far, thinks something bad is going to happen. She strikes me as the nervous type, looks over her shoulder all the time when she ventures to the shops. Never takes any of them with her. Oh, I tell a lie as the latest one, a boy finally, is pushed there sometimes in his pram. I think she waits until her mum comes to look after the girls. There's a nanny, but she looks too young to be left with so many youngsters. Adam's a bonny baby and Susan looked pleased when I showed an interest.

Sorry not to be more helpful, but that's about all I can tell you. Sad isn't it that we've been neighbours for so long yet have so little to do with each other. Jim says at least they're a quiet pair and never cause any trouble. His brother had the most horrendous people next door to him and had to get the police involved. Oops, going off on one of my tangents.

I know you can't tell me too much, but I do hope neither of them is in trouble, though I heard about the ambulance and then the police being at the house on Monday morning. We were away with friends last weekend and not back until Tuesday, so that's hearsay, and I don't know if anything was different over the weekend. Gemma's the one to ask. Jim says she's a one-woman Neighbourhood Watch.

Tara Summers

Ms Gemma Norton

I live opposite Susan and Gerald. I've been here for fifteen years and when they moved in, it must be getting on for a decade ago now, I went across to welcome them to the area. They'd not been married long but she was already showing, pregnancy not suiting her. She looked washed out and exhausted.

They were polite but made it obvious they didn't want to become involved with any of the neighbours. We all get together a few times a year, adults and children. I've got three, reverted to my maiden-name when Nick and I got divorced. The parties are fun and to start with we always invited them, but there were a variety of excuses: Susan was pregnant again and not well, he was away with work, or one of the children was ill. In the end, we stopped trying to include them.

You don't see much of the children, just occasionally a glimpse in the upstairs window. Their toys are sometimes left on the front path, so they must go out to play. I think they prefer the back garden, it's huge and very private. I only know that as a parcel was once left when they were out, and I took it round to the back door. The back garden was littered with discarded toys. I always make mine tidy up after themselves, but each to their own. Come to think of it, that day Susan looked shocked when she saw me there.

It's strange that you see the children so seldom. However, one day I did see two of the girls going to town with Susan. Pretty little girls, both dressed in smocked dresses, the kind Kate dresses Charlotte in: you know the royal look. They were some distance away, so I didn't speak to them. Not even sure it was them.

Last weekend? I saw and heard Gerald come home. Her parents had been there all day, but they usually leave before he gets home. He drives as though he's at Brands Hatch, must give his gears a real bashing. His car has blacked out windows and when I commented one time, he said Susan didn't want the girls to be seen when they all go out. Apparently, she thinks someone might take photos and place them on the internet. Talk about paranoid!

Anyway, last Friday, when he got home there was a lot of noise from inside the house: raised voices and slamming doors. That was unusual as you never normally hear them. The kids can be noisy, but not Susan and Gerald. I was in the garden dead-heading the early daffodils and planting bulbs...probably too late as I'm no expert.

Anyway, it – the argument - lasted about half an hour, then stopped. Gerald stormed out, looking like thunder (pardon the weather analogy) and drove off again; a bat out of hell moves slower. He must have returned sometime before midnight as when I looked out before going to bed his car was in the drive. I haven't seen Gerald again, but on Monday morning I saw an ambulance arrive and a bit later her parents coming to collect the kids. Then she was taken in the back of a police car. It's certainly got all the neighbours talking. Nothing exciting ever happens on this road. Sorry, that's a bit gossipy and I hope nothing bad has happened.

Gemma Norton

Mr Sid Brown

Oh, the Winters! Strange pair if you ask me. I inherited this corner shop from my father. He still helps-out and we've both remarked at their behaviour, especially hers. She comes in once a week to pay the papers. Saturday morning, ten o'clock; you could set your watch by her. Twice a year she leaves a tip for the paper boy, a kind gesture that not many seem to think of. Never says a word, apart from "I'd like to pay the papers," and "Thank you." Most people comment on the weather, or the lurid headlines some papers delight in, but if I ever say anything, I get no response.

The wife has commented that she always looks awful, especially when she's expecting. That's a regular occurrence, though Mary said now she's got her boy that might be the end. He's a lovely little chap, always smiling and showing off the latest teeth.

Never see the husband. Don't think I've spoken more than two words to him. He works away a lot, that I do know. Mary says it must be hard for her with so many children to look after. We only had the one and that was hard enough, even with both of us here all the time.

You asked about last weekend. Susan Winters came at ten on Saturday to pay the papers. Same as always. There were a couple of girls in the shop, we were busy, so I don't know if they were hers. They were certainly making a fuss of the baby. They had their spends, bought some sweets - they were ever so polite - then left before her. Mary commented that they were too young to walk home on their own, but maybe they waited outside, if they were hers.

Sid Brown

Chapter 13

New Hope was a private healthcare establishment on the outskirts of town, the fells in view a short distance away. Serena remembered the facility being built a few years ago. The approach was up an impressive drive. Gardens fronted the house, overloaded with spring flowers. Sandstone brickwork was interrupted by large windows, many of them impressive bays, giving the building an opulent look.

As the automatic door opened, a disembodied voice directed her to the reception area. Thick carpets and soft music accompanied her; it all felt a world away from anything the NHS provided and reminded her of Parkside.

Showing her ID to the receptionist whose face turned from welcoming smile to grimace, Serena said that she was here to see Catherine Trowbridge.

'Do you mean Doctor Trowbridge?' the voice was as unwelcoming as the look that had lingered. Serena was tempted to say her face would stick like that if left too long. 'The doctor is with a patient and has a full list today. I'm not aware that you are one of her appointments.'

Hiding her surprise that the woman she had come to see was a doctor, not a counsellor, she asked what kind of doctor she was.

'Doctor Trowbridge is our leading psychiatrist. I'd have assumed that you'd have known that if you want to see her.'

Duly chastised, the DI said she needed to speak to the doctor on police business.

'As I said, she's fully booked, but she may be able to spare you ten minutes between patients.'

Knowing the surly woman was only doing her job, she thanked her and went to sit in the waiting area. Tea, coffee, soft drinks and an array of small cakes and biscuits were displayed with a prominence that suggested that they were there to be enjoyed.

Forty minutes later, she was shown into the doctor's room. Catherine Trowbridge was small and so dumpy she could have been Humpty's partner. Oh dear, how I judge by appearance Serena thought, but perhaps it's just as well this woman deals with the mind and not the body.

'Thank you for seeing me, I know you have a patient waiting.'

'Indeed. You have ten minutes. I assume it's a matter of great importance. It's not often a senior police officer seeks my attention.'

Taken aback by the doctor's abrupt manner, Serena began. 'I'm seeking information about one of your patients. Obviously, anything you are able to tell me will be treated as confidential.'

Fiona Trowbridge's face spoke volumes and the DI knew she had stated the obvious.

'The woman I want to talk about is Susan Winters, a patient who was referred to you by her GP, Doctor Lennon. I am hoping you will be able to tell me about her problems and the treatment you suggested.'

'Absolutely, categorically NOT! Anything divulged within these walls is for my ears only. I see people at their most distressed, their most vulnerable, and I would be in dereliction of duty if I repeated a single word. It seems you have wasted your time and I must ask you to leave.'

'At risk of sounding like a second-rate television cop show, Susan Winters is a "person of interest" and anything you are able to say might help both her and the investigation.'

'If you knew what my job entails, you would be aware that anything I might say would almost certainly be to the detriment of the individual in question. No one seeks my help if they are happy and well adjusted, finding life easy. Each patient I see is suffering. Mental pain, in my opinion, is at least as horrendous as the physical variety and often more debilitating. All are in turmoil, distress, and often contemplating suicide. To disclose an iota of a patient's anguish could, and indeed should, have me disbarred. My licence to practise medicine would be taken from me. I am extremely sorry when any patient with mental health issues is being investigated by the police. It can only exacerbate their problems. All I will say is please tread carefully with Susan Winters.'

Standing up, looking even more minute, the psychiatrist now spoke in a voice straight from the Arctic: 'Good morning DI Peil. I'm sure you can find your own way out.'

Failure. Abject failure. The frown on her boss's face told her he agreed with the DI's rather prosaic summing up of the morning's meeting.

'Interesting though, she's a psychiatrist, not a counsellor, so there must have been a strong reason for her GP to refer her. However, I know he's not going to be any more forthcoming than she was.'

'We need to speak to Susan's friends. She must confide in someone. I'll ring her parents and see if they can supply any names and hopefully, they will feel able to enlighten us as to their daughter's problems last year.'

Twenty minutes later, Serena knocked on her boss's door. 'No luck, sir. Susan's mother got quite upset, something of a euphemism, when she told me that once her daughter got married, she broke all contact with her old friends, and she's almost certain she's never made any new ones.'

Her rather colourful words were, 'That man ruled her life; told her he was all she needed. Even we didn't see as much of her as we'd have liked. We tried to help, but all our offers of assistance were rejected. Over the years we've watched as our darling girl has been dragged down. She was at the lowest point we've ever seen her last autumn and that's when we asked her doctor for help. We thought professional assistance might improve her mood. Nothing changed! I once suggested that she'd endured enough pregnancies and her reply was that Gerald wanted a son. Well, he got one, but one seemingly wasn't enough.'

Grimacing, Serena said that following that rather esoteric statement Sylvia Page had put down the phone. No goodbye.

Pausing for a moment, Serena continued. 'I felt she was about to say more and I'm sure she knows something that she's either not willing or feels unable to disclose.'

Harvey's unhelpful rejoinder was, 'It's what parents do: protect their offspring.'

Finally. We're all in our own house. It feels strange, sullied by so many unwelcome visitors. I've not ventured into the dining room, and I dread to think of the mess the plods have left behind. I watched a documentary once about the lack of care the police take with people's things. One woman said her house looked as though a horde of teenagers had staged a drunken party sullying every room.

The children are delighted to be home and are being so well behaved: no arguing or hair pulling. Gerald is away again, and I must admit life is so much easier without his constant nit-picking. The rugs can remain skew-whiff (a phrase my best friend Abi used to use) dust can gather unchecked, meals presented as and when (another of Abi's phrases) and a break from his telling me about the *need*...yes, he used that word, for his son to have a playmate. Why, after he sired so many girls, does he assume that the next would be a boy? Does he assume he's cracked it? That he now knows how to produce the male of the species?

The only cloud on my sun-drenched horizon, DCI Tarquin's final words: 'We are releasing you, pending further enquiries. You are not to leave the country (fat chance: Gerald has my passport secreted somewhere, that is assuming it's still valid) and must inform us if you plan to leave Fordway (can't imagine why I'd want to).

Mum and Dad are coming later with a Chinese takeaway. Bliss. I'll leave the empty cartons and dirty dishes in the kitchen overnight!

Chapter 14

If Imelda Simpson had been surprised to be contacted by the police, she hadn't shown it. One phone call and the DI was invited up to Keswick. Serena smiled as she drove up to the Lakes. Only the innocent or the long-time guilty, full of experience and unwarranted bravado, reacted in such a manner.

She had taken the young PC with her, using the journey to tell him about body language and how useful it could be in interviews.

'We're not treating Miss Simpson as a suspect, but look for signs that she's prevaricating, or uncomfortable with our questions. It's often what's not said that's as powerful as the answers a person gives. No one we've spoken to so far has told us everything they know about the two deaths we're investigating.'

'Not murders? I thought they were both being treated as such.'

Keeping her eyes on the road, farm vehicles now impeding their progress, Serena smiled. 'Both could be. One might be. Maybe neither is.'

Imelda Simpson lived in a small cottage in the middle of the town. Hills could be seen behind the row of similar houses opposite, but there was no view of the lake.

'If I lived here, I'd want a better view, though they're probably an exorbitant price, especially as so many people buy them up as second homes.' The young constable realised he should have kept his thoughts to himself.

A tiny entrance hall led the way to an equally minute living room with barely enough room for the two-seater settee, matching chair, and television. A tray with cups, saucers and freshly made scones, accompanied by jam and cream in china bowls was in position on the low coffee table by the window. The former matron was a tall woman with broad shoulders which must have been useful at times in the delivery room. Her hair had retained its dark brown colour, perhaps aided by the attention of a hairdresser. She was smartly dressed in a pale blue cashmere jumper, off-set by a stylish scarf in a variety of darker blues and purples. Well-cut grey trousers completed the outfit. As she welcomed them in, she looked upset, and Serena realised they were here to talk about her friend.

'I can't believe what happened to Nora.' Imelda hadn't waited for any preamble. 'She was just the loveliest person, so kind and caring, and one of the best midwives I ever worked with. She was a slip of a girl, newly qualified, when she came to work at Parkside, but she was better, far more professional, than some of the more experienced nurses.

'Although I was many years her senior, we became friends and I'm godmother to her elder son. I was sad when her marriage broke down, but nothing compared to this. It's tragic, and I don't use that word lightly.'

Attempting to control her voice, she continued, 'I want to help you to find out what happened, but I can't think of anyone who knew Nora who would want to do her harm.'

Time allowed for the matron to regain some self-control, Serena said that what she was about to say might be difficult to hear.

'We have been told that Nora received several pieces of hate-mail in the post. Unfortunately, she destroyed them. She assured her son that they meant nothing, that women get very emotional and need someone to blame when anything goes wrong with a delivery.'

Imelda nodded and took her time before deciding what to say. 'Over the years I had my fair share of complaints. One woman threatened legal action, saying I'd failed to resuscitate her new-born. The poor little girl had been stillborn, a tragedy the mother wasn't able to accept. In such appalling circumstances women are inclined to act impulsively, often regretting their words later. If blame can be apportioned elsewhere, then it's not their fault; something that's too awful to contemplate.

'It's never easy to be on the receiving end of a woman's distress. Unfortunately, it is part of a midwife's job. I am so sorry that poor Nora received grievances at home. In every job you need to be able to leave it behind; go home and forget about it.'

Pretending to drink more of her tea, the DI knew that worse was to come. How much did Miss Simson know about the suspension?

'We spoke to the present matron, Petra Moreton.'

Interrupting, Imelda said she had been so pleased to hand over the running of Parkside to such a competent woman. 'I helped to interview her and knew she was the one the moment she walked through the door. Nora has always spoken highly of her, though I don't think they became friends outside work. Not like us.' Breaking down, she asked to be excused, and told her visitors to enjoy another scone.

Returning a few minutes later, she apologised. 'It's just so hard...so incredibly difficult to think I'll never see her again. When I retired and bought this cottage, Nora would come to stay, usually about once a month. We always said we were closer than family. Neither of us had many relatives. I never married and my sister lives in London, so we don't meet up that often. As you know Nora got divorced and one of her sons, Ralph lives abroad. He's been everywhere: America, Germany and now I think it's Australia, though I'm not sure. She used to get upset as he made so little effort to come back to see her, though she did manage trips to see him, especially when he was a bit closer. I seem to recall that she had several holidays with him in Berlin. Sorry, you haven't come all this way to listen to that.'

'Thank you, Miss Simpson, it's all background and we never know what might come in useful.' Pausing again, the DI asked if Nora's suspension was common knowledge.

'Yes, or at least I was aware of it. When a complaint becomes formal, the accused is suspended automatically, pending an internal investigation. Poor Nora was beside herself with worry, thinking it might be the end of her career. That would have been such a loss to Parkside.' Realising what she'd said, tears erupted. 'Oh dear, oh my, that's now happened. They will miss her...so much. In the end the complaint was withdrawn, no case to answer. However, the weeks waiting for that to happen took their toll and Nora looked awful when I saw her afterwards.'

'When did you last see her?'

'Three weeks ago. She came for my birthday weekend. The weather was horrendous, typical Lake District downpours, but we had a great time until she received some text messages.'

Intrigued, Serena asked if Miss Simpson could remember their content.

'Indeed. One doesn't easily forget such hateful missives. I wrote them down in case it ever became necessary to quote them. I'll just pop upstairs and get them.'

As she left the room Edward spoke for the first time since entering the cottage. 'Wow. This sounds interesting, or as my little brother would say, "The plot thickens!"'

Handing over the piece of paper, Imelda Simpson said that she had told Nora to ignore them, that they were the ramblings of a disturbed mind. 'How I wish we'd gone to the police. Nora might still be alive.'

'Is this your handwriting, Miss Simson?'

'Yes. Poor Nora was upset and didn't want to copy the foul insinuations. I wrote them in capitals as that's how they were received. I believe that's the modern equivalent of shouting.'

Thanking the former matron for her time and asking her to contact them if she thought of anything else that might help, Serena apologised for upsetting her.

Thick clouds and intermittent rain spoilt the views. The whole world seemed to have chosen the same moment to vacate the Lakes and most of the journey consisted of hold-ups interspersed with traffic moving between first and second gear.

Serena and Edward spent the time discussing the poisonous words Nora had received.

'I may be new and naïve, but doesn't this change everything? The woman was threatened just weeks before she ends up dead.'

'Let's wait and see what the DCI has to say, but they definitely put a new slant on her death.'

'Is it too late to find out who sent them? Have we got Nora Ederson's mobile?'

Serena had been wondering the same thing. Would she have kept such vile messages, or had her immediate instinct been to delete them? If so, one of the lab technicians was going to be extremely busy. The sender must be identified. Had they carried out the threats implicit in each abhorrent text? If so, it was murder. She was now certain that was the most appropriate word. If, that tiny word again, *if* the sender could be identified they would have the murderer. Surely it couldn't be that easy?

The day was fading; the rain that had followed them down the M6 blocking what little light was clinging on. Night-time still arrived too soon. Serena preferred the summer months with many more hours of daylight to enjoy.

'The clocks go forward this weekend; should extend the day. Silly thing to say as all days are the same length, they just seem so much longer in summer.'

Edward smiled, 'My mum always says she's lost an hour of her life when we spring forward, the same when we go abroad and change our watches. I tell her that we get it back in October and when we return to the UK, but she still moans.'

The station was unusually quiet, three cars in the carpark and only one officer, not involved in either of Serena's cases, on a computer in the main office.

Looking up, he informed Serena that Detective Chief Inspector Tarquin and Detective Sergeant Jennings were in Interview Room Two.

As there had been no mention of an interview, Serena asked the young detective if he knew who was being questioned.

'That woman who found a body in her dining room. Sorry, don't know any more.'

'It's been a long day, Edward, so you head off home. I'll wait to see the DCI and tell him what we found.'

'Before I go, I'll just ask the Evidence Management bods if they've got Nora Ederson's mobile and if they have, I'll ask them to provide us with a printout of all texts including any deleted ones. I'm sure they can retrieve those. We need a list of all the senders.'

Delighted with the young officer's enthusiasm, she thanked him and congratulated him on his day's work.

An hour later, Harvey strode into the room, Clare Jennings several steps behind. 'In the name of all that's holy, she's one peculiar person; battered fish minus the chips!' Staring at Serena he shouted, 'She expects us to believe it's her brother-in-law, Eric, who was dead on her dining room carpet. Reckons her dearly beloved husband is alive and kicking and enjoyed breakfast with her this morning. She looked really shocked when I started the interview by repeating that I was sorry for her loss.'

"DCI Tarquin, I've lost nothing. I hardly knew my husband's twin; we haven't met since the wedding nearly nine years ago. They were identical twins: Gerald and Eric. Some people couldn't tell them apart, but I know my husband. A wife can tell the difference."

'When I asked what Eric Winters was doing, life extinguished, in a prone position on her dining room carpet, a tray of untouched food by his side (yes, I did become rather verbose) in her house when he hadn't visited for the best part of a decade, she just looked perplexed.'

"My dear inspector, I have no idea. Imagine the shock I got when I opened the dining room door and saw him lying there. Thank goodness one of the children didn't see him."

'I felt like a fish floundering out of water. I told her that the man in her house was her husband, that fingerprints and dental records have proved that: beyond the proverbial shadow of a doubt. I added that Eric Winters had been to see us, very much alive, unlike her husband, the man whose death she failed to report for at least forty-eight hours.'

"Twins have identical fingerprints, so that doesn't prove it was Gerald."

'I think I almost lost the plot. No! No, they are not identical.' I realised the woman was irritating me. 'Similar, but not identical, and dental records are very unlikely to be even similar. The man whose death you reported…eventually…was your husband. Gerald Winters: formerly of this Parish. I must add that we have Eric's fingerprints, and none were found in your house.'

Clare butted in, 'Susan Winters maintained her story for almost two hours. I don't know if that's the only way her mind can cope, by not accepting that her husband has gone. Easier to think it's his brother, a man she hadn't seen for years.'

Harvey took up the reins again. 'Get this, (he wondered when he had started to use such appalling

English) I asked who had put the food beside him. Her answer was that she had. "Eric had come a long way to see us, he lives somewhere in France, and he obviously needed to sleep before eating. I thought that it would be good for him to have it beside him when he woke up." I thought I'd caught her out admitting she'd seen the body some time before reporting it, but, oh no. She said that the food was only placed on the floor on Sunday evening and Eric had most definitely been breathing then.'

'So that's her reason for not reporting the body for two days. That she thought he was Eric and was still alive. It's the best one yet for not admitting that there's a corpse on my dining room carpet!' Serena felt like laughing, but nothing about the situation was even remotely funny.

Sighing, Harvey continued, 'She really has no valid explanation for that time lag. The doll placed by the deceased's head received a similarly surreal response. "Eric looked rather lonely." She point-blank refuted the idea that she had moved the body, even when I informed her that the pathologist was adamant that had happened post-mortem. I told her that people who are very much dead, don't normally end up lying peacefully on their backs, fully dressed, limbs arranged artfully by their sides!'

Clare summed up the meeting: 'We were at the Mad Hatter's tea party, only the dormouse was missing! It was when Harvey asked her about her husband's health that it became even weirder.'

Harvey repeated the words he'd used, 'Mrs Winters, were you aware your husband had visited the doctor… very recently?'

Clare smiled. 'I'll swear she jumped, just a small levitation, like a Jack-in-the-box running out of oomph. She stared around the room, as though she was seeking someone to answer for her, then said, "My dear Mr Policeman, (how Harvey hated to be addressed like that, common courtesy demanding the use of proper names) I don't know whether or not you are married, but if you are you will be aware that not everything is shared between partners. All couples hide some secrets; aspects of their lives they are reluctant to divulge even to their spouse. Gerald may have visited the doctor, but if he did, he did not inform me. I am not aware of any problem. None whatsoever. He's a man who has enjoyed the rudest of health. In all the years I've known him I can only recall one winter when he had a cold. He's never had a day off work."

'I told her that the post-mortem indicated that her husband broke a bone recently, the injury so severe it required surgery.'

"Oh, that. He fell in the garage, trying to move a ladder, and I drove him to A and E. Yes, he had a small surgical procedure, but that was later in the afternoon when he went to our private practice. He never trusted the NHS. I cannot recall him going to the see the doctor at any other time. As I said, he enjoys excellent health and remains very much alive. Eggs and bacon for breakfast this morning. I don't think the dead enjoy that."

'That was her final comment. She either believed everything she uttered or is a consummate actress.'

Chapter 15

Following a prolonged period discussing the bizarre interview, Harvey asked how Serena had fared in the Lakes.

Placing the texts on the table, Serena explained the situation. Few words were necessary: the transcripts spoke for themselves.

YOU KILL BABIES

A LITTLE GIRL WOULD BE ALIVE IF IT WASN'T FOR YOUR CARELESSNESS

SOME PEOPLE SHOULDN'T BE ALLOWED ANYWHERE NEAR THE MATERNITY UNIT

MURDERER: THE BABY WAS STILLBORN. YOUR FAULT

SLAUGHTERER

YOU ARE THE ONE WHO SHOULD BE DEAD

'These were received over several days and Nora told Imelda Simpson that she had been sent similar messages in the past. Some by post and more recently by text. She didn't know how anyone, other than staff, would have either her address or mobile number.'

The DCI interrupted: 'Her son spoke of her receiving hate mail which unfortunately she didn't keep. Apparently, they were hand-delivered, so no helpful postmark.'

'The technicians have been asked to find the sender of the texts, but when young Edward spoke to Henry Brown, he said it would take some time. But if anyone can sort it, Henry can.'

Serena then continued with the rest of the information she had gleaned from Nora Ederson's former matron. 'Imelda repeated what we've already heard. Nora was well liked, good at her job and personable. She added that the patients loved her and second and third timers asked for her as their personal midwife. Interestingly, she said that everyone in the maternity unit received complaints at some time or other, mostly unfounded. She's sure Nora never received many, but the ones that did arrive were highly personal. One thing she said struck me as pertinent: "As she was so skilful, she was often left to deal with the really tricky deliveries: the breeches, twins, or on one occasion triplets who almost didn't make it, extended labours and the mums who were likely to panic. That all meant a higher likelihood of something going wrong. Poor Nora, she took it all to heart. Midwifery was her life." Are we assuming she might have been murdered because of an event at Parkside, or are we heading down the wrong road?'

Shaking his head, Harvey muttered that the vile texts must be of interest. 'The sooner we hear from the lab the better. The person who sent them needs to be investigated.'

The phone interrupted their thoughts, the ring tone set to maximum. Answering it, Serena laughed, 'Good heavens, Henry are you psychic? Your name is still in the ether. The room is full of it. Your name not the ether!'

'Good to know I'm so popular. At least with some people, I've stayed late to avoid the missus, we had a humdinger this morning and I'm definitely persona non grata.'

'OK, sorry to hear that. Take as long as you like telling us what you've found, but I fear it's not much as we only asked about Mrs Ederson's phone two hours ago.'

'Indeed...indeed, sorry but not much at all, in fact nothing of any use. I managed to retrieve all her incoming texts. There were a lot of local calls. Most of those were obviously from her son, Nigel Ederson. Some were from a friend called Muriel, and there were numerous work-related ones. Then there were a few from abroad from Ralph Ederson. But the nasty ones in capital letters were sent from a mobile which is untraceable.

'All phones should be traceable, but if you buy a pay-as-you-go, say at a petrol station, or local newsagents and pay in cash, unless you get caught on video there's no proof you purchased it and no way the mobile can be traced. Mobiles are tracked through Tower Triangulation. It was invented by some clever clogs in the Second World War as a pre-radar device, but it's now used for cell phone tracking. Shall I continue?'

'Please do, I'm with you so far.'

'If you're technologically minded, you can buy a phone that changes its IMEI, its serial number, randomly with every call, that means individual calls can be traced, but it's not possible to link a series of calls or texts, especially when the SIM cards are changed. However, the simplest and most common way of avoiding being traced is ditching a phone after a single use. Expensive, but effective.'

'Totally frustrating but thank you so much for accessing her texts so quickly. Could you email a list of all the mobile and phone numbers you were able to access? Oh, and good luck when you go home. Would flowers or chocolates help?'

'Absolutely not! Sasha would think I'd got something to apologise for and that would never do.'

Relaying the gist of the phone call, Serena said that at least following Henry's labours they had a few more leads. 'There's a friend called Muriel who texted regularly, and a lady called Briony. We could do with asking them to come in. They might be able to tell us something that puts a new slant on the woman.'

It had been a long day and Harvey called time.

Arriving home, the DCI was greeted by two moggies who seemed inordinately pleased to see him. 'Don't try it on you two, no cupboard love. I know George will have been round to feed you: on the dot of six.'

When Chopin and Grieg had commandeered his house, Harvey's elderly neighbour had volunteered to feed the composers, as he called them, any time Harvey was late. 'As you know Kathleen and I have three cats and they don't like waiting for their food. We've always had three, always with names starting with J, our daughter Jen's idea. At-the-moment it's Juno, Jasper and Jane. In the past there was Jade, Joe and Jupiter. They've all been long livers. Jade was twenty-one and the others late teens.

The old man had obviously wanted to talk. 'Jenny was our firstborn and has been a blessing to us, giving us two wonderful grandsons. Her little brother died when he was just eighteen months old: meningitis. Healthy in the morning and dead by midnight. We didn't know the signs and took him to A and E too late.' Harvey saw George's eyes moisten and thought how often he encountered tragedies from which individuals never recovered fully. Life continued, but with a gaping hole that nothing could fill, the pain ever-present. 'Ever since our loss Kath and I have been involved in raising awareness of the signs of meningitis. If it's caught early, there's a chance of a full recovery. I think most surgeries and hospitals now have information posters in their waiting areas.'

Hotly pursued by loud meowing, Harvey went into the kitchen and put a few biscuits in each bowl. 'That's all you're getting. The vet said you were both at the top end of normal weight.'

A note sat on the kitchen table telling him that there was a homemade lasagne in the fridge: five minutes required in the microwave. George fed the cats several times a week, and his wife their owner at least once. The kindness of the couple never failed to touch him. As he ate the delicious food, he wondered how the bewildering Susan Winters was faring.

Thank goodness Gerald is away leading an important conference in Manchester, fifty of the bank's representatives hanging on his every word. I'd be in trouble if he walked in now. The rug in the hall is too near the front door and his dinner isn't on the table.

Most lives can be viewed in segments. Seismic shifts re-route people's plans: leaving home, marriage, children, divorce, a new job, illness, bereavement to name but a few of the events that catapult one down a different path.

My life can be viewed in two parts: the first eighteen years and the last nine. Had you known me during my early years you would have seen a confident, popular, outgoing young woman. Fast forward. Times interminable tock following tick has reduced me to the woman you see before you today.

My ears are burning. The police officers must be talking about me, and the kindest epithets will be unusual, strange or a one-off. Perhaps they are being honest and calling me loopy, crazy, half-baked or a couple of ribs short of a cage, a cruel description Gerald used recently of a new employee.

My attempt to make you understand what happened to me will not be easy to write, or I fear to read. Will you empathise with my account? Will you even believe it? Will you find enough in it to forgive me for the decisions I have made; the ones others would find inexplicable?

I have, as the saying goes, let myself go. My once shiny hair (people commented on it) is now lank and flecked with grey. My eyes (once noted for their brightness) are dull and surrounded by lines not caused by laughter. Network Rail could use them to lay new tracks. Numerous pregnancies have wreaked their revenge and I now have the shape of the bag-lady who sits outside the library most days. No one would believe I have not yet reached thirty.

Now that Gerald is going to be away so much, I have time to resurrect the old me. I need to do something after the recent traumatic events. Being incarcerated, then questioned for what felt like hours, was horrific. It will take time to recover. Mum says she will pay for trips to the new, and inordinately expensive hair salon (far too posh to be deemed a hairdresser's) which has opened recently in Preston. It's called *The Look You Deserve* and has a beauty department attached. I'm booked in for a Japanese Hair Gloss which apparently was extremely popular with the geishas, and a series of facials involving deep cleansing. I can also choose from an Asian Purifier, Italian Skin Glow and the one Mum said she's had and makes one feel fantastic, the Russian Coffee Body Smoother. My husband won't recognise me when he gets back.

I had a blissfully happy childhood. By the time I arrived my mother was forty-three and Dad a few years older. They had given up hope of having a baby and Mum has told me often of the surprise she got when the doctor told her she was not going through an early menopause but was pregnant. I arrived five months later. An only child, my mother's age and an extremely difficult labour decided that. So, growing up I had no siblings to annoy me and parents who doted on me. I was never spoilt: Mum and Dad were all too aware that a child's every wish shouldn't be fulfilled. I have followed that example with my own children.

Unfortunately, I didn't inherit either of my parents' looks, or intellect. I'm small to their tall, dark skinned to their fair, and was always on the dim side academically. They've retired now, but Dad was an actuary, and a magistrate, and Mum did research in the Nicholson Laboratory in Manchester. When I arrived, she gave up work and devoted her days to me making sure I was given every experience, from messy craft sessions in the kitchen to visits to theatres and museums.

A fairy tale childhood.

Chapter 16

We saw Susan yesterday and she seemed so unsure of herself. On returning home, I sat and shook, every iota a quivering wreck. Richard poured me a strong drink which didn't even see the edge, let alone take it off. The voice in my head keeps repeating the same words: I lied to the police. I lied to the police. I employed words that were far from the truth and even more were omitted, entire sentences remained trapped in my head. When I was a child, my parents took me to church every Sunday morning and I would listen to the vicar, Reverend Michael Haughton. At the time he looked like Methuselah, or Abraham who is said to have lived for one hundred and seventy-five years. I used to joke that God must have been on his side, adding that Dorian Gray employed a rather different sponsor for his longevity.

Every single week Reverend Michael would ask God to forgive us, using the Morning Prayer from the 1928 Book of Common Prayer: "We have left undone those things which we ought to have done and we have done those done things we ought not to have done. And there is no health in us." How appallingly apt that sounds today.

Susan was never an easy child and almost impossible as a baby. Was it her background? Shall I finally say the words: she was adopted. There, the words are out, released after almost three decades. No one knows, apart obviously from Richard. None of her grandparents had made it past their mid-sixties, so didn't live to see a grandchild, and we avoided making close friends. I never told Susan and now it's too late. Far too late. I used to tell her the story of her birth, the one that with constant retelling I came to believe: the long labour, the knowledge that there would be no brother or sister, our joy when she arrived. At least that last bit was true.

The adoption workers advised us to use the word "adoption" early on, to make it an everyday, comfortable word, and to tell Susan from the age of two that she was adopted, and no later than four. I can remember exactly what Mrs Torrington said: 'Telling her when she is young will stop her finding out from someone else. Be positive about why she came to live with you and couldn't stay with her birth parents (how I hated those last words). Explain that being adopted means Susan is loved just as much as if she had stayed with her…those words again. Tell her how thrilled you were when she came to live with you and what a special member of the family she is.'

Two and four came and went. There was never the right time. As I said, she wasn't an easy baby and although I hadn't been told of any problem with the woman who had given birth to her (a teenager, not able to look after a baby, dad in absentia) I sometimes wondered whether drink or drugs had been taken whilst she was pregnant. I read everything I could find on foetal drug and alcohol syndromes. Her refusal to sleep and daily tantrums weren't mentioned but other indicators were present in our beautiful daughter: impulsiveness, hyperactivity and difficulty concentrating being three I remember. When she started school and found learning difficult, I attributed it to her experience before she came to live with us.

When she was nine, a new girl entered the class: an American called Tiffany. Her father had come on a twelve-month contract with his wine importing firm. Susan and she became friends and the two were inseparable.

'Tiffany is adopted. She said that makes her special. Her Mom (my daughter was picking a lot of Americanisms which until that moment had sounded rather cute) and Dad couldn't have their own baby, so they chose her.'

All the words we'd been told to use. My mouth had become so dry that speaking was beyond me. Susan didn't notice my lack of response and added, 'Are babies adopted in this country, or is it only in America?'

I couldn't bring myself to have the conversation that should have taken place so many years ago. I had practised the words so many times: in my head, in front of a mirror, to Richard, but had I told her then she would have been distraught, for she would have known we had lied to her. Once again lies of omission. They could be my specialist subject on Mastermind.

I muttered something about a few babies being adopted in England, but far fewer than in such a vast country as the United States. The mention of her favourite television programme meant that I was left alone to get dinner: fish fingers, baked beans and waffles, her favourite. Strange how some things live on in the memory.

Chapter 17

Statement from Amanda Collins

I came to the station today as Mrs Page told my mum you want to talk to people who knew Susan Page. I realise she's Susan Winters now but when we were friends, she was called Page.

We started primary school together. I remember sitting on the carpet next to her on the very first day. I'd stood at the classroom door, not wanting my mum to leave, and Susan marched up and grabbed my hand. That was it. We became best friends, all through Harrington Road Primary and then Fordway Academy, well it was just Fordway Comprehensive in our day. Apart from Year 5, when Tiffany landed from the good old US of A, it was always just the two of us. Girls don't really work in threes and that year Susan and I didn't spend as much time together, but thankfully Tiffany (what a ridiculous name, we had such laugh about it afterwards) flew back at the end of the year.

Susan was such a laugh. We often got into trouble for talking and giggling, but we found most lessons boring and neither of us enjoyed them; too much like hard work. At secondary we were in the lower sets and couldn't see the point of "trying our best". We knew our best wasn't good enough. My work was both inadequate and appallingly presented, unlike Susan's. Her handwriting was beautiful and her work always, and I do mean always, looked fabulous. I remember some work we had to do on Queen Victoria. It had been set as homework and when Mrs Lee handed it back the following week, she said mine looked slapdash and the content matched.

There was a long comment on the bottom of Susan's page in bright red ink: "If the content of your work had matched its presentation it would be truly outstanding. Anyone merely looking at your work would be impressed. Unfortunately, the moment they started to read it they would realise that you have absolutely no idea about the subject matter. A, for handwriting; D, for effort or any hint of an understanding of the subject matter."

I remember Susan saying that her mum had wonderful handwriting and that she spent a lot of time working with her developing her fantastic style. Having kids of my own now, I realise that Mrs Page wanted to help her daughter as much as possible but as Susan failed at every academic subject that was the only way she could assist her. Susan just didn't "get" anything else.

We were both OK at sport (I seem to think she was chosen to represent the county at something, maybe netball) and played together on several school teams. All you needed was energy, some skill and to turn up to the practices.

It's the times we spent together away from the stultifying restrictions and tedium of school life that has left the best memories and will give you some indication of what Sue was like as a child and then a teenager. Although she wasn't academic, she had the most amazing imagination. Even as teenagers, we spent hours dressing up. Her mum had an awesome (a word we learnt from Tiffany) array of beautiful clothes: fancy dresses, high-heeled shoes, lace shawls, long scarves and fur coats. Sue said that her parents went to a lot of posh dos, and that her mum went out looking like the Queen. Mrs Page never minded us borrowing them for our games and I don't recall anything getting spoilt.

We remained little girls for a long time, probably longer than girls do today. We played fantasy games, the clothes turning us into princesses, witches, or damsels in distress! In later years we became pop stars or the leading ladies in the latest blockbuster movies. We both loved teddies and dolls and would dress them up as well and pretend they were in our class (we were far stricter than most of our teachers) or were off to a Garden Party at the Palace.

For many years the Page's had a dog, Rufus, a mild-mannered golden Labrador. He was patience personified when we included him in our make-believe games. I can still see him sitting looking at us with doleful eyes when we had finished dressing him in a strange selection of clothes: a red beret, blue waistcoat and Sue's pyjama bottoms. I still have the photo we took.

Happy days. Susan Page was brilliant company. Funny, full of energy (when schoolwork wasn't on the agenda) and probably the best friend I've ever had. It's such a shame that things changed when she met Gerald.

We'd both escaped school at sixteen, the Sixth Form viewed as a type of purgatory we had no wish to experience. I went to Kingston College to do a hairdressing course and Susan started working in the shoe shop: Gordon's on the High Street. For eighteen months we still got together at least once a week, but that stopped the day she met her future husband. A few months later I was her chief bridesmaid and that was the last real contact we had.

I can't say I took to Gerald, and he wasn't right for Susan. He had a surface charm and was quite good looking, but from the get-go he was in control, and a free spirit like Susan needed her autonomy. Once she met him it was all, 'Gerald says this; Gerald thinks that; Gerald doesn't want me to go out with my girlfriends!' She was only eighteen when she met, then married him, far too young, though I know some people make it work and are still together fifty years later. I wasn't the only one to suggest she waited before committing herself, but she was bamboozled (the most appropriate word) by him and did exactly what he wanted. By the time she returned from honeymoon I'd been relegated, a member of a poor team, one which was in receipt of too few points. Sue was pregnant and she had no time for anyone but Gerald and the impending child.

Over the past decade, living in the same town, we've bumped into each other occasionally, but I don't think we've exchanged more than a dozen words. Over that time, I've seen her decline, both physically (I had to look twice to recognise her last month) and psychologically. Her exuberance vanished, leaving a pale shadow of her former self.

There's just one more thing I think you should know. Susan Winters remains a fantasist, but where she used to be able to distinguish between the truth and make-believe, I don't think she is able to do so now. I'm not saying she lies deliberately, but I'm not sure she knows when she is making something up.

Sorry, I don't intend to be mean, I still like her, but the police should know what she's like.

Amanda Collins (nee Trotter)

'Interesting reading, sir. Mrs Collins was quite emotional at times…obviously sorry the way things have gone for her friend. I think she knows why we're questioning Susan Winters. At one point she said her parents are still friends with the Pages. Serena waited for the DCI's reply.

'I think it's what she said at the end that is the most telling, that Susan can't differentiate between fact and fiction. I think we already knew that but it's good to have it confirmed. We need to question the perplexing Mrs Winters again, this time challenging everything she says. We'll leave it a couple of days, give her time to feel comfortable at home, then call her in. Make it formal. There's no way on this earth that she didn't know her husband was lying dead on her dining room floor, surrounded by food and a doll. No way! Making her admit it, though, might take some careful manoeuvring. Catch her at her own game.'

'Sir, did you read the second statement that I took yesterday?'

Looking at his desk, Harvey was horrified to see a statement written by a Scott Cuffe and left in pole position. How the blazes did I miss that? The words remained in the DCI's head. He wondered if trying to investigate two murders was proving too much.

Thanking Serena, he picked up the A4 page.

Statement written by Scott Cuffe

Thought I should come in. Mum said I ought to tell you what I know about Susan Page, well she's Winters now. You might know my mum; she works in the canteen here and she heard someone say the coppers were looking for info on Susan.

We were in the same year at Fordway Comp. She was dead pretty, and a lot of the boys fancied her, but she just went around with a group of girls. She could be a right laugh and used to annoy the teachers, especially the strict ones like Ma Street.

Anyway, we didn't have much to do with each other at school, but a few months after we both left - I got an apprenticeship with Tom Wilkins, the plumber, still work for him, he's a good boss, and Susan started selling shoes - we hooked up. Never serious, just a laugh and we didn't go out for long.

One day, a few weeks after we got together, she invited me to her house. Her parents were both out and she asked me to go upstairs to see her bedroom. As you can imagine my hopes rose! Now, at the time I had two teenage sisters and their rooms were nothing like Sue's. It was like a child's: Roald Dahl posters of James and the Giant Peach, Charlie and the Chocolate Factory and the BFG on the walls and teddies everywhere and I do mean everywhere: on her bed, chair, the windowsill, the floor, and they covered every inch of a huge chest of drawers.

The content of her bookcase had stopped about age eleven. In one corner of the room there was the biggest doll's house you've ever seen, a little girl's dream. Sue opened the front and there were three floors of furniture and tiny figures. I got the impression that she still played with it.

When we heard her mum come home, we went downstairs. For want of something to say, I asked if she'd enjoyed their recent holiday in America.

She looked a bit confused. 'Oh, Scott, that's still being planned. It'll be our first visit and we're thinking of seeing the east side of the country: Virginia, the Carolinas and Georgia. We'll probably go in the autumn, see the Fall colours.'

The thing was Susan had told me all about the trip they'd just had to Washington, New York and San Francisco. I should have twigged when she was unsure how long the flight had been from one side of the country to the other.

We broke up soon after, not that there was much to break, and I didn't see much of her after that. She didn't go around with the crowd who met up in the pubs or nightclubs, not her scene. I do have to say that I was surprised, well gobsmacked, when about a year later I saw the announcement of her wedding in the local rag. Mum read it out and we had a right laugh: *Richard and Sylvia Page are absolutely thrilled to announce the forthcoming wedding of their precious daughter Susan Natasha to Gerald*

James Winters, a local bank manager. I learnt the word pretentious that day!

So, how to sum her up? Beautiful, witty, fun but a few colours short of a rainbow if you get my meaning. Not top of the class but there was never any malice in her. She seemed like one of life's innocents and although people change, I'd lay money on her not being a murderer. As her husband's dead I assume that's what she's accused of.

Hope that's some help.

Scott Cuffe

Harvey sat bemused. Was the lad's rather rambling account of any use? It was well over a decade since he'd known Susan Winters and his recollections were probably distorted by the time lapse. It was an accepted fact that even something that happened yesterday was remembered differently by different people. The police, though not always juries, knew to take witness accounts with the proverbial dose of salts, so a young man's view of a girl he hadn't seen for ten years was almost certainly of little use. One thing he said had been interesting, that the lady in question had been extremely immature and had the propensity to make up things, with little correlation to the facts. Almost word for word with Amanda Collins account. That trait appeared to have had stood the test of time.

Chapter 18

Morning arrived full to the brim with sunlight. Having decided he wasn't going to watch the weather forecast Harvey was annoyed to see it was still in full swing when he switched on the TV. It was the hyper young man again, this time delivering a forecast for good weather with the enthusiasm of someone on a cocktail of uppers. Dressed in pink shorts and a Hawaiian shirt featuring every colour known to man, he held sun cream in one hand and a large bottle of water in the other.

'Great news folks, you'll need these over the next few days. Drink plenty and lather yourself in Factor 50.' When did life become so frenetic, and why did people need to be given advice that a ten-year old already followed?

Walking to work, he envied the rest of the world, all of whom appeared to be getting ready for a day off. It felt as though everyone else had the time to enjoy the unseasonably warm weather that had returned. He wasn't looking forward to his day: an interview with the woman who didn't appear to know fact from fiction and making sure the team were making progress with the Nora Ederson case. The former might or might not have killed her husband and the latter might or might not be murder. Harvey thought he had never had such a double conundrum.

Hardly pausing to say good morning, the DCI launched in, a ship that was determined not to stay becalmed. 'Now, any progress with Nora Ederson?'

Clare Jennings had been busy. 'I've contacted Briony Hughes and Muriel Woods, the names that appeared regularly on Mrs Ederson's mobile phone record.

'Briony only met Nora recently when they both did an evening cookery class at the Community Centre. She said they got on well and started to cook for each other about once a month, trying out the dishes they'd learnt. She spoke warmly of Nora and described her as "happy and well-adjusted with a great sense of humour." Unfortunately, she didn't say anything significant.

'Muriel Woods, however, painted a rather different picture. She and Nora had been friends since secondary school and had remained close. I wrote down her final comment: "Nora endured a troubled eighteen months. The divorce hit her badly; it came as a tremendous shock and I don't think she ever got over it. Then one day she told me she was being stalked, her word for someone who kept approaching her asking her to do something that she said would be both immoral and illegal. She never furnished further details and wouldn't follow up my suggestion to involve the police. I said eighteen months, but one day she told me the "abhorrent request" had first been mooted several years ago but it was starting to feel like more of a command and was delivered with threats attached. I do hope it had nothing to do with her death. She was such a lovely, caring person." She said she'd be in touch if she thought of anything else.'

Thanking Clare, he turned to his DI.

'Just before you arrived, sir, the former matron, Imelda Simpson, rang me. She sounded perturbed and has asked me to go to see her again. For some reason, she wouldn't tell me over the phone and asked me to go up to Keswick.'

'Another jolly, Serena? Looks like a decent day for a trip to the Lakes, scenery should be impressive. Take young Edward again and give him the experience of asking some follow up questions. You can always take over if he's floundering. Promise him some Lake District Delight if he does well. It's a new confectionery and is *"A Must Try"* according to the advert.

Good weather had obviously encouraged others to drive north to view the lakes and hills. Once they left the motorway the journey became slow, heavy traffic and slow-moving farm vehicles hindering their progress.

Serena realised she had done most of the talking and decided to engage Edward in the conversation. 'What do you do in your spare time, Edward? A girlfriend on the horizon?'

As soon as the clumsy words had escaped, she longed to recall them, the ensuing silence uncomfortable.

'No, no girlfriend. None for ages. Not since university.'

The short, stuttering sentences ceased, and Serena was desperately trying to come up with a change of tack when the young man carried on. 'Hannah. That was her name. We went out for two and a half years and I thought she was the one, you know, that we were destined to spend our lives together. I'd bought a ring and was planning to pop the question when she informed me, yes notified me as it obviously wasn't up for discussion, that she wanted us to part.'

The following silence was so long that Serena thought Edward had said enough.

'She'd always suffered from periods of anxiety: essays due in, exams, parents pushing her, but at the time she'd been having a good spell... or so I thought... and I couldn't understand what had gone wrong: where I had failed. She said that I should forget her. That she was going away. That I wouldn't be able to contact her. That she was leaving uni. That I wasn't to worry. That she'd be alright.'

Serena knew to give him time to continue. 'The last thing she said was that I hadn't done anything wrong and on no account should I blame myself. Two days later her roommate found her in the bath, wrists slashed and two empty bottles of Vodka on the floor. No note. No explanation. That's what she'd meant by "I wouldn't be able to contact her" though for months I was sorely tempted to join her. The pain was unendurable, and I ended up repeating the year. Why hadn't she talked to me, shared some of the anguish she was feeling? That's what haunts me. That was three years ago, and I've never been brave enough to start a new relationship. Sorry, that's all more than you bargained for. I'd rather no one else knows my tale of woe.'

Assuring the young man that she wasn't one to share other people's private lives, Serena concentrated on driving, the rest of the journey conducted in silence.

Imelda Simpson was standing looking out as the officers arrived. Ushering them into the living room, she asked them to make themselves comfortable whilst she fetched some refreshments. Serena thought the woman had aged since she had last visited, just a few days ago.

Entering the room, the elderly woman asked Edward to take the tray from her. 'I'm so wobbly I might drop it.'

Time allowed for the tea to be poured and the cake cut, Serena asked the former matron if she was OK.

Bursting into tears, she thrust a piece of paper at the DI. 'This arrived two days ago. If that had been the only one, I'd have left it, not bothered you.'

Donning disposable gloves, Serena took the envelope. Imelda Simpson's name and address were written on the front in capital letters. Inside there was a single sheet of paper. Three words were written in the middle of the page:

REMEMBER NORA EDERSON

The matron said that at first, she had thought it was meant as a strange form of condolence, reminding her to remember a good friend. 'It felt like a command rather than a question, especially as it lacked the necessary punctuation. The post mark is Preston, so I assumed it was sent from someone who knew both of us and was aware that we had remained friends. Then yesterday this arrived. Same type of envelope, paper, and writing:

BABIES DIED

MINE DIED

YOU WERE THE MATRON ON DUTY

REMEMBER WHAT HAPPENED TO NORA EDERSON

Shaking, she dropped the third envelope. 'This arrived half an hour ago, the postman was late today.'

YOUR FAULT

YOU WERE IN CHARGE AT PARKSIDE

REMEMBER WHAT HAPPENED TO NORA EDERSON

YOU WERE BOTH UNCARING

YOUR TURN NEXT

The paper handkerchief in Imelda's hand was shredded and Serena passed her the box that had been sitting on the coffee table. 'Imelda, I can see you're upset, and the messages are foul, but the chances are they are a prank; a particularly nasty one, but I doubt the sender intends you any harm. We still don't know for certain that what happened to Nora was anything other than an accident.' Looking at Edward, she gave a look warning him not to challenge her last statement. 'We will, however, take these letters very seriously. I'll take them back with me and we'll let the fingerprint experts see if they can lift any prints.'

Nodding, Imelda asked if they thought she was safe staying in her house. 'The person who sent them obviously knows where I live. I didn't sleep a wink last night and kept getting up to check the doors and windows.'

'Is there anyone you could stay with for a few days?'

'No relatives near, but I'm still in touch with Janine Mortice. She's another midwife in Fordway. I'm sure she wouldn't mind me going to her house and I'd feel safe nearer to you.'

Although Serena didn't think the arrangement sounded ideal, she said she'd wait until Imelda had spoken to her friend. 'We'll take you back with us if you want. I doubt you feel up to driving.'

An hour later, the arrangements in place, Imelda was sitting in the front seat of the car.

'Imelda, when you're ready, maybe over the next day or two, I'd like you to make a list of all the women who might have held a grudge against you and Nora. Especially anyone at all you can recall whose baby, or babies, didn't make it when you were *both* on duty. We can look through the Home's records which might jog your memory. The lady definitely says she lost a baby at Parkside which should aid our search.'

After what felt like several minutes, the matron spoke so quietly that Edward, relegated to the back of the car, couldn't hear her. 'There will be some. So sad. One baby not making it is awful, but a few poor souls end up suffering multiple miscarriages or babies who are stillborn. I'll do my best to recall names, but we dealt with hundreds of women each year.' After a pause she continued: 'One springs to mind, a young woman whose first pregnancy ended at thirty-eight weeks and the next was full term, but the baby only lived a few hours... Annabelle Borodin: that was her name. I remember as it was an unusual name and was spelt like the composer. Nora and I both dealt with the second delivery. I left Parkside soon after, so have no idea whether or not she went on to take a baby home.'

After a further pause, she continued. 'The letters I've received must be from the same person who sent the horrible texts to poor Nora: both sets written entirely in capitals. Not many people do that. I thought at first that mine had been done on a computer, but when you look closely, they're handwritten. Unusual these days, though I still prefer not to word process, so impersonal.' Realising what she'd said, she added, 'Oh dear, these are certainly personal!'

Chapter 19

'Good morning, everyone. Sorry to call you in so early, but there have been developments in the Nora Ederson case. As you know, Mrs Ederson received several unpleasant, indeed threatening, texts and letters in the weeks and then days before she died. Her son, Nigel, told me that his mother had ignored the letters that she received a few months ago and the texts which arrived days before her death were treated more seriously by her friend, Imelda Simpson, than by Nora. When DI Peil visited the former matron yesterday, she was informed that she has also been receiving similar messages. Three letters have arrived this week, posted with a Preston postmark which as we know also covers Fordway. We must therefore assume they were sent by someone local.'

Serena turned on the whiteboard, the screen a luminous white. The contents of the three letters appeared, accompanied by gasps from DS Jennings. 'Oh my God, they're just the same as the ones we know Nora Ederson received. I don't know about anyone else, but I'd lay money on them coming from the same person.'

Harvey was used to his sergeant's statements and reminded her about the danger of jumping to a conclusion that may be erroneous. 'Only horses should be blinkered. We need to approach this latest development cautiously...'

Clare Jennings interrupted, 'Is the matron in danger? Are we taking these threats seriously? If I were her, I'd be petrified.'

Speaking more calmly than he felt, Harvey assured everyone that the threats were being taken extremely seriously and that Serena had insisted that Miss Simpson wasn't alone.

Serena continued. 'She has come to stay with a friend in Fordway: Janine Mortice, 24 Alders Close. I know that doesn't sound ideal, coming back here, but no one apart from us knows she's returned, and at least she can't receive any more hateful letters. Clare, I'd like you to organise a rota of patrol cars to make their presence felt on Alders Close and I've told the ladies that you'll visit twice a day. The moment they feel uncomfortable in the house, we will find alternative accommodation.'

Looking even smarter than yesterday, wearing a dark navy pin-striped suit, a shirt so white it could have come straight from an advert for washing powder, and a pale blue tie, Edward Stones asked the question all assembled were longing to ask. 'Do these latest threats make it even more likely that Nora Ederson was murdered? She received horrific missives immediately prior to a totally unexpected demise. Also, the messages the two women received are identical in looks: capital letters that appear to have been positioned on the page for maximum effect. And the content: talking about losing a baby and blaming the tragedy on the midwives.'

'Thank you, Constable Stones, and yes, this development would lend credence to the idea that we are dealing with a murder. I'll hand you back to DI Peil.'

'At risk of repeating what has been said, I am now convinced that Nora Ederson's death was murder. Sadly, it seems that the murderer is now targeting the ex-matron, Imelda Simpson.' Louis Armstrong's version of *What a Wonderful World*, Serena's ironic ringtone, sounded unnaturally loud in the large room. 'Sorry, everyone, this is a call I must take.'

Phone call from Imelda Simpson to DI Peil

S.P.: Good morning Miss Simpson.

I.S.: So sorry to bother you, Serena, but you did say I could call at any time.

S.P.: Indeed, and I'm pleased to hear from you, though you sound rather upset.

I.S.: I feel so silly, I keep telling myself it was nothing.

A long silence ensued.

S.P.: It's obviously something bothering you, so not nothing. Take your time and tell me why you're so upset.

I.S.: As you know I'm staying with Janine; she's been so good to me. I'd been inside the house since I arrived, afraid to go out, and Janine suggested a trip to the shops and a coffee. We wandered around, didn't buy anything, then went to the café, the one on Weighbridge Road. We had drinks and cakes and it was all going so well. For the first time since receiving those letters I felt relaxed…

S.P.: You're doing well, Miss Simpson.

I.S.: As I said everything felt normal and I was sure I was coping. It was as we were leaving the café that I saw the woman. She was entering as we were leaving, and we crossed in the doorway. I got such a shock. I knew her face, though it's been a while since I saw her. She glared at me, such a venomous look, and then she came right up to me and just stared. I was about to say hello, though I couldn't remember her name, when she spoke so quietly that I didn't know if I'd misheard. Oh dear, oh dear.

S.P.: Don't rush, I've got all the time you need When you're ready tell me what the woman said.

Another prolonged silence.

I.S.: She said that it was fortuitous (her word) that I had returned to Fordway; it would make her job so much easier. It was uttered with such hatred that I was speechless and didn't ask what she meant. She then asked if I'd received the letters. She must be the one who sent them and now she knows where I am. I don't know what to do, I'm so frightened.

S.P.: Imelda, you told me that you recognised her. Is it the lady you mentioned yesterday: Annabelle Borodin?

I.S.: Oh, I'm not sure. Not certain. It might be. I do know her, but I can't think of her name. She's younger than me, so might well have been a patient at one time.

S.P: Did Janine get a good look at her?

I.S.: No, she'd left the café ahead of me and didn't realise I wasn't following her until the woman had walked off. She obviously changed her mind about going into the café and strolled off up Weighbridge Road as calmly as anything. I was too shaken to follow her and by the time I'd told Janine what had happened there was no sign of her.

S.P.: Are you back at Janine's?

I.S.: Yes. We came straight back, and I phoned you. I do hope I'm not wasting your time, but I didn't know what else to do and my friend told me to report the incident.

S.P.: Imelda, you've done the right thing. I'll be round very soon to take a statement and I'll ask one of our officers who is excellent at producing facial composites to come with me. With your help he will produce a likeness of the woman who spoke to you. All you need to do is give him as much detail as possible. To start with we can show it to Janine and the staff at the Nursing Home. Someone might remember her.

Serena returned to the station with the matron's statement and a facial composite showing a woman with darkish hair, a round face, the eyes hidden behind tinted glasses. Apart from that last feature Harvey moaned that it could be almost any female between thirty and sixty. The DI continued, annoyed by her boss's negativity. 'Her statement didn't tell us anything new. She knows she's seen the lady before but can't remember the circumstances. One thing she did add was that she's sure she can recall all the ladies who lost a baby. "It's so traumatic that their faces are etched in my memory. The lady at the café this morning did seem familiar, but I don't know if she was ever a patient at Parkside. Maybe she worked there. Over the years a lot of nurses, doctors, cleaners, admin staff and social workers came and went."

'Unfortunately, she then became extremely confused and murmured that it might be the woman she mentioned once before: Annabelle Borodin. "I think, though I can't be certain, that she wore tinted glasses and had similar hair colour. Oh dear, I'm all of a dither and not much help."'

Harvey moaned that her last statement was almost certainly true. 'However, we'd better follow up this Borodin woman. An unusual name, so she should be easy to locate. I'll ask DS Jennings to find her and it's about time we looked into Mrs Henderson's complaint. We really need to speak to them and find out what happened: what their complaint was against Nora Ederson and how it was resolved. Be interesting to see if they were satisfied with the outcome, though I've a feeling it didn't disappoint them so much that it led to murder.'

'A good idea to keep Clare busy, it might stop her discussing the colour of the bridesmaids' dresses! The wedding isn't for ages, so I've got months of hearing every single detail of the big day.'

Chapter 20

For so long now, my life has resembled a game of chess; one in which I keep making the wrong moves. I'm the one defending the ultimate secret, the one that if disclosed would lead to checkmate. So much dishonesty, people behaving disingenuously. However, it all becoming public knowledge is unthinkable. I can only imagine the lurid tabloid headlines.

Two murders to my name (they are treating Nora Ederson's demise as such, though that is unfair). A third one may become necessary. I believe three is the point at which I'm labelled a serial killer. Me: ordinary, boring me. Lying has become like a second skin. Should I shed it like a snake performing Ecdysis so that another one can grow? I can't remember when I last told the truth, if I even recall what that word means.

Poor woman. If she'd listened, if she'd acknowledged I had a valid point, if she'd accepted that she could help she would still be alive, home from the holiday she'd planned and refreshed ready to return to work. She was the one who could have facilitated the necessary change. Had she done so there would have been no need for people to get hurt. My pleas fell on ears that refused to listen. Year. After. Year.

That last time: her point-blank refusal stays with me: 'No. I can't possibly do that. It's not within my remit as a midwife to get involved. My job is at the Nursing

Home and is one I believe I do well. I look after my patients and deliver babies. Anything beyond that must be dealt with by others. Please don't ask me again.'

Telling me to leave so that she could get ready to drive to the airport made me beg. I almost wept with frustration, cajoled, almost got down on my knees but she stood as firm as the Rock of Gibraltar.

'I am truly-sorry for your dilemma...' That was the word she selected. It was like calling a hurricane a passing shower. That word was her undoing. That was the moment when self-control went AWOL. I had never struck anyone. I had never been unable to restrain myself. Until that moment. A punch. A fall. An appalling crack as her head hit the cupboard. The strange thing is that apart from that there was no sound; none-at-all in the kitchen. Nora fell silently, dead with an immediacy that seemed unbelievable. After what felt like hours, but was probably seconds, I jumped as her phone broke the silence. How strange I thought, a call that would remain forever unanswered.

Having been responsible for one death, the second was easy: and inevitable. But this is not the time to think about Gerald.

It's Parkside's former matron who requires my attention now.

Nora Ederson said no. So did Imelda Simpson. Will she remember the request I made just before she retired? The same plea: the same response. Her reply lives on: 'I am the matron of a well-respected and successful maternity hospital. Such a request is abhorrent, and I could be struck off should I carry out your insane idea.'

Will she make the link? The connection: my asking both her and then her friend the exact same thing.

I can't believe they didn't discuss it. The danger is that she will remember and talk to the police. Far too dangerous.

Clare Jennings said she had located Annabelle Borodin. 'Zoe and Alastair Henderson will have returned from their holiday and can also be interviewed, sir.' Mr and Mrs Henderson had moved to Dorset, so the DS suggested a Skype call.

Failing to acknowledge her excellent work, Harvey said that any interview would have to wait until the next day. 'I'm due to see Superintendent Talbot. He'll want updating on our progress, or lack of it. No doubt he'll have something to say about the fact that Imelda Simpson has returned to Fordway. I have to say, that I don't think that was the best game plan in the world.

'You can also organise a meeting with Mrs Borodin. That'll have to be tomorrow as well. I presume she's Mrs, though could be Miss or Ms. Make sure you know how to address her, I've been caught out in the past and it makes for a poor beginning to any meeting when you get their title wrong.' Neither officer realised that by the following day none would remain persons of interest.

Scowling, the DCI stormed off to the meeting he assumed would be difficult.

Light was streaming through the office window, making the dust motes look as though they were performing a disco dance. Harvey thought how unhealthy they made the room look.

Having knocked rather tentatively, Harvey was surprised by the ebullient, 'Come in, DCI Tarquin, Harvey. Very good to see you. Thanks for finding the time to meet me. I know how incredibly busy you are. Two murder investigations to pursue is so much harder than one. My wife always reminds me how hard she found it when our second daughter was born. She'd thought one toddler was hard work, but she assured me that was a doddle, her word, compared to a toddler and a baby. Coffee?'

Superintendent Talbot, call me Henry, was new to both the area and the position. Well over six feet and with a bushy beard and mane of black hair he looked more like a bouncer at a nightclub than a senior policeman. However, his reputation had arrived before him and had made him sound like Sherlock Holmes, Poirot and Morse all rolled into one. Harvey had met him once before, very briefly, and had been impressed by him. He hadn't pulled rank as so many people at the top did and had assured the DCI that he intended to remain "hands on" whilst supporting "from a reasonable distance".

A desk can look organised, as though its owner has the papers, folders and memos under control. Others are somewhat more erratic. Superintendent Talbot's desk was most definitely in the latter category and looked as though a tornado had swept across, leaving total disarray. Dossiers were stacked at a precarious Leaning Tower angle; documents were distributed higgledy-piggledy in no discernible order and the entire surface was subsumed under paper and folders of varying sizes and colours.

Seeing the DCI's expression, he smiled. I know what this looks like, but the chaos is organised, I could put my hand on anything at a moment's notice. My wife despairs as I'm just the same at home: old receipts, junk mail and catalogues follow in my wake, and she knows not to go anywhere near my desk. Periodically she mumbles about helping me to organise it but then I'd never know where anything is. Fortunately, she's in charge of my clothes and they all have their designated spots in the wardrobe. All colour coordinated so I can get dressed in thirty seconds should one of those dreaded phone calls come at two in the morning.

Harvey said he had always been meticulously tidy. 'I want to know where everything is: the old a place for everything and everything in its place routine. My mother used to annoy my brothers by telling them they should look at my bedroom...then theirs...spot the difference and do something about it. As you can imagine that didn't make me Mr Popular. The trouble is untidiness makes me feel so uncomfortable I'm almost ill. Must be to do with a fear of losing control, but as I've been like it for ever, I'm not likely to change.'

'Down to business. Anything of import to report? Sorry, that sounded rather facetious.'

'Unfortunately, nothing concrete. Lots of interviews, discussions – my DS and DI are both excellent and provide insights that aid inquiries, but we're at the stage it's one step forward half a step back.'

'The memo you sent, and thank you for making it so thorough, has given me the background to both Gerald Winters' and Nora Ederson's untimely demises. Another unfortunate phrase, but correct me if I'm wrong, but I got the feeling you're still undecided about Mrs Ederson. Accident or murder?'

'To start with we weren't sure, but we're now treating it as murder. The PM highlighted the bruise on the lady's face which wasn't consistent with a fall, so it looks as though someone either pushed or punched her. We're trying to find out who sent her hate mail in the months before her death. That person may or may not be the killer but is someone we want to interview.'

'Yes, you sent me those repulsive missives and he, or probably she, definitely needs to be questioned. At the very least she'll be charged with harassment. They must have been extremely disquieting to receive. I believe the former matron has also been plagued with something similar.'

'So similar, we believe they are from the same person.'

'Now, Gerald Winters. The transcript of Susan Winters' interviews made for interesting reading. Is she your main person of interest?'

'At this moment in time (where had that ridiculous phrase come from?) she is. She remains in total denial and even claims that the body she *discovered*, her somewhat esoteric word, wasn't her husband but his twin brother Eric Winters, a man who says he has never been to their house. As you know, there's a nanny who did a vanishing act when the police first arrived and who we will want to interview again.'

'Is she being treated as a suspect?'

'She has an alibi for the Saturday of that weekend, but not the Sunday, or indeed the Friday night. Despite her I'm-going-to-tell-you-just-enough-to-stop-you-asking-anything-else interview I feel it's doubtful that she had anything to do with Gerald's death.'

'As always and as you know only too well Harvey... keep an open mind.'

'Indeed. It would be progress if my mind felt a bit more open or was even in full working order!'

Following a pause, the Superintendent said that he wasn't treating Harvey as a grandma learning how to suck eggs. 'However, can I suggest something that I find works. Well, most of the time. When I'm stuck, as is the case far too often, I forget everything I think I know and return to the beginning. Like starting a new investigation. It's not always easy but means that you approach it all again with no preconceptions. I interview everyone as if for the first time and even if the same questions are asked it is amazing how different the responses can be. Worth a try?'

'Anything is worth a try.'

'Good. Keep me informed of your progress. I'm sure there will be some soon.'

Chapter 21

Imelda was sitting, her hands held firmly in place on her lap. 'I wish I could remember the name of the lady I saw in town earlier. She looked at me with such venom I should be a hundred feet under. It's so annoying as I do know her. I'm now almost certain she was a mum-to-be at Parkside, attended all the ante-natal classes and was happy to have me as her midwife. She went into labour and all seemed well until the baby's heartbeat stopped. No warning. No prolonged labour. No obvious reason. I called Doctor Rose immediately, but it was too late and the little girl (yes, I know it was a girl as she was named Natasha by the distraught parents) was stillborn.'

'I think it was before your time, Janine, so not much point describing her again. I know I've kept on, but I keep almost recalling her name, it's almost there, then disappears in a swirl of fog. I think if I keep talking it will come.'

Janine looked serious. 'Maybe let your mind rest, sometimes things pop into one's head when one is *not* trying to recall them. Let's eat. Nothing fancy, I'm no Mary Berry as you might have noticed. Cheese and egg salad and a shop-bought apple pie. The good news is I do have some double cream. Enough to drown the pie!'

'You've been so kind, Janine, but I'll go home tomorrow. I don't want to outstay…That's it…Zoey Carpenter. You were right, the name appeared like car headlights approaching round a bend, just when I wasn't expecting it.'

The meeting with Superintendent Talbot had gone better than feared. Harvey had been assured that his superior had every faith in him, a phrase that Harvey wasn't sure he'd have used. Going over the two cases hadn't helped much, both men already cognisant with every-last detail. It sometimes helped to verbalise any findings, but that didn't appear to be the case today.

Walking home he felt exhausted. Moggies needed feeding and a ready meal microwaved. He knew it had to be in that order. Placing the cats' food in their bowls he was amused to see that Chopin was ready to bolt his sachet of *Just What the Cat Ordered,* bought in a moment of madness, the price far in-excess of his meagre meals, and move onto Grieg's. 'No wonder the vet suggested that a little weight loss might be in order. You'll eat yours, then go outside until your less greedy brother has finished.'

'Damnation!' Harvey swore only rarely, but his mobile's raucous tone was the last thing he needed.

Ten minutes later, he was feeling slightly more positive. Imelda Simpson had come up with a name. Tomorrow's interview should be interesting. They might just have their killer. Could it really be that simple?

Chapter 22

Tomorrow started at a time that shouldn't be experienced by anyone not working a nightshift, Harvey all too aware that his night's attempt at sleeping was over. He'd spent the night tossing and turning, the sheets feeling as though they were on a never-ending cycle in the tumble dryer, and he knew the advice to get at least eight hours rest was now redundant. Never the best of sleepers (cocoa, oils on his pillows, heavy duvet, non-prescription tablets from the local pharmacy all tried) he knew this had been one of the worst.

At 03:41, (his bedside clock informing him how little remained of the night) he had gone downstairs to make a hot drink, pursued by two moggies, hopeful of an early breakfast and disappointed by a meagre allowance of *Dreamies*.

Once back in bed, names kept appearing, standing to attention like soldiers on parade. The final list was in alphabetical order: Edna, Eric, Gerald, Harriet, Imelda, Richard, Susan, Sylvia. He knew they were all linked. But how? What was the common denominator? Parkside Maternity Home? But what did such an establishment have to do with murder?

Once the birds began their noise, (the most-polite word he could muster) he dragged himself out of bed much to the delight of his friends who expected the Full English, or at least the feline equivalent.

His mind felt fuzzy. What did other people do after such insomnia? Read, do puzzles, drink tea, watch TV, talk to the cats? Only the last one appealed. Surely it was far too early to start work. In the past that had been the preferred option, but experience had taught him that when he did that he felt ill later in the day and was of no use to anyone. Least of all himself.

Although it wasn't yet light, he had a shower, shaved, and got dressed. A walk felt essential. Dawn would break soon. The birds had obviously set their watches far too early. He felt like one of his clients, stalking victims or casing houses. A few solitary souls were returning from work, whilst others in their evening attire of mini-skirts and elongated heels were tottering along still the wrong side of too much alcohol. He felt pleased that they would feel worse than he did once the day woke up.

As the sun made a tentative appearance, he returned home. His two cats were curled up together, fast asleep on the settee, and Harvey thought if he came back (not that he believed in reincarnation) he would probably opt to be a pampered pussy. Their needs were few and easily accommodated. Not a bad life.

'Good morning, sir.' Harvey was amazed that it hadn't morphed into afternoon.

'I had no trouble contacting the lady Imelda Simpson remembered: Zoey Carpenter. Apparently, it was the tinted glasses that brought her name to mind. Miss Simpson said her friend was polishing hers and it reminded the matron of the woman in labour who had insisted on keeping her glasses on. They were a special prescription, and she wouldn't part with them. Strange the things that jog our memories, that make the neurons go into overdrive.'

'Quite so, DI Peil. You said you contacted Ms, Miss, Mrs Carpenter.'

'Yes, late last night and it's Mrs Carpenter. She sounded on the scared witless side of frightened when I told her it was the police. She's coming in at ten. Interestingly, she asked if she needed the services of a solicitor.'

Harvey smiled for the first time that morning and said that she might well do. 'Shall we see how the interview starts and what she has to say for herself. She will, of course, be offered one. Makes it all sound far more serious.'

Zoey Carpenter was in her mid-thirties but looked considerably older, her obvious disquiet adding unwanted years. She looked even more exhausted than Harvey (he would have said that was impossible) and had obviously not bothered with her appearance: unwashed hair and a face devoid of make up the clues that didn't need Miss Marple's deductive skills.

Before the DCI had a chance to begin the interview, Mrs Carpenter broke down, loud sobs filling the room. 'I did it. I sent the texts and the letters. I'm sorry, I just wanted to make them feel as bad as I did. I know it was a horrible thing to do. My husband doesn't know, and I didn't tell anyone else. It was just something I had to do.' Each utterance had increased in both speed and volume.

'Mrs Carpenter, shall we begin at the beginning. I assume you are talking about the hate mail that Nora Ederson and Imelda Simpson received.'

'Yes, yes, I sent them both the texts and letters: Nora Ederson and the matron, Imelda Simpson. They were equally culpable.'

Allowing time for the woman who was sitting shaking and throttling the life out of a paper handkerchief to become calmer, Harvey asked her again to begin at the beginning.

'Liam and I had always wanted a baby. We were childhood sweethearts, met at school and married as soon as we could. It took me ages to get pregnant, but when that happened, we were both so happy. I'd been left some money, my godmother leaving me the bulk of her estate, so we went privately, and I was to give birth in Parkside Nursing Home. It's got an excellent reputation.'

'Take your time, Zoey, we can see you are distressed.' Serena received a don't interrupt her whilst she's in full flow look from her boss.

The story continued: 'My midwife was Nora Ederson and she was great, just what you want for a first pregnancy: reassuring, informative, kind and caring. She even gave me her mobile number so that I could contact her with any worries. Everything was fine until…until, oh dear I can hardly talk about it.'

Serena knew not to fill the ensuing silence, her boss giving her a glare that would have stopped an avalanche in its tracks.

'Labour…at thirty-five weeks…rather too early… began late at night, but I hoped it was all a false alarm and didn't go to Parkside until the following morning. Nora kept saying how well I was doing, but it was taking ages. I can still see her face the moment she realised the labour wasn't progressing as it should. When someone so experienced looks ready to panic you know there is something seriously amiss. She asked the matron, Miss Simpson, to come in and a doctor was summoned with a speed that made me know my fears were real. I was immediately transferred to a theatre and they delivered Natasha by Caesarean section and...'

Tears streaming down her face, Zoey stopped mid-sentence. 'They hadn't done their job. I should have gone down to surgery much sooner. The following day I heard laughter from the next room. My door was open so I could hear it very clearly. A few minutes later, Nora and Imelda Simpson walked past my room still chortling over whatever the joke had been. They must have known I'd seen and heard but walked on. So callous. Utterly without caring. I was feeling so totally devasted that I decided I would give them some of their own medicine. At the time, it seemed like an appropriate adage!'

Allowing some time for the woman in front of them to regain some composure, Harvey asked if she knew the Winters' family: Gerald and Susan Winters.

'No, I don't know anyone by those names.'

'Thank you, Mrs Carpenter, I realise how upsetting it is to relive that experience.'

Harvey paused, one of his interviewing techniques that upped the tension, not that it was needed in the room that felt ready to explode. 'As you know, Nora Ederson died recently, and we are treating her death as murder. You have admitted sending her the hate mail, which in-itself is sufficient to charge you with harassment, but I must now ask where you were the weekend of the 12th of March.'

Blanching, Zoey murmured, every word an effort. 'You don't think I had anything to do with her death! I only sent the texts and letters to make her feel awful. I never intended to do anything physical. That's not me, not me at all.'

'But it is *you* to put the fear of God into people. Nora's missives were repugnant and the ones that Imelda Simpson has received recently are not only obnoxious but also extremely threatening. One says that what happened to Nora will happen to her. That's more than just trying to cause a few sleepless nights. Vindictive is a word the CPS might use at your trial. So, Mrs Carpenter, I will repeat my question. Where were you the weekend of the 12th of March. The weekend the woman you harassed was murdered?'

Wondering if he had overstepped the boundary, his hands were shaking so much he spilt his coffee. It had been a horrible hour, one he wanted to forget. He knew he had used emotive language. He knew he had allowed her to rile him, something that a DCI should be able to control. However, her behaviour was unacceptable. He knew she had suffered, but that was no excuse for what she had done, how she had hounded two innocent people whose worst sin had been to enjoy a moment of humour with another patient. Her texts about unprofessional failings hadn't been raised and almost certainly wasn't the main grievance. No formal compliant had been made and thanks to his DI's research Natasha had such underlying problems that she wouldn't have survived anyway. The pathologist's report indicated that the catastrophic complications were undetectable before birth. No blame at all was attached to either Nora or Imelda.

Clare Jennings had been tasked with following up the alibi Mrs Carpenter had provided for the weekend in question. Efficiency personified she had done so with admirable speed.

'Sir, the dates don't correlate. Zoey Carpenter claimed to be in Tenerife from 10th to 17^h March. Her husband has just informed me they went the week before, the 3rd to the 10th. They returned to Manchester airport in the early hours of the 10th.'

Thumping the desk, and spilling more coffee, Harvey exploded. 'She lied, she bloody well lied. Did she not think we'd check? The more I know about that woman, the more she irritates me.'

'She may have made a mistake I know once I'm home I can't always recall the exact dates of a holiday. Maybe she knew the 10th came into it.'

The look Serena received told her he thought that most unlikely. 'No time like the present. We need to see her at home. Preferably with hubby there. He might as well know what his dearly beloved has been up to. Serena you're with me again. Clare, have a look at Mrs Carpenter's background. Anything you can find on her. Despite what she said about not being a killer, she's definitely on my list of suspects.'

Chapter 23

The Carpenters' house was a new build in an area that had, until recently, been open fields. There had been numerous adverse comments in the local press about yet more green space being given over to "top-of-the-range houses". Letters criticising the council for allowing the development had filled the letters' pages for weeks. The houses certainly deserved their impressive accolade: four, and five-bedroom properties with double garages and enough space surrounding each one to erect further dwellings. Harvey hoped the occupants enjoyed gardening or could afford the services of a groundsman. Gardener hardly seemed appropriate.

It was obvious which had been the first to be occupied, the area surrounding the properties well-stocked with spring flowers and small bushes. Two large cars parked on the wide path matched the house for opulence, no ancient Hondas on show. The ones further into the new estate looked unfinished and a large sign advertised the fact that not all had been sold. A Show House was open for viewing and favourable mortgage rates were advertised.

Number nine was one of the few that looked occupied at the rear of the new estate. Large wrought-iron gates had been added at the front of the drive (Harvey wondered where the stone lions were). The officers were surprised to see that there was an entry code on one side, with a buzzer beside it and a notice asking for any visitors to "make themselves known".

'Not exactly welcoming,' was Serena's rather blunt comment. 'I'd say they don't like visitors.'

'Definitely not us!' Leaning out of the car, Harvey managed to press the buzzer which made no external sound. A disembodied voice asked what they wanted.

'DCI Tarquin and DI Peil. We'd like to come in and speak to you and your wife, Mr Carpenter.'

'It's not convenient. Not convenient at all. My poor wife has come home in a terrible state. She has just told me what she's been doing, but it sounds as though she was being treated like a criminal this morning. I'm thinking of making a complaint. She's been through enough, so I'll ask you to leave.'

'Mr Carpenter, many people would say that your wife is a criminal. Harassment is an extremely serious crime. I must inform you that she has broken the law and that will, in due course, be followed up. However, we are here on another matter and we would like you to open the gates.'

Moving slowly and smoothly the gates slid noiselessly apart, allowing the officers to drive through.

Liam Carpenter looked like a bad-tempered employer, ready to sack the unwelcome visitors. Well above average height he loomed over Harvey. 'I'm not sure what you want as you've already interrogated my wife this morning and turned her into a wreck, but you don't have long to do it. I'm due at an extremely important meeting on the other side of town in less than an hour and I am not leaving you alone with her again.'

Standing aside he allowed the unwelcome pair to enter. 'Please come into the kitchen. I need to talk to you before you see Zoey again. She has admitted what she did and is now extremely sorry, not to say ashamed. I'm sure her actions were all part of her illness. Since we lost the baby, my wife has not been herself and has never recovered from the tragedy...and I use that word advisedly. She is constantly anxious...about everything... always waiting for something else to go wrong. If Natasha could die when the pregnancy had been so normal and Zoey so well, then she assumes that anything untoward might happen at any time. She was diagnosed with a paranoid personality disorder where you see danger everywhere, even in the most benign of settings.

'Her doctor has prescribed many different tablets, none of which have worked. A few months ago, he admitted her to Waterfront, a hospital in Carlisle dealing with psychiatric problems. At the time I was afraid she was suicidal and there were occasions when I was reluctant to go to work. Her sister came to stay with her when she was so down. I run my own company and cannot afford to be away from the factory too often. When she came out of Waterfront, we thought a holiday might help. We hadn't been away for a long time, and as I told your DS, we went earlier this month. Tenerife, a lovely hotel and good weather made no difference, and she came home in a distraught state.'

'Thank you for that background, Mr Carpenter, but we do need to see your wife again.'

'Please be as brief as you can. Sandra, her sister is due any minute and I need to go.'

Zoey was sitting wrapped in a duvet, the gas fire on its maximum setting, making the room feel stuffy. Despite the warmth, she was shivering so much her whole body shook.

Knowing he might be about to speak to someone who had killed two people, Harvey didn't bother with introductory niceties. 'Mrs Carpenter, when we spoke to you earlier today, we asked about March 12th. You told us you were in Tenerife from March 10th to the 17th. Apparently, that was wrong. According to your husband you went on the 3rd and returned on the 10th. So, in fact, you were in Fordway on the 12th, the date we asked about.'

Leaving a short period for Zoey to answer, he continued, 'Mrs Carpenter, why did you lie to us?'

'I think my wife just made a mistake. Why would she lie about the dates we went on holiday?'

'Because, Mr Carpenter, Nora Ederson, the woman your wife had harassed over many months, was killed sometime around the 12th and rather than being thousands of miles away you and your wife were at home in Fordway.'

'That is the most ridiculous thing I have ever heard. Zoey is as far from being a killer as it is possible to be.' Liam was blustering and Harvey wondered how much he believed what he was saying.

The DCI was becoming frustrated. 'People commit murders for a variety of reasons and those who know the people involved are often amazed, saying they never dreamt the man or woman they thought they knew was capable of committing the most serious of crimes.' Turning to Mrs Carpenter he said, in a voice determined to have an answer, 'So, I must ask you yet again exactly where you were on the 12th of this month.'

Sobs filled the room. Serena was to say afterwards that she wondered whether Zoey was giving herself time to think up a plausible reply.

Staring at the floor, the exact shade of the carpet burned into her retinas, she whispered, 'I was at home. I didn't go out for over a week once we got back.'

As it was obvious that was to be the extent of his wife's input, Liam took over. 'Zoey was tired after our journey. We got back early on the 10th. I stayed to help her unpack then I had to go to work. My factory makes cardboard boxes, all shapes, and sizes, and just before my wife and I went on holiday we'd received a huge order from a business that makes light bulbs. Four different sizes of boxes had been ordered and I wanted to see how much progress there had been whilst we were away. I have an excellent team, but probably like you, Detective Chief Inspector, I like to be au fait with all aspects of my business, and I wanted to ascertain how the order was progressing. My factory operates seven days a week, so I was there every day. We were behind with the order, not good for our reputation and that is something that is vital in any business.'

Turning to the woman who was shaking so much she made a whirling dervish look calm, he asked if she could provide an alibi. A brief shake of the head told him all he needed to know.

'Your sister didn't come to be with you?'

Liam spoke for his wife. 'No, she was on holiday, went when we did but was away two weeks.'

Knowing he would probably gain little more from the meeting, he said he had one final question.

'You told us that Nora Ederson was a wonderful midwife and that she gave you her mobile phone number. Did she also invite you to her house?'

'No. I never went there. I just phoned when I had a query or was worried about something.'

'We will need your fingerprints Mrs Carpenter (he refused to use her Christian name). Please come into the station sometime later today.'

Returning to the station, Harvey was furious, and Serena wished she had offered to drive. The journey was conducted in a deafening silence, the DI knowing from bitter experience that there were times not to speak.

Storming into the incident room, Harvey yelled at Clare Jennings. 'Phone that bloody woman and say she's booked in at 3p.m. to have her fingerprints taken. Then ask forensics to check them against any found at 120 Rose Avenue.'

Chapter 24

Superintendent Talbot had advised Harvey to "take a step, or many steps back"; to return to the beginning and look at each case as if for the first time. Frustration ruled. All too aware that he never coped well when stressed he knew that the lack of progress was getting to him. He had allowed Zoey Carpenter (vindictive, stupid, selfish, self-obsessed woman. Had no one ever lost a baby before?) to infuriate him today and was experienced enough to realise that he had been unable to hide his displeasure. He now knew who had sent the hate mail, but had she lied to them deliberately, to put them off her trail?

Speaking aloud, the habit more pronounced when his stress levels rose, he shouted, 'No bloody alibi! Claims she was alone in the house once they returned from holiday. Now that's what I call interesting.'

Evening briefing: the team were informed that each case was to be reviewed. Serena was tasked with noting everything they knew about Gerald Winters' murder and Clare the same for Nora Ederson's. They were not to be discussed or shared with others. 'Now, we all need an early finish. Go home, relax and start again in the morning.'

Henry Talbot had also advised Harvey to trust his team. 'Too many people can confuse the issues being reviewed. Leave the detectives you know can complete

155

tasks to work unaided. Then when they discuss them with you, you will be able to look at their results with fresh eyes. Take a day off. Clear your head. Your team will cope without you for twenty-four hours.'

Although the day was overcast, Harvey decided to go to the seaside. There was nothing like walking by the sea. Blackpool or Morecambe? The latter would almost certainly be quieter, though neither would be crowded mid-week in late March.

Morecambe had changed since the days his parents had taken him and his brothers there for days out. More sand had been added, the beach more appealing, allowing children to build castles and fill moats with seawater. New play areas seemed to spring up each time he came, and he thought how he and his siblings would have loved the swings, slides and climbing frames. Unfortunately, the Winter Gardens, the venue for so many shows - *The Wizard of Oz* and *Charlie and the Chocolate Factory* were two he recalled - had gone along with the bowling alley and most of the shops. The town looked in need of rejuvenation and he had been pleased to hear that the Eden Project North was likely to become a reality, attracting thousands who would spend their money in the cafes and hotels.

Driving through the West End of Morecambe, he decided to carry on to the village of Heysham. He remembered his first visit when he was about eight. At the time it had been awarded the *Britain in Bloom's Gold Small Village!* award and even as a child he had been impressed by the abundance of flowers on show. Today's display wouldn't win any accolades, but the daffodils, tulips and hyacinths in gardens brightened the gloomy day.

He had been too young to appreciate the seventeenth century cottages, or the ancient church dedicated to St. Peter. Every time he came back, he walked out to visit the church, set overlooking Morecambe Bay. He remembered being told that there had been a place of worship on that site since the 7th century. As a child he had been intrigued by the medieval sandstone coffin (disappointingly empty!) and the sundial of the same material dated 1696. However, the best part of any trip was a cream tea in the village, sometimes followed just before they left by an ice cream from a van on the beach. Smiling to himself, Harvey knew that these days such a double indulgence would give him a night of uncomfortable indigestion.

Huge waves were making obvious headway across the vast area of mud flats, though high tide was a few hours off. The Morecambe Bay tidal range was one of the biggest in the world and low tide meant that no water was visible. It was a treacherous bay, the speed of the incoming tide trapping many an unsuspecting tourist walking too far out. "Faster than a horse can gallop" was the local boast. No one would ever forget the disaster of 2004 when a large group of Chinese workers sent out to pick cockles were cut off at 9.30 p.m. by the incoming tide. Twenty-one lost their lives. Quick sands added to the danger and although they were mostly situated further round the coast Harvey never ventured onto the sand, preferring the safety of the long prom.

Determined not to think about work, he wondered, yet again, what pastime he should adopt. Something was needed to make his life less limited: work, work and more work consumed every week. Others managed to have a social life and interests beyond the working

day, (he often wondered where they got the inclination...
or the energy) so surely, he could, and indeed should,
organise some me-time, a phrase he had read in the
weekend Leisure and Relaxation supplement. He loved
singing and had once joined a local choir. Unfortunately,
he had been forced to miss so many rehearsals that he
felt unable to participate in the concert that was put on
in the town hall, afraid his ignorance of many of the
songs would mar the performance. The same had
happened with the evening classes he had signed up for:
far more missed than attended.

No cream tea or ice cream, but fish and chips, eaten
as it should be straight out of the paper.

'It's a tad chilly for eating al fresco.' The elderly man
smiled, making it obvious he was joking. 'But they do
taste even better like that and look at the view! Might
be a dour day, but one never tires of looking at this
panorama.'

Harvey didn't feel in the mood for conversation, but
good manners forced him to respond. 'Not the best of
days, but fresh air is always welcome.'

Pulling his black Labrador away from a smell that
had entertained him for long enough, the man sat beside
Harvey. 'It's definitely fresh. Rain forecast later, so
we're lucky to get out whilst it's dry. What would the
British talk about if the vagaries of the weather weren't
so endlessly fascinating?'

Half an hour later, the old man, call me William,
had told his listener his life story: one of eight children;
a life spent working on the railways; a long marriage
to Edith; children and now grand and even great
grandchildren. Knowing he was lonely, Edith long since

departed, Harvey pretended to listen, making what he hoped were appropriate noises.

'Well, lovely to talk to you. Hope you enjoy the rest of your day.' Rufus had sat patiently but was obviously glad to be on the move, straining at his lead as the pair moved off. Will that be me one day? Talking to anyone and everyone. Not the most positive of ideas, but perhaps preferable to letting cases wander through my brain like a meandering river that's adopted a more convoluted course.

Having completed over ten miles, the sign at the edge of Heysham informing him that it was 5.3 miles from Heysham to Bare at the other end of the bay, Harvey felt in better spirits by the time he returned to his car.

'Hell, and damnation, what now?' The utterance filled the empty car park and accompanied his *Dies Irae* ring tone which sounded true to its translation: The Day of Wrath! Who the devil needs to phone me? Can't it wait until tomorrow?

'Sorry to bother you, sir.' How often did DS Jennings begin any conversation with those five words?

'You asked me to bring Mrs Carpenter in yesterday afternoon so her fingerprints could be taken.' Another pause, the young officer obviously taking her time. 'Well sir, they match a set found in Mrs Ederson's kitchen!'

'She bloody well lied…again. Make another appointment to interview her, as early as possible in the morning. Tell the damned woman it will be under caution this time, so she might want to engage the services of a solicitor.'

Failing to thank Clare, he cut the call. Reviewing the cases would have to wait.

Chapter 25

It was an extremely discombobulated Zoey Carpenter who walked into the station at 8 a.m. the following morning, her husband two paces in front, like Moses parting the Red Sea.

The P.C. on the desk almost took a step back as the pair approached.

'My wife has been summoned to see DCI Tarquin. Let him know we are here at the appointed hour.'

Liam Carpenter expressed his displeasure when told that Zoey would be questioned alone by thumping the nearest wall. Harvey was pleased to see it must have hurt.

Interview Room One was small but no one could describe it as cosy. Its meagre dimensions highlighted the seriousness of the situation: predator, and prey too close, adding to the latter's discomfort.

Introductions and the standard warning, "You do not have to say anything. But it may harm your defence if you do not mention when questioned something which you later rely on in court. Anything you do say may be given in evidence" were read aloud for the tape, its red light shining brightly in the gloomy room.

'Mrs Carpenter, you have declined the assistance of the duty solicitor. If, at any time, you wish to change your mind, you are entitled so to do, and one will be appointed for you.'

'I do not and will at no time in the future require the help of a solicitor.' Zoey sounded more confident than she looked. A sleepless night had aged her even further, and she was so pale that the DCI wondered if a doctor might prove more useful than a lawyer.

'Mrs Carpenter, you have admitted sending hate mail to both Mrs Ederson and Miss Simpson. Unfortunately, the rest of your story has been a whole pack of lies, all fifty-two cards present and incorrect! Your first fabrication was about the dates you went on holiday. Now, experience has taught me that when a person tells lies to the police it's generally because they have something to hide. The dates *you* supplied indicated that you were out of the country when Nora Ederson was murdered. Unfortunately, we ascertained, (where did that word come from?) that was not the case and that you returned home on the 10th, sometime before Mrs Ederson was killed.'

Looking slightly more confident, Zoey sighed. 'We went over that, and I told you I had made a mistake. Liam always deals with our holidays, books the flights and the hotels and my only task is to pack and be ready when the taxi arrives to take us to the airport. I merely made a mistake. Easy to do.'

Harvey left a long gap. When he spoke, the room seemed to reverberate, the words bouncing off the walls. 'Easy to do! And had we not followed up the dates you *mistakenly* supplied, you would have had the perfect alibi: 'Couldn't possibly be me guv, I was sunbathing by the swimming pool!' The look his DI gave him warned him to keep this line of questioning under control. The best was to come.

Zoey took her time, then repeated that she had made a mistake. 'A genuine error.'

'Well, here's another error: genuine, or maybe not. You told us that Mrs Ederson was such a caring midwife that she gave you her phone number. When we asked if she had also supplied her address for you to visit her, should the need arise, you said no and that you had never been to her house.'

The pause this time was even longer, all that was missing was a drum roll. Zoey had stopped all eye contact and appeared to be finding the worn table a thing of beauty.

'If you've never been to her house how did your fingerprints magically appear in the kitchen and the hall? Once again, I cannot understand why an intelligent woman would tell such a transparent lie; one that can so easily be checked.'

'I've remembered. I did go once. I had genuinely forgotten. It was when I was pregnant. Nora had been so kind at the ante-natal class that when she asked if I wanted to go to back to hers for a cup of tea I jumped at the idea. It was the end of her shift and she said she was going home to an empty house and some company would be welcome. She'd baked a coffee cake. I remember it was delicious.'

'Interesting that you are able, suddenly, one might almost say in extremis, to recall the visit you denied having taken place. And in such detail. A delicious coffee cake...is that meant to make your story sound believable? They say that someone lying adds erroneous *add-ons* to detract from their fibs. You seem to either forget, get things mixed up, or embroider your lies rather too often for your own good. Why should we believe this version of events? You must see our problem. To misquote Oscar Wilde, "One lie might be regarded as a misfortune, however, to lie twice is extremely careless". The carelessness is entirely yours. Lying to the police twice. Is that *really* the best you can do?'

'I went to her house, but not the week she was killed. I am not your murderer.'

Staring at the woman who had faded into an even whiter shade of pale he yelled, 'Well, where is your alibi? Until you provide one...' He halted, like a driver suddenly seeing a red light, then spoke so quietly Serena wondered if the tape would pick up his words. 'Until then, we are charging you with harassment: putting people in fear of violence. A pattern of two or more incidents of unwanted contact: starting point six weeks custody. Deliberate threats, persistent action over a longer period: starting point eighteen weeks custody. That will, given time, begin to sound horribly familiar and I must warn you that the charge if proven, which seems as likely as night following day, always carries the punishment of time spent in jail. And that's before we consider a murder charge!

'The details of your case *will* be sent to the CPS and you *will* need the services of a lawyer. You *will* be informed of any future interviews and a date *will* be set for you to appear before the local magistrates. They then have the jurisdiction to send you to Crown Court should they view the texts and letters as sufficiently shocking to the two innocent victims who were on the receiving end of your foul missives (another look from Serena) to warrant the power of the higher court.'

Standing so quickly he upended his chair, he stormed out of the room.

DI Peil caught up with her boss in the long corridor leading to the canteen. 'Tea and coffee cake would seem appropriate, sir.' Harvey didn't appreciate her attempt at levity.

'That woman is a liar. We need any CCTV coverage of the area between the roads from her house and 120 Rose Avenue. We know there are no cameras in the immediate vicinity of Rose Avenue but if she even went in that direction on the 12th, we'd be able to apply more pressure. Bloody well have her. Harassment will be the least of her problems.'

'Sir, DS Jennings and I have put our summaries of the cases on your desk. Not sure they're much help, though there is one interesting piece of evidence we'd all overlooked.'

Chapter 26

Gerald James Winters: Case number 37892307.
Review by DI Serena Peil

- On the morning of Monday 18th March
  Mr Winter's body was found on the dining
  room floor of his house: 14 Wordsworth Avenue,
  Fordway. The PM indicated he had been there
  for some time, rigor mortice almost gone He
  was lying on his back, fully clothed. A tray with
  a three-course meal lay beside the body, with
  a doll sitting on his opposite side.
- N.B. listen to the 999 call, made by his wife
  (widow) Susan Winters where she claims to
  have just discovered his body. 09.18 hours.
  Monday 18th March
- The PM, performed by Alfie Morrison, said
  that Mr Winters had died due to ingesting the
  fatal combination of Temazepam (to help
  him sleep) and Oxycontin Oral (pain relief
  following a broken elbow). Both had been
  prescribed by his doctor, but he knew not
  to take them together. They had been
  consumed in extremely large quantities which
  may indicate suicide. However, someone had
  laid out his body post-mortem and failed to
  report his death.

- Susan Winters was taken to the police station and interviewed. She denied any involvement with her husband's death and seemed unsure it was him. She gave a largely no comment interview.
- Interview with Mrs Winters' parents was "unhelpful", but they did admit there had been long-term marital discord in the Winters' household. They were reluctant to say too much, though they obviously disliked their son-in-law and showed no remorse that he was dead.
- Interview with the nanny, Harriet Devizes, was once again mostly "unhelpful", though she indicated that her parents wanted her to leave the job. No reason was forthcoming.
- Neighbours spoke of a quiet couple who kept to themselves. Pleasant but not interested in socialising. Children were said to prefer staying indoors but sounded lively and noisy at times.
- Susan's doctor informed us (eventually) that Susan had received psychiatric help. He described her as fragile.
- Eric Winters, the deceased's brother, hadn't seen his brother or Susan since their wedding almost nine years ago. He said there was always some reason he and his partner were told they couldn't visit. Photographs of the children were sent each Christmas and he had come to England (he lives in France) hoping to meet them.
- He sent presents which were only barely acknowledged by his brother.

- Every interview felt unfinished, incomplete, as though the people being interviewed had vital information; information that they wanted to remain hidden.

People not yet interviewed: Gerald Winters' employers, colleagues, and friends. None of the last category have come to light.

No one spoke warmly of the deceased, but who hated him enough to kill him?

Possible suspects; possible motives.

Susan Winters: an unhappy marriage. Worn out with childbirth and five children all under eight.

Sylvia and Richard Page: worried about their daughter. She had changed from a bright, outgoing girl to one suffering from anxiety and depression. They blamed Gerald.

The nanny: had Mr Winters made unwelcome sexual advances? Was he the reason her parents wanted her to leave?

Eric Winters: had the brothers got a long-term feud?

Person or persons unknown?

Suggestions: re-interview each of the above. No one has disclosed all they know.

Nora Ederson. Case number 33076218.
Review by DS Clare Jennings

Nora Ederson's body was discovered by her son on the morning of March 19th. She had died approximately one week before. Her son assumed she had gone on the holiday she had planned, and her suitcase was found half packed ready in the bedroom.

The PM, performed by Alfie Morrison, concluded that death had occurred due to the "traumatic injury to the back of her head". A bruise on her left cheek indicated that, in-all- likelihood, she had been punched.

Mrs Ederson was a well-respected midwife at Parkside Maternity Home. The matron, Petra Moreton spoke highly of her but said there had been a complaint several months ago which led to Nora's suspension whilst the matter was investigated. She was fully exonerated. The couple, Mr and Mrs Henderson, who made the complaint have alibis for the weekend in question. See report by DI Peil.

Neighbours spoke of an extremely pleasant woman. One elderly lady said that Nora had done her shopping for her when she was ill, and another spoke of her willingness to feed her cat when she went away. No one saw or heard anything unusual the week in question. All appeared to be shocked.

Hate mail had been arriving by text and letter. We now know the sender was Mrs Zoey Carpenter and any involvement she may have in the midwife's death is being investigated.

The former matron, and good friend, Imelda Simpson, said that Nora had been upset by the hate mail, but refused to involve the police, saying it was all part of the job when things went awry. Miss Simpson has also been the victim of Zoey Carpenter's letters.

N.B. Are we looking for the same killer? The only link between Mr Winters and Mrs Ederson would appear to be Parkside.

Suspects: it is hard to see who would hate Nora Ederson enough to murder her. Was it an accident? An argument that became heated. A push that resulted in the fatal injury to the back of her head.

Both sons have alibis for the relevant period.

Next step: any further links between the two deaths need to be investigated.

On finishing his reading, the DCI was surprised to see both Serena and Clare walking into his office and he remembered to thank them for their exhaustive reports.

'Sir, I think you should listen to the 999 Call made by Susan Winters. I indicated in my report that it is, to say the least, interesting. I've brought it along. Clare and I have listened to it several times and each time it gets weirder.'

999 Call: Monday 18th March 2021. 09.18

Emergency. Which service?

He's asleep and I can't get him to wake up.

Madam, do you require an ambulance?

I think so, he just refuses to wake up.

Is your address 14 Wordsworth Avenue, Fordway?

Yes. He's lying on the floor and hasn't eaten his dinner, and it's his favourite: roast beef.

An ambulance is on its way, madam. Can you tell me if he's breathing?

He's lying down asleep.

Is it your husband?

The doll has been guarding him, looking after him, and I think she's been crying.

Can you tell me your name?

Susan Winters.

Well, Susan an ambulance will be with you very soon. Stay on the line and try to remain calm.

But it must be bad if his favourite doll has been upset. You can see the tears on her cheeks.

Try not to worry, just let me know when you hear the ambulance arrive.

He'll be so hungry, and the meal has gone cold. He won't like that.

I think I can hear the paramedics at the door. Let them in and they'll take over.

The line goes dead.

All three sat in silence. The words on the recording speaking volumes. Susan Winters was even more disturbed than they had originally thought.

'She knew about the meal and the doll. She's admitted placing them there. The thing we don't know is, was she the one who laid out his body? In fact, did she murder him?' Harvey was all too aware that there were no answers to his questions. Or not yet.

Clare leant forward. 'Sir, my report didn't take long, well let's face it there wasn't much to say, so I decided to look at phone records for both the deceased. I went back six months. Gerald Winters' calls were mostly work related. However, rather interestingly, he phoned home at least twice every day during the working week. Always at 11a.m. and 3p.m. Was he checking up on his wife? Susan's parents spoke of him being controlling. Two days before he died there were six calls. Had she had enough of being hounded?

'The vast majority of Mrs Ederson's calls were to her sons, one or two to each of them most weeks. Both sons phoned her on Sundays. There were regular calls to and from Imelda Simpson and others were to Parkside, the hairdresser, and the dentist. All as per normal. Then it got more interesting when I noticed a number that appeared on both phone records. An 0161 code: Manchester. I tried the number and got the answer phone, so I said who I was and asked for my call to be returned.'

Pausing for breath, Clare continued. 'Late yesterday afternoon my call was returned: a Barry London. He's a money lender, all legitimate, he explained at great length, registered for two decades under the name *You Need Cash*. He admitted having been contacted by Mrs Ederson and Mr Winters. It didn't seem appropriate to say any more on the phone, so I asked him to come to the station. He's due in an hour. Shall I interview him?'

'Let Serena be there as well. Have we found our link?' Staring at the paperwork on his desk he added, 'I'll start to follow up your reviews, and organise further interviews with our gallery of rogues; the people who so far have failed to tell us what was really going on. I think I'll start with Richard and Sylvia Page. This time they are going to tell me the truth about their daughter.'

Chapter 27

Barry London arrived early and seemed anxious to start the interview, not waiting for a question before launching in, his speech obviously well-rehearsed and self-serving.

'As I said on the phone, my business is one hundred and ten per cent legit. People need money in a hurry; they contact me. I do the appropriate background checks and lend it. Up to ten thousand pounds. We arrange a repayment strategy, and it gets paid back: with the agreed, and acceptable to both parties, add on. My interest rates are amongst the best in the business: three percent.'

Harvey smiled, thinking the man obviously had something to hide. Whether or not it was pertinent to the two deaths remained to be seen.

'Mr London,'

'Call me Barry, no one uses my surname.'

'Barry, as my DS indicated when she spoke to you on the phone yesterday, your number appeared on two bank statements and phone records that related to two people in Fordway...'

'Well, I do business all over the place, mostly in the North West, but sometimes as far away as Cornwall. Only yesterday a bloke asked for ten-grand, to set up a workshop in Aberdeen, not the first request from north of the border. My fame has spread far and wide. As

I said I've built up a good reputation and my online profile is as good as they get. Five stars for punctuality, repayment interest and all-round service. My staff are careful with the punters, they know people are upset, even in floods, when they phone. No one wants to need money and often the poor souls are in dire straits and we're their last resort. I emphasise the need for empathy, though there are occasions when we are forced to turn someone down after checking their credit rating. Only last week a woman got very shirty when we refused her request for two thousand. She'd got a list of debts as long as your arm.'

Attempting to get the interview, which felt like a Manchester tram in danger of becoming derailed, back on track, Harvey interrupted the man's verbal onslaught. 'Over the past six months the two people I mentioned have phoned you and we need to know why.'

'Funny you should mention that. As soon as your DS ended the call, I got my records out: not Status Quo or Take That, oops, showing my age, but my firm's detailed accounts covering the last year. Anything you want to know I'd be more than happy to assist you with.'

'Thank you very much, Barry, (what was the man hiding?) that sounds most helpful. The first is a Mrs Nora Ederson. She contacted you on the 8th of November last year and again on February 16th.'

Pages turned with the speed of a man fleeing arrest, Barry found the appropriate entries. 'Yes, 10.15 November 8th Sandra took details from a Mrs Ederson, 120 Rose Avenue, Fordway. She asked us to lend her one thousand. Background checks proved O.K. and she received the money the following day. We like to be quick, one of our great selling points. The money was repaid before the start of this year.'

'Do you have a record of why she needed the money?'

'Not for that particular transaction. Sometimes they say, like the bloke in Aberdeen, but mostly they keep the reason to themselves. I think a lot are too embarrassed to let on.'

'And the 16th of February?'

'Yep, there she is again. There's a record of her phoning. Tommy took that call. It says here she needed another loan but then Tommy's written, "The lady needs time to think about it and she'll get back to us if she decides to continue with the loan." No note of her doing so. People do change their minds, realise the money will need to be refunded and with a little extra on top. As I said, we're not in the business of fleecing folks, but we only make our living with the interest we charge.'

'The other person we need to ask about is a Mr Gerald Winters.'

Colour draining from a face was something Harvey had heard about but never seen with such rapidity. From ruddy to white in zero point one of a second.

'Are you alright, Barry? That name seems to have upset you.'

'Like I said, most people are good at repaying their loans and we are sympathetic when it takes a little longer than agreed. But our Mr Winters was a totally different matter. Totally different.' Pausing to think how to proceed, he stared at the wall, avoiding the eye contact that had so far been ever-present. 'The man was a liar. Wouldn't have known the truth if it was a Sunday sermon.'

Another prolonged pause. 'You don't need to tell me the dates: 5th November he asked to borrow the full Monty: ten grand the most we lend at any one time. We're always careful when it's such a large amount as people have got to realise how much they'll be paying back. Three hundred added, that's the initial three per cent, doesn't sound like much, but they forget that's the basic amount if they coughed up after a week. Any delay and more becomes due. It's then three percent of ten thousand, three hundred and so on. Soon mounts up. We warn them about that. Harvey thought it would be in the small print that very few people read. A lot of people borrow small amounts to see them to the next pay cheque and then three percent is easy. The problem starts when it's a large amount and not back to us pronto.'

'And that was the case with Mr Winters?'

'You could say that. Let me just check the details. He's got a dossier all to himself.

November 5th requested ten thousand, as soon as possible. Check completed: he had a first-class credit history and at the time was a bank manager. He assured us he was due to be promoted early in the new year: Area Supervisor for the whole of the North West, a post which came with a huge salary increase, so the money was transferred two days later. The understanding, I use that word loosely with what subsequently happened, was that he would repay a thousand a month. The interest would be taken with the final payment as we'd know how much the add-on was by then.' Barry looked uncomfortable, knowing that it would have been a considerable amount. Harvey recalled the horror story in the paper about a young woman who had borrowed a thousand pounds, only to find it had increased fourfold by the time she could pay it all back.

'December 5th the first repayment came. Then not the proverbial dickybird. Tommy was in charge up until that point, then I took over. Phone calls went unanswered, letters and emails received no reply, so it got serious. When I threatened him with the bailiff, he sounded upset. Let me just check, yes, March 1st. He begged for more time and I gave him a week, told him any further delay and it had the propensity to get serious. I like the word propensity, usually works, makes it sound like old Damocles and his sword!'

'What exactly do you mean by get serious?'

'In my line of business, you sometimes need to put on a bit of pressure. I've got a man who makes his presence felt, nothing illegal (why do I doubt that Harvey thought) just a visit and a warning.'

'Does the warning include physical intimidation?'

Barry London knew he had backed himself up a cul-de-sac. 'Threats maybe, but we don't carry them through. Usually we get a court order, all legal, absolutely legit, for the bailiffs to go round and remove goods to the value of the amount that's outstanding.'

'Can you tell me what happened with Gerald Winters?'

Making a show of studying his notes, Barry spoke in a voice that had lost all its previous bonhomie. 'March 8th came and went. No money. No contact. So, Jimmy paid him a visit. Laid it on the line. Mr Winters' wife answered the door and took Jimmy through to the lounge. Her husband was not at all pleased to be visited at home and ordered my bloke to leave. He did so after delivering the final warning letter. The bailiffs would be calling in two weeks.'

'We need Jimmy's full name and a contact number.'

'Of course. Can I add that Jimmy was adamant that Mr Winters was in total denial, didn't take the situation seriously, seemed to think it would all go away, vanish into some benevolent ether, all debts paid.'

'Mr London, I'm not sure if you are aware that both Mrs Ederson and Mr Winters are dead and in both cases murder is suspected.'

If Barry had been growing paler as the interview progressed, he now looked as though he had been dug up. 'You don't think I had anything to do with it? With either of them? Not me. We might get a bit heavy with those who think repayment is optional but murder, not our scene. Not our scene at all.'

Harvey knew that to ask the man where he was the weekend of the murder would be useless, that someone lower down the food chain would be ordered to take on the heavy work, but he did so, if only to further discombobulate the money lender whose blustering attitude was beginning to annoy him.

'I know where I was the weekend of the 16th. Me and the missus were in Cheltenham, my goddaughter's wedding. Went on the Friday night for a knees-up with the groom, nice chap, though he doesn't know what he's let himself in for with Sharon, then the wedding on the Saturday and a second night in the Ambassador. Home late on Sunday after we'd sobered up.'

Harvey knew it would be a waste of valuable time to check his story. Thanking the man for his time, he said they might need to be in touch again.

'Well, Serena, what do you think?'

'A slimy character. I remember my Sunday school days and hearing the story of Jesus in the Temple overturning the tables of the moneylenders. He told them they had turned the house of prayer into a den of thieves. Nothing new two thousand years later. He was too keen to tell us what a legitimate business he runs, then he kept opening his mouth only to change feet as he explained the rules of the *add-ons* as he so euphemistically called the outrageous interest rates.'

'Almost certainly not our killer, but we need to find out why Nora and Gerald wanted money. Most of our law-abiding citizens would rather commit hara-kiri than use the dubious services of Barry London. So, what did Nora Ederson and Gerald Winters intend to do with the loans? New car? Cruise? Credit card bills? Or something far more sinister?'

Chapter 28

Serena had volunteered to contact the Pages and asked when Harvey wanted to see them.

'I thought we'd interview them separately. Sylvia Page bothered me last time, the way she kept looking at her husband for reassurance.'

'Yes, she glanced his way and paused before she said *anything,* making every sentence seem like an oral test, one she needed to pass, and then when she finished speaking, she always looked at him. It was as though she was making sure her words were the ones they'd practised. Was she afraid of getting it wrong?'

Clare Jennings intervened. 'Maybe not. My mother hasn't had a single original thought or voiced her own opinion for thirty years. She's like a spokesperson for Dad. What he believes is good enough for her and he might as well be the author of her scripts. The Pages might be like that: extremely old fashioned, the man of the house rules. That won't happen when I get married!'

Ignoring his DS's ramblings, Harvey asked Serena to invite Richard Page in at 8 a.m. 'Let's make it a really early start, upset his morning routine. Then we can see Sylvia Page an hour later. That should give them an uncomfortable evening.'

'It also gives them time to work out what they are willing to say. I hope Sylvia's good at remembering her lines.'

Interview with Mr Richard Page
Present: Richard Page, DCI Tarquin and DI Peil

DCI: Thank you for coming in this morning, Mr Page.

R.P.: I don't somehow think I had much choice.

DCI: As you know we are still investigating the murder of your son-in-law. When we last spoke, it was obvious that there were aspects of his marriage to your daughter that you didn't like.

R.P.: Didn't like? Didn't like? What kind of mealy-mouthed phrase is that? I loathed the man. He made my daughter's life hell. He was single-handedly responsible for changing her from a sweet-natured, outgoing, sociable girl to a woman who requires psychiatric help. Because of him, she lost her friends and almost her family. That man tried to stop Susan seeing us. So, no, I didn't *like him*. However, I am not responsible for his death, even though I'm glad he's gone as Susan will be much better off without him.

DCI: Mr Page, can you tell us the last time you saw Gerald.

R.P.: The Friday night of the weekend he died. We'd gone to see our daughter and grandchildren. We always went when he wasn't there. Unfortunately, he came home early and made it obvious he wasn't pleased to see us. The feeling was mutual. We had a blazing row which lasted ages, upsetting Susan.

After about forty-five minutes he drove off again, in a dreadful mood. We stayed to calm Susan down, then went home. Sylvia didn't want to leave her, but I thought it would only exacerbate the situation if we were still there when Gerald returned.

DCI: Can you tell us what the argument was about.

R.P.: The usual: his lack of care and concern for our daughter. She was going downhill again, faster than an Olympic skier, and we were genuinely worried that she might do something silly. She once said that she thought the only way to escape was to slit her wrists, though we know she loves the children too much to do that and would never have left them with *him*.

DCI: So, you didn't see Gerald again that evening, or over the weekend. The exact time when he died is uncertain, but it was sometime between the Friday night and the early hours of Sunday morning.

R.P.: No, just after 6 p.m. was our final sight of that abhorrent man.

DCI: Did you know about Gerald's accident?

R.P.: You mean the broken arm? Yes, we knew he'd been to the hospital and then went privately to have a small operation. Susan was upset; she can't deal with any change to her routine. I must add that we've been quite amazed at how well she's coped with everything recently once he, I can hardly bring myself to say his name, started to spend time working away. We thought that might worry her, but maybe it was a relief. Time without him; just her and the children. Unfortunately, his phone calls continued at least twice a day and sometimes more. He liked to know what his wife was doing. The words control freak were invented for dear Gerald.

DCI: Did you also know he'd been prescribed some drugs? One type for pain relief and the other to help him sleep.

R.P.: No, I can't say we knew that. Susan might have told Sylvia, but I wasn't informed.

DCI: I don't know if you are aware of this, but Gerald went to a money lending company in Manchester last November and borrowed ten thousand pounds.

R.P.: Yes, of course we know *now*. The man was a fool. We'd have lent him the money had he asked. We weren't aware he needed money. We only found out last week when we were going through his desk, looking for his Will. There was a threatening letter from *You Need Cash* informing him the bailiffs would be engaged. Apparently, he'd had his final warning. The bastard, pardon my language, hadn't been keeping up with the repayments. He'd borrowed ten thousand pounds, a ridiculous amount to borrow from those sharks.

DCI: So, sorry to labour the point, but you had no inkling he needed money?

R.P.: No, absolutely none. If you'd asked me before, I'd have said that the one thing that family didn't need to worry about was money. The man was on a good wage and my daughter is careful with money, good at budgeting. They didn't waste a penny. No meals out, expensive wine or foreign holidays. I'd describe it as a frugal existence.

DCI: Five children must prove expensive.

R.P.: Indeed, but Sylvia and I were the only ones who spoilt them with expensive clothes and toys. My wife is the archetypal grandma, can't pass a children's shop without popping in to buy something.

DCI: Mr Page, is there anything else you can tell us that you think might be useful. I know you had no time for the man, but I imagine you want to find his killer.

R.P.: Well, my dear inspector, you think wrong!

'No love lost between Richard Page and his son-in-law. Any thoughts Serena?'

'A lot of anger. That was obvious last time, but even more pronounced today. He blames Gerald for all his daughter's problems. As we know she is a most unusual character with obvious psychiatric difficulties which the parents claim happened after she got married. It sounds like an unsuitable union, but there are lots of those that don't result in mental breakdowns.'

'Or lead to murder. He admitted to a humdinger of an argument, perhaps only hours before Mr Winters died. He knew about the injury to Gerald's arm, and if his wife was aware of the dangerous combination of pills it's likely she told him, though he claims no knowledge of those. He claims not to have known about the money Gerald borrowed, but that was the one time he looked unsure of his response.'

Serena asked the vital question. 'Did he hate Gerald enough to kill him?'

Interview with Mrs Sylvia Page
Present DCI Tarquin and DI Peil

DCI: Sorry you've had a bit of a wait. I hope you managed some refreshment.

S.P.: No, I didn't. This is the last place I want to be, and I have no idea why you want to speak to my husband and me again. We told you everything we could last time. I should be with Susan and the children They are all extremely upset, and my daughter hasn't fully accepted her husband's death.

DCI: Could you explain what you mean by that.

S.P.: You must have noticed Susan doesn't enjoy the best of health. Her problems started as soon as she married Gerald. As I told you last time, she was a happy, well-adjusted girl until he came on the scene. It has not been a good marriage. She now finds it hard to differentiate between fact and fiction and there are times she is certain that Gerald is still alive. She told me he had been home last night.

DCI: Mr Page told us about the argument last Friday night and I'd like to hear your version of what happened.

S.P.: We had gone to see the family, to spend time with them at their house. We only did that when he wasn't there. Unfortunately, he came back a lot earlier than expected and was not pleased to see us. When he asked us to leave, Richard went berserk, shouting and yelling that we must be allowed to see our daughter and grandchildren. Gerald informed us that it was his house, and we should, "Get the hell out and don't come back".

DCI: So, you left.

S.P.: Not immediately which just prolonged the fracas. I thought it might become physical so said we should leave, at which Gerald shouted, "At least your moronic wife has some sense." With that he stormed out. Poor Susan was becoming distraught, so we felt we had to go before he returned. We asked if she wanted to come with us, but she said she should stay.

DCI: Mrs Page, I have to ask you if that was the last time you saw your son-in-law?

S.P.: Yes. A horrible way to remember him. Sadly though, the damage he's done lives on.

DCI: Now, on a slightly different tack, Gerald had an accident recently which required a short stay in hospital. What can you tell us about that?

S.P.: Yes, he needed a small operation after breaking his arm, I think it was his arm.

DCI: What happened afterwards? Was he on any pills?

S.P.: Painkillers, I think.

DCI: Anything else you are aware of.

S.P.: No. Is it relevant?

DCI: Maybe. Leaving that aside, it has come to our attention that Gerald went to a money-lender last year. Were you aware of that?

S.P.: That's not a surprise. He came to see us - in October I think it was. He'd been gambling and it had got out of hand. He told us he owed nearly twenty thousand to several bookmakers, including the one on Albert Street in town, and they were demanding payment. He said he could manage half if we could give him the rest. You'd have thought we'd be the last people he'd ask for money. Richard refused to help him. We asked if Susan knew about his "problem" and he told us she had no idea, that he'd been going to the bookies during his lunch hour. I expect it will have to be paid back at some point. Another worry for her. He returned in early March, saying the moneylender was now after him for the final payment. He'd gone to one of *them*! We didn't think even he would be so stupid. Of course, we didn't want to have anything to do with such a lowlife activity. However, Richard was right not to lend him anything: you give money once and you're asked for more. Again, and again.

DCI: Mrs Page, are you sure you didn't see Gerald after the row on the Friday evening?

S.P.: We went home, extremely upset. On the Saturday we phoned Susan to make sure she was alright. She said she was and the next we knew was when she called us on Monday morning to say she'd rung 999 and that the police and an ambulance were there, and she needed us to take the children.

Not waiting, Harvey launched straight in, the coffee and cakes Serena had brought into the office left untouched.

'I'd say she'd learnt her script: every answer word perfect. The answers sounded practised. I'd bet a million dollars, or ten thousand pounds, with *add-ons*, that Richard told her what to say. No hesitation, no prevarication, just immediate and very straightforward replies to the questions she must have been expecting. The only discrepancy between their accounts was over the money. Did Richard not think we'd know about Barry London and his involvement with Gerald. According to Mrs Page, they were asked for money in October and again at the beginning of March when the heavies started to visit their son-in-law. Gerald must have been desperate to go to them again and admit how foolish he'd been using the services of a money lender. Mrs Page's version is far more credible. However bad the relationship with his in-laws, the people he'd initially ask for financial help would be them. And in-all-likelihood more than once.'

Serena intervened. 'It must have felt like the final straw when the man they loathed, the man they blamed for their beloved daughter's problems came cap in hand to beg for money... and a rather large amount. Their social circle definitely doesn't include people who need the assistance of outfits like *You Need Cash*.'

Having listened to her colleagues, Clare said she'd found observing Sylvia Page's interview amusing. 'Talk about a turnaround. One hundred and eighty degrees if my GCSE maths is remembered correctly. Last week he was the dominant, confident player and today it was her turn to win the Speaker of the Week prize, even if she did give us too much information for her husband's liking when she admitted they knew about Gerald's gambling debts.'

'The question is: do we believe her whole story?'

After a moment spent pondering, Serena looked at her boss. 'Do you mean, did she see Gerald again that Friday night? Did she know about the fatal combination of the drugs in the house? Was she the one who hated him enough to kill him?'

'Or was it a joint enterprise?'

Chapter 29

The Pages were sitting in their open-plan kitchen-diner that overlooked the back garden. It was the entire width of the house and had been added, at great expense, eighteen months ago. At the time, Richard had balked at the cost and still made comments about the *self-indulgent extras* that had taken the venture way over budget. Why they needed top of the range units from Germany and Italian marble surfaces had never been explained to his satisfaction. 'It's a kitchen, for God's sake, and you're not exactly a contestant on *MasterChef*. Tinned spicy parsnip soup and a bought lasagne hardly qualifies as cordon bleu.'

Looking irritated, he continued as though he was addressing a child with learning difficulties. 'Why, did you have to tell them that we knew about Gerald's money problem? I can't believe you embellished the story, telling them that we also knew about the loan he'd taken with one of those sharks. Don't you see, you stupid woman, it makes us look guilty. At the very least they'll be salivating over the discrepancies in our stories. This morning, I thought we had all answers ready; we'd been over every possible question. Spent all night on them.'

Almost in tears, Sylvia said, 'But we didn't think they'd know about the money, let alone ask us about it. When they brought it up, I thought honesty was the best policy. You were the one who lied. And lying to the police is bound to make them suspicious. If I'd known what you were going to say I'd have said the same.'

'So, it's my fault. What it means, Sylvia, is that they'll want to see us again, if only to ask why we gave different versions of the debt our recently departed son-in-law accrued and our participation in the sorry story. It also gives us another motive to kill him.'

It was only the middle of the morning, but the day was beginning to feel endless. Where to now? The reason Gerald Winters needed a moneylender had been solved, but Richard Page had been reluctant to admit that until this week he had known about the desperate need for twenty thousand pounds. Sylvia's version of events had rung true, giving them another reason to loathe Gerald. It spoke volumes that they had refused to help him.

Nora Ederson had also sought the assistance of the appallingly named *You Need Cash*. She had borrowed a much smaller amount and had paid it back within the agreed time.

Ordering DS Jennings to come into his office, he told her to contact both of Mrs Ederson's sons and see if they knew about the loan. 'Maybe we'll get some semblance of the truth from them. Everyone else seems to be telling porkies.'

Speaking aloud, no one left to hear him he yelled: 'The nanny.' The pleasant girl who had looked so uncomfortable first time around, her brain the custodian of things she could not/ would not/ must not/ dare not say? Yes, Harriet Devizes. And this time she'd be here until she told them everything.

Two hours later, Clare Jennings walked in to update her boss. 'As you asked, I got in touch with both of Nora's sons. To say they were surprised their mother needed money would be an understatement. Nigel said that when their parents got divorced, their dad was very generous, paid off the mortgage and made sure the boys always had enough ready cash.

'Ralph Ederson has come home for the funeral and is staying with his brother. He told me that his mother was always careful with money. She didn't earn much but managed by sticking to a careful budget. Her only extravagance appears to have been an annual holiday, but even then, she took it at a time of the year when they were less expensive. He was adamant that either of them would have loaned her the money had she asked. He finished by saying, 'The person to ask is Imelda, Miss Simpson. I think Mum told her everything. Far more than she said to us. Maybe she was embarrassed by needing money' (I never said how much) 'but I'm shocked she went to a moneylender.'

Edward Stones walked into the evening briefing looking like an extra from *Sixth Sense*, his face so pale it appeared to have been coated in white paint.

'Sorry I didn't come in earlier. Hope you got the message about my migraine. They don't happen very often, the last was about four years ago, but when they do, I'm floored, absolutely washed out. The only thing to do is retire to the infamous dark room and ride it out. I managed to get up late this morning and stagger around the flat, then a few hours vertical having helped I thought I ought to get back in.'

'Not sure that's a good idea, you still look washed out, like a shirt that spent too long in the machine: bleach added. Stay if you want to hear the updates, but then it's an early night.' Serena knew her boss was irritated by her mother hen act. If someone had come to work, then they would be expected to be on top form. No place for second rate in a murder enquiry.

'Thanks DI Peil, I'm fine to be here.'

Updating the team on the day's events, most notably the interviews with Mr and Mrs Page and the explanation of Gerald Winters need for money and the involvement of *You Need Cash*, Harvey said that the nanny, Harriet Devizes was coming for a second interview in the morning.

'I set that up, and I'll observe through the window, but Edward (the use of the first name a surprise) I'd like you to be in on that one. Let Clare lead, but have some supplementary questions ready. Most people find it far more difficult to cope when two people are involved with the questions; tend to get fidgety, not knowing where the next one is coming from. A bit like the old Westerns where the cowboy is surrounded, and unsure which Indian is going to shoot next.' Serena and Clare exchanged glances wondering where such an esoteric remark had originated. Very un-Harvey like.

'Tomorrow, as they say, is another day (more surreptitious looks) and one where surely there will be more progress.' How he hoped that would prove more than a possibility.

Chapter 30

Tomorrow was indeed another day: a rather unexpected one. DCI Tarquin had absented himself from the investigation, only Serena knowing the reason after an early morning call. Manchester and Salford Magistrates' Court felt like a busman's holiday and would not have been his choice of venue.

The building was in Spinningfields in the city centre and knowing how hard, and indeed how expensive, it was to park nearby, he had arrived by train at Piccadilly Station and caught one of the free buses that took him right to the courthouse door. The impressive building, with its huge glass windows and sandstone brickwork looked ready for business. Harvey knew the vast array of court rooms would be busy from 10 a.m. until close of play.

He had been to Crown Court in the city, but this was his first time at the lower court. A gigantic sign proclaiming that it was the *Magistrates' Court and Coroner's Court* told him he was in the right place. Having arrived early, he went to the public café in the John Rylands Library next door.

Late last night, he had received a phone call from Jeremy, his youngest brother.

'Hi bro, I need your help.' No preamble, no catch up, just straight to the point. 'I'm at the police station in Flixton and I'm in a bit of bother.'

From long experience, Harvey knew that meant his brother had done something stupid. Keeping as calm as possible, he asked the obvious question.

'They've breathalysed me, and I need you to come and get me out of this.'

'Jeremy, take a deep breath and start at the beginning.'

'I was out with some mates this afternoon and had a few drinks. I was fine to drive, but apparently, I drove across a zebra crossing when someone was on it. I just didn't see the old biddy and I didn't hit her. Bet she set off too early, not giving me time to stop. Her daughter was with her and took my car's number and phoned the police. Bad news: there was a CCTV camera nearby and it caught me as well.'

'So, Jeremy, bang to rights! How much over the limit were you?'

A long silence told him it wasn't good news. 'As I said, over the limit: a reading of 126 mg.'

Harvey knew that was in the top bracket, 120 mg the starting point, and his blood and urine samples would also be unforgivably high. Jeremy was in trouble.

'And you thought you could drive a car? It's a lethal weapon, for God's sake. Thank goodness you didn't hit the lady...or her daughter.'

'Can you help, Harvey? Come and talk officer to officer.'

Since their mother had died when both were still teenagers, Harvey had assumed a parental role. Over twenty years on he was still expected to stop everything and give whatever assistance was needed. Sometimes it was money or a place to stay. Being asked to bail him out of serious trouble was a first.

'Have you asked for a solicitor? There's always one on duty and they will come and talk to you; give you advice.'

'Why can't you come? If you say you're a Detective Chief Inspector that's got to carry some kudos. They're threatening to keep me here overnight and it's horrible.'

Overcoming the desire to yell at him to grow up, that he'd brought this on himself, Harvey took several deep breaths. 'I'm not sure what I could say. Your reading is so high it carries a disqualification, a large fine and in all probability, as you almost knocked someone down, a jail sentence. The fact your brother is a policeman won't have them bowing down and saying sorry they made a mistake. My presence will not encourage them to say you can leave.'

'Well, what can you do? There must be something. They say I'm due before the magistrates tomorrow.'

'I'll see you there.' Putting down the phone, Harvey realised it was the first time he had refused to dig Jeremy out of whatever hole he'd dug. About three years ago, Jeremy had started to drink too much, and Harvey had organised counselling sessions, warning him that the next step would be Alcoholics Anonymous or a liver transplant. The last time he had seen his brother he had been assured he was staying sober. Obviously there had been a relapse. Of the three brothers, Jeremy had taken their mother's sudden and totally unexpected death the hardest. But he was an adult now and needed to stop using the same excuse. Harvey sat and talked to Chopin, a good listener. 'Was I too soft on him at the time? Dad was no help and Sam seemed to cope so I assumed Jeremy would come through the loss.

'Well, Chopin, I wonder what happened to Liz? They were together the last time we spoke, but no mention of her this evening. No doubt she's gone the way of the others, got fed up with his immaturity.'

He had tried to warn his brother of tomorrow's possible consequences, though doubted that Jeremy had understood.

His copy of the Magistrates' Guidelines was well-thumbed, the hard copy preferable to finding it on the internet. He liked to be able to warn miscreants of the likely outcome of an appearance before the Bench, often adding that the case being forwarded to Crown Court meant the likelihood of far more stringent punishments.

120-150+ mg was indeed in the top range. At 126 mg his brother was comfortably within that worrying section. The starting point was twelve weeks custody, and the punishment ran from a high-level community order (how Jeremy would benefit from that, hours of unpaid, unglamorous work might make him think about his actions) to twenty-six weeks in custody. Reading on, Harvey saw that under the heading *Higher Culpability* one thing was *Evidence of Unacceptable Driving*. Almost knocking an old lady down on a zebra crossing would almost certainly qualify.

The final section on *Factors indicating a greater degree of harm* sited *being involved in an accident*. There but for fortune...

Courtroom Number Five was busy, the previous case still being heard. One of the trio of magistrates, William Thomas, was well known to Harvey, a regular at both Lancaster and Preston courthouses. Today he was the chairman and was flanked by two female wingers.

Finding it strange to be in court but not directly involved, Harvey wondered how his brother was feeling. He knew he'd been kept in the cells overnight, perhaps a foretaste of things to come.

'The next case on your list Your Worships is a drink driving matter: Mr Jeremy Tarquin.'

When his brother was led into court, Harvey's heart sank. Jeremy looked awful. He was wearing yesterday's crumpled clothes and hadn't accepted the offer of a shave. Bloodshot eyes and a jaded expression shouted that the hangover was still winning.

Giving his name, date of birth, address and ethnicity seemed like a monumental effort. As the charge was read out, he whispered 'Not Guilty' without waiting for the legal adviser to finish.

William Thomas wrote something on his sheet of paper and passed it to his colleagues who nodded in agreement.

'Please stand Mr Tarquin. As you have pleaded not guilty, we must set a date for your trial. We considered sending this case to Crown Court: you were appallingly over the limit and unfit to drive. Fortunately, an accident was avoided, but only narrowly. We have decided that this case will be heard before a Bench of Magistrates, with the codicil that should the Bench consider their sentencing powers to be insufficient, the case will be sent up to Crown Court for sentencing. In the meantime, you will be released on bail until your case is heard on May 4th at 10a.m. Please be here half an hour before and I advise you to keep in touch with your solicitor. As from this moment, you are disqualified from driving.'

Waiting outside for Jeremy to appear, Harvey doubted that his brother had taken in a single word. He had stood throughout the hearing looking totally bemused. Hopefully, his own case would be solved long before then and he would be able to lend moral support to the brother he could, at that moment, happily disown.

Chapter 31

A cold north-easterly wind had everyone retrieving their winter clothes. Parents were accompanying children to school, all dressed in hats, scarves, and gloves. Harvey remembered as a child having his mittens dangling from the end of his sleeves, the pair joined behind his neck by a long piece of plaited triple thickness wool. He wondered if these days that was far too old fashioned an idea but wished he had thought to bring some more modern ones today, his hands going blue with the cold. Surely, the weather forecaster had been exaggerating when he had mentioned late snow. It had been a mild winter, so maybe the weather gods were reminding everyone of their power.

His first job was to contact Imelda Simpson, the one person who might know why her friend had wanted to borrow money. The phone was answered on the second ring.

Explaining why he was calling he was met with a long silence. 'Oh dear! Oh dear! I thought that was all in the past. It was hush money. I suppose you'd call it blackmail. A young girl had come into the Home in advanced labour, though she was only twenty-five weeks pregnant, far too early. The girl was only fifteen and had no one with her. She said her parents didn't know she was pregnant. Her story was that she'd been raped by her uncle, and she hadn't told anyone. In those circumstances Nora should have informed the matron who would have called her parents and probably social services.

'Having a baby that young, has its problems and the poor girl hadn't had any ante-natal care. The baby died and the girl haemorrhaged and only just made it. When her parents found out they were apoplectic. They were adamant they should have been notified as soon as Miranda arrived in the labour ward. A payment was demanded to stop them going to the papers. Nora would have been in trouble if it became public knowledge that she had allowed a minor to go through labour with no appropriate adult present. I must admit that at the time I thought that it was the parents who were afraid of the adverse publicity. Rape, and a child of fifteen pregnant, wouldn't go down well at the golf club!

'I told Nora to go to the police. Yes, she had made a mistake, a terrible error of judgement not telling them, or at least informing her line manager (the modern idiom sounded strange coming from the elderly lady). I offered to lend her the money, but she said she could manage it. Obviously not. Poor Nora using one of those awful moneylenders. She told me later she'd cashed in a small Bond and that she should have done that in the first place. We don't always think straight when under pressure.'

Thanking the former matron for the information, he added, 'Mrs Ederson phoned them again this year but didn't follow up the initial phone call. Are you aware of her need for more money?'

'Oh yes. That's a much easier one to talk about. Her car failed its MOT, and it was going to cost a lot to repair it. I advised her to get rid of it. Once things start to go wrong, cars need so much spending on them. A car I once owned drank money instead of petrol after every MOT. Nora did as I suggested and got one of those hire arrangements with the local VW garage.'

'Once again, thank you, Miss Simpson, this is all most helpful. To return to the family who extorted money, do you know Miranda's full name?'

'An easy one, Inspector Tarquin: Miranda McWhinney. She and her family live on the Fell View estate at the edge of town. People who can afford to live there don't need hush money. I got the feeling she was being vindictive, wanting to hurt Nora.'

Thanking Nora's friend yet again (Serena would be proud of him) for her time and the helpful information, Harvey ended the call. So, our well-respected midwife had her secrets. The victim of blackmail, guilty of a professional misdemeanour. How many other skeletons were rattling in her cupboard? And were any of them the reason she was dead?

Without wasting any time, he looked for the McWhinneys' address. Fortunately, they were the only ones of that name in the book: 34 Beech Avenue. Imelda's statement that they were well off had surprised him; he had originally been expecting an address on the Orchard estate where teenage pregnancy was almost a rite of passage, the next generation of single mothers and absentee fathers a perennial production line of poverty, lack of ambition, failure - and all too often a life of crime.

Approaching the house, he felt the familiar goosebumps that made his skin tingle when there might be a breakthrough in a case. Had the parents visited Mrs Ederson that fateful weekend with further demands, the meeting resulting in a physical altercation?

The McWhinneys lived two roads away from the Pages. Surely a coincidence. He wondered if they moved in the same social circles.

Throwing the door open, the lady Harvey assumed to be Mrs McWhinney informed him that the notice about cold callers was in place for a reason.

After introducing himself, he asked for a few moments of her time. Some people are good at hiding their feelings, but Mrs McWhinney was not one of them. Guilty as charged before another word had been uttered.

'I know why you've come. I think I've been waiting for this moment since it happened. Can I assure you neither my husband nor I normally behave like that, and I am...'

Loud sobs now obliterated the words. 'Sorry, but Cal and I were going to return the money. Then we saw the notice in the paper about Mrs Ederson and it was too late.'

'You demanded one thousand pounds. Can I ask the reason for the extortion?'

'When we found out Miranda had had a baby, though the poor little thing didn't make it, Miranda going into labour too early, we were shocked. She'd hidden it well, and we assumed her moodiness was just a typical teenage thing. Sorry can't think of better words. Then when she told us her uncle Saul had raped her our world fell apart. Mrs Ederson told us we should report the rape, but that would have meant a court case and a lot of publicity. It soon became obvious that the midwife herself was in trouble: she hadn't told us our under-age daughter was in labour or got in touch when it all went wrong. So, for everyone's sake it was better to keep it all quiet.'

Another pause, the handkerchief in use again. 'I'm sorry we told her we'd report her to the NHS Complaints Department unless she paid for her mistake another way. She gave us the money and that was the end of it. Miranda returned to school with no one the wiser.'

'Your daughter was raped and impregnated, and you did nothing about that.'

'We have dealt with that in our own way. Nothing illegal, but his marriage is over, his kids want nothing to do with him and he lost his job as a teacher. So, he's had his comeuppance.'

'Mrs McWhinney, you said that you've had no contact with Mrs Ederson since you blackmailed her. Can you tell me where you and your husband were around about March 12th?'

'Was that the date Mrs Ederson died? Oh no! Really? You can't be treating us as suspects. Did she not die of natural causes? How awful. I've admitted to the demand for money but since then we haven't seen or heard from her. Yes, we're blackmailers but I can assure you we had nothing more to do with her. That weekend we had gone to my parents' house. It was their wedding anniversary; not a big one, but we always celebrate with them, go for a meal and stay for a few days.'

As he left, he thought he had probably been told the truth and her alibi was easy to check. Goosebumps returned to cold storage. Parents fearful for their reputation, and that of their teenage daughter, indulging in unfortunate and indeed criminal behaviour. But from extortion to murder felt like a pole-vaulting leap: a whole different ball game, a phrase one of his brothers employed. Thinking of Sam, he realised how long it was since he'd seen him. I wonder if he knows about Jeremy.

Making a mental note to ring him that evening he returned to the station.

Busy recording the morning's events, he was surprised to see Clare at the door. 'Sir, Miss Devizes, the absentee nanny, hasn't turned up. She's totally absent! When I rang her yesterday, she was extremely reluctant to come. I suggested 10 a.m. and she said she had a dental appointment, so I tried midday, or any time in the afternoon, and her excuse for not attending those sessions was that she was taking her parents to visit her maternal grandparents in Macclesfield. In the end I told her it was a murder enquiry, and I would expect to see her at 11.30, allowing her time to get here after her *visit to the dentist*.'

'No doubt you've tried to contact her again.'

'Yes, sir, I've rung every fifteen minutes, but no response. Her phone goes to voice mail. I've left messages; no reply.'

'If she doesn't appear in the next hour, we'll contact her home address. Thanks Clare, I'm sure you and Edward have other things to be getting on with.'

'One thing, sir, she asked yesterday why we wanted to see her again. When I said we needed more information on the Winters she gasped. Very loudly. Eventually she murmured that as an employee she couldn't be expected to snitch – that was her word – on them.'

'Sounds as though we really do need to have a chat with Miss Devizes. Let me know when she shows up. This is one interview I want to observe.'

PC Stones was still feeling the remnants of his migraine. The knowledge that it was a common phenomenon, known as the postdrome phase, was of little comfort.

He seemed to be viewing the world through a fog, making logical thought on the impossible side of hard. Utter exhaustion ruled the day. Experience from past episodes told him he had two choices: stay in bed or try to do something to take his mind off it.

Surely the phone call he'd been asked to make was possible. 'Good afternoon, Mrs Devizes, PC Stones at Fordway Police Station here. We were expecting your daughter, Harriet, to come in for a chat (no need to worry them) this morning, but she hasn't arrived.'

The only reply, jagged crying.

'Are you OK, Mrs Devizes?'

Moments of silence were interrupted by a man's voice. 'This is Ted Devizes. Who did you say you were?'

Edward repeated the words he had spoken to the mother.

'My wife and I have just been informed that our daughter, our wonderful Harriet, is dead. The hospital has just rung to tell us and we're leaving to come down to Preston. She's in the Royal Preston. They said they'd tell us more when we got there. She was dead on arrival, but we don't know any more at the moment. A cab driver has just arrived, so we must go. I'm not fit to drive, it's all too much.'

Phone still in hand, the dialling tone hurting his ears, the young constable stood unable to move. The nanny was dead. She's dead. Harriet Devizes is in hospital, dead. Dead. The words on repeat, slight variations on a sombre theme.

Clare found him minutes later slumped on a chair, receiver still held in a vice-like grip.

'Are you OK, Edward?'

'She's dead. Harriet Devizes is dead.' He wondered if he would ever think or say anything else ever again.

It took several seconds for his words to be fully understood. 'Harriet's dead? How do you know?'

Explaining that he had phoned her parents, he managed to convey the conversation. 'Oh, God, I think I sounded belligerent when I said we were expecting her, and she hadn't shown up. Callous in the circumstances.'

As the senior officer, Clare had to take control, telling Edward that he couldn't possibly have known the reason for her no-show. 'Mr and Mrs Devizes will have been too shocked to register your tone of voice. We need to inform the DCI then you and I must go to Preston.'

As they approached the hospital, traffic was at a stand-still. Two cars had collided, one now beyond repair. The journey felt interminable, made even longer as neither officer was in the mood to talk. Arriving, the plethora of car parks was bamboozling, and the illuminated signs indicated there were few spaces available in any of them. Twenty minutes later they stood at the main entrance, neither relishing their need to be there.

Reception was near the door. Explaining who they were, the woman booking people in asked them to take a seat and she'd get someone to come to talk to them.

'Are Miss Devizes' parents here?'

Looking at the computer screen, she said they had been informed that their daughter had been admitted but the couple had not yet arrived.

Ten minutes later a harassed looking doctor stood in front of them. 'I believe you're here in relation to Harriet Devizes. Very unfortunately she was dead on arrival but more than that I cannot say. We're expecting her parents to arrive very soon. Sorry I can't be more helpful.'

'What the hell do we say when they get here?' Edward sounded fraught. 'We need to ask to speak to them later. We can't intrude here but do need to find out if they knew where Harriet was before 11.30.'

Forty-five minutes later, two people rushed in, looking distraught. 'We're Harriet Devizes's parents. We were told she'd been brought here, that she'd been taken ill (the truth too unpalpable). Can you tell us where she is? We need to speak to someone who knows what's happened.'

Receptionists in a hospital are used to dealing with people in distress and the young woman behind the counter had done the training. 'Mr Oliphant will come to speak to you. Would you like to come to the relatives' room, and he'll meet you there?'

Waiting was something the police accepted as part of the job, but Clare and Edward found their time in reception endless. Finally, Shirley and Ted Devizes were back with a middle-aged man in scrubs. He was speaking to them gently. 'As I said the post-mortem will be tomorrow and we'll have a better idea of what happened. I'll be in touch as soon as I know.'

'We know what happened. We don't need a PM to tell us. But, but... she was normally so careful, that's what we don't understand. She knew what to do if it happened, she was so, so careful. Why? Why didn't she help herself? She's always been so good at that, ever since she was a small girl. Oh, God, how are we going to live without her?' Leading them to the exit, like a crossing lady helping children across a busy road, the doctor shook their hands and bade them a soft farewell. Edward thought he had never seen people look so despondent.

'Let's leave it. The doctor will establish time and hopefully cause of death and we can attend the PM. We'll contact them when they've had some time to understand what's happened.'

Clare looked at the young PC. 'That will take some time. I wonder what they were talking about. No doubt the wonderful Alfie Morrison will enlighten us tomorrow. If any pathologist can give us all the details, he can.'

Chapter 32

Harvey was woken by a very hungry Chopin patting his cheek. He was always the dominant moggy when he thought the time had arrived to alert his food source. He was forever of the opinion that breakfast was overdue, Grieg benefiting from his brother's lack of patience.

'And an exceptionally good morning to you.' When did I start to talk to them as if they could understand me? 'I'll be down in two minutes. I don't think you'll starve in that time.' The increasingly loud caterwauling emanating from the moggy indicated that Chopin didn't necessarily agree with that last statement.

A day in court was the last thing Harvey felt like, especially after his experience with Jeremy. Today's case was a particularly unsavoury and frustrating one. It was many months since he had been the officer in charge and sent the details to the Crown Prosecution Service. Belinda Northwich had appeared in the Magistrates' Courthouse before Christmas, charged with the murder of her husband. The DCI recalled the acute embarrassment he had felt when he saw the chairman of the Bench was Emma Carrodus, a woman he had treated as a suspect the previous year, following the death of her friend. She had been professional and not given Harvey a second glance, sending the case straight to Crown Court. He had been amused to realise that he was the only one feeling awkward.

Gravitas: the word that always sprang to mind when he entered a court room in Preston Crown Court, gowns and wigs adding to the solemnity of the occasion. He knew the judge that day was Lady Cecilia Hanover, a woman of great experience whose reputation for *taking* prisoners and locking them up for as long as possible went before her. Recalling the newspaper report accusing her of sentencing beyond the guidelines, (in some cases extensively so, life sentences meaning life, with the American-style penchant for no hope of parole explained to the miscreants in detail) had led to weeks of letters in *The Times*. Most copied the Facebook mantra of *liking* her attitude. Others believed in second chances and the hope that the possibility of parole, however far in the future, led to better behaviour in prison.

'Bloody do-gooders, they need to study what the evil bastards are capable of,' had been one comment he'd overheard in the station.

Courtroom Number Two was packed, the trial having attracted media attention: a wealthy husband who made Midas look destitute; a glamorous "trophy" second wife; the vacuum created by marrying the mistress filled; a jealous rage; a carving knife. Journalists were outnumbered by those who thought a day in court would be more exciting than the re-runs on BBC 2. All that was missing was the knitting.

Belinda Northwich was a stunner. A former model, she had retained the poise and looks that had made her one of the most sought-after models of her generation. Appearing from the underworld of the cells she made what could only be described as a show-stopping entrance. Her face was well known from the giant-sized hoardings and television adverts that had promoted the latest Armani fashion, and many people felt they knew her. The months leading up to today's starring role had not diminished her beauty.

Harvey sat trying not to stare. He knew her barrister had advised her that she would, in all probability, be found guilty, so a plea to that effect would lessen her sentence. The man had obviously not considered the possibility that the judge would be Lady Hanover.

A guilty plea would mean the judge hearing the details of the case, though everyone over the age of ten knew them all, the papers revelling in lurid headlines and libellous (the lawyers must have been busy) versions of the story. They delighted in disclosing the incriminating evidence on Boris Northwich's mobile phone, hotel receipts in his jacket pocket, ridiculous amounts of money transferred each month to the account of an "escort" and the wronged wife taking her revenge. All so prosaic. All selling extra copies.

The 999 Call made by Mrs Northwich at 02.39 on December 18th merely recorded that she had asked for the police to visit her house, no reason given. When interviewed, Mrs Northwich had remained silent. Not a word spoken. Harvey couldn't recall interviews where a suspect remained totally incommunicado. He was used to "no comment" being adopted ad nauseam, but selective mutism (the term suggested by the psychiatrist who had been asked to see her) was a new and altogether unsatisfactory phenomenon.

The police had found her husband's body, the knife still in situ, both the bed and Belinda covered in blood. Forensic evidence showed the knife had her fingerprints all over it and no one else was sought in connection with the murder.

'Mrs Northwich, you are charged with the murder of your husband, Boris Northwich, on the night of the 17th/18th December 2020. How do you plead?'

If a room can hold its breath, Courtroom Number Two did so. The question was repeated. Following a further period of silence, Belinda's lawyer stood and said that his client wanted to plead guilty.

Harvey had had enough. *I've got better things to do than sit watching her play acting. She's guilty as the proverbial hell and I'll find out what sentence she gets later.* As he left the court, he felt bad about haranguing his colleagues over their wasted trip to Preston yesterday afternoon. Today he was at least as culpable.

'Total waste of time. Her looks exceed her intellect. Let me know when we hear the verdict.' Harvey had stormed into his office, wondering how much worse the day could get. The nanny's interview might have been illuminating. He was sorry she was dead, a young life cut short, but he had been sure she had held the key to knowing about - and understanding - the Winters' strange lives.

PC Stones had recovered, amazing how the thought of a PM could raise the spirits. 'I don't mind going on my own this morning, sir. I know Clare and Serena aren't too keen on the cutting and sawing.' He was too tactful to mention his boss's loathing of the whole thing.

Smiling for the first time since talking to Chopin, the one-sided conversation that morning feeling like a distant dream, Harvey said that when DS Jennings had phoned him last night with an update, she had said that the parents had sounded adamant that they already knew the cause of their daughter's death.

'Yes, sir, it sounded like a long-term condition that she could and indeed had always controlled.'

'We'll see what the official verdict is. Come to see me as soon as you get back.'

Blue scrubs, overshoes and hairnet in place, Edward stepped inside the examination room, Alfie Morrison ready and waiting.

'Good morning to you, young man. You just can't stay away. If you get tired of being a policeman, I'm sure I could use you. Most of my team aren't quite so enthusiastic. I notice you're on your own, today's show has obviously not sold too many tickets.'

'No, just me. Too much excitement for my colleagues.'

As they approached the table holding Harriet Devizes's body both became serious, the time for light-heartedness at an end.

'And a good morning to you my lovely girl.' Alfie's Liverpudlian accent reverberated off the walls. 'You look too young to be receiving my dubious, and totally unwarranted, attention. Terribly sad when I have to deal with one robbed of so many years.'

'I don't know if it's relevant, but...'

'Sorry, don't mean to be rude, but let science say what is and isn't relevant.'

'Doctor Morrison, are you aware that she was the nanny to the Winters? We were expecting her to come to the station yesterday to hopefully tell us a lot more about that household and...'

'Once again, I'm sorry to interrupt, but who she was and how she might have been of interest to the police has no room in my world. My priority is to ascertain the cause of death. Shall we begin?'

Duly chastised, Edward took his place near the table.

'The body, (the time for personal remarks had passed) is that of a young woman. She looks well nourished. There are red patches on her cheeks and raised welts on lips, eyelids, hands and feet, all signs of anaphylaxis, or a severe reaction to nuts. I will now undress the body.'

Two hours later, the PM complete, Alfie addressed the young constable who had once again found the process utterly fascinating, remarking cheerfully on the secrets a post-mortem could reveal, then looking embarrassed by his unwarranted remark.

'Don't feel too guilty, once a post-mortem begins, one is dealing with a body. Science takes over. It's before and after one remembers she was a daughter, granddaughter, sister, friend, and only yesterday a living, breathing individual full of life and hope for the future.'

'DS Jennings and I were at the hospital yesterday and we overheard her parents say she had always managed her condition.'

'I expect she did. Until yesterday. Unfortunately, a nut allergy is a lifelong affliction. The main problem is that however much one safeguards against it, taking every precaution not to come-into-contact with nuts, the tiniest trace of say peanuts can cause a severe reaction, which if not treated immediately can result in anaphylaxis and, as we have witnessed, death. The immune system goes from zero to the speed of light in seconds. It's programmed to launch an attack anytime it senses the proteins in the nuts. This releases the chemicals which trigger symptoms like nausea, itchy raised welts, and facial swelling. We observed the redness and swellings before we began. What we couldn't see was the tightened airway. When that happens breathing becomes difficult, then impossible. Unfortunately, that can happen in a matter of seconds.'

'So, no hope of reversing the situation?'

'Yes, everybody with this allergy will carry an EpiPen which if administered quickly is the saviour. The question for you is why did she not use it? She was an intelligent girl and would have known to carry it at all times.'

'Could anyone else be involved in her death?'

'If someone knew about her allergy, then yes. Easy to put some nuts near her. The question then would be why didn't she use her EpiPen?'

Returning to the station, Edward went straight into Harvey's office. The DCI was chortling. 'Thank you, very much for letting me know, I was sure Judge Hanover wouldn't disappoint. Guilty as charged: a life sentence, minimum eighteen years.' Putting down the phone he beamed at the young PC. 'Sometimes this job feels worth every frustrating day and sleepless night. Now, any more good news?'

As succinctly as possible, Edward explained the results of the PM.

Harvey muttered, 'A nut allergy. Interesting. A woman who has lived with such an allergy all her life would have known what was happening and would have known what to do. I want you and Clare to go to visit Mr and Mrs Devizes. Not a good time for them, but we need to know as much as possible as soon as possible.' Harvey hated the abbreviation ASAP and chose the extended version. 'Ask about the allergy and how she coped with it, I know you overheard them yesterday, but we need a lot more detail. And, this is important, find out as much as you can about their daughter's experience at 14 Wordsworth Avenue. That house has secrets, and we want to know what they are.'

'The thing I keep thinking, sir, is that Harriet told us that her parents wanted her to leave.'

'Exactly and we need to know why.'

Chapter 33

Six months ago, had anyone told me I would commit two murders I wouldn't have believed them. How many are the police investigating? One, two or three? I don't count Nora Ederson. That was an accident.

I cannot feel anything but relief that Gerald Winters has been removed from this earth (removed my choice of word) anything else makes it sound overly serious or unduly important, which his ending (another one I find acceptable) is not. Nora was unfortunate, as I say an accident. Had she fallen in a different way she would still be alive.

Harriet Devizes was a necessary incident (occurrence, occasion, happening, event). She was about to divulge information best left hidden. Such a pleasant girl, so hard working and so lovely with all the family, but she could not be allowed to blab (gossip, tittle-tattle, sneak, snitch, tell tales) I think I like sneak. She knew everything and had until now been the soul of discretion (prudence, diplomacy, tact). Should the police duo, the rather dour DCI and his intense DI, be cognisant (have full knowledge, heaven forbid) of the situation, it would be disastrous. Yes, I have been using a Thesaurus. I'm not normally quite so erudite: another new word!

Mr and Mrs Devizes lived in a 1930's semi-detached on the outskirts of Kendal. Clare's satnav had taken them past the Mintsfeet Industrial Estate where the world-famous Romney's Kendal Mint Cake was produced. 'I tried that once, rather too strong for me, but must be good as it got Sir Edmund Hillary and Tensing Norgay to the top of Everest in 1953.'

'Could do with some now. Might help calm my nerves. Maybe we should have phoned ahead.' Edward knew he was sounding inexperienced.

The man who opened the door looked ashen, devoid of all colour. He stood leaning against the door frame. Apologising for intruding at such a sad time, Clare introduced herself and explained the need to speak to him and his wife.

If it was possible, Shirley Devizes looked even worse than her husband. She sat, slumped on the sofa, the gas fire turned to maximum making the small room feel like a sauna.

Good manners prevailed and coffee was offered and declined, the officers knowing they were not welcome.

'We are so sorry for your loss', the routine words uttered on such occasions a million miles from touching the tragedy the parents were experiencing. 'We'll try not to take too much of your time, but it would be helpful to know how much Harriet told you about her time with Susan and Gerald Winters. We know she'd been employed as their nanny. As you are no doubt aware, we are treating Mr Winter's death as suspicious. Your daughter had agreed to talk to us again yesterday (a tsunami of tears from the mother) and anything you can tell us would be helpful.'

Ted Devizes began talking, a monotone all he could manage. 'When Harriet said she had been asked to speak to the police for a second time we advised her to tell you all she knew. We were aware that there was something not quite right about the Winters' set-up, and at times it made our lovely Harriet feel awkward and indeed on one occasion extremely upset. Shirley suggested she leave, but Harriet was adamant that Susan Winters needed her.'

Mrs Devizes took over, the sentences interspersed with sobs. 'Harriet would never say what was wrong, though she did once describe it as a "strange situation that we'd find hard to believe". When I questioned her further, she clammed up and said she was sorry she'd said anything; that Susan Winters was a lovely woman, a kind employer who suffered from depression. Harriet was always so kind, wanting to help.'

'Did she mention Gerald Winters?'

'Only to say he was the reason everything was as it was. Once again, she didn't elaborate.'

'This is all most helpful, just a couple more questions. What were Harriet's duties? We know she looked after the baby, Adam, but was she also involved with the older children, the girls?'

'Just Adam. She adored him said he was the sweetest little thing. She didn't sleep at the house, had her own flat in Fordway, though when Mrs Winters was bad, she sometimes stayed over to look after him during the night. Not quite sure why his dad couldn't have done that occasionally. Susan looked after the girls: home schooled them. Harriet said they were very well behaved and clever. So, her only job was to care for the baby. Apparently, Mrs Winters suffered a bad bout of post-natal depression after he was born and that was when they employed Harriet.' The sentences had exhausted the woman who sank further back, the cushions the only things preventing her becoming horizontal.

'One more thing, then we'll leave you,' Clare knew not to add in peace, 'do you know what Harriet was planning to do yesterday morning before going to the police station?'

'She was meeting Faye Thornton, another nanny she'd got friendly with in Fordway. They used to meet in the park with their prams and they'd go to the café at the top of the hill for coffee or lunch. It's a nut-free establishment so suited our Harriet. She's had an allergy all her life and is always so careful.'

After stopping to mop up the tears running down her face, she continued 'Oh God! She *was* always, always so careful. She had her EpiPen with her at all times and we just can't understand why she didn't use it yesterday, or how in a café like that she came-into-contact with any nuts...oh dear God...'

Taking over from his wife, Ted said, 'She's probably the one to talk to, girls tell their friends more than they tell their parents.'

'Do you happen to know who Faye works for. We could do with seeing her.'

'I think their name is Newman. They're both lawyers in Fordway. I hope the girl can shed some light on what happened. Please let us know if you find out anything.'

'That was awful, the poor souls losing their daughter. They were distraught.' Clare knew Edward would need to toughen up, that conversations like that happened on a regular basis.

'We need to find the other nanny and hope the remark about girls confiding in their friends proves accurate. I know I still tell friends far more, and I do mean far more, than I ever discuss with Mum and Dad.'

As the pair were driving back from Kendal, Clare said she knew Toby and Jennifer Newman.

'They're both solicitors, working mostly in Fordway and Preston. With their family commitments they share the work. Toby Newman was in court the last time I was there, defending a young man up for GBH. No one was surprised that case was sent straight to Crown Court, a nasty attack on an innocent bystander. The couple live up on the Canterbury Estate, I remember them telling me about all the teething problems with the house when they first moved in. At least it's going to be easy to locate the nanny.'

Whilst their colleagues were driving up the motorway, Harvey and Serena were sitting in the Northern Allied Bank, waiting to speak to the manager. 'We should have come sooner. So far, we've got a very one-sided and probably skewed picture of the man. Gerald might not be as black as his in-laws have painted him.'

'Even black comes in shades these days,' was Serena's unacknowledged comment.

Shown into the room, both were surprised by the size of the desk. Was it to intimidate people seeking a mortgage or overdraft; make them feel small and insignificant? Recently polished, it appeared to dazzle the room and reflected the ornately decorated ceiling, the elaborate plaster swirls reminders of a bygone era, the building having been built by an extremely affluent Victorian as a family home. The room's dimensions suggested it might have been a dining room, ready to accommodate a banquet.

Elizabeth Gordon didn't bother to stand. Indicating two chairs she said she had an important meeting but could spare them a few minutes.

Harvey tried to hide his anger. 'Mrs Gordon, we are here to talk to you about one of the bank's employees: Gerald Winters. His death is being treated as suspicious and we are in the middle of a major police investigation, so your *important meeting* may have to be delayed.'

'I was sorry to hear he had died.' A pause, so long Harvey wondered if she was going to say anything else. 'Mr Winters was the manager in this branch before me. I was his deputy and was appointed in his place when he became Area Supervisor, involved in training new recruits and sorting any difficulties that arose in our branches across the North West. He deserved the promotion. Gerald was utterly professional and an excellent manager, dealing with staff and customers appropriately.'

Harvey thought that was an odd word to use and asked the woman sitting belligerently across the table to explain.

'As a boss there are times when one must take control, bring others into line, to act like a parent or teacher. To reprimand.' Serena thought how glad she was that she had never had the pleasure of being in Mrs Gordon's classroom. 'I must add that Mr Winters (why did she not call him Gerald?) also gave praise when he deemed it appropriate (that word again, the woman was devoid of emotion?) and indeed started our internal newsletter which included praise for any employee who had come to his notice for excellent customer service.'

'Thank you, Mrs Gordon, we won't take too much more of your valuable time, but can you tell us anything about Gerald as a person, maybe outside of work?'

'No. We were colleagues, not friends. I never saw him outside this building. Neither of us was interested in any of the social events some of the younger members of staff organised. I do know that the person he talked to the most was Molly Cornwell, one of our longest serving tellers. She might be able to furnish further details.'

Managing to thank the woman, they showed themselves out.

Attempting to curb the feeling of distaste the woman had engendered, he asked to speak to Mrs Cornwell.

'She's on the counter over there but I'll relieve her and ask her to meet you in the staff room. I'll let you through, everything is on a code here, but I think I can trust two police officers to go behind the scenes unattended. The door you need is third on the right.' The young man scurried off. At least someone was being helpful.

Ten minutes later Molly Cornwell walked into the room. She was not what either officer had been expecting: nearing retirement age, she looked every minute of her advanced years.

After brief introductions, Serena explained the reason for their visit, Gerald Winter's name making the woman flinch. 'Poor Gerald, such a dreadful thing to happen. We were all really upset, especially when we heard that the police were involved.'

'Mrs Cornwell, we believe that you knew Mr Winters better than most of the staff and we are hoping you'll be able to tell us something about him as a person.'

'I got on with Gerald really well. Really well. He was a lovely person, so kind when my husband died, made sure I was OK to come back to work and wouldn't allow me across the threshold too soon. Once back, I worked behind the scenes for several weeks, so I had no interaction with the customers. Some can be awkward, belligerent, and Gerald didn't want me to be upset. He was my boss, but I think he thought of me as a surrogate mother and would talk about a lot of personal things.'

'I'm sure you don't want to break any confidences, but anything you do feel able to tell us will help with our inquiry.'

'Is his death being treated as…suspicious is the word I think you use.'

'As I said, anything you can tell us might help.'

'Gerald was an excellent boss. He was punctilious, conscientious to a fault and expected others to be the same. He hated it when he had to reprimand someone: for bad time keeping, repeated absences, inappropriate language when speaking to a customer. I'm sure you get the picture. He was also ready to give praise where it was due and was most supportive of new appointees.

'He was also a caring family man and proud of his family. He loved his wife and four girls, but you should have seen him when Adam was born. That morning when Gerald came in, I'll swear he made a peacock look humble. He told everyone that it was a boy. Finally, he had a son. Don't get me wrong, as I said he loved his daughters and had photos of them on his desk. Susan wasn't well after Adam's birth, two weeks in hospital, then a bad bout of post-natal depression. At times, poor Gerald was at his wit's end. She'd found every pregnancy hard, ill all the time, but this was something else.'

'Can we ask if you knew about his money trouble last year.'

'Yes, indeed. He was annoyed with himself, said the gambling had started small, just the odd flutter to forget how hard life was with Susan. It got out of hand and he ended up owing a rather large amount. I offered to lend him some of it – I couldn't afford all of it, but he said he valued our friendship too much to take it any money from me.'

'Final question: did you notice any change in Gerald's behaviour over the past few weeks?'

'I suppose nothing I say can harm him now. I've never been one to tittle-tattle, some of the younger members of staff love nothing more than a good gossip, but I have always stayed well away from the false news and hurtful innuendos.

'There *was* a change in Gerald, but it was over a long period. When Susan was pregnant with Adam, she left the family home for a time and took the girls back to her parents. I found Gerald close to tears in his office one morning and he told me she'd left. His exact words were, "Her bloody parents have succeeded, they have been trying to get their precious daughter back for years and now they have."

'Mrs Winters had tough pregnancies. Morning sickness that lasted all day and throughout the pregnancy. That's not easy with older children who need looking after and indeed home tutoring them. She once told me that each labour got worse, that it became an experience to dread. Following each birth, she was advised not to have any more babies. I can't verify that last statement as that was something I overheard in the staffroom. Here I am passing on something that might be false.

'He told me there had been an horrendous scene when he went to his in-laws to persuade Susan to return home. I don't think there was much love lost between him and Susan's parents. He thought they hated him, and I think the feeling was reciprocated. Susan did go home, but things were bad until Adam was born and then all was fine for a time, at least for him. As I said he was overjoyed to have "a son and heir" such an old-fashioned idea, but Susan was so ill after the birth and never seems to have recovered. I dread to think what the poor man went home to each evening.

'Soon after Adam was born, they employed a nanny who eased the situation a little. Gerald always said she was wonderful with his son, which was what he really wanted: Adam cared for.'

Pausing, Mrs Cornwell asked if she was saying too much.

'Anything you say is in the strictest confidence and it is giving us a more rounded picture of the man.'

'The last thing I will say, and this is hard for me to divulge, is how surprised I was, when a few months ago he thought that a brother for Adam would be the solution to his wife's problems. "Another son would take her mind off her imaginary tribulations. Give her something else to think about and in a few years, he would be a playmate for Adam." I never did discover how that idea was received by his wife.'

Saturday morning but not a weekend, Friday merely fast-forwarding into another working day.

'Rick and I went to visit The Manor last night. We were supposed to go today but when I said I was working they fitted us in at 8 p.m. It's where the reception is being held, can't believe it's only a few months until I'll be Mrs Richard Cohen. I'm old-fashioned and want to take his name, though I suppose

I'll really be Mrs Clare Cohen. Not a great improvement on Jennings. We looked at menus, such an incredible variety, almost too many to choose from. It was hard as not only did they want us to decide on the sit-down meal in the afternoon, but also the buffet at the disco in the evening. I do hope you'll be able to come to the evening do; your invitation will be with you soon.'

Edward felt mean not asking more about the upcoming nuptials, but knew if he did, they'd have arrived at the Winters' before discussing the plan for the day.

'Is Susan Winters expecting us?'

'No. Don't want her to be forewarned and forearmed, much better to turn up unannounced; spring a surprise, see how she responds.'

Richard and Sylvia Page were sitting with their daughter in the kitchen, breakfast not quite over. The large pine table was littered with the morning's debris, dirty dishes and unwashed cups waiting to be moved to the dishwasher. Adam was fidgeting in his highchair, growing noisier by the second. His sisters were all sitting staring at him, looking amused by his antics.

'Thanks for staying, Mum, Dad, I don't know how I'm going to cope without Harriet.'

The exaggerated pealing of the doorbell, one that had sounded interesting in B and Q, stopped further conversation.

'Who the-devil is calling at this time of day? I'll take the girls upstairs, don't want them more disturbed than they have been. The last week has been hell for them.'

Upset by the sudden commotion, Adam began to cry, the wail overriding the doorbell's repeat performance.

Storming back downstairs, Richard yanked the door open. 'Oh, it's you. Can I say that this is not a good time! Not good at all. We are all devastated by poor Harriet's death. Coming so soon after Gerald it's doubly traumatic and our daughter needs time to mourn; to grieve for them both. The last thing Susan can cope with is another interrogation, another hundred questions she can't answer. Noises could be heard from upstairs, the girls obviously unhappy at being sent to their rooms. Squabbles and shouting filled the house, forcing their grandmother to say she must go up to calm them.

'The entire family has been affected by recent events (a strange choice of words) and I'd be most grateful if you could take that into consideration, before you come poking your noses in...yet again.'

Fifteen minutes later five adults had assembled in the lounge, the curtains opened and the gas fire on. Adam was squirming on his mother's knee. More pleasant sounds, children laughing, and giggling emanated from upstairs.

'We're sorry to upset the girls, but they seem to have settled.'

As there was no response, Clare continued. 'PC Stones and I have come to tell you the post-mortem results for Harriet. We are sorry for your loss (those facile words seemed to be on repeat these days) and thought you'd want to know the cause of death. You seemed very close to her and...'

'Very close. Very close. What in the name of all that's holy does that mean? Does your training include employing the most meaningless phrases known to man? Just say whatever it is you've come to say and then leave us in peace.'

Managing not to react (police training indeed utilised) Clare said that Harriet had died from an anaphylactic shock.

'But she was always so careful. We all knew she had a nut allergy and carried her EpiPen with her everywhere she went, she even carried it in a cardigan or trouser pocket in the house. Why didn't she use it yesterday? Oh, how awful, the poor girl.' Tears prevented further words Susan hugging Adam closer.

'Mr and Mrs Page, did you know about Harriet's nut allergy?'

'Yes. She told us in case she had a reaction and explained what to do. As far as we know she hadn't had any reaction whilst she was working in this house.' Richard seemed irritated by the line of questioning.

Clare knew her next question would almost certainly annoy him even more. 'Harriet was due to speak to us yesterday. We had arranged a meeting with her at the station.'

The atmosphere in the room changed, looks were exchanged; no one appeared willing to speak. 'Were you aware of the meeting and of anything your nanny might have wanted to say?'

'Good God. Whatever next? How the devil could we possibly know what the girl was going to say. Employees aren't exactly known for their discretion, so no, she could have said anything; anything we wouldn't have been in a position to deny.'

Clare left his outburst hanging, the use of the last word causing a dozen elephants to rampage around the room. His reaction needed analysing and like a politician he hadn't answered the first part of the question.

'Mrs Winters, did you know about the intended meeting?'

'No, yes, I'm not sure. She did say something about the police needing to speak to her again, but I don't think she told me when.' Clare thought that sounded as clear as a window covered in condensation.

'Mrs Winters,' Susan jumped, causing Adam to scream. She looked at Clare like a convict facing the firing squad. 'Would it be possible to have a look in the rooms Harriet used here to see if we can find the pens.'

'Absolutely not.' Richard spoke for his daughter, his voice rising with each word. 'Not unless you come back with a search warrant.'

Laying a hand on her husband's arm, Sylvia intervened. 'We will all look and let you know if we find them. She had at least two, said one was a back-up in case the first didn't work.'

Taking the baby from his mother, Sylvia Page said she must go up to the girls again. 'As you can hear, they are getting restless. We have promised them a trip to the playground, and I'll let them know we're going as soon as *you people* have left.'

Once back in the car the two officers sat bemused. 'Do you remember that line from the first *Men in Black* film when one of them has just delivered an alien in the back of a car, the one that looks just like a giant squid, and as they're leaving the other one asks, "Did you notice anything strange back there?" That's how I feel now. Strange and then some! Another way of putting it is to ask how you think the last hour went.' Edward's attempt at humour bringing a smile to Clare's lips.

'Do you mean on a scale of one to ten?'

'Probably have to involve some minus numbers. Boy, were they defensive!'

'Makes you think they have something to hide.'

'Or two or three somethings.'

'Do you know, young Stones, we'll make a copper of you yet. I think this next meeting might go better, but you never can tell. I'll let you lead on this one, then good experience for you to write it up.' Clare grinned. It was one way to avoid a task she hated.

Statement from Faye Thornton
(friend of the Winters' nanny, Harriet Devizes)

Harriet and I met pushing prams in Elizabeth Park. We were both nannies in Fordway. Last summer Harriet had just begun to work for Mr and Mrs Winters whilst I had been with the Newmans for five years. I live in and during the day I look after the baby, Jacob, but I am also responsible for Jake who's just turned six and Amanda, three. I often go to the park with the baby once I've taken Jake to school and Amanda to playschool. In the school holidays we all venture out, too hard to keep them occupied all day indoors.

I can't believe what's happened. She was just the loveliest girl and we had become great friends. It's too sad, her parents must be devastated. I met them once, such a delightful couple and they were so proud of Harriet. Apparently, she'd had some problems growing up and they were pleased to see her living independently and holding down a responsible job. I think she was bullied at school, had some kind of breakdown, and moved to a Sixth Form College her secondary school not willing to help her. Mr and Mrs Devizes told me that she'd always loved being with children. As a teenager she babysat the neighbour's offspring and helped at the local Scouts' meetings.

When Harriet was appointed by Mr and Mrs Winters, she'd only just qualified. A first job is always hard and there were times she was nervous, but I think it was more than feeling anxious about whether she was doing the job well. There was something awry, something wrong with the Winters' household. She adored little Adam. He is a gorgeous, contented baby and easy to love and she said the girls were growing up (there are four older siblings) and keen on their schoolwork. Harriet wasn't involved with them. Mrs Winters, Susan, looked after all four. Harriet said Susan was unwell following Adam's birth and Harriet was appointed to take care of him during the week.

There were times when I think Harriet was ready to say something, but then she seemed to hold back at the last moment. She once spoke of the danger of being disloyal and of saying things she'd later regret, things that would get her sacked.

I shouldn't say this, but she didn't like Gerald Winters; described him as overbearing and controlling. He checked up on his wife all the time, phoning several times a day to ask what she was doing. Apparently, he was always civil to Harriet, but he was the one who was uncomfortable that she knew too much about the *situation*, her word which I found strange, but when I asked her what she meant, she told me she'd already said too much. Far too much. Mr Winters once told her that an employee sees all and says nothing. Could it have anything to do with yesterday?

The thing is everyone knew about her nut allergy. She wanted people to know so that if she had a bad reaction, they'd know what to do. She carried two EpiPens: one in the front section of her handbag and the other in a pocket of whatever she was wearing. She used to laugh that she was being over cautious. Not funny now. When I asked how quickly she'd need to use one she said immediately, but that when she'd had incidents before she'd managed to locate the pen and administer it with "loads and loads of time to spare".

That's what I *cannot* get my head around. She never, and I mean never, went out without them and it's why we tended to go to the café in the park as it advertises itself as an allergy free environment. I only saw her use her EpiPen once when we were sitting on a bench and a child started eating a bag of peanuts. She applied the pen with the speed of a rocket being launched. I was impressed. So, what happened yesterday? That's what I keep asking.

If only I'd been on time. We were due to meet at ten, but I got delayed when I met a mum from playschool who kept me talking about the fund raiser next week. She asked if I could be on a stall. By the time I walked into the café Harriet was gasping for breath. She'd emptied her bag and her pockets were inside out, the jacket slumped over the back of her chair, but she obviously hadn't found either pen. The thing is...one pen not there, but two? She just wouldn't be that careless. The waitress said that Harriet had been to the counter to order a tea, which was strange as she never drank it, and when she sat down again had immediately started to make "funny noises" and was "scrabbling around in her bag asking where *it* was in a very loud voice." I looked everywhere but there was no sign of either pen. By the time the ambulance came she was unconscious.

Why had we agreed to meet? She'd rung the night before to say the police wanted to talk to her again. To say the least she sounded totally disconcerted, in a right state. She kept muttering that she needed to talk to me to ask if what she was going to tell them was acceptable or was breaking employer/ employee confidentiality. She added that there were things she'd never told anyone. Now I'll never know what she wanted to talk about, but it was bothering her. Really upsetting her.

Chapter 34

No other senior officer on duty, it fell to Harvey to deal with a particularly bizarre robbery. Jim Gunnis was an elderly gentleman whose house had been burgled. In the early hours of the morning, he'd made a citizen's arrest and the person who had entered his property was in a room waiting to be interviewed. Mr Gunnis was being detained in an adjacent room.

The duty sergeant, a man nearing retirement age, who had seen and done it all, had chortled when Harvey walked into the station, earlier than intended having driven at the last moment, the inclement weather not conducive to his usual walk.

'Good morning DCI Tarquin; you're going to love this. At least it'll make a change from hunting murderers. A house invasion at a time when all good people are fast asleep; so far nothing out of the ordinary. An old man alone in the house; ditto. Then it gets slightly more interesting: the thief is an elderly lady, in receipt of her bus pass and pension for many years. You won't believe this, but she gained entrance to the property via the kitchen window. Climbed in!'

Enjoying telling the tale, Sergeant Andrews paused. 'Once upon a time, as all great stories start, she was Mrs Janice Gunnis, in fact for fifty years that was the situation. But all good things come to an end and the decline and fall of the house of Gunnis happened six months ago.'

Looking at Harvey to see if he was still listening, the officer continued. 'Our Janice left the family home and moved to Manchester to be near her daughter, (she called the woman hers not theirs) whilst hubby stayed in Fordway, in the house they had lived in for over half a century. Now as we know all too well, break ups are not always amicable, even when people are old enough and ugly enough to know better. Things deteriorated faster than a land-to-air missile and the pair haven't spoken or been in contact, apart from via their rather well-reimbursed lawyers, for months. Not until last night!

'Not being in the first or even tenth flush of youth, and no doubt unaccustomed to entering a house via the kitchen window, she stumbled as she clambered across the draining board beneath the aforementioned window and ended up sprawled on the floor. (Harvey was used to the sergeant's long-winded stories and knew nothing would either stop him or speed up the tale.) Her ex-husband had been in bed asleep but was woken, first by the thud as she descended rather heavily and painfully to the floor, then by her fortissimo use of some rather choice Anglo-Saxon language.

'This is where it gets even more whacky, strange, unbelievable. He goes to see who it is, though as he told me he'd recognised her not so dulcet tone, so was pretty sure it was his dear and unfortunately at this moment not departed ex-wife. She's lying injured on the slate floor, a fact he found amusing as she was the one who had insisted on the hard tiles, when the kitchen was fitted. He not only leaves her there, first aid unforthcoming, but he tells her he's arresting her and locks her in! It sounds as if all the internal doors have locks. I told you this was a one-off, and I thought my days of being surprised by people's behaviour were over.

'Mr Gunnis then phones us, and we dispatch a car: blues and twos and for some unknown reason the siren blasting out its cacophonous racket, waking the local innocents enjoying some slumber.

'So, over to you DCI Tarquin. Janice Gunnis charged with Breaking and Entering and Jim Gunnis with Unlawful Imprisonment. You couldn't make it up! The best bit is, she'd gone back to retrieve her engagement ring which is worth a few Bob, and all the jewellery her husband bought for her over the last half century. Since the split, he'd always refused her access to the house and told her he was the one who'd paid for the rings, earrings and necklaces so they belonged to him.'

Morning briefing began on a light note with Harvey relaying the Gunnis' yarn. Although he knew he hadn't told it as well as Geoff Andrews it still made everyone smile. 'PC Stones, I'd like you to take charge of this: two charges, both admitted, shouldn't take too long.'

Edward Stones looked like a Wild West bandit who had just been told the vigilantes were about to catch him, hanging the likely outcome.

Not wanting to prolong the young man's anguish, Serena said, 'I think the DCI is joking. They've been dealt with; sent away with severe warnings about future behaviour.'

'I enjoyed my interviews with that pair: don't know which of them was the more cuckoo. They both require several appointments with psychiatrists, not the police. I'd loved to have charged them, but the CPS wouldn't have been interested in pursuing either case and it would have been a waste of court time if by some strange, convoluted route it had got that far: turn right at lunatics anonymous, pass go as quickly as possible, do not collect five hundred pounds, or whatever amount one gets these days. Still, I've had far worse starts to the day. Now down to some proper policing.' Harvey almost wished more of his time was taken up with the odd, the peculiar, the eccentric and not the serious matter of murders.

The information he had gleaned on Gerald Winters only filled a few minutes. 'He was obviously good at his job and deserved his recent promotion. His confidante, a Mrs Cornwell, spoke of him as an empathetic listener and a loving family man who was proud of his children. So, we have another take on the man.'

'Not totally surprising, most of us have more faces than Janus and it's well known that our personality changes according to the situation. We appear to have one persona when interacting with those close to us, like members of our family and friends, and quite another when relating to work colleagues when we need to be professional. The question is who was the real Gerald Winters and who wanted him gone?'

'Thank you, DI Peil, or should that be Doctor Freud, for that esoteric input.'

Copying Clare Jenning's habit, Edward stood to speak. 'I know, I'm inexperienced,' the look Harvey gave the young PC told him he wondered what was coming, 'but I've been thinking. Are we sure Mr Winters *was* murdered? Could it have been a deliberate overdose? Suicide.'

A long silence followed, all wondering how the boss was going to respond. 'Contrary to popular opinion, most people who commit suicide don't talk about it beforehand, or indeed leave a note. So far, so Gerald

Winters. However, most people who end it all don't find themselves laid out, with a doll and a three-course meal beside them. Susan Winters confessed to those bizarre additions, so I think it's fair to say the man was murdered.'

Duly chastised, Edward sat back and let Clare report on their interviews.

Clare stood. 'I understand Edward's thinking as we had another unusual, to say the least, session at his house. The whole family is strange, but none of them seem capable of murder.'

Seeing the look on her boss's face, she continued before he could state the obvious: that individuals who commit the ultimate crime don't have *I am a murderer* emblazoned across their foreheads.

'At the Winters' house we were treated like vampires, ones who had managed to enter without being invited in. I'm sure they thought we were there for blood, which I suppose, metaphorically speaking, we were. Susan's parents were there, not surprising as she looked most upset and in need of help following Harriet's death. All three acted like a team that only has defensive positions. Richard Page almost threw us out and here's an interesting thing, when we asked to look for the missing EpiPens he was foaming at the mouth – again speaking metaphorically – and told us we'd need a search warrant. To look for the pens!

'Both grandparents went, on separate occasions, to see to the older children who were making a racket upstairs and when one of them was out of the room Susan looked most uncomfortable and seemed afraid of what we were going to ask her.'

Looking at Edward for corroboration, she continued. 'Susan Winters was obviously upset about the nanny, though whether that's because she'll now have to cope with the baby on her own or because she genuinely liked the young woman, I'm not sure. However, there was little emotion from the Pages, or not about Harriet. Plenty aimed at us.

'They all knew about Harriet's nut allergy and agreed that she was always prepared in case of an attack. Also, they were aware that she was coming to talk to us. Richard Page said something that we thought was curious: "Employees aren't exactly known for their discretion". Did he think she was going to tell tales out of the nursery? And one is left wondering what he thought she might say that was inappropriate, or worse.

'Now to move on to our second interview. You've all got copies of Faye Thornton's statement. She knew something was amiss at the Winters' house. I'll just read her final comments as we thought they were particularly telling. "Why had we agreed to meet? She'd rung the night before to say the police wanted to talk to her again. To say the least she sounded totally disconcerted, in a right state. She kept muttering that she needed to talk to me to ask if what she was going to tell them was acceptable or was breaking employer/employee confidentiality. She added that there were things she'd never told anyone. Now I'll never know what she wanted to talk about, but it was bothering her. Really upsetting her." Frustrating to think we might never know what it was she wanted to say.'

Harvey exploded, 'That's what we are being paid to do. To find out what the hell is going on in that house. We've got three people dead. Gerald Winters, the Winters' nanny and Nora Ederson. They *are* all linked, and I now believe the link isn't Parkside but the surreal trio: the two Pages and their daughter.'

As soon as the police left, the trio plus children were dressed in warm clothes, ready for the promised outing. The play area near Preston was a favourite haunt. It looked like a young child's idea of heaven with its slides, roundabouts, climbing frames and tree houses accessed by a variety of ladders. Rope bridges crossed artificial rivers, and swamps which had alligators and hippos placed at strategic points. Some of the equipment had warning signs saying that children *Must be Supervised* and several had age limits. Being a popular venue, it was invariably busy.

Glad to be outside, the adults took turns pushing Adam on the swings, those suitable for the under twos. Anyone looking at them would have seen a mother and grandparents appreciating sometime in the park. Had they looked closer they might have been surprised to see that for over an hour not a word was spoken. Seventy minutes of silence, the only sounds the shrieks of excited youngsters with the occasional cry as one fell over.

Chapter 35

No one could miss Clare's voice as she gave a blow-by-blow account of her meeting with the vicar. Most listened politely but would be glad when the wedding was over and normal conversation could be resumed.

'Rick is a believer and wants us to be married in church, so we are going for a few meetings with the Rev. Baldwin. Yesterday it was about the sanctity of marriage and how important is to understand that our relationship and our love will change over time. One thing made me smile when he said that at the moment love is all about planning our life together and is full of "wedding bells and honeymoon bliss" but one day it will manifest itself as making sure the beloved (yes, he used that word) remembers to take their pills each morning. Not the most uplifting picture, but I suppose if you love someone, you'll keep loving them when they're old, bald and in need of Statins!'

His phone ringing gave Harvey an excuse to return to his office and escape the Mills and Boon chit-chat. 'Two young men are here to see you DCI Tarquin. They say it's important.'

'Have either of them got a name?' Harvey hated the unprofessional style of some of the youngsters who manned the front desk. He could hear the constable asking for their names.

'They say you will know them. They're Nora Ederson's sons: Nigel and Ralph.'

'I'll be down in a minute.' Calling Serena, he informed her about their visitors and said that he would see the men in his office, and that he'd like her to sit in.

Ralph Ederson looked the more confident of the two, Nigel looking around for an escape route. Taking them upstairs, Harvey asked how they were coping.

'Not too good. It's all such a shock. One minute, Mum was alive and well and looking forward to her holiday, the next she's dead and under strange circumstances. We know you're looking into her death, though we've not come to ask for any progress as you told us we'd be kept informed of any developments.'

Taking time to think of the appropriate words, Ralph continued. 'We've been sorting Mum's things, a horrible task. Well...yesterday we were clearing out her bedside cabinet and found some diaries, well more like notebooks, that she wrote in every so often. The entries certainly aren't regular, about two or three a month. I've brought them along with the relevant pages marked.'

Nigel interrupted. 'At first, we didn't want to read them, too personal, but we thought we'd look at the most recent pages, see if there was any hint that something was wrong, or was bothering her. Most of the things she wrote were about various outings, visits to the cinema, trips up to the Lakes to see her friend Imelda and books she'd enjoyed reading. But ... and this is the reason we've come in today: there was an entry two days before she died, in red (the others were in blue or black) that said "CM bothering me again. How many times must I insist that I cannot, simply cannot, do what she is asking. It's totally unprofessional and I would be struck off." That made us look back to see if there were similar entries.'

Allowing the young man time to compose himself, Harvey asked him to carry on.

'Over the past few years, the letters CM have occurred on a regular basis. Always followed by similar wording and all written in bright red. The first one we found was dated roughly four years ago and says, "CM approached me as I left work and said I needed to help her. She told me I was all too aware of the situation and knew what had to be done. What she asked is impossible. I was then informed that should I not do what she requested I would be responsible for a life in ruins and possibly ended. I told her not to approach me again as the answer would continue to be no."

'Similar entries appear over the following years, then the situation seems to have escalated, with CM coming to the house. The first time that happened, Mum sounded extremely upset. "CM was at the front door and barged her way in. She was more disturbed than I've ever seen her and was yelling at me to get a grip and do my job. When I told her that I did that every day and loved being a midwife, she broke down and begged me to help."'

Ralph took over the story. 'One week before she died, there was a long entry. "CM. What should I do? How many times must I say no? I asked her if she'd sought help from anyone else. She said she hadn't, but I'm not sure. She told me I am the saviour of the day. I am the one who knows the whole story. I do, but my job is to deliver babies and look after the new mums. If she comes again, I WILL phone the police." Before you ask, we have no idea who CM is. None of the family or any of her friends have those initials. Might it be someone at work?'

Thanking the sons for coming in, he asked to keep the diaries, promising to return them in due course. 'We will keep you abreast of any developments and the entries you have highlighted sound interesting.'

Once the Edersons had left, Serena was instructed to contact Imelda Simpson. 'She was still the matron when the mystery woman appeared on the scene, so Nora might have spoken to her, told her what CM had asked her to do.'

If Imelda was surprised to hear from the police again, she didn't show it, though Serena knew in her working life she must have had a lot of practice at hiding her feelings.

After enquiring how Imelda was, she explained the reason for her call.

A long pause, the former matron could almost be heard thinking. 'CM. The initials don't ring any bells, but over the years I must have come across literally thousands of women: patients and staff. Nora never spoke to me about anyone harassing her in that way and she never mentioned anyone asking her to do anything that made her feel uncomfortable. I have no idea what she could have been asked to do, though I was once asked to be involved in something unprofessional, something I never contemplated doing, and I certainly never shared the request with anyone.

'I don't recall Nora using those initials. I'll have a think, but it will be quite a task. As I said it could involve thousands of names. We kept extremely detailed records at Parkside and every mum would be logged in there. Do let me know if you find anyone with the initials CM and I'll try to fill in some details.'

Head needing to be cleared, Harvey left the car at work and walked the long way home. People were hurrying, a pavement rush hour, and Harvey took a few seconds to study them. Serena's words about multiple personalities occupied his mind and the fact we all have at least two faces we present to the world.

After his mother died, he had felt like the survivor of a war, suffering from Post-Traumatic Stress Disorder: flashbacks, nightmares, extreme anxiety, and uncontrollable images consumed every second. On his first day outside, a trip to the shops a necessity, his brothers seemingly incapable of filling the depleted fridge, his father catatonic on the settee, he had been amazed to realise that no one had any idea what he was feeling. The world was continuing to turn and for most normal life remained uninterrupted. That day he knew he looked as he always did, his face fixed in a neutral expression when all he felt like doing was sitting outside the shop and weeping. He'd known that had he started he wouldn't have mustered sufficient self-control to stop.

Was he passing the bereaved this evening, their faces fixed as his had been? Was that woman rushing back to a house full of noise, the elderly man to a lonely tin of baked beans, the single slice of bread placed carefully in the toaster? The young woman in the bright red coat might be in the first raptures of new love, the man on the opposite side of the road pleased with his promotion.

Who were the innocent? Who the perpetrators of a crime? Ninety-five per cent were likely to be in the former category and it was a statistic he tried to keep at the front of his mind. The accepted figures were that ninety-five per cent of all crimes were committed by five percent of the population. Only a twentieth! Smiling he re-did the maths, yes five per cent was one twentieth; five times twenty equalling a hundred. Mrs Cotton, his teacher in Year 5, had berated him when he'd got an entire page of fractions and percentages wrong. He had been hauled to the front of the classroom and rebuked for his "sheer carelessness". He'd love to be able to tell her that thirty years on he'd cracked it!

He dealt with the criminal underclass every day and always found himself wondering why they did such unspeakable things. He was often tempted to ask, 'What in the world made you behave like that?' The words had been spoken aloud, leaving his lips before his brain's red light could halt them. A lady smiled at him.

'Sorry, talking to oneself is a sign of something. Not sure what.' Harvey felt embarrassed.

'We all do it, love. Get yourself home and have a nice cup of tea: the answer to everything.'

If only life could be remedied that easily. Wishing her a pleasant evening he walked on.

There were times he was afraid he was following his father down the same one-way path. For many years, the old man talked to himself, usually asking where he had put the house keys (discovered in the bin) or his gloves (the fridge). Words, then entire sentences began to be mislaid with no hope of their being discovered in the bin, or the fridge.

'Unfortunately, the decline is inevitable and irredeemable. On occasion it's a steady adagio, at other times it's an unbearable presto. There will come a time when all speech will be lost. Try to enjoy the now, the conversations, however limited and esoteric that he remains capable of undertaking.' The doctor, a kind, empathetic specialist in Dementia, had been warning what lay ahead.

'For a period, there will be moments of complete comprehension. That is good for the onlooker, but not always for the one with Dementia as it can make them aware of their cognitive deterioration.' Almost to the end, that had been the case with his father.

Arriving home, Harvey was pleased, almost inordinately so, to be greeted by friends. I suppose cupboard love is better than none. It didn't matter that he was still talking aloud, only Chopin and Grieg to hear his maudlin comments. As the duo chomped their way through their *Cat's Delight Gourmet Meal* (why in the world do I fall for the latest trendy sachets and not the cat food on special offer?) he continued the one-sided conversation, telling them that he was disappointed in himself: once again he had asked Serena to visit Parkside Nursing Home, the letters CM ringing in her ears. He knew his reputation as a dinosaur was well founded!

Was it too late to change? He'd done a totally unwarranted chameleon-like transformation once. That had been utterly detrimental and had affected the rest of his life. We all have twenty/twenty vision when we look back and would all choose different paths if time could be rewound. Specsavers' vision told him that he had made a colossal mistake staying at home for eighteen months after his mother died. At the time it had seemed like the correct, and in many ways, the only thing to do. His father had been so depressed and unable to cope (even putting a meal on the table beyond him) that

Harvey was always afraid when he had to leave the man alone, fearing what he might find when he returned home. All pills had been removed from the bathroom cabinet and Harvey had dispensed the man's prescription medication each morning and evening.

A suicidal father and two wayward teenagers who thought that attending raves and playing truant was the way their mother would have wanted them to behave forced the younger version of himself grow up too fast. At nineteen he'd been the only adult in the house, no helpful manual available.

It was when he returned to university to repeat the second year that he'd been forced to abandon the day his mother dropped down dead, no advance warning, that he realised how much he had changed: from a sociable, life of the party, lock up your teenage daughters, to a morose introvert, one who favoured his own company. Almost a quarter of a century on he knew it was down to him: no one could make the necessary adjustments. He didn't want to look back in another twenty-five years and realise that he had done nothing about it.

Chapter 36

DS Jennings stopped on her way to work to visit the café in Elizabeth Park. She knew it opened early to catch the dog walkers who popped in on their morning stroll around the grounds.

A young woman was serving a group of three men. It was obviously a regular occurrence as they all chatted happily whilst waiting for their coffees. After what felt like an eternity, Clare approached the counter. Introducing herself, she asked if Thelma, the name badge prominent, was working two days ago when a customer was taken ill.

An older lady (name badge Jane) who had been making the men's coffees turned round and told Thelma to take over and she'd speak to the Detective Sergeant. 'I'm the manageress and I was here when Harriet was taken ill. So sad. Harriet was a regular and was always so pleasant and chatty. Her parents came in with her once and seemed like such a lovely couple. They'll be distraught.'

'Can you tell me what happened.'

'We were ever so busy, unusual for that time of day, we're not often full by ten o'clock, it's usually closer to half past, but we were chock-a-block on Tuesday. Harriet came up to the counter and ordered a pot of tea and I think it was either toast or a toasted teacake. Now that was different: she never drank tea, said she'd never liked it, but we were so busy I just took the order. She added that she'd be back later as she was waiting for her friend, probably the other nanny, they met up here at least once a week. They've both got the most gorgeous little boys to look after.

'Anyway, the next thing I knew she was crying out, almost screaming, it sounded as though she was panicking. She kept asking where it was, that she needed it. I went over to her and could see she was distressed. Her lips and face were going a funny colour, so I asked Thelma to ring for an ambulance. I sat with Harriet until they came, by which time she was in and out of consciousness. They took over and tried to help her and asked me if I knew where she kept her EpiPen. I must admit I didn't know she needed one. We are a nut-free café, so we've never had anyone have an allergic reaction before.'

'Thank you, Jane, you're being most helpful. You said Harriet said she was waiting for someone, but had anyone been with her before she became unwell?'

'I can only think she ordered the tea for someone else, but I didn't see anyone with her…as I said we were extremely busy, every table taken. The paramedics tried to help her for ages and ages, by which time the café was quieter, the coffee brigade had gone, and it was too early for the ladies who lunch. When the ambulance left there was a lull, so I decided to do a bit of tidying and sweeping, little ones and the elderly can drop more food than they eat. Beneath the table where Harriet had been sitting, I found several salted peanuts. As I said we are nut-free, and I can only imagine that a child had opened a packet and dropped some on the floor. Shame the parents didn't see. Just a few nuts to cause that reaction.'

'Just one more thing, Jane, do you by any chance have CCTV in the café?'

'No, sorry and there's none outside. We used to have some in the park, installed when the down-and-outs were being murdered a couple of years ago, but people objected and said they wanted to enjoy the park without Big Brother watching their every move.'

'And here's the thing that's strange,' Clare was in full flow, telling the DCI about her visit to the café, 'there were peanuts underneath the table where Harriet had been sitting. Jane, the manageress, thought they'd been dropped by accident, but what if they were put there deliberately to stop Harriet coming to see us.'

Waiting for a moment to gauge her boss's reaction, she added, 'We've been told she was so careful to carry her pens, two for good measure, so why in the world didn't she have either of them on Tuesday?'

'You're thinking someone removed them? That would make it murder.' Harvey thanked Clare for her visit and asked if they were now investigating three murders.

'If we are, we've got one cold-blooded murderer. To kill a young nanny in that fashion takes a certain kind of person: one without empathy.'

'Or one so desperate to curtail our line of questioning. Now who knew she was coming to see us? And what did they think she was going to say?'

Harriet was so trusting, such an innocent. The café was surprisingly busy for that time in the morning, the coffee brigade not usually assembled so early. That served me well as no one gave me a second glance.

When I went up to her, she didn't seem surprised, perhaps thinking I'd come to enquire what she was planning to say. I asked her if she'd mind getting me a tea and a toasted teacake and she scuttled off without a backward glance. There was a short queue, but long enough! Sufficient time for me to spread the peanuts under her chair and remove the EpiPens from where she always kept them. A creature of habit. Such a shame, but essential. This time she would have said too much. Far too much. She had to be silenced.

Do I feel like a murderer? YES.

Am I sorry? NO.

Richard and Sylvia Page had taken their grandson for a walk. He was at that adorable age when he took an interest in everything. Today it was the turn of the swans gliding down the canal on the outskirts of Fordway that he was finding fascinating. One pair had nine tiny mini-me versions following in their wake.

Having explained the new word signets to Adam, they gave him the feed pellets they had acquired from a local pet shop. Once he was happily engaged in aiming the pellets in roughly the right direction, they began the conversation, the one that was repeated daily.

As usual Sylvia was the first actor to speak the well-rehearsed lines: 'I'm worried about Susan she doesn't look well.'

'We've both been more than worried for the past nine years, ever since she met that man.'

'Yes, I know, but I was hoping that now he's out of the picture she might start to improve, to regain some of her old bonhomie.'

'That, my dear Sylvia will take time. With our support, it will come, and we'll have our delightful, bubbly daughter back. For now, we will just have to be patient.'

'It's so wonderful to think that he has gone forever.'

'That goes without saying. Now is it time to go back for tea and some of your date and walnut cake?'

Chapter 37

A copy of this week's *Fordway Gazette* was lying open at the appropriate page.

WINTERS
Gerald James

Died peacefully at home.
Husband of Susan.
Father of Hannah, Abigail, Lara, Esther and his beloved son, Adam.
Son-in-law of Richard and Sylvia.

Funeral to be held at Fordway Crematorium for immediate family only.
No flowers
No donations

'Good morning, Harvey, I see you've read the notice. Bland, to say the least.'

'Almost funereal!' Harvey was pleased he was still able to see the humour, albeit the black variety, in the situation. 'Very little detail. They obviously don't want people attending, no mention of when it's happening.'

'I'll ask Edward Stones to ring the crematorium and find out the date and time. I know you always want to attend the send-offs of our victims.'

'Indeed. Like most people, I hate funerals, but as the adage goes the murderer is often in attendance to see his victim taking their final journey. We'll both go. Watch and listen.'

'I don't think I've ever seen a notice in the Family Announcements section that didn't have the words beloved, much loved, loving husband of, sorely missed. At least they managed the fact he died peacefully. I expect that was true after ingesting a pharmacy's entire supply of drugs!'

Harvey smiled, pleased by his DI's levity. 'Interesting list of children, the girls named, but only Adam called beloved. Backs up what we've been told about his obsession with a male offspring.'

Ten minutes later, Edward appeared at the door saying that the crematorium had the funeral booked for 11.30 this morning. It's the new building out on Ash Tree Road. I don't know why a town the size of Fordway needs two, but as my Dad always jokes, and I do mean always, people are dying to get there.'

'The family really didn't want anyone else going along. The paper only came out two hours ago, so few people will have had the chance to read the announcement. Well, we have!'

Serena had dashed home to change, the red jacket she had been wearing deemed inappropriate. Meeting Harvey outside the doors of the crematorium, they were pleased to see that they had arrived before the mourners, though neither of them was sure that was the most appropriate word.

'We'll watch them go in, then follow and sit at the back. I suspect it's going to be brief.'

The hearse, led by the funeral director in traditional black and top hat, came slowly up the path that led from Ash Tree Road to the crematorium, erected last year following complaints about the length of time people had to wait to "get a slot", the unfortunate phrase employed in a letter to the paper. A black coffin, devoid of a floral tribute was lifted from the vehicle.

One car pulled up behind the hearse. As the door opened, the waiting officers were surprised to see only two people emerge: Susan Winters and Richard Page.

'Where's Sylvia Page?' Serena hoped her aside was quiet enough that only Harvey heard. Answering her own question, she added, 'She must have stayed at home with the children.'

Richard looked so angry when he saw the two uninvited, and from the look on his face most unwelcome extras, that Harvey expected him to go over and remonstrate with them. Instead, he said, in a voice that Serena suggested afterwards was in danger of waking the dead, 'What the hell are you doing here? This is a private affair, and you are not welcome. Susan has enough to contend with, so I'll ask you to leave. Get out of our lives. Go!'

Without replying, Harvey indicated that they should follow the coffin indoors. The waiting room was more spacious than the rather cramped one in the original building. With so few mourners it felt cavernous. Real flowers were an improvement on the plastic variety that had bothered Harvey when he had last had cause to attend a funeral.

The chapel itself was beautiful, cream walls and a matching carpet creating a calm atmosphere. Stained-glass windows had been created in a mosaic of pastel colours, devoid of religious references. Many religions would be represented within these walls as well as funerals for non-believers. Someone had been tasked with no causing offence. Susan and her father walked tentatively and sat at the front, to the right of the coffin.

As unobtrusively as possible Harvey and Serena took their places at the rear.

Half an hour later, they were back in the DCI's office, Clare and Edward looking like puppies waiting for a ball to be thrown.

'So, tell all.' Clare realised she hadn't sounded very professional and apologised.

'Five minutes from start to finish. Not much of a goodbye. No hymns, no eulogies, no readings, no nothing. A man, no dog-collar, but obviously the one in charge, stood by the coffin and said we were there to say goodbye to Gerald James Winters and then indicated to some unseen person to close the curtains. Susan and Richard stood and walked out.' Harvey shook his head. He still hadn't worked out what they had just witnessed.

'Golly, not very emotional. Even I wouldn't have needed a handkerchief. How did they look?' Clare sounded desperate for more details, maybe some snippet to aid the investigation.

'Serena will tell you the only interesting bit.'

'Both Mrs Winters and Mr Page were wearing black. Very traditional. Head to toe completely black. So was the doll!'

'What? The doll was there? The same one that was beside Mr Winters when he died? The one we said was the most gorgeous one we'd ever clapped eyes on. That doll?' Each question seemed to go up several semitones.

'It looked like the same doll but had been changed out of its lovely dress into a black jacket, and matching trousers. It was even wearing a black beret and a pair of tiny sunglasses.'

'No! What in the world is going on?'

'We know Susan finds it hard to distinguish fact from fiction and maybe she thinks the doll is in mourning. I suppose grown men play with train sets and sail toy boats on paddling pools, so maybe the odd woman still plays with dolls, dresses them up and takes them out.'

'I think odd is the word.'

'You've not heard the best, Clare. As they walked out after the oh so brief farewell, Mrs Winters took out a tiny lace hanky and wiped the doll's cheeks.'

'Did she think she was crying? This just gets more and more weird.'

Serena said she just had one more thing that puzzled her. Sylvia Page was in absentia. No doubt she was on babysitting duty but surely any normal family would have been able to find someone to look after the children whilst she attended the funeral, if only to show support for her daughter.

'Ah, but Serena, as we are all too aware, especially after this morning, we are not, and I do mean not, dealing with anything like a normal family.' Harvey was beginning to think he no longer recognised normal.

'I'm off to Parkside, sir, see what names with the initials CM they can come up with. The trouble is we don't know if the letters belong to a patient, nurse or someone on the admin. side. The entries in Nora Ederson's diary go back years, so I'll have to do the same. Even if they give me access to all their data it could take hours to sift through.'

'Take PC Stones with you. He might not be in his comfort zone there (Harvey felt himself go red, knowing others would say that about him, his nickname of Tyrannosaurus Tarquin all too appropriate) but he is keenness personified so will be a willing assistant.'

CM: Clara Morris, Christine Masters, Corrine Monks, Charlene Millstone, Clare Muir. The visit had at least supplied a few names with the appropriate initials. Access to the Home's records had been given with surprisingly little resistance. Edward and Serena had spent hours poring over lists of names going back a lot further than the entries in Nora's diary. Thanking the young man for his help she told him to go home and have a quiet evening. 'I'm off to see a friend, another one of us, so no doubt we'll talk shop. I'll let you know if she has any insights. We need some. She's very bright and often has the most amazing take on things. We first met at police training in Manchester, and we've kept in touch ever since. She's just caught me up, got her Inspector's badge a few weeks ago, and tonight is a celebration. We both know anything we discuss will be kept under wraps, so I feel safe talking to her. Keep your fingers crossed…unless you're tiddly winking!'

The journey to Lancaster was quick, rush hour over. Mikayla lived in an apartment overlooking the canal named after the town. After parking, Serena noticed a new sign giving some information on the waterway.

Lancaster Canal
The canal that travels through Lancaster is
a waterway of approximately 73 miles
50 chains in length.

The line of the canal was first surveyed by <u>Robert Whitworth</u> in 1772 and work began in 1794.
By 1797 it was in use; horse-drawn boats
an essential means of transport.

The North End commences at Kendal, from where it passes almost due southward through Burton-in-Kendal, Lancaster, Garstang, Fordway, and on to Preston.

Linking Preston to Kendal, the **Lancaster Canal** is one of the country's few coastal **canals**. Built along the natural lie of the land it offers 41 miles of lock free cruising - the longest stretch in the country. As the canal is naturally level, it also lends itself to gentle walking and cycling as well as canoeing and other outdoor activities.

Please enjoy our beautiful canal.

As she walked to her friend's apartment, she remembered that they had said they would walk the entire length one day. It was one of those things that was a really good idea, when they could find the time.

Mikayla was waiting, dressed to go out. 'No, you're not late. I saw you park and thought we'd go out straight away. Don't know about you, but I'm starving.'

Dinner was at their favourite Chinese restaurant: The Great Wall. Laughing at the fact they didn't need to study the menu as they always had the same dishes, they were able to begin gossiping a few seconds after they sat down.

'So, Mikayla, how's the love life? Still Ma'mun?'

'Yes, Ma'mun.'

'Sounds serious, he's lasted longer than any of the others. Is he the one?'

'I think so. As I've said before the one drawback is the fact that he's a Muslim. Doesn't bother me, not for a second, but it definitely upsets his family. They want him to settle down with a follower of Islam, not a non-believer. When he met my parents, it went really well. Then I went to his house. It's one of the big ones in Alderley Edge. His whole family was there waiting in an enormous lounge: parents, two brothers, a sister and one set of grandparents. All his siblings have married or are engaged within the faith.

'I thought I'd dressed appropriately, arms and legs covered, but they gave me a headscarf to wear! The atmosphere reminded me of one of those disaster movies where the world is overtaken by a perma-frost, ice slowly encroaching over everything. I became so devoid of conversation they must have thought I had developed selective mutism.

'Ma'mun was so apologetic afterwards. He kept saying they were living in a time-warp. It was all a throw-back to their upbringing in Pakistan where the eldest son married a woman from the village, chosen by his parents. "I've told them I was born in this country, became a doctor here, will stay in England forever and want to adopt the Western tradition where a man marries for love." It was the first time he'd mentioned getting married and I was as lacking in a rejoinder as I'd been earlier.'

'Do you think you will marry him? Is it that intense?'

Following a long pause, tears threatening to join the fried rice, Mikayla spoke so softly Serena had to lean across the table. 'I love him. Enough to say yes. I've considered converting, but it would be totally hypocritical, and I can't imagine wearing a hijab when I'm nicking someone!' Her friend was pleased to hear some levity.

'We need to spend more time together, but our jobs interfere: he's still a junior doctor and has a dreadful shift pattern and well…you know what our lack of routine can do to relationships. Think of the times we've planned to meet, only for one of us to cancel. The other thing that bothers me is that we both want children, but he is insistent that they would be brought up as Muslims. I've never liked introducing children to any form of religion too early, I think they should be allowed to find their own path when they are able to understand all the arguments.'

'I'm sorry there are problems. Hope it works out soon – one way or the other. Do phone any time you need a chat.'

'Anyway, how about you? Work isn't everything you know.'

'I don't seem to find enough time to get involved with anyone and my sisters aren't exactly role models, both separated.'

'Don't leave it too late and regret the missed opportunities and most marriages still work.'

Returning to her friend's flat, the curtains drawn to keep out the night which had turned nasty, the gale force winds and torrential rain that had been threatened arriving early, Serena told Mikayla about the initials she had been investigating and read the list of names matching them.

'CM? You've got a reasonable list of names to follow up. However, thinking outside the box, one of my favourite sayings, might I suggest Claude Monet if she's a painter. Charlene Manson if she's a serial killer!'

Smiling, Serena said she'd keep those suggestions in mind, though she didn't think her boss would be very impressed.

'Have you considered that the letters might mean something else, a code for words that were understood by your Nora Ederson. The trouble with that scenario is that they could stand for anything and from what you've told me Nora does indicate that it's a woman who is bothering her. However, Cretinous Moron if she's not very bright! Cooked Meat for a chef. Chlorine Magnesium if she's good at chemistry or, I will stop in a minute, Cliff-edge Mountain if she's into geography.'

'I know you're being silly, but you might just have a point. They might not be the person's name but indicate something about the woman. Obviously, Nora couldn't or wouldn't accede to her request so it might be Constant Mitherer - my Mum used to tell me not to mither when I was wanting something; I had to be patient.'

Having consumed rather too much wine, Serena stayed the night with her friend. At two o'clock in the morning they were still discussing cases they were involved in, and of course Ma'mun and the wearing of the veil.

Chapter 38

CM: Clara Morris, Christine Masters, Corrine Monks, Charlene Millstone, Clare Muir.

The list was sitting, waiting to be tackled. Having suggested to DCI Tarquin that the initials might be a code Nora had used to identify the woman who had harassed her, Serena was reminded to start with the more obvious scenario. Her boss was, as she had feared, not impressed with her thinking outside the box, and hadn't found any of last night's suggestions amusing. Had she had too much to drink and got to the point where anything had been viewed as funny?

'Flights of fancy do not sit well in the middle of a murder investigation. Now get down to some proper policing and find these women. One of them might be the one we are looking for. Let me know what you discover. Sooner rather than later.'

Three hours later, Serena knocked loudly on the door and entered without waiting for Harvey to say come in. It was a habit he hated. Edward Stones followed behind, looking like a dog waiting for its master to say it was walkies time. Harvey wondered if he had ever been so enthusiastic, bright-eyed, and bushy-tailed.

'Sir, we've contacted all the names we got from Parkside yesterday. Not much to excite us. Edward has written them up for you. Let us know if you think any are worth pursuing further.'

Muttering a muted thanks, he took the paper and began to read.

C.M.

Summaries of phone calls to women with the initials C.M. who had connections to the Parkside Nursing Home. These are the initials that appear in Nora Ederson's diary, the person so named appearing to threaten her. The entries span several years.

Clara Morris

Married, two children, both born at Parkside Nursing Home. Nora Ederson the midwife both times. Mrs Morris described her as, 'Outstanding, a wonderful professional. Kind, caring and excellent at her job. I recommended her to my friend.'

Christine Masters

Moved to Exeter four years ago. Twins delivered at Parkside, but not by Nora Ederson. Had no recollection of anyone by that name.

Corrine Monks

N.B. interesting reaction on hearing the nursing home mentioned. Extremely unhappy memories. Early labour but told the baby should have survived. Midwife wasn't English, but she thinks she was Polish. Made a complaint against Parkside and the midwife and received a substantial pay out! Gave birth a year later at Waterfront Maternity Unit in Preston. No knowledge of Nora Ederson.

Charlene Millstone

Mr and Mrs Millstone have been living abroad for a decade, her husband working in Brussels. They returned to Fordway a week ago. Positive memories of Imelda Simpson as the matron and most complimentary about Nora who was the midwife when her son was born. He's now fifteen, so going back some time.

Clare Muir
Worked on the admin side of the Home. There for almost thirty years and spoke highly of both Nora and Imelda. 'Nora was always so friendly, and both the staff and the mums loved her. She was Midwife of the Year at least twice. Imelda Simpson was an exemplary matron, and I didn't wait to see her successor.'

No bloody use. Realising he was talking to himself Harvey thumped the desk. Where to now? Had Serena and Edward discovered all the people with those initials? Edward had said they had gone back as far as the records allowed. Records allowed? What the hell does that mean? Everything was recorded on computers these days, but what about paper records pre-dating the modern technology? He was standing ready to storm out and find the duo when Serena appeared at the door, once again knocking and entering leaving no gap in between.

'Sir, what a coincidence.'
'In my experience, there's no such thing.'
'Well, sir, whilst you were looking at Edward's notes, I had a phone call from Imelda Simpson. I'd told her the names of the women we'd found and asked her to let me know if she could think of anyone else. The call is recorded and it's worth listening to.'

Phone call from Miss Imelda Simpson to DI Peil:

I.S.: Good afternoon Serena. I'm sorry to bother you and it may be nothing, but you said I was to phone you if I thought of any other ladies with the initials C.M. whom we knew at Parkside.

S.P.: And a good afternoon to you Imelda and thank you for calling. One never knows what is important.

I.S.: It was just before I retired, so several years ago now. She was just the most awkward woman. Nora was her midwife; it was the only time I ever heard her say she didn't like any of the mums. The woman had a permanent scowl on her face, and nothing was good enough. I think because she was going privately, she expected to receive preferential treatment, but we dealt with all the mums in exactly-the-same, utterly professional, way.

S.P.: And did she have the initials C.M.?

I.S.: Well, that's the thing and the reason I didn't think of her because she did, and she didn't. Her surname was double barrelled: Carter-Monmouth, Delia Carter-Monmouth. She insisted on being addressed by both surnames and went for one of the young nurses when she called her Mrs Monmouth. We all called her Mrs Complaining big Mouth behind her back: not very professional, but fun.

S.P.: I bet it made you feel better.

I.S.: Oh, it did. The woman complained about everything: if an appointment was a few minutes late, if

269

*the doctor was busy and left a midwife to attend to her.
The worst was when she claimed that Nora had used
the word "he" during a scan. I know that can't have
been the case as Nora always said "baby" in case the
parents didn't want to know the sex. After that Nora
and I always saw her together.*

S.P.: Did she follow up the accusation?'

*I.S.: No, but things didn't improve. She had a small
pelvis, and we suggested an elective Caesarean. She
wasn't having that! Demanded a birthing pool which
we knew wouldn't work, not for her. Great for some
women but we advised strongly against it for
Mrs D.C.-M. When the time came it was a long labour
and she was soon out of the water! In the end the doctor
had to perform a forceps delivery...of a girl! She went
mental (sorry rather colloquial) saying they'd bought
clothes for a boy and her husband had painted the
nursey in pale blue.*

*S.P.: I imagine that caused some hilarity behind the
scenes.*

*I.S.: Indeed, and of course Nora was vindicated. She
might not have had a crystal ball to foretell the character
of a baby on a scan, but she did know the difference
between a boy and a girl! Mrs Complaining big Mouth
threatened a lawsuit which never materialised, a wise
lawyer no doubt telling her to save her money. But
here's the reason she came to mind: a few months later I
was in town with Nora when we saw her. She marched
up to us and looked daggers at Nora. I can recall her*

words verbatim: 'You're not fit to be a midwife and one day you'll get your comeuppance.' We laughed at the time but it's not so funny now.

'Interesting. I think we need to talk to the woman.' Harvey wondered if they were clutching at the proverbial straws but kept the pessimistic thought to himself.

'Edward is finding her details. There can't be many by the name of Carter-Monmouth in the system. We'll ask her to come in, make the "talk" more formal. Do you want to be there or are you happy for Edward to interview with me?'

'Discuss it with him beforehand but let him lead. Good experience and he's champing at the bit to make his mark.' Oh dear, so many colloquialisms, his use of the glorious English language was receding faster than his hairline.

Mrs Carter-Monmouth strode into the station and announced her presence to the young constable on desk duty. 'I have been summoned. Someone called Stones wants to speak to me. He said it was important, though what can be so important that I have to leave the new nanny with a three-month old baby she doesn't know, I can't imagine.'

Thanking the woman for coming Edward managed not to laugh. She reminded him of the cat made famous by its miserable expression and the catch phrase "This is my happy face".

'I have no idea why I'm here and it had better not take too long. Francesca is new, and I don't want to leave Hooper with her too long. Wondering if that was a dog Edward gave a non-committal smile and said she was here in connection with an on-going inquiry, and they wanted to eliminate her from the investigation. Thinking he hadn't put that very well he took a deep breath before continuing.

'Mrs Carter-Monmouth, you may have seen the sad news about a former midwife at Parkside Nursing Home: Nora Ederson. She died recently and we are looking into the circumstances surrounding her death. We are speaking to the ladies she nursed at the Home. I wonder if you remember her.'

'Remember her? Remember her? That woman almost ruined my life. She was rude, incompetent, unprofessional, and told me I was having a boy, when the baby was a girl. Thankfully, Hooper is male and was born at a far superior establishment. I wouldn't have repeated the experience and set foot in any hospital where she was a midwife.'

'I think the birth of your daughter...'

'Fleurette, that's her name.

'Yes, the birth of Fleurette was several years ago.

'Fleurette is now six.'

'Quite.' The interruptions and the names made him want to guffaw: Fleurette Carter-Monmouth, sister to Hooper Carter-Monmouth were some monikers. Would the children bless their parents when they got older, or even in Reception when they had to learn to write them!

'As we've established, your dealings with Parkside and Mrs Ederson were several years ago. Have you been in touch with her since?'

'Why in the world would I want to get in touch with that awful woman? So, to answer your question, no, thankfully no dealings with her.'

'It has come to our attention that you threatened her in the street, warned her that she would get her comeuppance.'

'That was soon after Fleurette was born, and I was still annoyed by the way I had been treated. It was a phrase that meant nothing.'

'Well, here's the problem: you made a threat and Nora Ederson ends up dead. I will ask you again, have you had any contact with her more recently?'

'No. None. I'm assuming she didn't die a natural death, and if you are insinuating that I had anything to do with that then I think I need a solicitor present.'

'As I said we are hoping to eliminate you as a person of interest.'

'It didn't mean anything. I loathed the woman but wouldn't have taken it further than a few ill-advised words.'

'If you want the services of a solicitor, this talk can be suspended until one is present. Otherwise, there are just a couple more questions.'

The silence, accompanied by an even more pronounced scowl, and a dismissive wave of a hand indicated that he could proceed.

'Could you tell us where you were on and around March 12th.'

'For goodness-sake, are you really asking me to provide an alibi? I have absolutely no idea without looking at the diary on my mobile.'

Exaggerated movements made the retrieval of the phone from her capacious handbag, the ones Serena hated saying they were ostentatious, look like a scene from a BBC drama. The movement was accompanied by dramatic sighs.

'March 12th I was in hospital, thankfully not Parkside, having an in-growing toenail removed. Not the most attractive of alibis, but as I couldn't then walk for a week, I think that removes me from your list – no doubt an extensive one if others suffered as much as I did when under her care – of suspects and I would like to go home.'

'Final question: do you know a family by the name of Winters? Gerald and Susan Winters? They live on the same estate as you.'

'It's a Garden Village, and no, I don't. Humphrey and I don't socialise locally. Now can I return to my son?'

'You did well PC Stones. That wasn't easy. What a character, no wonder Imelda remembered her. But I don't think we have our killer, and I can't see a link to the Winters, especially as they weren't in the same *social circle* as Humphrey and Delia Carter-Monmouth et al!'

'You said you mentioned to the boss that the initials might not be a person, but a way of describing them. I know DCI Tarquin wasn't keen on that idea, but I think it's a possibility, though goodness knows what they might stand for. It is worth asking Miss Simpson if Nora used acronyms when speaking of any of the ladies at Parkside? Maybe they had a secret code. At school we used B.F. for our science teacher: Bumbling Fool, he was always upsetting the chemicals and rendering the experiments useless. G.T. for a young, rather attractive, and very well-endowed English member of staff. I'll let you work that one out! And in my defence, we were fourteen.'

Laughing Serena said that she had intended to phone Imelda to let her know about the flame-breathing dragon they'd just survived. 'I will ask about any acronyms.'

Chapter 39

Susan Winters was enjoying a few peaceful days. Her parents had taken all the children and said they'd keep them as long as she wanted. She loved her family, but it was hard work on her own. She hadn't realised how much help Gerald had been. He'd overseen bedtimes and read stories and had been willing to get up in the middle of the night when one of them had a nightmare.

The marriage hadn't been all bad. Yes, he had been controlling and his constant checking had worn her out, but she had known that he cared for her and for the children, not something she knew always went with fatherhood. Some men would have walked away from the situation. If only he hadn't been so insistent on producing his heir, the boy that became the be-all-and-end-all. Each pregnancy had left her weaker; both physically and mentally, and she had begged him to be satisfied with what they had. The knowledge that as each daughter arrived, he became even more determined to have a boy, a child who really counted, had been soul destroying.

The seemingly endless washing and ironing were done and as Gerald wouldn't be coming home (she couldn't recall when she had finally accepted that) the cleaning could wait. Taking a ready meal out of the fridge she sat down and waited for the ping of the microwave. Bliss: an easy meal then some mindless television. What would her now departed husband say? Probably something along the lines of, "You need to eat sensibly, ready for the next pregnancy. We need you well for son number two." If only he'd listened when she said that with their track record it was more likely to be another girl.

It was a terrible shame about Harriet. She'd liked the girl and she had been so good with Adam. Secrets had remained hidden. If only she had stuck to that promise, she'd be here now, and they'd be enjoying the evening together. Such a terrible shame.

Harvey had been blessed with one of his neighbour's meals, left ready to heat up, the note on his kitchen table informing him that it was a casserole that needed thirty minutes in the oven. A portion of apple crumble sat beside it accompanied by a carton of double cream.

The cats had been fed, though they were hoping he didn't know that. His meal was delicious. 'I must put a note through their door, thanking them. Yes, pussies, I am talking aloud, yet again.'

All three arrived in the living room at the same time. Me and my shadows. 'If only you could help solve these murders. The humans are getting nowhere.'

An evening off had been planned. As "Dies Irae" yelled into the silence, Harvey thought of the famous Robert Burns quotation: *"The best laid schemes o' mice and men gang aft awry."*

'Good evening Harvey, as always sorry to bother you at home, but we've got another body.'

DCI Tarquin was glad he hadn't had anything stronger than tea to drink as he hurried to the alley behind the Nine-To-Nine store in the middle of town.

By the time he arrived SOCO had begun to cordon off the area and erect floodlights.

Serena was standing a few feet from the body. As he approached, he saw that she was crying. Asking if she was alright seemed like a superfluous question but greater erudition escaped him.

'Sir, oh sir, I can't believe it. Not her. She was lovely. Who'd want to kill her?'

'Who is it, Serena?'

Stumbling over her words, she mumbled, 'Imelda Simpson. Why? Why her?' Through ever increasing sobs she added, 'She told me she was coming back to Fordway, to a retirement party at Parkside, one of the midwives who was there when she was the matron. Someone must have known she'd be here, but why was she in this back alley?'

Out of the corner of his eye, Harvey saw a familiar figure approaching.

'And a good evening to all assembled, though it's not so good for some poor soul.' Alfie Morrison's jollity sounded out of place and the pathologist looked abashed when he saw Serena's face and apologised. 'Do we know who it is?'

'Imelda Simson, retired matron of Parkside Nursing Home and a close friend of Nora Ederson. She also knew the Winters' household. The lady has been helping with our enquiries.'

'Dear goodness, are *all* these deaths linked?'

'Not the time for guessing games,' Harvey tried to hide his irritation, 'we just need a time and cause of death.'

Duly chastised, Alfie walked over to the body and knelt beside it. 'Cause of death fairly obvious, heavy bleeding to her chest, probably caused by a knife, though nothing is certain before the P.M.; time very recent, I'd estimate no more than one to two hours. Who found her?'

'A couple who'd been to the supermarket and were using the alley as a short cut. Called it in straight away but didn't see anyone in the vicinity.' Serena managed to relay the information, then burst into noisy sobs. 'No bloody cameras working, I almost throttled the manager when he said he'd been meaning to fix the one in the shop's entrance.'

Apologising once again for his earlier insensitivity, he added, 'I'll be able to tell you more after the post-mortem. Shall we say 10 a.m.'

I'm sitting shaking so much my glass of wine (which I need) has slopped onto the floor. There will be a stain that I need to see to as soon as possible. I keep seeing her face as she realised what I was about to do. How easily the knife went in, and she slumped to the ground with an almost inaudible sigh. How fortuitous that I had started to carry one. It's at the bottom of the canal now.

There was no choice. None. Imelda Simpson knew too much. When we met at the supermarket's checkout she looked as though she was merely going to smile, perhaps discuss some minutiae of life, until she saw it was me. She froze and her pleasant expression vanished to be replaced by what I can only describe as terror. 'Oh, it's YOU,' she said. She knew. Everything. It was like watching a car's windscreen clear, the wipers on maximum. Full visibility restored.

Imelda Simpson, former matron of the abhorrent Parkside Nursing Home, hadn't, until that moment, made four out of two and two, hadn't linked me to the trio of deaths. It would only be a matter of time, tonight, or at the latest, tomorrow morning, before she would be hotfoot to the police. I couldn't let that happen.

How fortuitous that as she ran out of the shop, she turned left into the alley. A quiet cut-through at that time of the evening. No one about.

'These murders are all about you and your problem,' she spat at me. Problem? What an understatement. Tragedy, disaster, lifelong searing heartache nearer the mark.

That afternoon, several years ago, just before she retired, I thought, so mistakenly, that if I made her fully aware of the situation that she could be persuaded to do as I asked. She listened, made all the right noises, full of false sympathy, but the response, as with Nora Ederson a few months later, and forever afterwards, was a resounding no.

'No, I can't do as you ask. Don't bother me again and don't ask anyone else. The answer will be the same. Why you think any professional would risk their licence doing what you want is beyond me. It's both illegal and immoral.'

For weeks after that conversation, I hardly slept. I'd told her everything; far more than I needed to. What headlines the papers would have enjoyed had she gone to them. When she retired and left Fordway I felt safe.

Did she and Nora Ederson ever compare notes? It seems doubtful, no nasty follow-up. Thank goodness they are now both removed from the scene. Normal, not the word most people would use, service can be resumed.

Wordsworth Avenue was deserted. 'Just think of all the fortunate people, safe in their houses. Preparing dinner, hearing the children read, bathing the baby, or sitting with a glass of wine. Every-day normality that happens every day. Few will witness or even be aware of the things we see and deal with.'

Thanking Serena for her esoteric input, Harvey knocked at number 14. Two knocks later, he knelt-down and shouted through the letterbox: 'DCI Tarquin and DI Peil would like a word, Mrs Winters. Please open the door.' As this brought no response, Serena said, in a voice that must have carried the length of the street, that they would have to go to visit Susan's parents.

Looking annoyed, Susan opened the door. 'I have nothing to say to you. For once I was enjoying a relaxing evening. Mum and Dad have the children, so I really don't want you going round bothering them. Mum just rang so I could say goodnight to them.'

'Good evening, Mrs Winters, we just have a few things we'd like to discuss. May we come in?'

The rhetorical question was answered by a loud sigh. 'I hope this won't take long. The doctor has given me some tablets to help me sleep and I'm due to take one soon.'

Changes had been made to the lounge. The furniture had been rearranged, an extra coffee table beside the settee and pictures of the children had been put on display.

'What a handsome family you have. Who's who?' Serena knew that mothers were always ready to talk about their kids.

Appearing pleased to have been asked, Susan explained all five. 'Gerald never wanted pictures around, but I love looking at them, so I fished out one of each of them as babies and then more recent ones. Mum bought me frames when she went shopping.'

Another addition to the room was the doll which sat bolt upright in the middle of the settee. This time she was dressed in a white sleepsuit. It was without doubt the same doll they'd seen beside Gerald's body wearing a beautiful dress, then at his funeral decked out entirely in black.

As Susan sat down, she picked it up causing tears to run down both cheeks. Removing a tissue from her sleeve she wiped them away then did the same to her face, tears having appeared in sympathy with the doll's.

'I had a doll that cried,' Serena received a look from her boss that spoke volumes: we are perhaps dealing with a killer, 'and I loved filling the water receptacle behind her eyes and then making her cry.'

Susan looked blank, like a child who is not following her teacher's instructions.

'I think she's crying because she's tired. The last thing she wants is visitors so please be quick. It's almost her bedtime. Each sentence seemed like an inordinate effort.

Taking the chair directly opposite her Harvey began. 'Mrs Winters can you tell us where you were between six and eight this evening.'

'Why do you want to know that?'

'Please just answer the question, Mrs Winters.' Harvey was growing tired of her games, her seemingly endless prevarications.

'I was here. I've not been out all day. Mum said I needed to rest.' She sounded like a child who knew she would be put on the naughty step if she didn't follow Mum's orders.

'I have to ask if anyone can verify that claim.'

Susan looked puzzled and both officers thought of the many times in court when defendants, and indeed witnesses, needed questions rewording using simpler words.

'Was anyone here with you?'

'No. Mum told me to relax. Not to speak to anyone. It's been quiet without the children…and Gerald.' More tears descended, this time from Susan.

Serena said she'd make a drink and went into the kitchen. All the knives were in the block beside the microwave. None had been found at the scene, but the murder weapon could have been washed and replaced. It might have been an individual knife, not part of a set and had been put back in a drawer. Getting out an evidence bag she secured the block. A quick search through the cutlery drawer revealed two smaller knives, most probably too small, but these were also removed. A glass that had obviously contained red wine had been left on the table.

'Can you tell me exactly what your quiet evening has involved' Harvey knew he had put the question badly, another simplification required. 'What were you doing between six and eight?'

'I always watch the six o'clock news. I did some knitting, Adam needs a new jumper, he's growing so fast. The doll needed a bath and to be put into her night clothes. I watched *Law and Order*. I like it, one of my favourite programmes, I usually try to see it.'

'I don't watch it. Too near to my line of work, a busman's holiday.' There was no response, Susan not appreciating the DCI's remarks.

'And what happened in tonight's episode?'

'I can't remember. They all blur. I know they got their man.'

Harvey thought that's more than we're doing. Changing tack, he said, 'Mrs Winters, we are aware that you have experienced some difficulties in your life and that Doctor Lennon has been your doctor from birth.'

Susan blanched. Where was this going?

Harvey was delighted to see the reaction and decided to ram home the advantage. 'Earlier this evening Miss Imelda Simpson was found behind the Nine-To-Nine supermarket in the middle of town. We believe you knew her when she was the matron at Parkside Nursing Home where you gave birth to your first two daughters.'

Shaking her head so vehemently that a hair slide became dislodged, Susan said she didn't know anyone by that name.

'You gave birth at Parkside and yet you claim not to know the matron, the one in overall charge.'

Serena appeared with the drinks, giving Susan time to think.

'Parkside was horrible, and I never went back.' She sounded like a petulant child and reminded the DI of her sister's six-year-old.

'So, are you telling us that you have no memory of the matron.'

'I don't know. I might have met her, but it was a nurse who looked after me. Very badly. She wasn't English, and I found her hard to understand. It was all horrible and Gerald said I didn't need to go back there.'

'But you did go back a second time, when Abigail, I think that's your second daughter's name, was born.'

'We didn't think it could be as horrible (the word on replay) again. But it was.'

'Mrs Winters, I have to ask you if you had anything to do with Miss Simpson's murder earlier this evening.'

'No. I've been here all day. I've not been out at all. Mum told me to stay in. Now please leave as the doll and I both need to go to bed.'

Not knowing what to make of the previous forty-five minutes, Harvey and Serena sat in the car in total silence. After what felt like an eon, Harvey suggested they discussed the visit later. 'Time to go to see Mum and Dad!'

Richard Page was furious at being disturbed. 'What time do you call this? Sylvia and the children are all in bed and I was going to join them. We're shattered. Looking after five young children is hard work at our age.'

'Please will you ask your wife to join us?' The look Harvey received indicated that it was the last thing Richard wanted to do.

Ten minutes later, Sylvia walked into the lounge, light blue dressing gown fixed firmly in place.

'Mr and Mrs Page, I would like to know where you both were between six and eight this evening.'

Richard exploded; a hand grenade that has had the safety pin removed. 'What the hell now. We are being badgered, harassed to such a degree that a formal complaint will be on your superior's desk in the morning.'

Repeating his question, Harvey added, 'We can do this here, or down at the station, the choice is yours.'

'Really? You'd march us out at this time of night. We have five children asleep upstairs.'

'Well then just answer the question. Where were you this evening?'

Sylvia took over, sounding calmer than her husband. 'We've been here all day and evening. The children were happy indoors and the weather didn't make a walk or a trip to the park look very appealing.'

'Is that it?' Richard was still wound up. 'Can you leave us in peace now?'

Serena gave a quizzical glance at her boss. Neither of the Pages had asked why they wanted to know.

'There has been another murder, one that yet again has links to your family. Miss Imelda Simpson's body was found a few hours ago.'

'Who the devil is that and what in the world has it to do with our family, a unit you seem hell bent on destroying.'

'Miss Simpson was the matron at Parkside when your daughter had her first two daughters. We find it hard to believe you didn't encounter her on either occasion.'

'Well, my dear inspector, you will be most disappointed to know that that is indeed the case. No contact with a woman of that name. No knowledge of the matron at Parkside. Susan was *dealt with*, the best words I can find for her experiences there, with nurses and midwives on a much lower pay grade than the matron. Maybe if she had become involved our daughter would have had an easier time of it.'

'Mrs Park, do you have any recollection of the matron?'

'No, like my husband said poor Susan was attended to by silly, inexperienced young girls.'

Richard asked how the lady *they didn't know* had died.

Normally, Harvey wouldn't have divulged such sensitive information, but the man had riled him. 'She was stabbed in the chest.'

'And you come here accusing my wife and I of such an horrendous crime? You really think Sylvia, or I are capable of sticking a knife into someone?'

Harvey smiled, further annoying Richard, 'If you'd done my job as long as I have, you'd understand that anyone is capable of anything given the right circumstances.'

Knowing they would get no further Harvey thanked them for their time and left, Serena in his wake, ten paces behind, giving the impression of a traditional religious observance.

'What an absolute waste of time. It's obvious they knew the matron. And, if Susan had endured so *horrible* a time, they'd have been beating down Miss Simpson's door to complain. I'd like you to write up both meetings and we'll discuss them tomorrow afternoon. I should be back by then.'

Chapter 40

Some days are best forgotten.
Some days it would have been better to stay in bed.
Some days the guilt gets to you.
Some days…

Harvey was woken by Chopin head-butting him, a sign it was breakfast time. The cat had never learnt to make contact in a more genteel fashion, instead wielding the side of his head like a boxer's glove, the one intending to floor any opponent in the first round. Greig wandered into the bedroom making strange noises in his throat, a far gentler way of informing the manservant that food was overdue.

It was the day of his brother's trial, one Harvey had been dreading, the outcome inevitable. Jeremy had sounded despondent on the phone the previous evening and there had been few words available to comfort him.

Moggies fed and sitting washing themselves on their favourite chair, Harvey switched on the television. He was disappointed to see that the oh-so-jolly weatherman was delivering the forecast dressed in his wet-weather outfit of sou'wester, mackintosh, and wellingtons. An enormous umbrella was being held aloft whilst he warned, in an inappropriately cheerful voice, that storm Erika had hit land. He made the torrential rain, gale-force winds, severe flooding, and disruption to the morning commute sound like an accolade to some mischievous weather god. 'Don't forget your brollies; not that you'll be able to hold them up!' was his final rejoinder.

Disruption was the word: roads flooded, traffic diverted, rail journeys delayed or cancelled, made for frustrated people trying and failing to get to work on time. Fortunately, the DCI had left early, catching the last train to make it into Manchester Piccadilly.

The courthouse didn't look as attractive in the downpour. Jeremy had arrived before him and was sitting with his barrister, Marie Borwick, the one Harvey had recommended, in the austere waiting area. The décor was bland, the walls painted an off-white, no pictures to enhance them. Grey metal chairs were placed in small groups, all fixed to the floor. A coffee machine in the far corner informed any would-be customers that it was out of order. The pair sat looking like actors hoping for a Bafta, the one awarded for acting the part of the most miserable character.

Feeling like the Grim Reaper, and knowing he would be as welcome, Harvey approached and attempted a light-hearted good morning.

Two pairs of eyes looked up. Ms Borwick managed a smile and made a comment about the weather. Harvey was pleased to see that his brother looked healthier than the last time they'd met. At least he'd dressed for the occasion in a dark suit, white shirt and navy tie.

Over the past few weeks, Alfie Morrison had been a wonderful friend to both brothers and had spoken to Jeremy several times. Harvey had overheard one conversation. 'When the wife (he never used her name) left I took solace in alcohol. The trouble is one is not aware when one bottle leads to two or eventually more, or how one goes straight to panic mode when none is available. The morning I arrived to perform a PM bleary eyed, with the hangover from hell and hands that looked as though I'd developed Parkinson's, was the one when I knew it had to stop. That morning my assistant asked if I was OK to carry on and I thought I was. I began the procedure then dropped the scalpel: twice. I love my job, but it was that or the booze.'

Harvey believed Jeremy when he assured him the drinking had stopped. He knew his brother was hoping Ms Borwick would use the weeks of abstinence as part of his defence. Harvey was all too aware that the magistrates heard such Road to Damascus moments far too often for them to hold much sway. The damage had been done: two witnesses and CCTV footage damning evidence.

His brother had needed a lot of assistance in the weeks leading up to today: many late-night conversations and several evenings at Alfie's house, the neutral ground deemed appropriate. He had been told, in the strongest words possible, that his comment that he couldn't remember a thing about the fateful journey must not be raised in court. 'But I recall getting into the car outside the pub, then the next thing I knew the police were hammering on my front door, demanding I accompany them to the station. Can I be guilty if I wasn't aware what was happening?'

Such naivety had angered Harvey. 'You weren't aware what was *happening* as you so euphemistically call it because you were totally impaired by drink. I hate to be the harbinger of bad news, but you must prepare for the almost certain fact that you will be spending time in prison.'

'Is that what you think I deserve?'

The silence spoke volumes.

What would our mother make of it? Would she blame me? Was I not strict enough when he was a teenager? Over the years, have I not been supportive enough? These and other maudlin thoughts accompanied Harvey as he returned to Fordway, the delayed train standing room only, the commuters complaining about the dreadful service that almost ground to a halt at the first sign of inclement weather.

Phoning Alfie as soon as he got in, he was horrified to realise that tears were cascading down his face. Controlling his voice, he told his friend of the horrific hour in court. 'They threw a whole shelf of books at him! Twenty-six weeks in custody: the maximum, followed by a long disqualification when he gets out. The chairman, someone I hadn't seen before, said he was handing down the full tariff for three reasons: his breathalyser readings were in the top bracket; he had nearly knocked down two people, an elderly lady and her daughter, who by his own admission he didn't recall even seeing on the crossing proving that there had been an unacceptable level of driving; and finally, his lack of remorse.

'Jeremy didn't do himself any favours. He came across as arrogant and kept saying he hadn't actually hurt anyone. "I was a bit over the limit, but I'm not the only one who has ever driven when they've had a drink. I got home safely, parked the car in the drive and was indoors when the police arrived."

'I could see his barrister wincing. She made the most of the fact he has stopped drinking and the chairman did acknowledge that, but as he said, "Had you done that a few months ago, you would not be here today, and two ladies would still feel confident crossing the road."

'So, Alfie, even with good behaviour, which I'm not sure he can manage, he'll be in prison for over three months.'

'Let's hope it's the making of him. His boss has said he'll keep his job open which is something. Now, my dear friend, you must, and I do mean must, forget today. Back to finding a murderer then you and I will go to the new Indian that's just opened on Prospect Street.'

Thanking the pathologist for all his support he ended the call, fed the duo (why were they always hungry?) and phoned Serena to apologise for not making it into the station. 'One hell of a day here, hope yours was better. Fill me in tomorrow.'

He hoped whoever once said, "Tomorrow is another day," had got it right.

Chapter 41

The morning news was full of a terrorist attack in London: a lorry full of explosives driven into a café, ten dead and many injured. No one had claimed responsibility, but the driver had been known to the police and had been under surveillance for several months. Great, thought Harvey, Joe Public will be castigating them for not locking him up and throwing away the key. The *Daily Mail* will have the proverbial field day. When the next news item was the rise in knife crime, the year's figures just released, he switched off the radio and made an extra slice of toast. Dear God, he thought, is that the best I can do to cheer myself up and prepare for another frustrating day. Even the cats have gone out and left me to it.

Walking into the incident room, he was pleased to see that a picture of Imelda Simpson had been added to the display board. Someone was ready to investigate the senseless killing of the old lady. It was a particularly flattering one, taken at her retirement do a few years ago. In it she appeared to be happy and relaxed, no doubt looking forward to a well-earned change of lifestyle in the Lake District.

Morning briefing was a sombre affair. 'Another murder, making four, and we're no nearer to solving any of them.'

Officers had been out conducting house-to-house interviews in the area around the supermarket. The alley where Imelda had been stabbed ran between the rear entrances of two parallel rows of houses. The staff at the Nine-To-Nine store had also been interviewed.

Serena was still criticising the lack of CCTV evidence. 'None at the front of the store or in the back alley. We did look at footage from the cameras placed further inside the store and Imelda can be seen putting chocolate in her basket, but no interaction with anyone is caught on camera.'

Dispatching a happy looking Edward Stones to attend the post-mortem, he asked Serena to update Clare on the meetings they had *enjoyed* with Susan Winters and her parents. 'Meetings isn't quite the word, but definitely not interviews; far too one-sided. That family could represent England on how to avoid tricky questions: employ never-ending silences, plead ignorance, misunderstand the question, get angry, say it's their bedtime, ask us to leave, threaten to make a complaint. They're all loopy and are playing us for fools. Enough. Time for a concerted attack. And I use that word advisedly.'

'Sir, Imelda was in Fordway for a retirement party. She was staying with her friend Janine Mortice for a few days. When I phoned Janine yesterday to tell her the awful news she was devastated. I said I'd go and see her this morning. I hope that's all right with you, sir.'

'Yes. Whilst you do that, Clare and I will speak to Doctor Lennon again. We need to get to the bottom of the paradox that is Susan Winters. We'll make it formal this time. It's far too late for him to hide behind the doctor/patient confidentiality nonsense. He needs to tell us all he knows about her and that cuckoo family! That's probably being rude to the birds, though they have some most unattractive traits.'

'Thank you for attending, Doctor. We asked you to come into the station as we think the time has come to take it all a tad more seriously. We understand your reluctance to talk about a patient, but we are now dealing with four murders; four people involved closely with Susan Winters. Two nights ago, the former matron at Parkside was murdered. Mrs Winters has links to Parkside having given birth there twice. Her husband, nanny and a midwife at Parkside are also dead. So, you see our problem.'

Looking most uncomfortable, Doctor Lennon mumbled about the need for confidentiality.

'No. Sorry that time has passed. Mrs Winters is a suspect in all four murders, so please tell us everything you can about her. Everything and anything which may aid our investigation.'

'I'm not happy, not happy at all about this. Susan Winters is an extremely troubled young woman who needs sympathy, not judgement.'

'We are not asking you to judge her, but anything you say might be helpful and will, of course, be treated as confidential.'

After a long pause, the doctor looking around the room as if he could find the words he needed written on the walls, began. 'You may or may not know that Susan was adopted.' Clare and Harvey glanced at each other; it was something they hadn't known.

'Her birth mother was an alcoholic and heroin user. When a baby is born to a mother who is an addict the baby starts life with the drug in their system. Almost every drug is passed from the mother to the foetus's blood stream during pregnancy, so the baby enters the world, not addicted in the usual sense, but with enough of the drug in their system to cause great problems. It's horrific to see the uncontrollable trembling, high-pitched crying and unsightly blotchy skin of those born having ingested heroin.

'The baby has withdrawal symptoms which include tremors, diarrhoea, fever, irritability, seizures and difficulty with breathing and feeding. They require an extensive stay in hospital to help them get better. I'm telling you this to give you some idea of how Susan started life.

'Unfortunately, the problems don't end once the baby has had the toxins removed. Long term effects include difficulty focussing and controlling behaviour. Fine motor skills and developmental delays are common. They are almost always behind their peers at school, both emotionally and in terms of academic progress.

'Richard and Sylvia Page were, and continue to be, wonderful parents who have dealt with a myriad of problems over the years. They have no doubt told you how fantastic Susan was as a child, that everything took a nose-dive when Gerald came on the scene. That is not the case.

'Susan found academic work almost impossible and was in the Special Needs' groups at school. She was often in trouble for misbehaving and the Pages were regularly hauled into school to discuss the way forward. She did, however, excel at games. Strange as motor control is often an issue with these children. At home she *played up*, a phrase I remember her father using.

'Over the years I have seen Susan on many occasions. She suffered from anxiety as a child, felt ostracised at school, and of course endured the usual childhood illnesses. But Richard and Sylvia are correct when they say that things deteriorated even further once she met Gerald. The main problem has been all the pregnancies. Some women, and Susan is one of them, are not well during pregnancy. It doesn't suit them. She suffered from terrible sickness, the all-day kind, and on each occasion her blood pressure gave cause for concern. None of the births was straightforward or easy and each time she was left with the mind-altering post-natal depression.'

The pause was so long the listeners wondered if he was going to add anything.

Looking embarrassed, he studied the far wall, the little eye-contact there had been had vanished. After extremely traumatic labours, I cannot emphasise that too strongly, poor Susan was left to cope, Gerald Winters didn't want to let her parents help. She stopped attending the surgery but there were frequent telephone calls. She was always paranoid that there was something wrong.'

Another prolonged silence, Harvey giving Clare a look that said wait.

'Susan Winters is one of the most disturbed women I have ever seen. She has severe psychiatric problems and unusual fantasies which have never been addressed. Not for want of trying on my part. However, I believe she is a sad soul; not a murderer.'

Harvey smiled, 'If I had a pound for every time someone expresses genuine shock when a kind, considerate neighbour, a pillar of the community, or the most loyal friend, does just that, I'd be a rich man.

Unfortunately, Susan Winters knew all four people who died and although a motive is eluding us, she is linked to each one.'

'I'm genuinely sorry to hear that. Susan is the keeper of a secret that if exposed would almost certainly end her already threadbare relationship with reality. She has dealt with it in her own way for almost eight years, a fact that others would find hard to believe.'

'Are you able to divulge that secret?'

'No, and I don't think it would aid your investigation.'

'I'd like to be the judge of that. In my work one never knows what tiny detail might break a case.'

'Chief Inspector, our jobs are similar in some ways: we both hear and see things that we must keep to ourselves, rather like a priest in the confessional.'

'You probably won't agree, but I've always believed that there are occasions when a man of the cloth is duty-bound to disclose what he's heard.'

'As you said, I don't agree. People have to be able to confess all, knowing their secrets will remain hidden.'

'Just one more question, doctor. You don't think Mrs Winters is capable of murder; would you say the same about the Pages?'

'Richard and Sylvia have been exemplary parents. When they adopted Susan, they knew she would have problems, but they can't have envisaged how extreme those problems would be, or what a toll it would take on them. They have stood by their daughter and supported her throughout. They will be all too aware that should they be imprisoned Susan wouldn't cope without them. So, I very much doubt they are your killers.'

Thanking the doctor for his time and the details he had supplied, Harvey showed him out.

Thirty minutes later, having listened to the taped discussion twice, Harvey and Clare sat through a prolonged silence.

Looking as puzzled as she felt, DS Jennings started the conversation. 'I'm not sure what to make of that, sir. I think he was being as honest as he felt he could be, but...'

'But indeed! Are we ever, in this damned case, going to end an interview knowing we've been told the whole caboodle, the entire and unexpurgated facts? The truth.'

'Susan is obviously even more disturbed than we thought. If she is guilty, we know where she'll be spending the rest of her life: Broadmoor!'

Harvey stood, the pins and needles from having sat too long bothering him. 'What in the world did the good doc mean by a secret? Everyone has those but he thought this one to be so important that should it get out, it would prove life changing. Life changing enough to commit four murders?'

Chapter 42

A few miles away, Richard and Sylvia Page were keen to escape the confines of the house. Five youngsters incarcerated indoors was making the house feel claustrophobic.

Still in a foul mood after the unwelcome visit two nights ago, Richard was prowling the kitchen, a predator seeking its prey. 'Calm down, Richard and for God's sake let's get out, take the children to the seaside. Susan is never keen on them going, afraid of all the germs that she thinks are just waiting to pounce.'

'Better than staying here all day, waiting for yet another visitation. The weather's improved, so we could take a picnic, let them have a traditional day on Blackpool beach: sandcastles, paddling and candy floss.'

Sylvia was relieved to hear some levity in her husband's voice and said she'd get the children ready, if he'd do the sandwiches. 'It's a treat for Adam, he was too young to appreciate the seaside the last time we took them.'

'Shall I phone Susan and see if she wants to come?' Richard hoped the answer would be no but felt he should ask.

'She needs more time to herself, a complete rest, and if we tell her we're going she'll only spend the day thinking something horrendous is going to happen. It was jellyfish last time they went anywhere near the water. I'm so worried about her, she's not coped well since Gerald died. I thought she'd be O.K. that she would feel relieved without his constant monitoring of her every move.'

'Give it time, Sylvia, give it time.'

PC Stones returned to the station in an upbeat mood. 'I don't think I'll ever get over seeing the inside of the human body; utterly fascinating. What a work of art – and science – we are.'

'Thank you, young Edward (Harvey realised that was an inappropriate form of address; somewhat patronising). Sorry, PC Stones, what happened at the post-mortem?'

'Alfie Morrison will send the full report later today but asked me to tell you that death occurred due to a deep knife wound in Miss Simpson's chest which lacerated her heart. The knife was plunged in a long way, then removed causing severe bleeding. Time of death between six and eight yesterday evening. She was in good health for someone of her age. As Alfie said, "She should have died hereafter. There would have been a time for such a word." I think the pathologist was impressed when I knew that was the beginning of Macbeth's Soliloquy. I studied the play for A level.'

'I never realised PMs could be such fun or include Shakespeare!' Fortunately, Harvey smiled as he said it.

Serena's entrance was far more sombre, tears not far away. 'Janine told me she met Imelda at Preston station on the morning she was killed, and they stayed in the town to go shopping and have lunch. Once back at home they sat and chatted, and Janine was pleased that her friend was more relaxed than she'd seen her for a long time. Just after the six o'clock news Imelda said she'd go to the Nine-To-Nine to buy some chocolate. It seems that she loved sweet things and Janine said when she was the matron at Parkside there was always a supply of bars of chocolate and fudge (her favourite) in her drawer. She's incredibly upset and can't think of a reason for anyone to hurt Imelda.'

'That's the problem with each of these murders: no motive, or at least not one we can see. My first boss always said, "Find the motive; find the murderer." The first case I worked on was a man in his early fifties who'd been hit over the head with a huge frying pan. Nothing else was awry in the kitchen, but the pan was streaked with blood and had been left on the floor. There were fingerprints, but not in the system.

'No suspects. No motive. The wife and grown-up children all had cast-iron alibis as did his friends and neighbours. He was, by all accounts an upstanding citizen, not even a speeding ticket to his name. He was an accountant and his colleagues spoke of a kind, gentle soul. He even did voluntary work at the local hospice.

'So, we were stymied, a word the boss used when it was like walking through treacle. Then, several weeks later the man's wife came into the station with a letter. She'd found it in a box of old memorabilia she hadn't known about. It was thirty years out of date and was from a woman who had been abandoned by Martin Jones, I've just remembered his name, and left her pregnant. Fortunately, we could trace the woman in the letter as she had a most unusual surname: Bukowski, Polish, I think, and she was still at the address on the letter.

'She'd had the baby, a boy called Oliver, and she said he'd recently become obsessed with knowing who his father was. She'd not included Martin Jones on the birth certificate, but as her son was so insistent, she gave in and told him the name. When Oliver went to meet his dad, to say the least, it didn't go well. Mr Jones wanted nothing to do with him and told him to leave and not come back. That must have hurt, and Martin picked up the pan and hit the man he wanted to be his father.

'We had motive and the assailant in one fell swoop. Another saying I got used to hearing!'

Clare fidgeted, unsure how to ask her question. 'Sir, are we looking for one motive that covers all four murders, or do you think each one has an individual trigger?'

Before he could answer there was a knock on his office door and a young PC stood waiting to come in.

'DCI Tarquin, I'm PC Belinda Taverstock. I was asked to return to the Nine-To-Nine store to ascertain if anyone had remembered anything pertaining to the incident.' Harvey realised the young woman was nervous, making her sound like a training manual.

Remembering how intimidating it was to speak to a senior officer he asked her to sit down and tell him what she had discovered (he managed not to repeat ascertained).

'I've got a witness statement from a Mrs Corrine Verdun. She works part time at the supermarket and was on duty from five to nine that night. I asked her to come into the station and she gave a witness statement which she signed. I hope that's OK.'

Assuring the young woman that she'd done a good job, Harvey asked to see it.

Witness Statement by Corrine Verdun, taken by PC Belinda Taverstock

I was working on the tills at the Nine-To-Nine two nights ago. I was on the till nearest the exit door and had just served an old lady who had bought three bars of chocolate. It was 6.35, I know the time as I'd just looked at my watch, the shift going slowly. As she walked towards the exit she stopped suddenly and yelled, "Oh, it's YOU," very loudly. She sounded scared and couldn't wait to leave the shop.

The other lady followed her out. Sorry, but I didn't get a good look at her as she had her back to me. I think she was wearing a dark jacket, but again I'm not a hundred per cent sure. Her hood was up so I didn't get a look at her hair. All I know is that the old lady was shocked when she saw her, looked as though she'd seen a ghost, or someone from the past she wasn't expecting to meet, and from the look of things didn't want to. She almost ran out of the shop door and turned in the direction of the back alley and the other woman followed her. If only I'd known what was going to happen, I'd have called security.

Corrine Verdun

'That's really helpful PC Taverstock. It gives us a precise time for the murder and tells us that the perpetrator (likely to be the person who followed Miss Simpson out of the shop) is female. Thank you very much, and for bringing it to our attention so quickly.' Serena was impressed by her boss's words; maybe he was learning the value of praising the younger officers.

Once the PC had left, looking as if she'd just been awarded an Olympic gold medal, they knew the field of suspects had been narrowed.

Harvey looked as though he was thinking aloud: 'Someone she knew; someone who frightened her; someone she wasn't expecting to see.'

'Or, sir, someone who knew Imelda had to be silenced. I've been thinking about what Clare said earlier about motives. We have four different victims: a well-respected professional; a midwife; a nanny and now a retired matron. Are we looking at *separate* motives or is it the *same* for all of them?' Serena looked round the room as if the answer might be suspended in the air.

Edward Stones cleared his throat, the nervous gesture he tried to control before speaking. 'I know I'm the least experienced here, but I think there's a motive that is common to all four. Did they all need to be silenced? Did they all know the secret that the doctor alluded to, the one that would force The Fall of the House of Winters?'

'More A Level reading, Edward? I seem to recall being terrified of *The Fall of the House of Usher*. Anything by Edgar Allan Poe had me hiding behind the settee!'

Goodness, two plaudits in a morning, I wonder what the boss is on. Instead of saying that aloud, Serena agreed with Edward. 'The cases are too linked; I believe we have one cold-blooded killer who believes it is vital to stop whatever is going on seeing the light of day.'

'Clare, are you of the same opinion?'

'Yes and no. Not helpful I know. I can see how it might be one killer, but each of our victims was murdered in a different way. Gerald Winters was given an overdose...Nora Ederson was pushed and hit her head...Harriet Devizes was made to suffer an anaphylactic shock...and Imelda Simpson was killed with a knife. The last one seems to be the odd one out. Far more violent.'

'Thank you all for your inputs. For the moment let's go with one motive. That means all four victims are linked. We know Imelda and Nora worked together at the Nursing Home, the one where Susan Winters had her first two babies. That is also the link to her husband. Harriet Devizes worked for the Winters. We know that Susan has psychiatric problems, but that's evident and hardly hidden away, so doesn't sound like a motive for murder.'

A pause allowed Edward to speak. 'We know Mrs Ederson felt threatened by someone she referred to as C.M. and her diary entries show this was the case over several years. I also got the feeling that the nanny was under some sort of duress not to talk to us. However, I can't see Gerald Winters being told to be the keeper of secrets, doesn't sound like him at all. He was a top man at his bank and according to his in-laws an overbearing character. That leaves Miss Simpson. The only threats she received have been dealt with and we know the sender of those isn't on our list of suspects.'

'Well team...who is?'

Chapter 43

Nothing on the television and she wasn't much of a reader: Susan was bored and scared. Silence ruled, a most unusual phenomenon. Five children filled the house with action and sound and Susan was ready for them to return. Used to every waking minute being devoted to her family, she found her own company unwelcome and needed a distraction. There was too much time to think. Beds were all changed, the sheets, pillows and duvet-covers washed, ironed and put away. Everything was spotless, even Gerald would have approved. Cakes had been baked and the weekly delivery from Sainsbury's put in pristine rows in the cupboards in date order.

She knew her life was at a crossroads. Gerald had been the rock she clung to. He had kept the secret and maintained the status quo. With him gone the fear was it would all become public knowledge. The whole charade exposed. The future annihilated.

House-to-house reports from the back alley continued to arrive on Harvey's desk. One couple said they'd heard noises at just gone half past six coming from the alley, someone sounding angry, but they couldn't make out the words. They had been in the kitchen at the back of their house but when they went outside the noise had stopped and they thought no more about it.

Unfortunately, they didn't open the back gate, so were unaware there had been an assault.

'Youths use the alley as a meeting place, away from prying eyes. They like to smoke and drink there. We did call the police once when they got rowdy, but we usually leave them to it; we aren't that old that we can't remember the need to experiment and have some fun. Trouble is, we often have to clear up after them: empty bottles, cigarette packets and occasionally syringes that they can't be bothered to take with them.'

Two other couples had heard "a commotion" but in both cases they thought it was people arguing "the way you do".

Once Imelda and the other unidentified woman had left the supermarket no one recalled seeing them.

'Sir, there's a phone call I think you'll want to take.' Clare had walked straight into the office without knocking.

'Put it through, DS Jennings. You could have done so without barging in.'

Making himself calm down he picked up the phone on the fifth ring. 'Good morning, DCI Tarquin here.'

'I'm sorry to bother you Chief Inspector and it might be nothing,' Harvey waited for the but, 'but I believe you are in overall charge of the investigation into the murders in Fordway. Do hope you are making headway. Anyway, the reason I'm calling is that we had a serious incident late last night which might be linked to your enquiries. Sorry, I should have introduced myself: DI John Green. I'm stationed in Preston, very near to you, but I don't think we've met.

'Just before midnight last night, two people were knocked down in a hit-and-run on Richmond Avenue on the outskirts of Preston. An eyewitness said it looked deliberate, the car mounting the pavement and aiming straight at them then escaping at speed. Hard to believe anyone would use a car as a weapon, but it has been known. Unfortunately, one woman died at the scene and her companion, another lady, is in hospital. She's stable but has several broken bones and rather a serious head injury.

'So far, you're thinking it's got nothing to do with you...however, here's where it might have. I remember hearing that you were interested in Parkside Nursing Home, you know how gossip spreads, and both our victims were nurses who now work at the Royal Preston Hospital but who completed their training at Parkside. Last night they had finished a late shift and were almost back at the house they share.

'The interesting fact is that a witness is adamant that it *was* a deliberate manoeuvre, the car swerving onto the pavement and accelerating, giving the unfortunate pair no chance to get out of the way. It was, as per usual, an elderly man taking his dog for a final stroll who saw it happen. He was extremely distressed when he came in this morning and the PC who spoke to him last night said the man was so upset that he sent for the police doctor to give him a sedative.

'We've appealed for other witnesses. No one so far. When we say there was a fatality it might encourage others to come forward. The driver of the car that followed the killer's must have seen something. With any luck he had a dash-cam fixed and can show us the relevant footage. Hopefully, that would provide us with a number plate, though when does one get that lucky?'

'Do you have the names of the victims? It's definitely interesting that they trained at Parkside, which seems to link our four murders.'

'Four? You've had another?'

'Yes, two nights ago, about half past six. The details haven't been released to the press yet and the gossip tom-toms are obviously not beating loudly enough to reach Preston! Our latest victim was a retired matron from the nursing home and that place is looking more and more like the link. There's very little else connecting them, but your news is of interest.'

'Morag Clerihew was the unfortunate soul who was killed instantly, and her friend is Jo Harris. As I said she's in rather a bad way. Parents of both women have been informed and are on their way here as we speak. Nothing worse than losing a child and in such an abhorrent way. If they can help us with the names of anyone their daughters had fallen out with, especially recently: ex boyfriends, patients, neighbours, we'll let you know. We'll also ask about their time at Parkside.'

Thanking the DI for the information, he called Clare into his office, told her the details of the phone call and asked her to go to the nursing home. 'Take Edward Stones with you and get as much information as possible on the two young women who were mown down. They probably didn't know Imelda Simpson, after her time, but if they trained at Parkside recently, they would have come into contact with Nora Ederson. I remember someone mentioning how good she was with the newer members of staff. I'm not asking Serena to go as she is still upset; she was very fond of the old woman.'

Despondency: that was the word that described the journey to the nursing home, both officers afraid of what they might discover. 'We need to keep an open mind; these latest victims might have nothing to do with our enquiries.' Clare hoped that was the case.

'But if they do, it might be the breakthrough we need.' For the first time that morning Clare smiled. He really was so incredibly naïve. She wished she had retained his optimism.

The receptionist gave them a look that could have frozen hell. 'I'm not sure if matron will have the time to see you this morning.'

'She must and she will. Please let her know we're here.'

Half an hour later the two officers were shown into Petra Morton's office, her greeting no warmer than the receptionists had been. Told they had precisely fifteen minutes before "an extremely important meeting", she looked surprised when the DS said their business was far more important.

Why were so many people unwilling to respond positively to a visit from the police? Surely, the woman sitting fidgeting had nothing to hide.

Aware that she needed to remain cool, calm, and collected, a favourite phrase her mother had employed ad nauseam during her daughter's teenage years, Clare explained the reason for their unscheduled visit.

'Oh, dear God, not more deaths. I heard about Imelda. I know someone who works at the Nine-to Nine, and now those poor, poor, girls. Sorry, that's not the best word but they were so young they seemed like girls to me. Morag Clerihew and Jo Harris were with us as trainee midwives last year. They were both excellent at the job and had we been recruiting we would have been more than happy to keep them on. We supplied excellent references and they both went to work in Preston.' The matron was speaking quietly, shock making her stop after every sentence.

'Did Mrs Ederson have anything to do with their training?'

Looking at the computer, the matron said she'd have to ask someone more au fait with the latest technology to give them what they wanted. 'It was only installed last week and apart from the obvious I'm finding it hard to access information speedily.'

Whilst they waited for the data expert to appear, Clare asked if there had been any incidents during their time at Parkside.

'Incidents? Incidents? I'm not sure what you mean.'

'Did either of them receive any complaints, from staff or patients? Did anything go wrong when they were assisting with a birth?'

This time there was no hesitation. 'No, as I said they were superb trainees, the kind the profession needs; passed their courses gaining top marks. They were based in Lancaster, at the University of Cumbria, and were with us for their final placement. They came by bus, the one from Lancaster to Preston that goes all round the earth. After a late shift they would have to stay at the nurses' home, the last bus leaving too early. Some trainees we've had come into work with a hangover or miss days for the weakest of reasons. Not them, they were utterly professional.'

Clare wondered if they were being made to sound like paragons; no one liking to speak ill of the dead.

Ten minutes later a woman in scrubs arrived, pressed the appropriate buttons, and gave Clare a printout of the trainee nurses' time at Parkside.

Thanking the matron for her time and apologising again for being the bearers of such bad news, Clare asked her to contact them if she thought of anything else.

As they approached the exit, soothing music and thick carpeting making the area feel like a bijou hotel rather than a place of blood and placentas, they were surprised to see the computer nerd following them.

'Can I have a quick word, maybe outside? There's a quiet garden that's not overlooked.'

The garden was as beautiful as everything else to do with the Home.

Obviously uncomfortable, the midwife spoke in sentences where each word appeared to be chosen with the utmost care. 'There's something I need to tell you that's not in the records you've just received. It's to do with Morag Clerihew. One day, not long after she started, she was on duty with Nora. In fact, Mrs Ederson was always acting as her mentor. The one named in the records, Florence Jones, was off as per normal, with one of her *illnesses*, the ones mostly in her head (she left us six months ago by mutual agreement) and that day something went wrong. Nora had gone to check on the delivery Jo was assisting with and left Morag to deliver the baby as it looked straightforward. Trainees are not supposed to be left unsupervised, but Nora said afterwards that she only left for two minutes. We were short-staffed and every baby chose that day to arrive.

'Unfortunately, the cord was around the baby's neck and Morag didn't notice. It's very common but can be serious and when Morag became aware - rather too late - she panicked. She should have slipped her finger in to disentangle the nuchal cord but didn't. The danger is that the blood flow to the baby decreases the longer the cord is around the neck and the brain doesn't receive sufficient oxygen. The baby was born, but with life-long problems.

'The parents demanded an inquiry and Nora took the blame. I remember her saying if she let Morag admit her mistake it could end her career before it had begun. I remember her comment: "And she's too good for the profession to lose." Mrs Ederson was suspended during the investigation which took weeks, then cleared of any wrongdoing. I think the fact she was so experienced helped. The two became close after that and on occasion Morag and Jo stayed with Nora after a late shift. I don't know if that's of any use, but the incident was never recorded in Morag's notes.'

'Can you recall the names of the parents?'

'Mr and Mrs Wright. They moved to Spain soon after the birth to be near her mother who's a doctor. They'll need a lot of help with the child.'

'Our Nora wasn't the angel people have been making her out to be. What she did was unprofessional, probably for good reasons but still reprehensible.'

'Trouble is, Edward, we're not the morals police. All that matters is whether her death and last night's hit-and-run are linked.'

DCI Tarquin was lost in his Impressionists, the prints on three of the four walls, causing one visitor to remark that his office was more like an art gallery than a policeman's workplace, one where the horrendous misdemeanours of people were discussed. He stood in front of his print of *The Yellow House* painted in 1888. It was one of his favourites. He knew the painter had rented part of the house in Arles for 15 francs a month. He had spent time furnishing it, the result being a series of bedroom paintings. The house had been destroyed by bombing in the Second World War, a sad end to a beautiful building.

Standing stock still he wondered if things ever changed? The beauty, emotion and colour in Van Gogh's paintings wasn't enough to stop his life-long struggles with mental illness, (he spent time in an asylum) and grinding poverty. He had been virtually unknown in his lifetime, a fact Harvey found tragic. However, he thought, his legacy lives on. Unfortunately, that was also true of the things he dealt with: the wrongs perpetrated by the guilty altering innocent lives forever.

Why am I thinking about one of the great painters when I should be working on the case, the one with an ever-increasing number of victims? It's easier, that's why.

Did the woman never knock? Clare barged in and sat opposite her boss, Edward entering in a more respectful manner. 'Our Mrs Ederson was in trouble and it was all to do with Morag Clerihew.'

'And a second good morning to you, DS Jennings. Would you like to begin again, or shall we ask PC Stones to do the honours?'

Duly chastised, Clare took a few deep breaths and gave a summary of their morning, finishing with, 'So, sir, not only did both Morag and Jo know Nora Ederson, but she acted as their mentor, and got Morag out of trouble.'

'So, there is a link, and we need to see whether last night's hit-and-run has anything to do with our investigation. Edward, see what you can find about the two girls, sorry women, involved and Clare and I will pay yet another visit to Susan Winters. We need to know if she knew either of them, be interesting to see how she reacts when we say their names? Serena can have the pleasure of asking the Pages the same question. She can wear her bullet-proof vest.'

Houses with young children tend to be noisy and as they approached the Winters' house it was obvious the children had returned. Raucous sounds were emanating through the open windows. 'Will they hear the doorbell? My friend's house was like this. She was the oldest of seven, yes seven, children and I could never get over the noise. I'm sure Bedlam was calmer.'

It took three rings before the door was opened. Susan stood looking aghast; visitors unwelcome. Bedlam would indeed have been quieter, the children obviously squabbling and hurling abusive comments at each other.

'I hope you won't be long. As you can hear the children are restless (a euphemism) and I need to see to them. They're supposed to be doing some schoolwork, so I'll just pop up and quieten them. Seconds later the raucous cacophony was replaced with laughter and amusement. 'She's obviously got a magic wand up there or can cast a let's-behave-we've-got-company-spell. When I had to be on my best behaviour, I was promised a late bedtime which worked. Funny to think that nowadays I long for my head to hit the pillow.'

Giving the DS a look that said let's concentrate Harvey led the way into the lounge. More photographs had appeared and now covered most of the walls. Before either could comment, Susan walked in, going straight to the settee and picking up the doll that sat on the central cushion. Same doll: new outfit. Today she had on a white blouse and grey skirt, making her look much older. As she was picked up, she began to cry, tears rolling down her cheeks.

'She's not used to visitors, though I thought she'd be alright now the children are settled upstairs.'

'Your parenting skills are most impressive. We hear that peace has been restored.'

Looking blank, Susan stood so still she hardly seemed to be breathing and asked what they wanted.

Harvey wasn't in the mood to waste words. 'Mrs Winters, we know you had your first two children at Parkside.'

Butting in Susan yelled, 'Yes and I wish you'd stop going on and on and on about it. I hated the place and never went back. Just the thought of it makes me feel unwell. Lara, Esther, and Adam were all born at home, in this house. Now I'd like you to leave, you're upsetting me and if I get upset it bothers the doll and the children.'

'We are very sorry to upset you, but we are now pursuing another line of enquiry.' The look he received told him she hadn't understood a word. 'The names of two young midwives have come to our attention (still too complicated). We wondered if Jo Harris or Morag Clerihew were names you are familiar with, that you know. Did either of them come here to assist in your home births?'

'No. My midwife was an older woman, very experienced, Gerald insisted that I had the best.'

'Do you know her name?' He didn't add that they would be contacting her.

'Gerald dealt with all that and when you give birth you don't really care about a name. She was lovely and very caring, but I haven't seen her since. I think she was from down south as she had a posh accent. I do know it wasn't either of the ones you said. Jo someone and...'

'Jo Harris and Morag Clerihew.'

Deciding a different tack was needed, Clare commented on the array of photographs that adorned three of the walls. 'I see you've added more pictures of the children.'

Looking nonplussed at the change of direction, Susan said, 'Gerald wasn't keen on photos on the walls, but I love them. I like looking at them when the children are in bed. Makes me feel close to them.'

'You've presented them in a clever way, each of the children shown in their own montage, from baby stage through to now. I know they don't go to school, but the photos look like the ones taken professionally at school. My school always organised a day when we had to look smart, ties straight and hair combed. The photos were taken in time for Christmas, so they could be sent to grandparents inside the festive cards. The more I look at them, the more they impress me. Someone's good with the camera. My pictures are often skew-whiff or out of focus.'

As no further comment was forthcoming, Harvey thanked the woman, who was now standing shaking, for her time. 'If you think of the name of your midwife, please give us a ring.'

Once back in the car they agreed that the names hadn't meant anything to Susan. 'Pity Gerald isn't here; he was obviously the one in charge.'

'Well, sir, if he were still with us, we wouldn't be pursuing four murders!'

318

As they drove away, Clare commented that the noise the children made was unusual. 'When we heard them, they went from fortissimo to pianissimo in a matter of seconds. I had piano lessons when I was young, and I can still recall the Italian directions ff and pp. Can't play a note now.' Stopping to consider what words to employ, she added, 'It's still strange for young children to go from one extreme to the other so quickly.'

Serena returned to the station a few minutes after Harvey and Clare. Convening in his office, the DCI asked Serena if the Pages had been any help.

'None, sir. The names Jo Harris and Morag Clerihew meant nothing to them and for once I believed them. They said that Gerald had taken charge of everything to do with the last three births: ante-natal visits at home with the midwife he'd employed, arrangements for the older children to go to their house as the pregnancy progressed, and the midwife present in good time to "oversee", apparently his word, the birth. Once again they called him "overbearing and a control freak" but they said in his defence - there's a first time for everything - that he had employed a very experienced midwife.'

'Susan Winters gave us the same information. The hit-and-run in Preston might be connected to Parkside, but it doesn't look as though the two young women had anything to do with the Winters.'

Edward Stones had little to add. He'd spent the morning trawling through phone records and social media sites. Neither woman had been in trouble with the police and their social media profiles showed two people with everything to live for. Their texts, emails and tweets were full of anecdotes from work and their nights spent having fun. Photos had been updated regularly and showed the youngsters enjoying life.

Phoning his colleague in Preston, Harvey updated him.

John Green had spoken to both sets of parents. 'Naturally, they are devastated. Neither could think of anyone who would wish to do their daughter harm. Jo had broken up with a long-term boyfriend recently, but Mrs Harris was sure it had been amicable. "It was one of those relationships that had run its course."

We've got CCTV footage which shows last night's incident and I've got one of my techno wizards (we all need one of those) to enhance it. He's hopeful that the number plate might become legible. I'll keep you informed.'

Chapter 44

The phone was answered on the second ring. 'Mum, the police have been here again. They asked about the midwife, the one who was here when I had the babies at home.'

'Yes, Susan, calm down. They've been here as well and asked the same question. Were you honest with them?'

'I told them I didn't know either of the names they said and that I couldn't remember the name of my midwife. I wish Gerald were here, he'd be able to deal with them. They seemed to be talking about a young midwife and I told them mine was an old lady. Did I do the right thing? I'm scared, I'm sure they're working it all out.'

'We said the same and it's a hundred percent true. I'm sure they're not interested in your midwife she's got nothing to do with any of this.'

'But what if they track her down; they're like bloodhounds following a scent.'

'They won't. Only your husband knew who she was and let's face it, even if they did talk to her what could she possibly tell them?'

'She was here for well over twenty-four hours each time, so she knows enough.'

'No one is going to work it out. Now I'll come and take you all out. It's a lovely day and I'll bring a picnic.

Be there in an hour. Stop worrying, it's all going to be OK.'

'John Green from Preston on the line for you, sir.'

'Me again, Harvey. We've, well I had nothing to do with it so it's the royal "we", have managed to read the number plate on the hit-and-run car. It belongs to someone called West, Trevor West. He lives in Fordway. Does the name mean anything to you?'

'Nothing springs immediately to mind. Has he got a criminal record?'

'Indeed, he has. If it was him driving last night - the techno wizard is still trying to enhance the video to let us identify the driver - he's doubly in trouble: disqualified from driving at Lancaster Magistrates' Court two weeks ago. I'm coming to Fordway in a few minutes and wondered if you wanted to go with me when I seek this gentleman's company.'

Elizabeth Gardens was a pleasant area, mostly comprised of 1930's houses with new builds added over the decades. The houses were rarely for sale for any length of time, the estate in-close-proximity to the park of the same name. 12 Sycamore Crescent was the far end of a cul-de-sac, the turning circle in front of it more like a mini roundabout.

'Funny, that looks just like the car I was watching on the CCTV video this morning: same model, same colour, same number plate. Even better, that looks like a dent on the front nearside. Now I wonder how that got there?' DI Green sounded pleased, maybe for once it was going to be straightforward: a crime solved in less than twenty-four hours.

Although not in uniform, the pair couldn't have been anything other than policemen (or Jehovah's Witnesses). Both dressed smartly in dark suits, the DI towered over Harvey and stood erect, his height adding to the moment. The woman who answered the door looked most uncomfortable. Still in her dressing gown, she stood awkwardly not knowing what to expect.

'Mrs West?'

Nodding her head slightly, she seemed to be having difficulty recognising her name.

It took several minutes for the two officers to gain access and be shown into the spacious living room, which was furnished in a style that shrieked money: local retailers not on show.

'Can you tell us who was driving your car last night, at about ten o'clock?'

'No one, it was parked on the drive all night.'

Harvey hated it when someone lied, and the last statement fell into that category.

DI Green continued, speaking as one would to a child who knows he's in trouble but is trying to lie his way out of any repercussions. 'You see the problem is, Mrs West, that is not the case. We have your vehicle, the one that *is* now parked on your drive, on a CCTV video on Richmond Avenue on the outskirts of Preston at just before ten p.m. last night.'

'No, it was here at that time. No one else drives it, the children have left home, and neither of us went out. I wasn't feeling very well and went to bed early and slept through until Trevor woke me with a cup of tea before he left for work.'

'If you were asleep, how can you be sure your husband didn't go out in the car?'

Looking embarrassed, she said that he had been disqualified. 'He was stupid, got in the car when he had been drinking. It was the first time, but he was quite a bit over the limit, so the magistrates gave him a fifteen-month ban.'

Always fascinated by the workings of the human brain, the pair watched as realisation dawned. No words were necessary.

'Would you be so good as to tell us where your husband works.'

'He's a doctor at Riverside Surgery. He walks to work, it's only ten minutes away.'

Following the route, the by-now distraught woman had indicated, Harvey spoke for them both. 'A doctor, the ones mown down were nurses. Is the dot-to-dot too obvious?'

'Will we have to wait for a fortnight to get an appointment? That was what I was offered last time I needed to see someone.' John Green sounded upbeat. 'When I told the receptionist that my diabetes was playing up (off the scale, it always happens when I get too stressed) I was told I could go immediately and would be seen. Must try that every time!'

Once at the surgery their warrant cards speeded up the appointment process and fifteen minutes later, they were shown into the doctor's room. Doctor West looked every one of his fifty-five years, with grey hair and a dour expression. Standing to greet them, he said, 'My wife phoned and said you were on your way.'

'And did she say why we want to see you?'

'Yes. Apparently, my car was on some camera in Preston last night. Well, as you must already know, I'm banned from driving, and I have to say I wouldn't be so stupid as to take the car out. As far as I knew it was on the drive all night. My wife has been driving it and she doesn't like putting it in the garage, finds the entrance too small. I tell her it's the same width as the rest of the garage, but the only time she tried to reverse in she nudged a wing mirror and that was that.'

The last bit was probably true but as for his story about last night the man was either telling the truth or was a consummate liar.

'Sheila went to bed early, she's started to suffer with migraines, and I followed as soon as the ten o'clock headlines were finished. I must admit I didn't look out, so have no idea if the car was there or not. It was definitely there this morning when I opened the lounge curtains.'

'The CCTV pictures are crystal clear. Your car was on Richmond Avenue on the outskirts of Preston at 9:58 last night.'

'Someone must have borrowed it and returned it before I got up this morning. As I said, my wife hasn't been very well and I was up first, about half past six, and took her a cup of tea, had my breakfast and came in to work early. Paperwork to catch up on, I expect you know all about that.'

'Dr West, I find it strange that you haven't asked why we are interested in the fact that your car was in Preston about the time you claim you went to bed.'

'I'm still getting my head around the fact that someone took it.'

'And returned it...with a dent on the front. I don't suppose you looked at it this morning before you made your wife a cup of tea and came to work early to do your paperwork.' John Green's voice oozed sarcasm.

The man was a liar and was trying to play them for fools.

'No, I didn't even glance at it. At risk of repeating myself, as far I'm concerned my car was on my path all night.'

'And I must inform you that your car, the one you claim was outside your house, was involved in an extremely serious incident. A hit-and-run, two women knocked down. One is in hospital in a serious condition and the other one was killed.'

Looking suitably shocked, the doctor took a few moments to respond. 'You can't honestly think I left my sick wife, drove the ten miles to Preston, knocked two women down and returned home, carrying on with life as normal.'

The DI's phone rang, disturbing the silence in the room. As he walked to the door he muttered, 'Sorry, need to take this.'

Three minutes later he was back. 'Doctor West, I am arresting you for the murder of Morag Clerihew and the attempted murder of Jo Harris.' Reading out the rest of the well-known caution, he gave his mobile to Harvey. The enhanced still from the CCTV footage clearly showed the driver of the car: Trevor West.

Chapter 45

Williamson's Park in Lancaster was quiet, most people at work. A few dog walkers strolled by, barely glancing at the three adults sitting on a bench facing the Ashton Memorial. The remnants of their picnic lay on the next bench. Adam was in his push chair, spreading a rusk liberally over his face and once that was finished, he'd want to be on the move.

Keen to break the uncomfortable silence, his wife and daughter having ended their usual argument, the one neither would win, Richard Page, sounding like a history lecturer, told them the background to the monument. 'It's a folly, took two years to build, from 1907 to 1909, by Lord Ashton, a local industrialist and millionaire – not bad in those days – in memory of his second wife, Jessy. It cost £87,000, or a staggering 8.4 million today! Some people compare the memorial to the Taj Mahal.' Realising neither woman was listening, he said he was going for a walk and would push Adam up to the swings. 'You can bring the girls in a few minutes.'

'Dad tells us those facts every time we come. As if we're interested.'

'At least he tries, more than you seem to do these days, Susan. I know it's hard without Gerald and with the police forever appearing, but you could show a little more gratitude. Your father and I have done so much for you and we only have your best interests at heart.'

'When are you going to start treating me like a grown up?'

'The moment you start acting like one. It's time, indeed more than time, that you grew up. I have to be honest and say that your father and I are finding the whole thing hard and the longer it goes on, the harder it gets.'

'Hard? What do you think it's like for me? I live it every moment of every day and it never gets easier. Nothing I do can change the past.'

'No, the past can't be altered, however, there are different ways of dealing with it. Maybe it's time to move on, to stop the pretence. Look to the future.'

'Move on? Pretence? Future?' Susan was aware she was repeating everything her mother said. 'What would I move on to? The life I have is all I've known for almost a decade. Gerald helped me maintain it, but now he's gone it's like a sandcastle that's about to be washed away by the incoming tide. If I change, I'll have nothing left.'

'Susan,' her mother sounded cross, 'you must see that Gerald was a large part of the problem.'

'Problem? Problem? Is that what you call it. You think my life is something that can be fixed? Tell me how.'

'When you're ready to change we can sit down and make a plan. It will take a lot of willpower, as you said it's been like this for a long time, and we all get into patterns of behaviour that are so entrenched they prevent us from seeing a better alternative.'

'There is no alternative. If there was one, I would lose everything. Everything I care about.'

'Once you get used to Gerald not being there...'

'No, that will never happen. I loved him and I miss him so much. Coping with the children without him gets more impossible every single day.'

'We all need to sit down and talk. The sooner, the better. Reality must...'

'This is my reality!'

Late that night, an email arrived from *johngreen1966 @ hotmail.com*.
Subject matter: Doctor Trevor West. Hit-and-run.

Good evening/night Harvey, greetings from Preston. Thanks for accompanying me today and as promised an update. Thought I'd use this mode of communication, a bit late to phone!

- Total confession. Little choice when faced with the CCTV footage!
- He had an affair with Jo Harris, met when she spent a few weeks working at the surgery as part of her training.
- Lasted two years and she was getting too serious, asked him to move in with her.
- He finished it and she was threatening to tell his wife.
- He went to try to talk to her.
- She laughed and said it was too late for that.
- Her friend had waited for her whilst he and Jo argued.
- As the women walked off, laughing, he saw red.
- Wanted to "give her a scare"!
- Drove off in a panic when he knew he'd "got too close"!!

- Nothing to do with Parkside, so sorry to have taken your time.

All so prosaic.

I always use bullet points, hope that's OK. Pleased to have met you and maybe we'll work together at some time in the future.
  Best wishes,
  John

Harvey sent a quick response, thanking his Preston colleague for his swift update. He then sat, almost relieved that the latest death had nothing to do with his murders. Yet another would have complicated his investigation, like extra paths added to a maze.

Chapter 46

Sunday: Harvey had given the team a day off. They were exhausted and frustration ruled. Lunch with Alfie Morrison was booked at The Weighbridge, a restaurant they both liked overlooking the canal. This would be followed by a walk. If they trudged (Alfie's choice of word) along the towpath to Brownswick and back, it would be a good (not the word the pathologist would select) ten miles. We will NOT talk shop. Alfie will, no doubt, need to tell me - in intricate detail - how Liverpool managed to lose yesterday despite having almost eighty per cent possession. Harvey was pleased he had watched that part of Match of the Day. Maybe I'll pretend I saw him on the Kop, effing and blinding as the third Everton goal went in.

Sunday: Serena was enjoying a lie-in; a rare luxury. She had brought breakfast back to bed and was reading the latest book by Dorothy Koomson, one of her favourite authors. It felt like sheer indulgence. I'd better read as much as I can. Goodness knows when I'll get the time to finish it. Most days by the time I get home my eyes are too tired to contemplate even looking at the words and as for following the plot...not a chance. I won't think about this afternoon, it will come soon enough. A shame no one wants to accompany me.

Sunday: Clare Jennings was at her parents' house making final preparations for the wedding, ('of the century', her father's sarcastic comment) which was less than a month away. A healthy discussion, or in this case shouting match, was in fifth gear about the flowers: bouquet, buttonholes and the ones in church which would, if Clare had her way, empty every florists' in Fordway. As the bride, Clare was determined to win the argument. Her mother was used to having her own way, but not this time. She had won one argument today, telling her husband to be that she would take his name, but at work she would remain DS Jennings.

Sunday: Edward Stones was catching up on jobs he'd neglected since joining the DCI's team. Washing and ironing was always up to date, but he was starting on the dusting and hoovering. He had to admit the flat looked a lot better, but thought it was a sad way to spend the day, time off so infrequent. Now I'm here, and it looks like I'm staying, fingers crossed, I must join something, make friends, do things outside work. Unfortunately, nothing sprang to mind.

Sunday: Richard and Sylvia Page sat glaring at each other. Both knew the situation had escalated and they felt at breaking point.

Sylvia spoke quietly, afraid of any sound, 'I'll go to Susan's later and stay the night, make sure she's OK.'

'I'll come as well; moral support.'

Sunday: Susan Winters was pacing, stalking every room. She opened the dining room door, stepped inside then retreated with an immediacy that told her she wasn't ready to face that appalling sight: Gerald remained on the floor, the meal uneaten and the doll unable to rouse him.

Mum phoned. I almost didn't answer, calls make me so nervous, but when I saw who it was, I thought I'd better as she'd only have kept ringing. Mum said they'd be round this afternoon so that I can go and visit. It will be the first time without Gerald, and I'm scared.

Sunday: No one could have foreseen that it was Breakthrough Day!

Still Sunday: It was the anniversary of her grandmother's death, the person she had felt closest to growing up. Nana had lived two streets away and from a very young age, Serena had taken herself to the house at every opportunity. 'Age is merely numbers, and you keep me young Serena.' For some reason, her sisters had never been drawn to the old lady, so she usually had her to herself. Hours were spent baking: fairy and cornflake cakes morphing into cheesecakes and gateaux. However, their favourite activity was painting. Nana had entered pictures, invariably landscapes using oils, in local exhibitions, and had been awarded several commendations. 'I'm no Constable, but it's such a relaxing pastime.'

Three years ago, Serena had taken her out for Sunday lunch. As they returned home, Nana said she was tired and would have a bath, change into her pyjamas, and watch her favourite DVD: Sleepless in Seattle. The next morning when her cleaner arrived, she found the old lady, dressed ready for bed, sitting in her armchair, the television still on. Everyone kept telling Serena it was a wonderful way to go, but three years on she could still weep whenever she thought about her. She had been denied the chance to say goodbye, though she hoped Nana had known how much she was loved.

A bowl of purple hyacinths looked colourful placed on the centre of the grave. It would last a lot longer than a bunch of flowers. The headstone read: '*Mabel Atherton, 10th July 1936 to 25th August 2018. Aged 82. Wife to Jim, mother to Sasha and Jane, sister to Mabel, and grandmother to Serena, Clare and Tasha. A life well lived. Friend to all she met.*' Tears streamed down her granddaughter's face as she sat on the grass. She was so engrossed in her many memories that she was only vaguely aware of a figure passing by on the next path. As she stood to leave, she noticed the woman walking towards the far corner of the graveyard. The person looked familiar, but out of context it took Serena several seconds to recognise her: Susan Winters.

Not wanting to intrude, Serena began to walk away then the need to see who Susan was visiting got the upper hand and she sat on a bench waiting. Had she not done so, the Parkside Puzzle (Edward's attempt at humour) might have remained just that and eventually become a cold case, hidden in the archives to be reviewed at a future date.

Serendipity. Two people in a cemetery on the same afternoon. Two women who until a few weeks ago hadn't met. A duo with nothing in common, apart from their involvement in four murders.

Still Sunday: The walk back from Brownswick was taking longer than expected, the pathologist admitting he wasn't as fit as he should be. 'I know it's important. After all, I see enough men go before their time because they didn't take care of themselves. Clogged arteries, carrying too much weight, livers in a state beyond repair, lungs filled with tar, all contributary factors that mean you don't reach your allotted span.'

Harvey was pleased to see that his friend had got on to his favourite topic; at least it stopped the increasingly heavy-going step after laborious step moan.

'When you said no more than ten miles it sounded doable. Not so sure now. At risk of sounding like a child, how much further is it?'

Glad not to have to depress his friend, (still three miles to go) Harvey was almost relieved when his mobile rang.

'It's me, sir. Yes, I know you gave us the day off, but this will not wait until tomorrow. And I do mean not.'

'If Alfie doesn't speed up it might be Monday before I get to the office. Be at least an hour, or with our much-loved pathologist in danger of performing a PM selfie this evening, nearer to two. Can you ask DS Jennings and PC Stones to meet us at five? Might as well spoil everyone's day.'

'It won't be spoilt. I can guarantee that.'

Still Sunday: Clare was furious. The first day off in too long to remember and now her presence was requested (demanded) at the station. It had better be good. I'm forty-love up on Mum. A rare occurrence. She's agreed to all my requests regarding the flowers and we're now debating the seating plan for the wedding breakfast.

Still Sunday: Edward was intrigued. What could be so important that their day off was being curtailed?

He bounded along, thinking he had the best job in the world. If curiosity killed the cat, he was a prize-winning moggy, though probably by now deceased.

Still Sunday: Serena was on tenterhooks, longing to start the meeting. She had gone straight to the station and was pacing the floor of Harvey's office. Sheer luck. Totally amazing. Being in the right place at the oh-so-unbelievably correct time. A Swiss watch couldn't have done it better.

Still Sunday: Fordway was in sight, like a mirage in the desert. The phone call had stopped Alfie's complaints and Harvey had instructions to tell all later that evening. 'If I'm asleep wake me up. Sounds like good news and after this afternoon I need some.'

Still Sunday: Harvey was trying not to get his hopes up. He knew his DI was prone to moments of unwarranted excitement, but she had sounded so upbeat that he thought she must have something important to impart. He hoped that was the case or certain people would not be pleased to have their downtime interrupted.

Chapter 47

Four people sat unable to speak. Each had a print-out from Serena's mobile in front of them: the photo taken at 14:58.

Clare was the first to utter. 'Good God. I mean crikey. What the hell does this mean?' Not normally prone to swearing, it seemed appropriate; other phrases deemed inadequate.

No one had an answer, baffled by the words on display.

'I know, totally bamboozling. I'm still not sure what to make of it.' Without going into too much detail, Serena explained how she had seen Susan Winters in the cemetery. 'I was intrigued as she stood by a grave for a long time, and I could see she was sobbing as she walked away. Once she'd gone, I went to see what she had been looking at, who she had been visiting. When I saw the headstone, I took a photo and called you.'

Four pairs of eyes looked down at the surreal picture. The memorial stone looked expensive: beautiful cream marble. It was the wording, written in an old-fashioned script, that held their attention.

*In loving memory of our cherished and
much-loved daughters.
May the angels look after them until we meet
once more in heaven.*

Hannah Elizabeth Winters aged 2 weeks

Abigail Veronica Winters stillborn

Lara Jennifer Winters aged 3 days

Esther Amelia Winters aged 1 month

*God gave you to us for too short a time
He took you to His beautiful garden
Where you will play
Until we meet again*

Silence ruled. A silence no one felt able to break. The words had mesmerised them and each waited for someone to act as a magician and break the spell. They hoped this was the breakthrough they had longed for, but logical thought was beyond them.

Serena was the first to find some words. 'I've had longer than the rest of you to look at this and although I still don't understand it fully, I can only surmise that none of the Winters' girls are actually alive. It makes for incredibly sad reading, three dying so soon and Abigail stillborn.'

'But who do we hear when we go to the house? And whose photos have been displayed so carefully on the lounge walls?' Clare sounded in a daze, and continued as though she was talking to herself, 'Is this the secret Susan has been so careful to hide? Are the children we hear not hers? Did she and Gerald adopt or foster? Is Adam theirs or did Gerald manage finally to adopt a boy?'

Jolting so suddenly that she sent her photo flying, she added, 'Does anyone else remember the babies who went missing? It started about the time Hannah was born, maybe eight years ago, and since then a new-born baby has been abducted with an uncanny regularity. If I remember correctly, at least two were taken from different hospitals in Greater Manchester, with apparently nothing to connect them. Others were abducted from their homes. All girls, all healthy, all to parents beyond suspicion. Women get desperate when they lose a baby, and stranger things have happened than taking someone else's offspring. Despite a nation-wide search none was ever found.'

An Arctic cold descended on the room; four adults sat stunned; the possibility raised too ghoulish to be acknowledged. Serena gasped. 'Let me look at our records, it's something one of the neighbours said.' Several minutes later she yelled, 'Yes. Here it is in Gemma Norton's statement: "His (Gerald's) car has blacked out windows and when I commented one time, he said that Susan didn't want the girls to be seen. Apparently, she thinks someone might take photos and place (I suppose she meant post) them on the internet." Then Mrs Norton added, "Talk about paranoid!" Well maybe not. If the girls grew up looking like their birth parents or siblings, they might have been recognised.'

'But if Gerald Winters was so keen to have a son, why kidnap four girls?' Edward looked around for the answer.

'Each baby Susan lost was female, so maybe she was trying to replace them. If the baby she had given birth to was female, then the substitute had to be the same. We know she calls them the same names as the ones on the gravestone. Maybe she has convinced herself that they are hers, that the ones she bore didn't die.'

Harvey spoke so quietly the others hardly heard him. 'Is this the secret that has led to four murders? Has Susan Winters killed a midwife, her nanny and the ex-matron because they found out what had happened in that house? Nora Ederson and Imelda Simpson must have known that the Winters' first two babies didn't make it. She had them at Parkside when they were both working there.'

Edward intervened, 'What about Harriet Devizes? Did she work out what had happened? Did Susan confess? Was that what the nanny wanted to talk to us about the day she was killed?'

Harvey didn't know the answers and asked his own question: 'Why did she murder her husband? He must have been part of the conspiracy. Had he had enough? Was he about to bail out or spill the beans? Too many questions and there's only one way to get the answers. Yet another visit to that bizarre house.'

'Sir, I think we need a search warrant. She's not going to allow us to meet the children, whoever they are.'

'Indeed, Serena, but search warrants take time, and I don't feel like waiting. You and I will go and demand to see the children. Clare and Edward find everything you can about the babies who went missing in Greater

Manchester. We need dates and times and any CCTV footage that the hospitals were able to supply. Then look further afield for any infants who disappeared or were snatched over the past eight years.

'Are we charging her with four murders?'

'One step at a time. I think we have our murderer, but I want to know what's going on at 14 Wordsworth Avenue. If children have been abducted, we need to deal with that first.'

Chapter 48

The house was in darkness, the curtains drawn against the dying light. Sunset was officially some time off, but the overcast evening made it feel later. The cheerless clouds felt appropriate. No one saw the police car pull up outside, or the two officers who sat wondering what lay inside.

'Maybe the children will be in bed.'

'We still need to see them and if necessary, wake them up. If Susan Winters has killed four innocent people just to hide the fact the children in that house aren't hers, she might decide the game is up, sorry, not the most appropriate phrase, and get rid of them. She will see them as evidence and if backed into a corner it might look like the only solution. I hope we're not too late.'

'Yes, sir, you remember the horrendous case of the father who smothered his three children to get back at his wife. Even parents are capable of the most heinous of acts.'

No answer to the doorbell, repeated loud knocks or shouts through the letter box. Giving the door one final battering, Harvey told Serena to call for back-up. 'Make sure they've got battering rams.'

'What the hell do you think you're doing?' An apoplectic Richard Page stood behind them, his wife on the path beside him. 'Our daughter is tired and went to bed early. We looked after the children this afternoon to let our daughter go out. When she came home, she said she didn't want us to stay. She told us she'd put the children to bed then go herself. She gets extremely tired these days.'

Yes, Harvey thought, prolonged obfuscation and murder can do that to you.

'Susan rang us a few minutes ago, at her wits end. She didn't know who was trying to get into the house and as she's on her own with five youngsters to protect she rang for our help. Now I must ask you to leave.'

Nonsense. He was certain that Susan had known who was at the door. Why, he wondered, hadn't she answered? Why send for her parents?

'Mr and Mrs Page, I must ask you to leave. We need to talk to Susan on her own. She needs to tell us about her daughters. We've seen the gravestone in Manor Hall cemetery with four names on it, the names she calls the children in the house.'

Both parents looked shaken. Pushing past the officers, Sylvia Page asked for a few minutes alone with their daughter. 'She will talk to you, but I must beg you to be understanding. Our beloved daughter has been seriously ill for many years and this may break her with a totality you cannot imagine. I need to make her accept that she cannot retain her secret any longer.'

Reluctantly, Harvey nodded. 'Ten minutes, then we *are* coming in.'

Light drizzle began to fall, the kind that soaks one without warning. Retreating to the car Harvey was annoyed when his mobile rang.

'Sir, it's Clare. Edward and I have been researching missing babies, those that have been snatched and never found. None have disappeared from local hospitals in

343

the past eight years, hardly surprising with their security systems. However, two baby girls were abducted in the area that fit with the appropriate time frames.

'One, a girl aged two months, was taken from her front garden six weeks after Hannah Winters was born. The baby was in her pram, the mother leaving her to rush back into the house to collect the purse she'd forgotten. Unfortunately, as she entered the house the landline rang, and she took a few minutes to answer it. By the time she went outside the pram was empty.'

'Where was this?'

'Chorlton-Cum-Hardy in Greater Manchester. 89 Riverside Close, a pleasant road of semi-detached houses so no CCTV cameras anywhere nearby. No one saw a thing, most residents at work, and the baby was never found. She'll be coming up to eight now, the age they claim for Hannah Winters.

'And the second?'

'Very similar in many respects, sir. A baby girl, just three weeks old, placed in her carrier on the front seat of the family car, the Volvo parked on the drive, near the front door. The dad this time, was taking the baby to her grandparents' house a few miles away, leaving her mum to have a short rest. It was the grandfather's birthday and Jonathan Riley, the baby's dad (sorry sir, I'm trying to give you the full picture) had gone back inside to collect the birthday presents. In the report of the incident he says, "I just couldn't carry everything, and I only left Sasha for a minute and that's all it took: she was gone. If only I'd put the bag in the car first. I can never forgive myself." No eyewitnesses, another leafy suburb, this time in Pilling, so no CCTV. That was almost five years ago which would coincide with Lara, the Winters' third born. Do you know Pilling, sir?'

'Yes, a very pleasant place and much closer to home than Chorlton-Cum-Hardy.'

'Baby abduction is thankfully rare and they're the only two in the North West in our time frame. Edward is widening the search as we speak.'

Remembering to thank his DS for the information, he relayed her findings to Serena. 'If those two girls are living here DNA will prove who the parents are. Might be time to reunite them with their birth families.'

Ten minutes mutated into twenty. 'Time to go in, they've had more than enough time.'

Stepping out of the car, Serena asked, 'Do you think the Pages know what's been happening?'

'I'm absolutely sure they do. They've been in on it from the start; they might even be the ones who took the babies. No wonder none of them wanted us to delve too deeply into their family. My only question is which one of them was so determined to maintain the status quo, to preserve the appalling set-up, that they were willing to commit four murders.'

'Or, sir, has it all been a joint enterprise?'

Chapter 49

A single day can alter people's lives irrevocably.

So much had happened in the twenty-four hours following the begrudging invitation to enter 14 Wordsworth Drive, the house that was about to become headline news across the country and probably the world.

Susan Winters had been committed to a psychiatric unit in a specialist hospital in Birmingham, the nearest establishment with places for someone who had suffered a total, catastrophic breakdown.

Baby Adam had been taken into care and was with Greta and Finn Small who had been delighted to be asked to undertake long-term fostering, their months of interviews and training completed, this the first baby in their care. They had already fallen in love with him.

Richard Page had been charged as an accessory to four murders and was being held in HM Preston Prison, awaiting his appearance in front of the magistrates. His lawyer had warned him that it was highly unlikely that he would be granted bail. The next few months would be spent incarcerated before the case was heard at Crown Court.

An hour after the officers had entered the house, Sylvia Page had asked to speak to DCI Tarquin and was now held in the bowels of Fordway police station. DCI Tarquin had wanted her close at hand.

Interview Room Two was one of the less salubrious ones, a small skylight the only source of natural light. The sign on the door had faded with time leaving it looking like something from a bygone era. Someone had once said the words, "Abandon hope all ye who enter here," should be added and today the phrase seemed most apposite for the person sitting and waiting, staring vacantly at the drab décor of peeling plaster and cobweb encrusted light fittings.

Marching into the room like a general about to lead his troops into battle (one Harvey was confident he was going to win) the DCI sat down and for the sake of the recorder announced those present: 'DCI Tarquin, DI Peil and Sylvia Page' He then added, 'Despite being asked several times, Mrs Page has refused the assistance of a solicitor.'

'How is my daughter? I've worried about her all night. Please tell me she's going to be OK, well looked after.'

'Susan is in the best possible place and I'm sure the staff there know how to help her.'

'I knew one day she would collapse, lose what fragile hold she has on normality, suffer in a way you or I can't imagine. None of it is her fault, you must believe that. I really want you to remember that no blame can be attached to someone so severely ill. She played no part in recent events. She is not a murderer. Life has been most unfair to her, but she has never hurt anyone.'

Pausing to stem the tears that were coursing down her face, she continued. 'Susan's illness means that she doesn't see the world the way others do. Richard and I did everything we could to help, but in the end, we had to go along with the life she lived (not the one any of us would have chosen for her) and pretend it was normal. Totally normal. It was truly beyond her control; she loved those children as if they were her own. I know no one will understand and we'll be blamed. It's been going on for so long and I suppose we just accepted it, though we knew it was wrong: so terribly wrong.'

Unable to hide his disdain, the woman in front of them guilty of four murders, Harvey spoke in a loudly enough for the rest of the station to hear. 'Enough of your self-pitying nonsense, Mrs Page. Let's get down to the reason you are here…'

Interrupting him, something Harvey deplored, Sylvia Page spoke as though she was reading a particularly boring passage from a set text, one she was being forced to study for an exam. 'You and I both know why I am here. I'm here to confess. I murdered my son-in-law, Gerald Winters; the midwife, Nora Ederson; the ex-matron at Parkside Nursing Home, Imelda Simpson; and my daughter's nanny, Harriet Devizes.'

Harvey glanced at Serena who was looking nonplussed. Neither had expected an immediate and full confession, all their pre-interview planning undone, like a football team determined not to allow the opposition to score in the first half, only for their full back to put the ball into his own net in the first minute. Plan B their only hope.

'You must want to know why it was so necessary to commit the ultimate crime. It's not what you are thinking.'

'Mrs Page, you can have no idea what I'm thinking, but do carry on and enlighten us.'

'Last night you learnt our daughter's foible, her weakness, her idiosyncrasy: the life she lives that others wouldn't understand. None of us wanted Susan's strange lifestyle to become public, though that is not the real reason for the murders: the ones that had to be undertaken.'

Attempting to control his sense of repulsion, Harvey yelled, 'No one, and I mean absolutely no one, *has* to end someone else's life. It's a self-serving excuse and one I've heard far too often. However much one abhors another person, what they do or stand for, there is always another route.'

'Another route? If only it had been that easy, like asking Sat Nav for directions. For eight years I have yearned to find a way to alter the drastic situation in which we found ourselves. I have to tell you that nothing worked. Nothing. So...I realise I won't persuade you... the murders became inevitable.'

'Inevitable? What all four? Why in God's name were any of them the solution?'

'You've both seen how my daughter was existing, I won't call it living. It started nine years ago when she met that man. Until then, we'd had our ups and downs as all families do, but the change in her was unreal. From the word go she was totally enthralled by him; he was like a sorcerer who had cast a spell, without doubt the wicked kind, on her.

'At the beginning the change was psychological. He played mind games, controlled her every thought, stopped her seeing her friends (there was a time she enjoyed a great social life) and tried to stop us seeing her. Then when she fell pregnant, a honeymoon baby - he insisted they didn't waste any time - the physical changes became apparent. Pregnancy has never suited her. The first time she was ill for nine months and then poor Hannah only lived for such a short time; just over two weeks. That is heart-breaking for any woman, but Susan never recovered. She wasn't allowed to grieve, just get pregnant again ASAP! When it happened a second time we remonstrated with Gerald, told him the toll on his wife was too much. His solution was to impregnate her again and employ a midwife at home, preferring that to Parkside. Two more tragedies followed. Susan appeared to shrink, both physically and mentally, and her problems exacerbated until all reality was gone. Her life was what you witnessed last night.'

Pausing, like an actor who needs a prompt, she looked straight at Serena. 'The pregnancies were so stressful, not only physically but emotionally: Gerald always insisted on knowing the sex of the baby when they went for the first scan. She felt she was failing him when the foetus was female. I once reminded him that the sperm decides the sex, not the egg. He didn't like that at all.

'A son. That was all he wanted, and she had to keep trying until he had his heir. He showed little emotion over the ones who died, in his eyes they were second class, not good enough. He was willing to accept the bizarre routine that began immediately after she lost Hannah if it meant it kept her pliable and willing to try again. Four times our lovely daughter went through the agony of full-term pregnancies only to be left empty handed.'

DS Jennings knocked and entered the room. 'Sir, could I have a word with you?'

Informing the tape recording that he was leaving the room, he followed Clare into the corridor.

'We've just been told that Richard Page tried to hang himself this morning. He's OK and has been taken to hospital.'

'Surely he was on suicide watch.'

'Apparently not, sir. One of the guards found him when he took his breakfast. He'd torn up his shirt and used it as a tourniquet. They found him in time, and he will make a full recovery.'

'Makes one wonder how involved he was with the murders. We were assuming he wasn't hands on, sorry not the best use of language, but it's a line of enquiry we need to pursue with his wife. Keep me informed if you hear anything else.'

Interview Room Two looked even bleaker when he returned, the little sunshine that had managed to creep through the high mesh earlier had vanished.

Without waiting, Sylvia Page continued, as though there hadn't been an interruption. 'When Adam was born and got through the first few days, then weeks and months, we were so hopeful that things would improve, that with a son, Gerald would finally be satisfied. All went well until a few weeks ago when Susan told us that he was making noises…her phrase…about a brother for his son. That was how he always referred to him: my son. Having produced one male, he was sure future offspring would also be boys.

'Chief Inspector, another pregnancy would have killed Susan. She haemorrhaged when Adam was born, and the doctor told us that any future pregnancies were to be avoided. Our son-in-law didn't listen…or didn't care. I begged Susan to come home, to bring the children and live with us. Our house isn't enormous, but we'd have managed and to know our daughter was safe was all we wanted. They all came for a month then he persuaded her to go back and in front of us informed her that Adam needed a male playmate.

'That was when I knew what I had to do.'

'Mrs Page, would you like a break?' The DCI was furious with Serena, but as she said it was either that or call for a doctor. 'She went drip-white and looked as though she was going to collapse. At that moment, we'd got as much as possible from her. Half an hour won't make any difference.'

Ninety minutes later, a doctor having checked on Mrs Page, the interview resumed, Harvey still irate.

'Mrs Page, the last thing you told us was that you decided to end your son-in-law's life.'

Once again, not waiting for the question, Sylvia continued her story. 'That Friday; that unforgettable day. We'd gone to see Susan and begged her to return home with us again. Gerald came home early and was, what's the word? oh yes, apoplectic. He ranted and raved, accused us of interfering, of making his wife doubt her own mind. He told us he was going for a drive and didn't expect us still to be there when he got back. Susan was upset and went to bed. Richard went home, but I stayed.

'When Gerald returned and saw me still there, in the kitchen, I thought he was going to hit me. I asked him to calm down, have a drink and we could talk. We went through to the dining room, Gerald still in his coat. I'd prepared the drink earlier, oh dear, that sounds like a macabre version of Blue Peter. It was his usual, a large whisky, but this time embellished with the drugs I knew shouldn't be taken together. Amazing what one can glean from the internet. The pestle and mortar had ground the entire packets into fine dust.

'I stayed until he was comatose and rang Richard to come and collect me. Please believe me Chief Inspector, he was not involved in any way. What followed was not in the script (did the woman think she was taking part in a BBC 2 drama?). When Susan found him, she was meant to call for an ambulance, thinking he'd committed suicide. However, she assumed he was asleep and laid him out on the dining room carpet with food for when he woke up and placed the doll beside him to watch over him. When he still wouldn't wake on the Monday morning, she made her phone call.'

Both officers were to comment later at the lack of emotion on display, the words delivered without any nuances, feelings, or regrets, and Serena would add that the admissions became more detached as each murder was explained.

'I now want you to move on to the death of Nora Ederson.'

Setting off, so slowly each sentence appeared to be in danger of having no ending, Mrs Page began. 'Over the years I begged her for help. Although she wasn't Susan's midwife at the nursing home she was there and knew about Hannah and then just eighteen months later, little Abigail. I begged her to ask a doctor to sterilise my daughter. A hysterectomy for medical reasons. I knew that was the only way she would be spared any more heartache. She point-blank refused. Told me it was unprofessional, that future pregnancies might have a different outcome. I recall her exact words: "Susan is still very young, and many women take babies home after suffering late miscarriages and still births."

'Following Lara and then Esther I once again sought her assistance. Each time the answer was the same.

I know she referred to me as C.M., told me I was a Caring Mum, but that what I was asking would never happen.' Serena looked at her boss. That was one mystery solved. 'She was full of sympathy. That was never going to ameliorate Susan's predicament.'

After an extended pause, the silence only disturbed by the loud ticking of the clock on the far wall, she continued. 'Nora told me she was packing, ready to go on holiday, when I called that last time. I told her about Adam and how ill Susan had been following his birth and that the doctor had warned that any future pregnancies might have serious consequences. When she asked me to leave and not come back, I lost my temper and punched her. As she fell, she hit her head and I panicked and ran out. When I heard she was dead I didn't know what to do. If I went to the police and explained, the whole story would come out. Everything was to protect the fantasy that was our lives.'

Another extended silence. 'Imelda Simpson. Such a pleasant woman. When we met that evening in the supermarket it was like a lightbulb coming on as she put two and two together and came up with four. She knew about my request as at one time I'd asked her for help. Once again, the answer had been a resounding no. I followed her out, knowing she would go to the police, and when she turned down the back alley it was so easy to make sure she didn't speak again. For weeks I had carried a knife, a weapon I never intended to use.'

'And the nanny, Harriet Devizes? Was she going to tell all? She must have known what was going on, the whole sorry mess that you played along with. For eight years!' The last three words were yelled, the DCI failing to maintain his composure.

'I am sorry about Harriet, such a lovely girl and so helpful to my daughter.'

'Sorry? Sorry? How dare you! In the name of all that's holy, do you really think crocodile tears and mealy-mouthed words will help your situation?'

Serena gave her boss a look that said she'd take over. 'Tell us about Miss Devizes.'

'She phoned me and told me she was going to the police, that she had to give them the information that would assist in their investigations. She was meeting her friend early to discuss it with her but was ninety-nine (her words) per cent certain that she would keep her appointment at the police station. I couldn't let that happen, so turned up at the café and asked her to get me a cup of tea. I had thought about trying to change her mind but knew that was futile. So, when she was at the counter, I spread peanuts under the table and took her EpiPens; she always kept them with her. I had gone by the time she returned with my drink, but I've been told her end was quick.'

Enjoying what he was about to impart, Harvey stood ready to leave. 'Mrs Page I have to inform you that your husband tried to commit suicide this morning and is in hospital.' Walking out he knew he was damned if he was going to add that he was likely to make a full recovery.

Serena remained in the room to gauge Sylvia Page's reaction.

'Richard has suffered over the years and last night was the painful denouement, his worst nightmare, and impossible for him to deal with. You saw his reaction, the tears and despair. He loves his daughter more than life itself and will never recover. I think he suspected I was involved in the murders, though he never asked, not wanting me to lie. He had nothing to do with any of them.'

Tears now pouring down her face, she added, 'Poor Richard. Susan may return at some point when the doctors think she will cope. Until then, he will be alone. Poor, poor man.'

There were to be many occasions when neither Harvey nor Serena would find the words to describe what they had found at Susan Winter's house that Sunday evening. It was so surreal, so unimaginable, that they never trusted their own judgement again, forever waiting for final proof before committing themselves to any hypothesis. They had been utterly wrong, misreading the signpost and rushing off down a blind alley.

On entering the house, Harvey had demanded to meet the children. 'We have reason to believe that the youngsters in this house were abducted as babies, each one taken following the death of a daughter borne by Susan.'

Sylvia Pages looked beaten. 'Please come quietly, Adam is asleep.' Then, with a shrug of her shoulders she led the way upstairs. The noise of children laughing and joking grew louder with each step. As the door was opened it became a cacophony of sounds. Shrieks. Guffaws. Giggles.

Each wall was filled with educational posters. All the multiplication tables, portrayed in lurid colours, filled the far wall with a large map of the world on the opposite side. The other two walls were covered in posters, one displaying all the Kings and Queens of England and others bright pictures of flowers and trees, all labelled.

A whiteboard shone brightly with work displayed in dark lettering:

Nouns are naming words, e.g. book, house, man, woman.

Proper nouns need to start with a capital letter, e.g. Hannah, Abigail, Lara, Esther, Adam.

In the centre of the room a large rectangular table was set up ready for tomorrow's lessons. On each of the four sides there was a set of books: exercise, text and reading, each set aimed at a different age group. Parallel to the books, pencils, rubbers, and rulers were placed with an almost mathematical precision.

The two police officers stopped in the doorway and gazed at the scene in front of them.

Neither spoke.

Neither moved.

Words and logical thoughts beyond them.

In the corner of the room the CD player stopped then started again.

The noise changed from laughter and joy to an ugly squabbling.

'Have you seen enough, Detective Chief Inspector?' Mrs Page sounded defeated.

Four highchairs were in place, one in front of each set of books.

On each chair sat a doll.

The largest was the one that had kept guard over Gerald's body and had been dressed in black at his funeral. She now bore the name badge Hannah.

The other three ranged in size from medium to small. Each had their name badge fixed to what looked like a school uniform of white blouse, red jumper, and grey skirt: Abigail, Lara, and Esther.

'Meet the children,' Susan said then fell to the floor convulsed in maniacal laughter. 'They are my babies: my four girls.'

'But the photos showing them at different ages?' The words left the DI's mouth unbidden.

Sylvia Page intervened. 'Amazing what a computer program can do. Enhance a baby's face to show how it would look, as the years go by.'

'My babies are always with me and I can see how they change as they grow up. Hannah knows all her times tables and is very good at reading, Abigail is going to be artistic….' Dramatic sobs curtailed the remaining words.

'Come on, darling, I'll see to the children.' One by one the four dolls were picked up and changed out of their uniforms into sleepsuits. Each one was then laid in the Moses baskets in the corner of the room. 'Let's get you downstairs, leave the children to rest then they'll be ready for their lessons tomorrow.'

'Good night, Hannah. Nighty night, Abigail. Sleep tight, Lara. God bless, Esther.'

Lightning Source UK Ltd.
Milton Keynes UK
UKHW011846171221
395826UK00001B/123

9 781839 757532